MW01121322

The Weed Killer

Greg Swiatek

ISBN: 1484081188
ISBN 13: 9781484081181

dedication: To Susie

prologue: If Albert Champion had to say when it happened, when the thought finally solidified in his brain, it was on a very ordinary day in April. He was taking a stroll around the neighborhood. Mrs. Kane, his neighbor down the street, was outside tending lovingly to her garden. Albert nodded to her out of mere politeness and muttered some inanity like, "Nice day, isn't it," then continued on his way.

"The weeds," the old woman shouted after him. "The weeds, they're driving me crazy. Where do they all come from? Every year it's the same thing, weeds, weeds, weeds. You got weeds on your lawn too?"

"No," Albert smiled. "I paved over the area. The only weeds I see are on the streets of Toronto holding out their hands for spare change and they're just as obnoxious and tenacious as the ones on your lawn."

Yes, that was it. The seed of Albert Champion's new purpose, his mission in life, got planted that day. Back home he immediately went into the basement and brought down a cigar box that was perched on a shelf in his workshop. Inside the box was an old .22 caliber pistol along with two boxes of bullets. "Yes, come to me my melancholy baby. Come to me and don't be blue."

And so it began, a reign of homicidal terror that plagued the streets of Toronto, Canada for one long hot summer. As the deaths of the city's homeless piled up, police were at a loss for clues and suspects. The killer seemed unstoppable. "He's so new at the murder game, he doesn't even know the rules. That's why it's so difficult to catch him," bemoaned Detective Sergeant Wright who headed the Toronto Homicide Division tasked with bringing the killer to justice. His career and family in tatters, the public and press berating him, the Sergeant's fate was inextricably linked to that of his antagonist until he was offered a way out.... by the killer himself.

During the carnage that engulfed the city, antipoverty groups, government officials, and citizens of all stripes joined in the battle, offering a plethora of opinions and solutions in an attempt to stem the tide of murder. Mary Monticello, a columnist at the *Toronto Star* and a community activist, found herself in the front ranks of the action and in the end wound up paying a high price for her well intentioned humanitarian efforts.

The stories of these characters and others are cleverly interwoven in a tight, action packed plot with that of the protagonist, Albert Champion. Neither the love of a new woman in his life, nor friendship, nor simple human compassion could dissuade Albert from his murderous course. "I have become Death," he proudly proclaimed. "I am the Weed Killer."

Follow the action, the crime investigation, and explore the many sides of the homeless dilemma that unfold in the pages of <u>The Weed Killer.</u>

chapter 1

STINKY EDDIE SETTLED in under the Spadina Ramp, his more or less permanent home at the intersection of the numerous on and off lanes of the Gardiner Expressway. This was his spot, the one he had managed to defend from all comers over the years. He forsook it only on those especially frigid winter nights when the temperature plunged below the survival level for anyone sleeping on a cardboard mattress and wrapped only in an old sleeping bag. Then he'd reluctantly head for the Salvation Army Shelter or the St. Christopher House on Queen West and Bathurst Streets for a night's rest.

Despite their comparative comfort, Eddie didn't like the shelters. He didn't like other people around him. They bothered him and stole from him. He preferred isolation and even avoided the sidewalk heat vents so prized by other homeless people when winter's cold breath swept clean the streets Toronto. The vents were too centrally located with too many people walking by, commenting, staring. Fuck them!

But Spring was now well established in the city and Eddie enjoyed his life. He foraged during the day, begging for change, and eating out of trash cans and restaurant waste bins. At night he headed "home" to his familiar steel and concrete lair with traffic rolling overhead and the odd headlight sweeping across his sleepy body. His shopping cart, holding his worldly possessions, stayed always by his side parked within arm's length even when he slept.

Stinky Eddie took a few sips from his bottle of wine. It helped him sleep. In the winter he'd drink at least a third of a bottle to get him past the cold and the aches of age and toil. After a few fleeting sepia toned images of an old life long gone by he'd fall asleep. No one complained of his snoring here.

Eddie did not at first feel the kicks to his body. His sleeping bag cushioned the blows. When he finally turned over and looked up, he saw a stranger standing next to him crouching slightly because of the slant of the roadway above the man's head.

"Fuck off," shouted Stinky Eddie. He found that a loud forceful voice, with a hint of drunken insanity mixed in, was a good deterrent to meddling strangers, do gooders included.

But the man did not move, but instead delivered another kick.

"You son of a bitch," hissed Eddie as he roused himself and sat up.

The stench that wafted from Eddie's body compelled the man to step back. At the same time he held his hand forward. He seemed to be holding something in it.

"I got enough to eat. Leave me alone. I don't want your goddamn help."

"I'm not here to help you," the man replied in a disembodied voice. Eddie could not see his face.

"Then what the fuck do you want?"

"I want you, gone."

"Ha, I ain't goin nowhere. This is my spot. Get your own or I'll smash you one. You don't scare me, you bastard!"

Eddie saw a brief flash of light and heard a loud bang before he was hit hard in the chest. He thought for a minute that the man had punched him, but the man had not moved. Eddie coughed and felt a warm liquid seep into his mouth.

"What the fuck?" he gasped as his head grew light and he had trouble breathing. He slumped back down lying flat on his back looking up at the indistinct undersurface of the road above him. When he died Eddie heard a truck roar by, loud, but unseen and heading nowhere.

***

Albert Champion drove down Lakeshore Boulevard heading east. He peered intently out his window scanning the intersecting labyrinth of roads and ramps that marked the Boulevard's approach to Spadina Avenue in downtown Toronto.

"Son of a bitch," hissed Albert. "He's still there. I can see his goddamn shopping cart from here. You mean to tell me after all this time nobody noticed that dead skunk laying there stinking to high heaven? What kind of city is this anyway? Doesn't anybody clean up around here? Where are our garbage men? Jesus, the bastard's dead and he's still irritating the shit out of me."

Albert talked to himself a lot. Companionship was scarce. He lived alone in a two bedroom bungalow on Niagara Street, his wife having left five years ago this past September, an early autumn. He could still remember her standing in front of their house on that last day with suitcase in hand, tears in her eyes, looking back over her shoulder, waiting for the cab.

"She was always such a suck. Whimpering over every little thing. What the hell was she staring at, expecting to see?" he wondered. "That song has ended. I don't love you anymore. Simple as that. Get over it."

Albert had no relatives in the city, few friends, and knew his neighbors only to say hello which he did as infrequently as possible. Simply put Albert didn't like people and frankly speaking the feeling was mutual. In light of his newly found mission in life that was just fine with him. The less he interacted and conversed with other people, the less conspicuous he would be and the less likely to shoot his mouth off and tip his hand, or so he thought.

As he continued to curse the inert presence of Stinky Eddie under the Gardiner Expressway, Albert made his way to the intersection of Lakeshore and Leslie Street where he stopped for a red light. At that point he was startled by the image of a young man dashing in front of the car. The boy had a squeegee in his hand.

"Hey asshole, they outlawed this bullshit years ago," Albert shouted through the closed window while shaking his head, No, no. "Nice outfit you got on by the way," he continued. "What did you do? Mug a clown on your way over here? I like that black shoe you've got on. The brown one looks good too."

Almost immediately and without warning his passenger door opened and a girl jumped into the front seat beside him.

"Hey Grandpa, you got any change in here?" she said rummaging through the console and grabbing the few coins that were lying there while Albert stared at her with his mouth agape.

"What the hell?" he finally stammered.

The girl was wearing ripped jeans and a tee shirt tied in a knot below her breasts. Numerous tattoos covered her arms and shoulders. Studs and rings hung from her ears, lips and eyebrows. She was pretty, but dirty as a dog's bone.

"Is this it?" she snorted viewing the few coins in her hand. "I thought you old timers had all the money. Where is it? Anything in here?" and she made a grab for the glove compartment.

Albert slapped her hand away, then reached in his pocket and pulled out a few dollars and some loose change.

"Here, take this and get the hell out. Otherwise when the light changes you can go for a ride with me and your boyfriend can drag the lake for your body."

The girl grabbed the money and bounded out of the car.

"Fuck you too, old man," she shouted, slamming the door behind her. She then joined her beau and the two of them took off laughing. In the meantime Albert's heart was pounding hard.

"Oh my God, the gentleman is a dope," he said to himself as he leaned over and tapped the button on the glove box. The door popped open exposing a .22 caliber handgun and a nine bullet clip alongside it. "Maybe you should keep it locked, dummy?" he added. "Jesus, what if I was stopped by a cop and he asked for my insurance and registration? Then what the hell would I have done?"

Albert turned onto the Leslie Street Spit. A parking place was available across from the idle community gardens. It was still early in the season and no one was tending the small make shift plots. A few committed runners and bikers passed by and the hot dog stand guy was setting up in his strategic spot at the gated entrance to the long peninsula. "Good," said Albert, "he will notice if anyone messes with the car," and he slung his binocular strap over his head, tucked his Peterson bird book in his belt and took off down the roadway, gated to the public all week because of the haul trucks, but open on weekends.

Today Albert was focused on the hawk migration which was in full swing. He had done his homework to get the timing down correctly. He read several articles in the *Toronto Star*, checked the birder hotline and even consulted with his one and only friend in the city, Norm Aspen. It was, of course, still too early for the warblers and vireos to arrive, those bright, energetic, insect eating sprites of the tree tops. They were his favorites.

"Without them," he complained, "we'd be stuck with those god-damn sparrows and starlings, starlings and sparrows. Interlopers! Some asshole actually brought them over from England and ruined everything here. Those feathered fuckers should be shot, eliminated, killed off. A good example of what happens when you drop your guard and let things get out of hand. Before you know it, the turkeys have taken over."

"Anyway, be positive, this should be good," he said as he made his way along the paved main road only to veer off towards the lake at the first bend in the path. Albert wandered around giving himself a chance to unwind from his traffic light surprise before he ventured out to see if his buddy Norm was at the Spit that day. Sure enough he found Norm sitting on a log beside a quiet bay located at the end of one of the many diversionary side roads that interlaced the man made peninsula. It was Norm's favorite spot, his sanctuary; a place of tranquility and natural beauty. "When I die I want my ashes scattered here," he often proclaimed to Albert.

Besides meeting happenstance like this at the Leslie Street Spit the men occasionally rendezvoused at the Rex Jazz Bar on Queen Street and a nearby coffee shop. Albert was a jazz fan. Norm preferred the blues. In their political outlook the friends were even more markedly different. Albert was as right leaning as a British sedan while Norm espoused the principles of the political left, the far left. "The labor movement died when the old IWW folded," Norm stated. "You couldn't break those old time unionists. Take your life in your hands if you ever tried to cross a picket line."

As Albert approached, Norm silently motioned him forward while staring intently through his binoculars.

"What yah got there?" whispered Albert and he pulled his own binoculars up to his eyes and tried to follow Norm's track.

"There's a hawk, looks like a merlin. He's sitting on the overhang of that dead poplar near the edge of the water. He's eyeing up that flock of starlings in the maple tree across the bay, waiting for them to fly off."

"OK, I've got him. Magnificent. Are they still moving through in any numbers? I guess the buteos are gone?"

"You just missed em. Were probably two hundred red tails and red shoulders last week. What were you doing anyway? I called and left a message."

"Oh, I was all fired up with a new project of mine."

"Anything I'd be interested in?"

"I doubt it. Just some trash removal you might say."

"OK, watch out! Here it comes," interrupted Norm suddenly standing up. "They've flushed out of the tree. He's after em. Look at that speed. My God, look at him go!"

"Talk about maneuverability. Once he zeros in on a target, it doesn't have a chance. Bye, bye blackbird."

"It's a wonder he can pick one out of that group. Seems so chaotic."

"Don't worry. He knows what he's doing. There it is! Bang! Holy Jesus, look at the feathers fly. You'd think that starling was hit with buckshot for God's sake."

"Yeah, he's got him now. Somehow it's sad though. I always feel sorry for the victim, eh," added Norm.

"For Christ's sake Norm, it's just nature's way. The strong prey upon the weak. Big deal! It keeps the animal kingdom healthy by, you know, eliminating the inferior individuals; the slow, the sick, the weak. That strengthens the entire gene pool. We humans could learn a lesson from all this because we're doing just the opposite. We coddle our weaklings so instead of declining, their population is exploding. The sons of bitches are overwhelming the rest of us and ruining the entire species. We're going to be a society of cowbirds if we don't watch ourselves. Our economy can't sustain this. We've got to do something before it's too late."

"What do you want to do? Go around knocking off every welfare recipient, every unemployed or homeless person who can't fend for himself like that hawk with them starlings? Eliminate the weak so only the strong survive?"

"I've thought about it. Just now at the traffic light on Lakeshore I ran into a couple of young punk losers. Little bitch actually jumped in the car with me. Fucking nerve, eh. If I had a gun in my hand I could have shot her. They're everywhere. I walked through the Music Garden the other evening and half the benches were occupied by the fucking homeless bunking down for the night. You get out of the theatre and there's some jerk-off sitting smack in the middle of the exit with his hat out for change. People have to step over him to get out of the show. What the fuck is that? They're at nearly every exit on the subway, every street corner and every laneway. You slow down for a red light and they got a squeegee out wiping your windshield before your car comes to a stop."

"I'd put up with squeegee kids if I could have a car," replied Norm. "And you know I ain't that far away from being one of them poor homeless bastards you're talking about. I'm only working part time, living in a dump of an apartment, no car, no money. You gonna want to shoot me someday too?"

"Hey Norm, you're not a free loading, parasitic, social leech bleeding the tax payers dry and ruining the city, shaking a goddamn Timmy's cup in everyone's face, or squeegeeing somebody's windshield. You're independent. Hard working. You got some pride. You've got ideas and interests." Albert slapped Norm on the back. "Look buddy, how about we grab a coffee down at the Starbuck's on Queen? I'm buying."

"Sorry, I'm meeting Claudia for lunch. She doesn't like you, remember? She thinks you're sinister and a bad influence on me."

Albert snorted in derision. "You can assure her I'm right handed, but no problem. I wanted to head down to the cormorant colony anyway. But I'm surprised you're still seeing her. She's got bitch written all over her face."

"Beggars can't be choosers to keep with the theme. Besides I like her and she's also the only woman to give me the time of day since Alice left. I'm happy for the first time in a long time and I don't want nothing to screw it up. I better go. How about the Rex next weekend? Check what's up and give me a call."

Norm waved good-bye over his shoulder. Albert turned and headed towards the lighthouse and the cormorant colony up the road. "I wouldn't mind seeing dear old Claudia on all fours whimpering like a dog," he said. "Don't know what she sees in old Norm anyway. He's a great guy and all, but he'd be more like a girlfriend than anything else.

I can't see him taking care of a woman like that. Too much for him. As far as I'm concerned, I prefer to pay for sex. Love for sale. Advertizing young love for sale. Love that's fresh and still unspoiled. Love that's only slightly soiled. Love for sale. That way I get what I want, when I want it and it goes home when I don't want it anymore and relatively speaking, it's cheap as hell. I can get four blow jobs for the cost of one dinner on the town, especially this town."

Far up the Spit Albert approached the cormorant colony with its thousands of black feathered, long billed, serpent like creatures screaming amid their stick stitched nests high in the dead and dying trees. The din from the multitudes and their gull neighbors was deafening. Albert almost reeled with confusion and awe tinged with a good ounce of admiration.

"Sure, sport and commercial fishermen, lot of birders too, condemn the poor bastards for their fish eating appetites and habitat destruction. Not me though, no way. I like em. They fascinate me. Why is it OK for man to haul tons of fish out of the lake and to build homes and businesses everywhere and anywhere, just look at all these fucking condos, but when a bird does it, it's an environmental catastrophe and they have to be eliminated. Hey, they're native birds. They struggle to make a living. They have a legitimate right to be here. You want to get rid of anything, get rid of the starlings and sparrows."

chapter 2

DETECTIVE GIGNAC OF the Toronto Homicide Division dropped a file on Sergeant Wright's desk. "The Captain said you might want to look at this when you get the chance."

"When I get the chance?" mimicked the Sergeant. "Sure, no problem and how about I stick a broomstick up my ass and sweep the precinct floor while I'm at it? Get the chance! I've got the Wellington Street murders along with the Brunswick House homicide fresh on the books. Community leaders and our so-called concerned citizens are screaming to high heaven and the Captain wants everything solved last week if I remember correctly. If he could spare a half dozen more detectives, maybe I'd get the chance to accommodate him."

Sergeant Wright leafed through the document as the detective stood by. "You're kidding, right? Some homeless asshole is dead and you're giving the report to me? Is this a joke?"

"Captain said it was unusual. The guy was shot."

"Jesus Christ, shot, stomped on, run over, thrown from a roof top, what do I care? It's one less loser to bother with. I mean, does anybody besides the Captain really give a damn?"

"I didn't read it, but don't shoot the messenger, eh. I'm on your side remember?"

"Thanks for the reminder," Sergeant Wright added. "Did the press pick it up?"

"Just Mary Monticello from the *Star*. She got wind of it somehow. Seems she did a past article on the murder victim and wanted to follow up. But we didn't release any detailed information mainly because we ain't got much. The coroner's report is pending. We used that as an excuse."

"Not her again, the "Champion of the Oppressed". Did the murder occur in Parkdale?"

"No, farther east, along the Gardiner at Spadina."

"Thank God for that. Monticello's got a pickle, dill, double garlic, up her ass for anything that happens in Parkdale. She lives there, you know. Thinks it's fucking Paradise with all her little Parkdalian neighbors flitting around socializing and looking out for each other. A real love in. Home sweet home for the great unwashed. I think she's a retired flower child still tip-toeing through the tulips. So what do we got here? A.k.a. Stinky Eddie? You've got to be kidding."

Sergeant Wright tossed the file into his briefcase. "I'll read it at home while I'm sitting on the john. A place worthy of its importance."

Unfortunately, home wasn't a place for relaxed reading of late for Sergeant Wright who longed for the days when his children, especially his now teenage daughter, Meaghan, were young and their problems consisted of lost baby teeth, diaper rash, and the choice between breast and bottle feeding.

"You better have a talk with that daughter of yours," said his wife before he got both feet inside the front door. "She sure as hell doesn't listen to me anymore. She's got a goddamn tattoo now after I expressly told her, No. I believe you said the same thing if I'm not mistaken."

"Mind if I get a beer first? It's been a long day."

Sharon Wright, a veteran police officer's wife, noticed the weariness and pain in her husband's face and toned down her attack.

"Have a seat. I'll get it for you. That Wellington homicide still got you jangled? It's been all over the news again. The families want answers. As though the police don't. What's wrong with these people? Don't they realize the police, you, are doing everything you can and want the case solved more than anybody?"

"Who knows? I gave up trying to figure them out a long time ago." Sergeant Wright took out the report Detective Gignac had dropped on his desk earlier in the day and skimmed through it. "Homicide, Edward Craig, a.k.a. Stinky Eddie. Jesus," he sighed.

"What's that?" inquired his wife handing him the sought after beer. "More homework?"

"Another murder to add to the list, some homeless bum killed under the Gardiner. Actually, I knew this loser. He was a regular down at #56. Brought in all the time for disturbing the peace. I could have shot the bastard a hundred times myself. He was a real pain in the ass, a complete and total pain in the ass. After a while we just ignored him and any complaints about him. It was a waste of time."

"So what's the big deal?"

As a rule Sergeant Wright tried to keep his family away from the conflicts and troubles his job created, but upon occasion he opened up a bit to his wife.

"Well, actually I see the Captain's point."

"Which is?"

"The guy was shot while he was bedded down for the night."

The Sergeant's wife shrugged her shoulders. "And?"

"And that means he was targeted and the killer was sophisticated enough to use a gun. It wasn't jealousy or robbery or some kind of argument amongst losers that caused good old Stinky Eddie's death."

"Then what was it?"

"I'm afraid to ask, but I'll tell you one thing. If there's another killing like this, some homeless guy shot to death, well then, the Toronto Homicide Squad will have a real problem on its hands, one far more serious than the Wellington Street murders. Now let me finish this beer before I have that talk with Meaghan."

Sergeant Wright knocked on his daughter's bedroom door and then immediately walked in. The family had an "open door" policy in effect before ten o'clock at night. No locked doors. No entry denied. The idea did not go over well with Meaghan. His son Josh at twelve was not yet a problem.

"You guys just don't understand. It's no big deal. All my friends have them. It's not like a piercing or something like that."

"Where exactly is that tattoo anyway?" asked the Sergeant, losing the mood for an argument if he ever had one in the first place.

"On my back."

"I don't see anything," replied Sergeant Wright, noting that his daughter had on a top that kept her entire back exposed except for a thin bra like strap between the shoulder blades.

"Lower, on the small of my back." The girl tugged her jeans down a bit until the edge of a colorful image appeared.

"I still can't see it. Looks like it's located more on your butt than on your back."

"Well, I'm not showing you any more, that's for sure."

"So then just who gets to see this tattoo and what is it? Not some bleeding skull with a knife through its eye socket, I hope?"

"Dad! Give me some credit. Actually, it's a butterfly, and it's small, delicate. I thought it was pretty and it's not like I'm walking around with my ass showing."

"Meaghan, nobody gets a tattoo so that it stays hidden and no one ever sees it. Tattoos are generally meant to be shown off, flaunted. And since yours is on your behind, I just wonder who it is you're trying to impress with it?"

"Please, you and Mom think I'm some kind of slut or something. You're both just too old fashioned, especially her."

"Enough said. You know we love you, and if you'd stop fighting us at every turn, life in this house would be a lot more enjoyable. You're grounded for three weeks."

"What?"

"I wanted six. It was your mother who talked me down to three. You can thank her when you come down for supper."

"I'm not hungry and I hate the both of you."

Sergeant Wright returned downstairs. At the same time Josh walked passed his sister's room and stuck out his tongue. A sandal came flying out the door.

"And I hate you too, you little brat."

In the living room Sharon handed her husband another beer while indulging in one herself. "Supper can wait a bit. Don't bother telling me how it went upstairs. It's alright. She'll get over it and we'll get through it. Does the music bother you? I can shut it off. I know you're not fond of jazz."

"Leave it on. I'll enjoy the pain," he replied with a smile.

"I don't know what's happened lately, this last year especially," Sharon continued. "I've lost control over her. We used to share things, laugh together. You know, girl stuff. Tease about you and Josh. Now nothing. I think maybe we should have stayed up north in Sudbury. It was more stable and secure. We even knew our neighbors. School had only a few hundred students. The house was nearly paid off. I don't even remember why we left now."

"Well, I wanted the promotion and the big city beckoned: the restaurants, the music, opportunity for you to work and better schools for the kids. And then there was your sister living in Rosedale. We had to keep up."

"Don, Come on. That's not fair. You wanted this house too, didn't you? It wasn't all me and you made sergeant. That was a great accomplishment and you deserved it. But let's not argue. Let's just sit here and talk. We haven't talked for a while and I miss it."

"Talk? I haven't slept, but you're right. We'll get over this and then I'll clear these cases and take it easy. No more promotions, climbing the ladder. I'm done with all that. I want more time with the family. Josh needs my attention too. It can't be all about Meaghan."

"Boys are easier to raise than girls. They're not as sensitive. He'll be fine. He adores you."

"Good, I need all the support I can get."

chapter 3

ALBERT TOOK A circuitous pedestrian route down Fort York Blvd. and over the Bathurst St. Bridge on his way to the Rex Hotel. He liked to walk and the semi isolated transitional neighborhood of old warehouses, construction sites, vacant lots and fields afforded a good opportunity to spot new victims. Yes indeed, his newly discovered mission had given Albert a new purpose for living and put a fresh, confident spring into his step. He felt exhilarated, alive for the first time in a long time. What a difference a day made.

"Quite the contrast from those years long ago when they told me about the cancer," he mused out loud remembering his near death experience. "Throat cancer? I never smoked or drank to any degree, the primary causes. Then it's a virus, they said. Sometimes it's just a virus that hits you at random. My luck. Fate. Maybe there is something to the phrase: Only the good die young. Of course, Maureen attributed "my salvation" to her constant church going and praying. Those goddamn votive candles of hers almost burned the house down. If she only knew the bargain I struck, I'm sure she would have wished me dead. Still, she kept me alive. I'd have to admit that much. Those special meals she cooked, the soups, puddings, and stews. Nice reward I gave her for her efforts too. Poor little butterfly in the garden waiting. I guess she really did hope I'd call her back that day she left, but sorry. Your man don't love you."

Albert tried to recollect the latest count of Toronto's homeless population. He had read it in an article in the *Star* and was sure it numbered in the thousands. Lots of losers to choose from, but, no doubt, he'd have to be selective. He couldn't possibly kill every one of them, but he would have to make enough of an impact to scare the majority off the streets and hopefully the hell out of Toronto altogether.

"I should concentrate here on the West End, he said. "Prioritize my own neighborhood. At least that way I can enjoy the fruits of my labor and not have to navigate through a minefield of panhandling losers every time I venture out the door. Of course, that holds risks. Narrows down the crime scene and gives the police an idea of where I live."

Albert didn't have to worry about disguising himself, or being careful not to slip up in front of others because basically there were no others. Besides Norm, and the occasional hooker, Albert was essentially a nobody, a nowhere man.

"That's what characterized a lot of the really successful guys, men like Di Salvo and Bundy and Casey. They were all ordinary, regular Joes. They didn't stand out." Albert carried the unloaded .22 strapped to his thigh underneath his pants. He had torn open the right side pockets on all his new "hunting" trousers for easy access. He kept the clip in the other pocket. He didn't want to take the chance of pulling a "Plaxico" and shooting himself in the leg.

"Damn, but I have to admit it's there, that feeling of power, omnipotence. Hard to explain, but it happens the minute you carry a gun. 'You talking to me? You talking to me?' I don't know. It's crazy. And then, of course, the real problem is that when you pack a gun, you just have to use it, pull the trigger. It's pointless otherwise like a camera whose shutter button you never press."

Albert made note of a developing pathway leading from the edge of Fort York Park's eastern entrance to under the Bathurst Bridge. The warm winds of Spring time were already carrying the migrant seeds of homelessness into the city. Soon they would sprout another patch of noxious weeds to mix with the perennials already rooted here and together they would spread and slowly choke off the life blood of the city he so loved. He couldn't let that happen. He had to stop them, eradicate them. He had to be the Weed Killer.

Queen St. was loaded with characters whose looks and dress fascinated Albert: the girl with the green hair, men and women with tattooed arms, legs, and necks, the low cut blouses and short skirts. He could walk that street forever and never get bored. It also provided him with many inviting targets since it was lined with panhandlers, many of them homeless, and therefore prime targets for eradication. That was where he first spotted Stinky Eddy pushing his way down the street using his cart as a battering ram knocking people aside like bowling pins.

"Fuck, I'd like to throw a bomb in there," Albert whispered as he passed the St. Christopher House on the corner of Bathurst and Queen. "Kill a bunch of them bastards in one fell swoop. Ditto for this dump," he added while in front of Johnny's Restaurant. "Hey, spare some change?" a bedraggled man with a cigarette dangling from his bobbing lower lip asked.

"Don't listen to him,' interjected a woman in her thirties, pushing the man aside. "He'll just waste it on booze, but me, I need fare money, eh, for the streetcar. Five bucks."

"Five bucks!" stammered Albert. "Jesus, what happened to asking for some change?"

"I got to get home. I live way over on the West End. Look, you can give me a loan. I'll take your name and address and send you the money later. I'm not like these losers here. Come on."

"Well, that's original," Albert chuckled. He paused, then reached in his pocket. "OK, here. More than my monthly quota for alms. Hope you get a seat."

"Hey, thank you, Thank you very much. If I run into you again, I'll repay you. You can trust me."

"You must be nuts mister," said the cigarette bobber. "Hey, by the way, I need plane fare to Calgary. You got two hundred dollars you can borrow me? Ha, ha, ha." On John Street an older man sat on a milk crate shaking a Tim Horton's cup at passers- by.

"Sorry," said Albert. "I gave up the street."

On the other side of Queen St. in front of Much Music two young lads and a girl sat leaning against the building, a dog curled up next to them. The dog looked like the cleanest of the bunch Albert noted. He could read the large print on the sign from where he was walking. "Cash for Hash. We won't lie."

Farther up at the East restaurant a young man squatted on the sidewalk. "Will Take Verbal Abuse for Cash." At the bank machines on McCall Street sat another man surprisingly well groomed it seemed to Albert. He silently held out his cap to pedestrians. Albert looked at him with a quick up and down and then said. "You look too well dressed to be begging. What's your problem?"

The man immediately stood up and shouted at Albert. "What the fuck do you know about me or what I'm wearing? I got fired from my job six months ago. I got two kids and a wife to feed, you bastard." He followed behind Albert gesticulating wildly. "So what am I supposed to do, dress in rags so you can feel sorry for me? Is that what you want? Maybe I should piss my pants, shit myself? Would that help? Here, wait a minute, maybe I can oblige you." The man stopped in the middle of Spadina Avenue and with his legs spread apart he squatted and moaned and grunted his face turning bright red. "There, how's that? That better? Do I fit the image now? Do I? Do I?"

The crossing crowd spread away from the man like waves on the Red Sea as Albert stepped up his pace and disappeared amidst the throng leaving the man to scream in the distance like a coyote baying at the full moon.

"Jesus Christ, this is getting goddamn ridiculous," Albert sighed. "Ridiculous."

Albert thought immediately of Stinky Eddie and the man's final minutes on earth. That's why I didn't feel any remorse. Nothing. Why should I? The son of a bitch deserved everything he got. His life was useless. I only regret that I killed him so fast, that I didn't stop and tell him what a worthless piece of shit he was before I pulled the trigger. How he contributed nothing to society. How his very existence, regardless of anything he actually did, thought, hoped for, or imagined was a defilement, a cancer, a blight on the city.

Yes, Albert reasoned, a more personal involvement would perk up the killing, give it a kick. He could savor the moment, actually enjoy it. Only now was he beginning to understand why killers left clues for the police and engaged them or a reporter in some kind of dialogue. It was exciting, a chance to match wits, taunt, brag, show his superiority. The whole exercise of murder was rather pointless if left unexplained. But wasn't it also true that such exposure inevitably led to the killer's capture? The murderer virtually gave himself away in an effort to challenge the police. Perhaps the real genius lay in keeping quiet with success and escape as the final rewards. Anyway, how many more killings would he be able to get away with before the veil would be lifted off his mission. The next shooting might well be the one that provided that spark of attention he was both dreading and anticipating, the beginning of the beguine.

Laura Hubert was on stage at the Rex when Albert arrived. He liked her detached animation and self confidence and her quirky voice. A good crowd was on hand. Albert was glad. He always felt an awkward unease for the entertainers if only a few patrons were in attendance. No one he recognized was around this evening. He sat at the bar. Since his radiation and chemotherapy the acts of eating and drinking had changed permanently for Albert. His saliva was gone making swallowing difficult. Food tasted bitter and metallic and alcohol burned his throat. Two drinks, White Russians preferably, were about his limit.

"Oh Baltimore, it's hard just to live."

He dropped twenty dollars in the jar when Laura brought it around. They can't make a living at this, he thought. Just doing it for pleasure probably and hoping for a break down the line. Must be frustrating. He bought her a beer.

"Jesus, don't give her a drink," someone shouted jokingly from the audience. "She's a mean drunk."

Albert didn't like the next group and he wasn't willing to pay the cover charge for the performance. The gun strapped to his leg also put him physically and emotionally on edge. He was constantly tapping at it from outside or surreptitiously slipping his hand down his pants to make sure it was secure. All I need is for it to fall out of my pant leg and have me kick it across the floor. 'Oh that old thing. I keep it for protection. Seen a couple of coyotes over at Fort York. Could be man eaters. You never know, eh?' At eight o'clock Albert walked out of the Rex. It was getting dark. Queen Street was busy with people as he walked westward back the way he had come turning south on Spadina to King Street. He thought of stopping at the Wheat Sheaf, but decided to pass it by at the last minute.

"Don't want to cloud my judgment," he reminded himself. "Clear thinking and quick decision making are essential. Anyway, there's no music there."

The gun itself was now burning into Albert's thigh, branding him. He had to get it out and into his hand. Albert turned up Strachan and crossed the railroad tracks. It was quiet, dark. He stopped and with an audible sigh of relief pulled the gun out and mated it with the bullet clip. The sound of the sliding metal and the click when the clip locked in place was an aphrodisiac to him, a fatal and exciting mating of parts that belonged together and had no functional separate existence. Albert felt a thrilling tingle course through his body. It was like an impending orgasm which he tried desperately to hold off, to prolong, in order to make it all the more pleasurable in the end. This was pure power he thought. No wonder God is so happy.

***

Jenny and Lefty passed the wine bottle between them as they sat behind the old Lighting and Standards buildings just below the northern side of the Strachan Street bridge. Since the city employees moved out six months ago this was the couple's favorite night time haunt. They regularly spent the night inside the building huddled in a corner where they couldn't be spotted by a casual observer or passer-by.

"We'd get more money if we went legit and had a place to stay. I'd really like us to move in together," said Lefty. "I mean you could still have sex with other guys, you know, do tricks and all that, but it would be nice to have someone around steady and we get along good, talk and share stuff, eh. And we could help look out for each other too."

"The sex thing, that's just for the money, eh," added Jenny. "When I was younger I'd get a lot of cash for sex. Guys didn't mind paying me ten, fifteen bucks for a lay and five for a blow job. Money was damn good then. Now I'm lucky to pull in fifteen bucks for a whole night's worth of work and that's fucking and blow jobs combined."

"Hey, you know what I seen today looked like a real good idea, eh? A guy at St. Christopher's, you seen him around I'm sure. He's a little guy from Parkdale. He hangs around behind the trash collection station. I think his name is Pete, Little Pete, they call him. Well, anyways, he was pulling around one a them big blue garbage bins they got now, eh, the really big ones."

"What's he want garbage for? Fuckin nuts or what?"

"No, no, wait. You see he has all his stuff in that bin. It carries everything he owns, and it's got a lid for when it rains and it's on wheels too, eh. Perfect. And at night, what do you know? He tips it over and sleeps in it, all comfortable and warm. He pops up that lid like a little roof too for extra room like a porch, eh. He sleeps in there all night long like a fucking turtle. I'm thinking of getting one myself. They're all over the streets. Just pick one up, clean it out and off you go. Hey, you got any wine left in that bottle?"

"Not much."

"That's OK, you finish it off. Maybe Common Johnny next door's got something. I'll walk over later. He probably ain't bedded down for the night yet. Hey, you wanna go tomorrow and get a meal at McDonald's after our allowance comes in? It's Thursday, eh. A little treat. They give you unlimited pop if you supersize."

"Yeah, but I ain't buying no booze until it's night time. You buy something early and every leech in town is suddenly your good buddy, eh. And if you get too smashed, somebody's bound to roll you too because they know you just got paid. I'm careful now. Last time I swear it was Stinky Eddie took my stash. I had fucking sixteen dollars saved up. He's a fucking little weasel that one."

"I haven't seen him lately. Somebody said he died."

"Good, I hope it's true. He was a fucking asshole. I'm sure he was the one ripped me off."

"Hey, look somebody's comin. Maybe it's Common Johnny. Let's see if he's got something to drink." It was beyond twilight. A couple of outdoor utility lights automatically went on farther down the alley. Lefty and Jenny had deliberately broken the lights immediately above them in order to secure more privacy. They had never encountered a watchman at this time of night so they weren't prepared to flee.

"This sure as fuck ain't Johnny. He's dressed too good," Jenny laughed.

"Hey man, I think you're lost or something," said Lefty to the strange man who nonetheless walked steadily towards them. "This don't go nowhere. Not a through street."

"That's for sure," added Jenny. "Fucking dead end. Hey, while you're here, you got any spare change?"

"It's a dead end for sure," echoed the man in a calm voice. Too calm thought the two vagrants as they peered up at the figure who now stood directly opposite them.

Lefty began to get an uneasy feeling born of many a past confrontation and he gripped the now empty wine bottle tightly.

"It ain't safe for guys like you to be around here," said Lefty. "You better get going. There's some rough customers bunk down here at night."

"Is that so? Rough customers. I don't think I'm too worried about rough customers."

"Hey, mister," chirped up Jenny. "Maybe you looking for sex, eh? How about a blow job? Ten bucks. That ain't much for a guy like you, eh. How about it? Help us out here."

"Sorry darling, my idea of sex is a twenty-five years old escort, naked and down on her knees sucking my cock in front of a full length mirror."

"Jesus, how much does she get for that?" asked Jenny wistfully.

"One hundred dollars."

"Holy fuck," said both Jenny and Lefty at the same time.

"I could live a month on that," continued Lefty.

"And have money to spare," added Jenny. "So how about it mister? I'll suck your cock right here for, for twenty bucks. That's a cheap deal for you, eh. Come on."

"I wouldn't stick a pig's dick from one of these passing transport trucks into that mouth of yours. Who knows what diseases you've got and your moronic mud puppy friend here doesn't look like he's got the highest standards of hygiene to provide a valid reference."

"Hey man, that's no fuckin way to talk to her," Lefty said and clutched at the wall behind him in an effort to stand up. He fell back down with a thud when he saw the gun in the man's hand.

"Eenie, meenie, minie, moe," the man swung the gun from Lefty to Jenny and back again. "I think I'll kill only one of you and let the other one go. A bit of uncharacteristic generosity on my part, but what the hell. That's the kind of guy I am. So which will it be? Sophie's choice with my apologies to the Jews."

"Who the fuck is Sophia? Why don't you just shoot her and leave us alone? We ain't done nothing to you. We're just sitting here minding our own business," pleaded Lefty.

"You should shoot him," interrupted Jenny pointing out her companion. "He's a guy. It ain't right to shoot no woman. And he don't do nothing but lay around and drink all day anyways. Me, I help out at the food kitchen. And I, I can still suck your dick. No charge, eh, No charge, Mister."

"You bitch. I let you have the last gulp of wine," complained Lefty.

"Shoot him!"

"Come on Jenny. We were going to McDonald's tomorrow remember? Please."

The stranger laughed. "The love of all loves, stronger than brotherly love, or the love of son for mother, is the undying, unfaltering love of one dead drunk for another." An old poem from somewhere. Anyway, just a minute now."

"What, what you waiting for? Shoot him. I won't say nothing. Not a word. I swear. Shoot him. Shoot," shouted Jenny as she slyly unbuttoned her blouse exposing as much cleavage as possible for the man to see.

The stranger ignored her and put his finger up and tilted his head. "It's coming."

"What? What's coming?"

"The night train."

And as the rumbling sound approached and drowned out all conversation and noise, the stranger's gun flashed out three times. He then knelt down beside Jenny who was crying and having trouble breathing.

"You said you'd shoot only one of us. Only one."

"Sorry, but tonight's the night I told you a little white lie. Ha, ha."

And Albert squatted there watching Jenny die, holding up her chin with the barrel of his revolver and staring into her eyes. He waited for some hint of remorse or regret to creep into his heart, but there was nothing. Not a pang, a murmur.

"Weeds," he said. "They're weeds. Ugly, foul looking, smelly weeds choking out the flowers in the garden, the garden that is my beloved Toronto."

He looked around in the dim light. Several plantains and a few dandelions were growing out of the cracks in the pavement. Albert pulled two out and stuffed them into the mouths of his victims.

"There chew on that in the afterlife."

On his way through Garrison Common following a meandering route back home to Niagara Street, he shot and killed Common Johnny.

"Bye, bye black bird," he said as he passed the old tombstones embedded in the memorial wall.

Inside his house, Albert kicked off his footwear in the hallway, shut the door and slumped against it wearily. He was shaking. During the walk home the calmness he had exhibited on the killing fields had turned to fright and anxiety. He was like an helpless animal frantically fleeing to its den at the approach of night and the inevitable emergence of nocturnal predators. Had he walked too fast, he wondered? Did he sweat too profusely? Had anyone seen or heard him? He tried to compose himself. "OK breathe deeply, once, twice, three times. Jesus Christ, I gotta piss. Can't hold it anymore." Albert snapped on the light and walked toward the kitchen entrance. Suddenly he stopped.

"Oh my God," he cried in horror. "What did I do? What the hell!"

Albert stared down at the floor where he saw a watery smear of red along the bottom side of the wall. He stepped back and lifted his shoes examining their soles. Nothing, but he noticed the cuff of his pant leg. It was damp, damp with blood.

"Son of a bitch, what an idiot! That's all I need. Leave a trail for some lope eared, sad sack bloodhound to follow right to my goddamn door. Jesus, what a fool am I. How the hell did I let that happen?"

Albert yanked his pants off and rushed into the basement, a certain panic still coursing through his mind. That was ironically one reason why he felt the need to keep his attacks unpredictable, to strike only when a target presented itself. That way he wouldn't obsess when his schemes went wrong as they invariably would if he plotted them out to the last detail.

"No plan to go wrong, no screw up to anticipate, no anxiety, just simple reaction," he had told himself. "Also the sheer randomness of the murders will make it all the more difficult for Toronto's finest to find and arrest me."

Albert emerged with a pail of sudsy water and some rags which were actually former tea towels that his wife had left behind. They had small flowers, daisies, her favorite, hand stitched on one side. He got to work cleaning off the baseboards. He next washed the floor, then rinsed the towels, spilled out the water and threw the towels and his pants into the washing machine. When the floor dried he applied a coat of wax.

"Goddamn good thing I didn't walk into the dining room. If I had gotten blood on that Persian rug I'd have to go out and gun down a dozen of those bastards just to get even. The shoes have to go though just in case."

Albert sat in his living room sipping a glass of sherry with a twist of orange peel. It was one of the few drinks he could enjoy after the cancer treatments had decimated his mouth.

Even so, one small glass was his limit. He listened to Billie Holiday, in his mind the best of the jazz singers. "My man don't love me. He treats me oh so mean. He's the meanest man that I ever seen," Albert repeated. "Yes, Billie Holiday. Listen closely. Simple, straight forward approach, but the pathos in her voice, the emotion, the suffering, it tears at you. That kind of feeling, that interpretation can't be taught or imitated. It's personal and unique. But poor Maureen, she never got the music. That was obvious from the start. Of course, she did like Chet Baker's, "My Funny Valentine". Probably the most smarmy, overdone, bullshit, tug at your heartstrings piece of musical crap ever written. She cried every time she heard it. After a while so did I."

Maureen, after all those years, he still remembered that blank, unblinking stare on her face the day of her departure. It reminded him of a frog he had shot with his pellet gun when he was a kid and hunting with friends at the old Brick Works. The frog had been shot several times, but still sat motionless on a lily pad with it's side torn open and its intestines hanging down into the water. Albert could remember its white throat pulsating up and down with each breath it took as it just sat there dying but making no sound nor giving any indication of its mortal wound. Maureen was that frog the day he said good-bye.

chapter 4

NEWS OF THE murders crashed through the Toronto media like a tsunami. The city was appalled, aghast, and in disbelief. From TV to newspapers to magazines, and the internet headlines trumpeted the tragedy. "Homeless Homicides," "Trio Targeted for Death," "Not Here. Not in Toronto!" "Homeless Slain in Gruesome Killings," "Innocents and Innocence Murdered."

People talked about the killings everywhere they met. The cafés and restaurants, the bars, Starbucks, and Tim Hortons, the City Donut Shops, were abuzz. In the subways and on street cars and buses passengers for once dropped their iPods and cell phones and actually conversed with their neighbors and fellow travelers. Little work was accomplished that day in the thousands of offices and businesses in Toronto. The Homeless Homicides dominated everything. Most of all and not surprisingly they were also the number one topic in the police stations throughout the city.

"So, it goddamn well happened," said Sergeant Wright to himself as he waited nervously to be called into Captain Donnally's office. "Stinky Eddie ain't alone no more. But three at one time? Is this guy crazy? He can't possibly hope to get away with it. Impossible. Once the evidence is gathered and our forensic crew gets done, we'll have this guy's sorry ass in the bag sure as hell."

Calculating the killer's chances of escape was not the Sergeant's only concern this morning, the day after the murdered bodies were discovered in the city's West End neighborhood. His more immediate and unenviable problem lay in explaining to his Captain how these homicides were related to the Stinky Eddie murder which had taken place several weeks before and which he had thus far failed to investigate.

"Yes, Sir, I've got it here," said the Sergeant taking out a folder from his briefcase. "These latest homicide victims, the two at the Lighting Standards Building on Strachen and the third at Garrison Common, were all homeless and had apparently been bunking down in the buildings or out in the Common on a regular basis. We don't have their full names just yet but they appear to be well known in the Queen West section of Toronto.

"They were all shot at close range with a .22 caliber handgun. There were no witnesses and no grieving family or friends have come forward as yet to help in the identification. The scene of the crimes was isolated, obviously selected to protect the killer who must have had some prior knowledge of the area. He came and went with no one observing his movements. The victims, as well as another found under the Gardiner Expressway a while back, appeared to be specifically targeted and all fit into the same modus operandi."

Sergeant Wright threw the reference to the first homicide in to break the ice on the Stinky Eddie case. The Captain picked up on it immediately.

"As well as the one found under the Gardiner Expressway? There was a fourth victim?"

"Yes sir, but it was actually reported almost a month ago as a separate case, one Edward Craig, a.k.a. Stinky Eddie whose body was found under the Gardiner Expressway Off Ramp at Spadina Avenue on April 25th of this year. He had been shot once in the chest and died at the scene."

"Yeah, I remember that now. The gun shot tipped me off. It was an unusual way for a homeless person to die. I gave the file to Gignac to pass along to you. I wanted you to look into it. You mean to say this Stinky, ah, whatever his name was, was a victim of the same killer?"

"Eddie, Stinky Eddie, yes, everything fits, but we didn't have Stinky Eddie's forensic report until weeks after his murder and on top of that he had been dead for some time before his body was discovered by a city construction crew doing some work under the Expressway. There was no bullet or casing found at the scene. It passed right through him so we had next to nothing on the gun itself. It was only after these most recent killings that I had anything substantial to work with and that's when the connection was made."

"So before that you let it ride, the Stinky Eddie case? You didn't bother to investigate it?"

"What else could I do? The Wellington murders were sucking all the oxygen out of the Homicide Squad and the press was eating us up. We gave it our top priority so when this Stinky Eddie thing came along, I mean a homeless victim with no evidence around and no motive, it kind of got lost in the shuffle. Plus, remember we also had the Brunswick case. We got our man on that one. No mean feat given our manpower shortage."

"Well, Sergeant, you've got quite a fistful of cards right now and, I might add, ones that you've dealt yourself. Weren't you the one who convinced me and the Chief to buy into your "All In" manpower scheme? When a homicide occurs throw everything and everyone into it, all twenty detectives and go at it en masse. Flood the case with manpower. That sounded great at the time, Sergeant, and obviously helped secure your promotion. Something I was not exactly in favor of I might add just so we have full disclosure here. But what happens to your scheme when we have multiple homicide cases, when a backlog develops and we've already got all our investigative eggs in one basket? I think that overload was a contributing factor in the Wellington and Brunswick cases, one of which is still unsolved.

"So I hope you're a good swimmer, Sergeant, because it's a long way to shore. Now, let me ask you another thing. Does the press know about this Stinky Eddie, the fourth victim who was actually the first victim if we straighten out the timeline?"

"No, but we've had one reporter, Mary Monticello, snooping around and starting to make connections."

"Just between the two of us, Sergeant, I can't honestly say I would have lost a lot of sleep over a few homeless assholes departing this world, but when this kind of thing gets into the hands of the bleeding heart media and out into the public, we got a nightmare on our hands. So what we'll do right now is concentrate on the three recent homicides. Give the press as much detail as possible without compromising the case. Hint at the possibility of other murders, then make the Stinky Eddie announcement in a week or so. Play up the forensic delays and claim we were already monitoring the situation and didn't want to tip our hand to the killer. In other words pretend you were actually doing your job. We'll stick to that story. In the meantime, is there anything else I should know?"

"Yes, the last three victims, those at the Lighting Standard Building and Garrison Common, they all had weeds stuffed in their mouths. After they were shot according to forensics."

"What?"

"Weeds, sir. The murderer, we're presuming he's alone since we have only one weapon involved, stuck weeds into the mouths of his victims. I forget what type of weed, but it's in the report. Only these last three. Stinky Eddie was untouched that way."

"Let's keep that fact to ourselves right now," said Captain Donnally. "The press didn't get hold of that information, did they?"

"No, the drunk who found the victims at the Lighting Standards Building flagged down a cruiser. The constable examined the bodies and found the weeds in the victims' mouths.

The drunk doesn't remember anything other than guessing who the two were from the location they were in. He said they slept there regularly for the two months. Later one of the cops found the Garrison Common body during a routine search of the area."

"Good, that piece of information can come in handy in later Id-ing the perpetrator. Also, I want you to handle tomorrow's press conference so let's go over all this again and get our stories straight. I don't want any surprises later on."

***

When Albert walked into the City Donut Shop on King Street he was immediately waved over to a table by Norm who had arrived ahead of him for one of their rare downtown rendezvous. Other than also visiting the Rex Hotel, Norm did not usually venture west of Yonge Street. Nevertheless, given Norm's more friendly nature he did know a few of the regulars at the coffee shop by name. Albert only recognized a couple people by sight. "I'd fucking well shoot myself if I had to associate with any of these assholes on a regular basis," he said.

"Where have you been? Hear the news?" stated Norm out loud. "Looks like we got a serial killer in town and he's targeting the homeless. Besides three down in your neck of the woods they found another one shot dead under the Gardiner. Yeah, Toronto made the big time. We now got our own mass murderer. We can join the ranks of the big US cities. And, hey, you should start dressing up a bit better before he mistakes you for a homeless person and guns you down too."

Albert grabbed a large coffee and a blueberry-cranberry muffin and settled into a seat and a conversation with Norm. The rest of the room was loud with argument and banter.

"It's a terrible thing," continued Norm. "Bad enough these poor people are forced to live out on the streets, but now they've got to be careful they're not murdered in their sleep. If we had a humane, responsible social system, this would never happen, never. Everyone would have decent, affordable housing, along with a good, secure job, as a right of citizenship, not a privilege of wealth and opportunity."

"I don't think the murderer was considering the ramifications of economics or government policy," said Albert. "Very few people look into this social study stuff as closely as you do, Norm, and if they did they obviously don't see it the same way. The killer too was probably just fed up with running into those demanding, dead end losers with their hands stuck out everywhere he went on the streets of Toronto."

"Yeah, because he blames them and not the system. He don't realize they're not the problem, only a symptom of it. People react to conditions rather than analyze them. If someone has a job, they're considered useful. If they can't or won't work, or aren't needed anymore, then society, capitalist society to be specific, dumps them out on the street to fend for themselves. That's how we got the homeless problem."

"Well, I, for one, don't have much sympathy for the unwashed masses. If they want care and comfort they can work for it like the rest of us. Certainly they can at least not make nuisances of themselves. Face it, whatever the reason, these jerks are a pain in the ass, and to date the city fathers, Mayor Milne in particular, aren't doing anything to solve the problem. Frankly, I think a few more of these killings and the homeless problem in Toronto will be solved without costing the public one more penny in social assistance or welfare. The killer is making a statement. If no one else will solve the problem, he will, his way. Not pretty, but effective."

"Ha, you're right there buddy," said a patron sitting at a nearby table. "This guy is cleaning up the streets. I bet the rest of those homeless bastards are leaving town as we speak."

"I hope so," added the fellow's companion. "Them bums are a pain in the ass. They shit up the sidewalks and chase people away. The tourists, they don't want to come here to Toronto no more because of the losers on the streets. In cities down in the States like New York and Chicago they got rid of all their bums. Probably all wound up here. Guess what, just last month there was a woman right here on King Street, she stabbed a guy who refused to give her some money. She killed the poor bastard and guess what again? She was homeless and from the States. What do you think of that, eh?"

"I can't believe I'm hearing this? Am I getting this right?" said Norm. "You people are condoning murder as a convenient way to rid the city of a serious social problem? Maybe we should start shooting the emotionally disturbed, the physically handicapped as well as the homeless? Let's clean house. Go all the way."

"Count me in if that's the case," shouted someone from another table.

"But what are we really losing here?" chimed in Albert. "Valuable citizens who have jobs and families, people who contribute to society, volunteer their time, pay taxes even?

No, these are people who contribute nothing. Now, sure I'm sorry they're dead, got murdered, but I don't grieve for them. How can you grieve or feel sorry for someone whose life is a total zero, who makes no contribution to his family or society. Make no mistake, there's no willow weeping for these losers."

"But these people are human beings. They don't need any sanction for their existence from anybody. They have an inherent right to life, liberty, and happiness," added Norm quickly.

Just then the store manager walked by headed for the front door of the shop. "I wish that killer man, he would come here to my store and shoot that, that bastard outside," the man mumbled nodding at the pan handler who was holding the door open for customers.

"Spare change? Thank you. OK, have a nice day anyway."

"Why don't you just hire him, and he maybe won't be homeless and broke?" said Norm.

"He's filthy and he don't want to work. Ask him."

"We'll take your word for it,' added Albert.

"Son of bitch sleeps on the sidewalk right across the street. Whenever he wakes, he come here. Back and forth all day. Then, he buy a coffee and use the washroom. I caught him washing feet in the sink. If I say something he start bitching and howling, raise a fuss and I lose customer. So I just let go. Live with it."

"That reminds me of that Mark Kelly special I seen on the CBC. I think it was last winter," said the man at the table next to Albert and Norm. "Kelly, he was in Winnipeg interviewing a bunch of homeless people, eh, and people that dealt with them every day, social workers, government people. Anyway there was this one guy, I think he called himself Superman or something crazy like that, and Mark Kelly, he sort of liked this guy and felt sorry for him. Figured he was smart, eh, and just needed a break in life. So Kelly goes out and talks some employer into hiring the guy, and even gets this Superman a long term room in some shelter. Kelly's got the whole damn thing arranged, and then guess what happens?"

"The guy, Superman, he turns down the job," volunteered Albert.

"Yeah, how did you know?"

"I saw the program."

"Not that you'd have to," continued Albert. "None of these people want to work. I've seen them begging in front of stores that had a "Now Hiring" sign hanging in the window right above their heads."

"How are any of these unfortunates going to qualify for a job, any job?" said Norm. "You ain't got decent clothes, no washroom to get cleaned up in. Who's gonna take a chance on hiring you? Get serious. You need a permanent address just to get welfare."

"Think they'll catch this guy, our killer?" said the story teller to Albert.

"Only if he trips himself up. The police don't have very many clues and no witnesses from what I've read. Anybody hear anything else?"

"Why would there be witnesses? These people are so socially marginalized that they're virtually invisible," added Norm.

"The victims were shot late at night and in out of the way places and that's why there ain't no witnesses. Who's going to go snooping around old warehouses and abandoned stores and under highway over-passes looking for trouble?"

"He only kills men."

"The last one was a woman. They said she was raped first."

"He only killed her because she was a witness. I heard that when he was done he arranged her body real nice and respectful like he was sorry he had to kill her."

"I wonder where this psycho lives?" said Albert.

"I bet he's from around here somewhere, the general downtown area, or leaning towards the West End. The murders all happened in this area, eh. Spadina, Strachan, four victims."

"That's exactly why he is definitely not from here," said Norm getting into the details of the argument and forgetting for a minute the social ramifications of the situation. "He's too smart to kill in his own backyard. All those killings here, that in itself is a guarantee he's definitely from some other part of town."

"Interesting," said Albert. "Very interesting. You might be on to something there, but no matter how you look at it, things ain't the way they used to be and Toronto will never be the same again."

chapter 5

MARY MONTICELLO SAT sipping her coffee listening to the conversation swirling around her. She rarely came to this City Donut. Just happened to be in the area doing a newspaper story on the construction lot across the street featuring the changing face of the city. The site was once the home of dry cleaners back in the Thirties. Now it was the new location of a luxury condo building which sold for multiple millions of dollars making the family of the original immigrant owner wealthy overnight. While she was at the City Donut, however, Mary did take the time to admire the shop's furniture. It was a special interest of hers. She noted: no fabric, cushions, pillows, plush couches or chairs, just plain, varnished wood everywhere. One can't take any chances with those sons of bitching bedbugs, she ruminated. They could be anywhere.

Mary largely ignored the cooling bagel next to her coffee cup. She wasn't hungry anymore. She was angry. Mary had done an article on Stinky Eddie the year before and had noted his recent death. She should have pressed the police for more information at the time because really, when did they ever volunteer anything? Then she would have had something, the seed of the most important crime story in Toronto history. A story like that could boost a career, move someone from an occasional columnist to a full time crime writer, maybe even syndicated, she thought. It wasn't just for the lack of remuneration or personal prestige that Mary was upset and disappointed. Sure, that mattered, but more importantly and in a much less selfish manner she was concerned about other people, her neighbors and fellow Torontonians. She wanted to do right by them and writing full time from a public media post such as the *Toronto Star* she could fight the good fight. At present her endeavors were spread across a broad spectrum of projects. Besides her bi-weekly column in the *Star* she also raised funds for anti-poverty groups, served as a part time receptionist at the Parkdale Mission, tutored underprivileged students and delivered Meals on

Wheels not to mention her on- going crusade against the most pressing, but largely unacknowledged, social problem in Toronto i.e. the bedbug infestation.

Now with these recent murders, events had taken a far more serious turn and her mission in life became more urgent. The poor, the homeless were being killed right on the streets of Toronto. Furthermore, judging from the conversation around her in the coffee shop there was precious little sympathy and certainly no justice being served by the public. She'd have to work harder.

"This is more downtown Toronto talking anyway," she said to sooth herself. "You'd never hear this kind of talk in Parkdale."

Mary's mood and her outlook on social progress and anti-poverty efforts were on a rollercoaster lately and her head was spinning from the ride. Last year, for example, had been the overall anti-poverty campaign's best year to date. The Canadian economy as a whole had expanded and with prosperity charitable organizations and anti-poverty groups put pressure on the local and provincial governments to do something about the poverty problem. A new coalition, an amalgam of numerous formerly independent anti- poverty groups, was even formed calling itself "The Ten-in-Two Committee" which advocated an aggressive new initiative in combating poverty and homelessness. Their statement of purpose was prescnted in a news release to the media during a rally at Nathan Phillips Square. Mary covered the event for the *Toronto Star* under the headline:

"New Coalition Takes Straight Aim at Poverty" and quoted directly from the group's manifesto: "The economic wealth of this great country was created by all its citizens and must be shared by all. The current disparity in wealth, due to inherent flaws in our economic system, is unethical, immoral, and indeed criminal. Now is the perfect time for new meaningful action to combat systemic poverty in Ontario. We have had plenty of studies regarding poverty in the province. We don't need further documentation of the problem. The Ten-in-Two Committee is therefore resolved to reduce poverty in Ontario by a full ten per cent in the next two years. To this end we demand that anti-poverty initiatives show measureable, verifiable progress and all projects must be done with the active participation of anti-poverty groups and locally affected citizens. Business lobbies are not welcome and sole government oversight regarding anti-poverty measures and their efficacy is no longer acceptable.

"With the goal of reducing poverty by ten per cent in mind, economic statistics will be checked regularly to monitor progress. What doesn't work will be scrapped. What works will be expanded. These programs will involve increased government spending and new taxes leveled in particular against the wealthier members of our society. This must be done to achieve a just and proper redistribution of wealth. The Ten-in-Two Committee welcomes any and all like minded groups to join our growing organization. Together we can and will make a decided difference."

Mary Monticello was happy with the spotlight this new group had shined on the anti- poverty fight although Mary herself didn't sign up as a member. She shunned organizations as such and didn't like the broad focus of the Committee's approach.

She preferred a more individualized, personalized attack. "Poverty is not an abstraction, a statistic. Poverty is poor people and poor people need help on a personal level. Individual volunteerism is central to the solution. If we all do our part, we can change the whole."

Nevertheless, Mary was heartened to see both the city and provincial governments cave to the Ten-in-Two-Committee's pressure and within the year a wide range of new programs were crafted. These included an increase in the minimum wage, a boost to welfare and unemployment benefits, job training, subsidized day care and after hours educational and recreational programs, an increase in the number of teacher assistants in elementary schools, and an emphasis on the construction of affordable housing.

Everyone in the city's charities was refocused and happy. Mary redoubled her efforts. The future in the fight against poverty looked winnable for the first time in a long time. Then in six short months the bottom fell out of the Ontario economy and the government reversed its course and cancelled its commitments. The Ten-in-Two Committee faded away with a whimper.

"The same old story,' cried one volunteer. "When times are good the government doesn't want to rock the boat, tip the scales and trigger a recession. Then later when the economy falters, it's, 'We can't afford these programs right now. We'll have to wait until the economy improves.' How are we supposed to make any kind of progress?"

"It's all bull shit, eh. Premier McGuiness and the rest of them were just waiting for this downturn, probably knew it was coming. If not they would have dreamt up some other excuse."

"You know, if we volunteers didn't always help out, if there was no one for the poor to fall back on, maybe the government would be forced to do more on its own. They couldn't be ducking the issue and dumping everything on us. What would happen if all our fund raising and volunteer work simply ended?"

"We can't close up shop and let people starve," Mary intervened. "I'm not prepared to quit and see people suffer like that. It's not right. We have to keep up our efforts. We can solve this problem one poor person, one underprivileged child, one unemployed adult at a time. The Ten-in-Two Committee may be dead, but the rest of us are alive and as long as I'm alive I'm going to fight for justice. I would, however, make an exception regarding the recent bedbug infestation that is sweeping the city. For that we could use some concerted governmental assistance."

On her way out of the City Donut Shop Mary gingerly dropped the wrapped, untouched bagel onto the homeless doorman's hand. "Toasted, light cream cheese," she smiled.

"Hey, don't you got no money?" he replied. "I ain't hungry. I already ate."

***

The Police News Conference at CP 24 Studios on King Street West, one week after the West End murders.

"Hello, and good afternoon everyone. My name is Sergeant Donald Wright of the Toronto Homicide Division. I think most of you already know me from our conversations regarding the Wellington Street and Brunswick House murder investigations, the latter of which, as you know, has ended in a successful arrest. We continue to actively pursue the Wellington Street incident. In the meantime, of course, our city has been hit by a terrible and senseless series of murders. I am here today to give you a brief over view of the crimes and then answer questions. Please bear in mind that this is an active investigation, the killer is still out there, and I can not divulge any information which might jeopardize the case. So, let me start.

"First off all three murder victims were homeless and living on the streets of Toronto. The attacks appear to be random. Each individual was shot at close range by a .22 caliber pistol. The murders occurred at night, roughly between the hours of nine o'clock and midnight in isolated urban areas of the city's West End. There were no witnesses and no security cameras to record the attacks and right now we have no suspects, or persons of interest. The two victims shot at the abandoned Lighting Standards Building on Strachan Avenue have been identified as Jennifer Belcourt, age thirty-six. and John Pots, age forty-two. I'll spell those names for you. Both were Caucasian and from the Toronto area with no fixed address. Families have been notified, but as yet no one has come forward with any useful information. The Garrison Commons victim is still unidentified although he went by the alias of Common Johnny from the information we have gathered in the neighborhood. If anyone has further knowledge of any or all of these people please contact the Toronto Police Department. The address and anonymous tip line are flashing across TV screens now and will be provided in a handout at the end of this news conference.

"In all of these murders there was no sign of struggle, no defensive wounds on the victims, no apparent evidence left at the scene by the killer. Of course, our forensic people are still working the areas. If they come up with something we will notify the media and the public. OK, if there are any questions I'll take them now. Please stand up, identify yourself and the organization you are representing."

"Mary Monticello, the *Toronto Star*. A year ago I wrote a story in the *Star*, a profile about life on the streets, centered around a homeless man called Stinky Eddie. He was a character in the downtown scene and well known to a lot of people there. Recently, Eddie was found shot to death in his make shift home under the Spadina Ramp of the Gardiner Expressway. Can you confirm the date of his murder and is there any link to it and the three you have just described to us here at the news conference. I tried to get some information from the police a while ago, but was denied any access to the file. Also are there any more victims out there at this time?"

"Yes Mary, you're right. There was another identified victim, Edward Craig, a.k.a. Stinky Eddie, whom we believe is possibly linked to this killer, but we do not have enough conclusive evidence at this time to make that claim. The lack of an autopsy report and forensic evidence is hampering our investigation. The body was in an advanced state of decomposition when it was found some time back in April of this year if I remember correctly. To your last question we are currently checking our files for similar homicides, and modus operandi, but have found nothing to date."

"Neil Strong from the *Globe and Mail.* Would you characterize these murders as hate crimes?"

"Yes, I would. The police department of Toronto as well as the Mayor's office and in fact all citizens are outraged by this brutal assault on our city's most vulnerable inhabitants. There does not appear to be any provocation for these attacks and no motive outside of hatred pure and simple."

"Karen French also of the *Star*. Are Toronto's homeless in imminent danger right now and what is the police department planning to do about it?"

"Well, I'd have to say Yes. Anyone sleeping on the streets of Toronto right now is in danger and will continue to be until this murderer is apprehended. This also applies to ordinary citizens who may by accident of location or misidentification be targeted as well."

"Bob Coleman from *The Sun*. The presence of pan handlers and the homeless on Toronto streets has grown substantially over the past few years, yet calls to do something about the situation have gone unheeded. Now these murders have highlighted the problem and scared the hell out of people. Because of your inaction on the homeless problem do you feel at least indirectly responsible for this new violence?"

"No one is responsible for this carnage except the heartless killer who perpetrated it. Let's get that straight first of all. Secondly, the police department does not make policy. We simply enforce the laws. No comment beyond that."

"Karen French again. You've admitted that the homeless aren't safe on the streets of Toronto, but you didn't really explain what actions are being taken to protect them and the public from this killer?"

"Police patrols are being augmented by squad car, horseback units, bicycle, and on foot with patrolmen paying particular attention to areas frequented by the homeless. The Mayor's office, I believe, will be holding a separate news conference to outline city wide actions to help ameliorate the problem. I will let them speak for themselves."

"Mary Monticello. Do you have a profile of the killer?"

"The investigation is obviously still underway so I can't comment. Remember, we also have other unsolved cases still on the books that we are actively working on. We are just now making connections and sorting things out. Our immediate concern is protecting Torontonians and getting this killer off the streets as soon as possible. As more information becomes available we will release it to the media."

"Karen French. Is there any connection between these recent murders and the killing of those two young men on Wellington Street? After all the crime scenes are not that far apart."

"No connection."

"Greg Ross, CP24. Is there more than one killer?"

"Right now we believe there is only one perpetrator."

"Joan DeLaney, with *Now Magazine*. "Will he kill again, you think?"

"I don't know. Maybe he has been spooked off by the sudden media attention. Also, like I said before, the Mayor's office will be initiating new measures to help the homeless get off the streets. Hopefully those will stop the killings, but I'm afraid as long as this individual is out there the threat will remain. We are committed to finding him and we will. You have my word on it. That's all for now. Thank you."

After the press conference ended Mary, along with her Editor, Karen French and several other attendees lingered in the TV studio drinking coffee and comparing notes.

"Where did Sergeant Wright go? I wanted to ask him a few follow up questions."

"You kidding me? Him and the rest of the cops took a second look at us and the mob outside the windows and ran out the back door the minute the microphone was turned off. They ain't saying nothing more than they have to, business as usual."

"Yeah, but wait till the case goes nowhere or we get more murders. Then the cops will be inviting us back and asking for help in tracking this bastard down. Wait and see if I ain't right."

"You know," added Janet Lockhart from the Ten-in-Two Committee who had sat in on the conference but did not participate. "If the authorities had only kept their bargain with us and stuck to those initiatives, which were beginning to work I might add, then we would not be in the situation we find ourselves in now. Most of the homeless, including those unfortunate murder victims, would probably have been off the streets. At least they'd a been in decent temporary shelters while they awaited permanent housing. The whole thing was a fiasco, an embarrassment to us all."

"Yes, so many great ideas, so little political will."

Mary Monticello's Article in that day's *Toronto Star* was entitled: "Do They Care?"

"Three innocent people, maybe four, are dead as the result of a murderous rampage by a cold blooded killer on Toronto's West side. The real question is: Had these people been from respectable backgrounds and well to do families would a full scale police investigation have taken so long to materialize? British Columbia had its helpless and hopeless women prostitutes, sad victims of a sick pig farmer named Robert Willie Picton.

Picton murdered with impunity because his victims were social cast offs, marginalized women of no apparent worth. Nobody cared about them even when they were alive. So who is it now stalking the homeless in Toronto and do the police here care any more than did the callous cops and RCMP of that Western province when the slaughter started years ago? How many other lonely and forgotten victims are out on our streets perhaps undiscovered in the city's urban jungle? More importantly, how many more are yet to come?"

chapter 6

ALBERT WATCHED THE news conference and the follow up report on CP 24 and knew right away that the police were withholding significant information, namely the weeds he stuck in the mouths of his last three victims. "They're obviously saving that for me in particular, a marker that only the killer would know about. I'll have to be extra cautious now, no false moves. From now on it gets tricky."

Yes, the police were alerted and on the lookout. Maybe Albert should lay low, give the situation some time to calm down? But it was already too late for that. The itch was on and Albert had to scratch it. He couldn't help himself. It just felt too goddamn good pulling that trigger. Furthermore, with the killings in the open, he would now be able to show the police and the public just how smart he was and how totally clueless and helpless the authorities were in stopping him. It would be fun, a contest of wits and wills.

"Ah, the good life," Albert said, "full of fun. Seems to be the ideal. But I can see already I've got too much activity centered around the West End, too close to home and always at night too for that matter. The cops will be out like mosquitoes ready to bite my ass at the slightest exposure. I'll have to try something new, something cool. Yes, I'll have to order something cool. Wouldn't it just shake them up if I eradicated one of these homeless weeds right in the middle of the day? Ha, ha. That would be something to brag about."

Albert packed his binoculars, his Peterson book, a light lunch and his reloaded .22 caliber pistol and decided to make it a day of trekking through High Park.

"A nice relaxing bird-watching hike would be perfect right now," he said. "I need the break and a little distraction. However, if some sprout does come up for a little pruning, that would be just fine too, and for the record, I don't care for the term "birding". It's too clipped, and sterile, too contemporary. Give me that old time religion of bird-watching.

It's good enough for me." It was indeed a beautiful early summer's day. Insects buzzed in the air. The warblers and vireos and all their diminutive bug eating comrades had by now established themselves comfortably in their northern homes and were preparing for the major nesting duties that were soon to follow. Albert moved off the well worn trails of the Park and wandered aimless of direction or destination for a while. He knew it was too close to the noon hour to spot very many birds. Eventually the weight of the day's heat and then the sight and sound of running water drew him to a speedy stream at the bottom of a cool, shady vale.

"Perfect to spot a water thrush, veery, or thrasher down here," he said as he sat on an outcropping of rock and partook of his sandwich accompanied by two bottles of water. He could not eat without the liquid. There was no saliva to help glide the food down his throat. It had been permanently blasted away by his radiation treatments. No problem. He was used to it.

When he finished Albert climbed back up an embankment fresh with new growth and emerged onto an almost indistinct foot path. At that point he unexpectedly came face to face with a young man. The fellow was shoe, sock, and shirtless wearing only shorts and looking as though he hadn't washed in a month. Albert barely turned his head and glanced down at the stream below, then did a quick 360 degree pivot. In the meantime, the young man just stood there more looking through Albert than at him.

"Are you OK?" Albert inquired.

No reply. The man merely blinked expressionlessly. Albert pulled out his gun and fired a shot point blank into the man's bare chest. He actually thought he saw the bullet enter, or at least he noted the perfectly neat round hole in its wake. Everything moved in slow motion. The man collapsed and tumbled down the embankment collecting a wardrobe of leaves, tendrils, and vines on his way to the bottom. The verdant foliage cushioned the fall and strangely muffled all sound. For a moment everything was encased in a profound silence like the frozen frame of an old time movie. Except for the gun in his hand, it appeared that nothing at all had happened and that Albert had just ascended the slope for the first time.

"When a tree falls in the forest, does anybody hear?" whispered Albert as he glanced over the edge of the ravine. There was no trace of the body. He took out his binoculars and scanned the area.

"What the fuck. Where the hell did he go? OK, just a second now. What is that? Come on. Show yourself. Yes, yes, yes, a water thrush, northern! Can you believe it? Jesus, it's been years since I've seen one. I think the last time was up in Algonquin Park with Maureen. Shy little bastard. Wonder if he's sticking around or just passing through on his way farther up north? I'll enjoy him while I can. Carpe diem. Too bad Norm's not here. Wait till I tell him. He'll shit himself."

***

A couple of nights later when Albert took a more direct route to the Rex going down Bathurst to Queen Street West, sans gun this time, he had already dismissed, virtually forgotten the lad up in the Park. It was more like a dream than reality, but his suspicions about increased police surveillance now turned out to be real enough. He spotted more cops than he'd ever encountered before. It was still not quite dark as two mounted patrolmen trotted past him on Fort York Blvd. heading to Garrison Common. Not unusual in itself, but immediately above them another two were crossing the bridge at Bathurst. Along Queen St. patrol cars cruised by at intervals with the occupants far more interested in their surroundings than at anytime in the past.

Yes, this was going to be a challenge because unlike some suicide bomber Albert had every intention of staying alive, alive to kill another day, and the day after that as well.

After all, wasn't that what made real crime so challenging, the fact that you had to get away with it? If you could taunt the police while doing so, all the better because it was the police along with the city government and even the media, with the *Toronto Star* in the lead, who were responsible for the mess the city was in. They let the homeless situation get started, develop, and then grow unchecked. "Like the guy at City Donut said, New York and other large US cities don't have this problem because their authorities don't harbor the same bleeding heart bullshit attitude that we have up here."

The Rex was only half full despite the fact that the 6:30 PM set was cover free and Peter Hill's quartet was on stage. Guaranteed good music. Albert took a seat in the back and was soon joined by Norm who emerged from the washroom almost immediately after Albert sat down. "Wow, great timing."

"I'm telling you, I had a creepy feeling coming down here," said Norm as they settled into conversation. "Kept to the brightly lit streets. You never know, the son of a bitch might mistake me for some poor homeless slob and put a bullet in my back. I look a bit bedraggled. Need some new clothes. I'm fucking dressed to kill right now."

"Jesus, Norm, you're not homeless. Don't worry."

"Tell that to the killer. How's he supposed to know? Maybe I should pin a sign on my back, 'I'm Not Homeless,' like them farmers do during hunting season painting COW on the sides of their cattle so those dumb ass deer hunters don't blast them full of holes.

42

"And another thing, I hate to tell you, but people like me, we ain't really that far removed from the problem. All I have to do is lose one of my part time jobs and all of a sudden I'm in trouble, big trouble. And remember, everything I do is under the table. If the government knew, they'd cut my benefits. I'd lose my rent subsidy and wind up not being able to afford my apartment no more. Then I would be homeless. Of course, those crooks I'm working for they figure if my income is all undeclared well then they can skin the hell out of me. 'You don't pay no taxes, eh. Government screws us businessmen regular with taxes. You're lucky.' Yeah, so lucky that they pay me less than the minimum wage and on the last minute tell me not to bother coming in when they figure they don't need me."

"Well then, I'll just call you Mr. Lucky, but seriously if that ever happens, just give me a call. I've got more than enough money to lend you."

"I'm not looking for charity, thank you."

"Who said anything about charity? I'm talking a ten per cent interest here, compounded daily."

"You bastard," Norm laughed. "But you know that's just how the goddamn banks operate too, always charging you up the ass for their money while giving you next to nothing for yours. They can't go wrong, can't lose. The whole thing is a scam. And the banks are protected and set up by the government. Yeah, they get to borrow federal money at real low rates and at a ratio of thousands of dollars of federal money to every dollar of their own and then, then, they turn around and lend that money to you for a mortgage, or a car loan, student loan, whatever. Of course, you've got to pay back their cheap borrowed bogus money with your own real hard earned wages. And if you screw up and can't pay, guess what? The bank repossess your real house and real car. Try to get a deal like that for yourself and see how far you get? Of course, you can't do without the banks. They supply all the credit without which nobody would be able to buy nothing. Think of it. What would most people actually own if they had to pay cash up front? Fuck all, that's what."

"I don't know," replied Albert. "That's life, as the song says. My banking stocks pay a good dividend, quarterly."

"Don't even bother telling me how many stocks you own, Mr. Broker. I bet if it's two, three hundred, that's a lot. In the meantime, the largest stock holders in these banks and companies own millions of stocks, millions. People always get sucked into this "people's capitalism" shit. They think because they own a few stocks and bonds suddenly they have a big stake in the system. It's an illusion. The next market fluctuation will wipe you out and you'll be a pumpkin again. Anyway, if you're so flush, you can buy the first round."

"No problem, my little fired up socialist comrade," Albert smiled.

The two men soon lost themselves in the music. During the second set Terra Hazelton joined the group on stage for a few songs.

"I used to listen to her at Healey's every Saturday," said Albert. "That was a great gig. Great musicians: Healey, Plok, Kaiser, Bray, Scrivens. The Jazz Wizards. Very tight, very polished. And no cover charge. But the bar, downstairs in a dingy basement was a shit hole, Hernando's Hideaway, and that location on Bathurst Street near the corner of Queen West, my God. It was a nightmare. You had to fight off an army of homeless losers just to get in the door. They had that Community Health Care Centre as a neighbor and the St. Christopher House across the street. But I had some great times there. Somehow the new venue on Blue Jays Way didn't have the same vibe."

"I liked his blues more," said Norm. "His style of jazz was too old fashioned. That stuff was all written in the Twenties and Thirties. But too bad he died so young. Cancer, eh."

"Yeah, that was a waste of talent and he had a young family too."

"And how are you feeling lately?" Norm asked.

"Well, I'll never be the same, that's for sure, but I'm alive and that's better than the alternative and perhaps I'll last long enough to get a few remaining goals accomplished. There's a few things yet I want to do before I can rest in peace. I've already died once so the second time around can't be too bad."

"She's got a good voice," interjected Norm pointing to the singer. 'Lots of character too and pretty as a kewpie doll. Of course, she is a bit on the large side."

"You think so? Just because she's wearing a six man Woods tent as a dress? Actually I do prefer a singer with a band. It adds a certain dimension, a depth, and I like the character singers; Billie Holiday, Dinah Washington, Nina Simone."

"Ella Fitzgerald," threw in Norm with a knowing smile.

"Son of a bitch, I can't stand her. That fucking voice of hers, so perfect, so clear, and so absolutely lacking in character. And she was stupid as a trombone slide too. She developed that goddamn scat shit because she could never remember the lyrics to the songs. One time I heard a recording of her doing "Mack the Knife". She butchered the shit out of it, and even admitted to it on the record. 'We're making a wreck of Mack the Knife.' OK, I thought it was an aberration. But then over the years I'll be fucked if I didn't hear another half dozen similar screw ups. 'Oops, we're making a mess of "Satin Doll". Oh, there goes "Smoke Gets in Your Eyes". "Love Me or Leave Me." Jesus Christ, I can't stand the woman. I'll take Billie Holiday any time."

"I like Ella. I'm sorry to say, especially when she's using words," said Norm.

Albert liked Norm and enjoyed a decent debate. Beats the "No opinion crowd", he thought. What do you think of the Afghan conflict and Canada's involvement over there?

No opinion! Abortion? No opinion! Gay marriage? No opinion! Shooting the homeless in the head? No opinion!

"How about our own Diana Krall?" asked Norm who seemed to be enjoying Albert's emotional rants and knew just what buttons to press.

"Her earlier stuff was good, straightforward and sincere. Her latest stuff is crap. You'd think she was fucking the microphone for Christ's sake the way she's emoting all over the place. I can't take it. Listen to her rendition of "Bye, Bye Black Bird" and you'll know what I mean. If I was a black bird, I'd fly into a goddamn jet engine to get away from that."

"Yeah, but you just can't keep singing the same classics over and over again in the same way. You need variety, interpretation."

"Sure. Look, I'm not wedded to the past. I can stand change, but within musical parameters. Look at Nina Simone and her "Mood Indigo". Perfect example. Old song, completely new interpretation. Excellent work, thank you very much."

Outside the bar Albert walked Norm to the nearest transit stop. The streets were not crowded. Evidently the news of the homeless killer had gotten around. Nevertheless, on the corner a bedraggled pedestrian greeted them.

"Hey, can I ask you guys a question, one question, that's all?"

"Hey, only if I can give you one quick answer. Go fuck yourself," Albert replied.

"Gees," said Norm as they walked away. "Still a bit hostile I see. You and that killer seem to share the same philosophy."

"That's right, the guy's my hero. He's my everything."

"Well, you know, a lot of those jazz characters you admire so much, if history informs me correctly, were pretty bad alcoholics and drug users themselves. At many points in their lives Billie Holiday, Chet Baker, and Charlie Parker looked a lot like the homeless. You and the city's new killer would have probably knocked them off back then and where would the jazz world be today?"

"You know, you got a point there, Norm. Sometimes adversity builds character, sometimes it kills it, I guess. Maybe if some of these losers got off their asses they might make something of themselves."

"So how would you know when and at who to pull the trigger?"

"Educated guess is probably the best you could do. If I ever meet the killer I'll ask him."

"I don't think you'd want to come across him. Might be the last conversation you have. You going to the Spit this weekend?"

"Probably, everything is back to the summer time normal. Nice to see color in the trees again. How about you?"

"No, I'm seeing Claudia. She's not into birding."

Again just what Claudia saw in Norm was something that Albert couldn't quite figure out. "Maybe she feels sorry for the guy, a charity fuck. Still, besides that, what do they do together? He doesn't have any money. Sit up in that little shit hole of an apartment of his and watch TV? Maybe he entertains her with all that socialist talk of his and she admires the liberal minded revolutionary type, a Che Guevara. Some women like to gravitate around losers. It brings out the motherly instinct in them. Anyway, good for Norm."

***

On Saturday, Albert decided to take the Queen Car to Leslie Street, then walk to the Spit and maybe grab lunch on the way back home. He remembered his last automobile drive there with dread and after all the Queen Streetcar route was one of the most iconic and longest in the entire world. It would be a great ride full of old architecture, unique shops and fresh weird characters. He hadn't been that way in ages. For lunch Albert fancied the "Green Eggplant" in the Beaches, good food, nice upbeat atmosphere, inside seating. He did not like patio dining, especially after one particular incident years ago when he was sitting outside the Bank Note on Queen West having a sandwich, sweet potato fries and a glass of iced tea.

"Hey man, you gonna eat all that?" said a raggedy looking young fellow leaning over the wooden railing. He carried a packsack and was wearing dirty jeans and a black tee shirt that read, "Jesus is a Cock Sucker".

"Probably not," replied Albert. "But what I don't eat, I'll gladly throw out rather than give to you."

"Fuck you!" replied the young man. "When the revolution comes we'll line up all you Old Yuppie bastards and gun you down."

"I doubt if you can spell revolution let alone organize one," replied Albert.

"Fuck you, wise ass."

"Pretty limited vocabulary you've got there. Maybe instead of roaming around with shit stained shorts you might try going back to school, improve yourself a bit, and increase your chances of gainful employment."

"Work is for losers like you, asshole," and the boy walked away shouting over his shoulder. "Yuppie assholes in Toronto! Yuppie assholes in Toronto!"

Today Albert once again carried no gun. He tried to tell himself that he was on a leisurely pleasure trip with a little bird-watching thrown in although he had to confess to the inner motive of doing some scouting along the way. Try as he would, it was getting more and more difficult to detach himself from his newly found mission in life.

"I could use an area outside of the West End to distract the police," he mused out loud. "And that young guy at High Park? Whatever happened to him? I haven't heard a word. Nothing in the paper or on TV. I hope to hell I killed him. Shot him straight in the heart. I mean, Killer Joe, the bastard has to be dead."

When the Queen Car passed St. James's Church and moved on to Jarvis and Sherbourne Albert's eyes popped open and his jaw dropped. "What in the fuck?" he mumbled under his breath. "The streets, they're full of losers and butt plugs strolling around like they own the goddamn place. The park, St. James Garden, has gone to seed. It's weed packed, weedified. It's Weedland! Jesus Christ, it wasn't like this when I took in those St. Michael's masses with Maureen; Christmas and Easter, my two concessions to her Catholicism. Then again I wasn't on my mission back then so maybe I didn't notice though I had to be blind not to. I do remember that idiot wife of mine dropping nearly as much money into coffee cups on the street as in the collection baskets in church."

"Poor thing looked so hungry. Probably hasn't had a decent meal in months."

"He's heading straight for the LCBO to buy a bottle of rye, no doubt about it."

Well, let me think, Albert ruminated. The last time I was down in this area was with Maureen actually, yes, but we were taking in the New Year's Eve party at the old Montreal Bistro. Damn, that was a fine spot, top notch, and I loved that Quiet Policy they had there. 'Shut the fuck up and listen to the music,' although I think they were a bit more subtle in their wording. Saw Jim Galloway that night. Great performance even though I'm not crazy about the soprano sax. Just use a clarinet and call it even. Was one of the last decent times Maureen and I had together. She was good in the sack that night too, I remember. Must have been the booze. It always made her more uninhibited.

Naturally when he finally got to the Spit and made it down along the shore, the first thing to catch Albert's eye was a make shift tent constructed out of a blue tarp and plastic sheets sitting in a line of tall grasses just off the beach. A plastic lawn chair with a missing leg propped up with a cement block sat next to a flat topped slab of concrete that most likely substituted for a table. A large, weathered barbecue stood nearby with a pile of charred wood thrown on top in lieu of charcoal. Litter covered the ground and seagulls circled. Common herring gulls,

Albert noted before lamenting out loud. "The sons of bitching homeless assholes are even out here fucking up nature. They're taking over the whole country. I should have brought my gun. This is ridiculous."

The incident spoiled Albert's day. He walked around in a grand funk, kicking the dirt and cursing at every opportunity. He did salvage something by tracking down an indigo bunting in some alders lining the gravel trail that led to Norm's favorite spot where Albert himself paused to calm down and collect his thoughts.

"I'm just going to redouble my efforts," he muttered to himself. "Every little bit helps. Eventually as the bodies pile up the message will get through and these scumbag cretins will abandon the city. On my way back I'll check out Sherbourne Street. I will need to do a little reconnaissance just to get my bearings. If I want to scout out some targets I'll have to at least know where the hell I'm going."

Albert got off the Queen car at the corner of Sherbourne across the street from the Salvation Army Hostel the front of which was littered with drunks and dysfunctional stumble bums chain smoking and passing a bottle of wine around. Further down the street several men slouched on steps and the sidewalk while others sat, stood, and crouched on the corner like ants on a sugar cube. Fellow homeless or itinerate travelers stopped to talk and reminisce and compare notes with their comrades in arms. Happiness, if not outright joviality, prevailed. Occasionally one or two people would break away from the group and move to the sidewalk to harass some passer-by.

"Got some change? Dollar, quarter, dime, nickel, a fucking penny? No problem. Have a nice day."

A multi tattooed couple tag teamed on squeegee patrol jumping out amongst the vehicles whenever the traffic light changed. They looked familiar. Maybe the couple at Lakeshore branching out to new territory? On the opposite side of the street a shirtless man waved his arms and cursed at a couple running for a street car.

"Yeah, yeah, fuck you too. I'll crap on your forehead. See how you like that, eh. Fuck!"

"And a good time was had by all," said Albert out loud to no one in particular.

"Why don't the police do something about this?" asked a woman standing next to Albert at the streetcar stop.

"Not enough room in the jails," he replied.

"It's a terrible image for the city," she continued. "Don't these people care?"

"I'd venture to say at this time of year half these people are not even from Toronto. They're here for the fun and excitement. The winter will drive them away except for the perennials."

"Oh, you're a gardener?" the woman asked.

"You might say that," Albert replied as he waved good-bye and entered the melee on the streets. He walked north on Sherbourne. Down and out looking characters littered the streets and sidewalks. It was a hot day and the buildings, many of them former mansions and grand homes turned into crowded rooming houses, had dozens of people sprawling in front of the entrances. Several tables were set up where a variety of pieces of junk were up for sale.

"The whole neighborhood is one giant shit hole," said Albert.

A couple of anorexic looking women strolled by in what would have been provocative outfits were it not for the dirt, rips and hanging threads that festooned the different items of clothing. They giggled at Albert and appeared ready to say something before one of them while lighting a cigarette fell into a paroxysm of coughing that turned her face blue.

"Fuckin Export A. I'm goin back to my DuMaurier Lights," she finally gasped after a belabored drag.

"There goes the health care system," Albert noted. "Why is it every one of these losers can afford to smoke, use drugs, and get a fortune worth of tattoos printed on their asses, but they can't afford to put food in their mouths?"

Albert made his way through the congested street to a large park with a conservatory sitting conspicuously out of place in the middle of the acreage. It was Allan Gardens.

"Wow, an oasis; the flowers are beautiful," he commented noting that the grounds, like the surrounding streets, were overrun with vagrants. Several men and one woman were playing some sort of game on a picnic table. Must be dominoes, Albert guessed from the hand slapping and cursing going on. No one spoke English. A black woman stood nearby washing her legs and feet with a succession of small alcohol wipes which she threw along with the wrappers onto the grass. A couple of men passing by whistled at her eliciting a coquettish reply of, "What the fuck are you pricks looking at?"

"Doesn't dish the dirt with the rest of the girls. That's why the lady is a tramp," said Albert to himself as he sat down on a park bench to take in the sights. The grass was littered with cigarette butts, discarded bits of clothing, scattered package wrappings and torn papers. A few crumpled newspaper pages bounced like tumble weeds across the lawn evoking an urban doomsday scenario reminiscent of the Terminator movies.

Opposite him on another bench a man slept outstretched using a packsack as a pillow. The next bench was occupied by a lone, heavily dressed man who was engaged in an animated conversation with himself complete with spasms of laughter. As Albert took mental notes a black squirrel, chattering on its way in fits and starts, nervously descended a large chestnut tree.

"I know the feeling," Albert sighed. "I'm pretty fucking nervous myself. There's more nuts walking around here than dangling up there in the tree."

Albert took off his Blue Jays cap, wiped his forehead and surveyed the park and distant streets. He shook his head in dismay. It was at that moment the man across the way suddenly shot out from his bench and at full gallop charged across the gravely pathway straight at Albert. He carried a long stout tree branch that had been apparently laying in wait at his feet.

"Die mother fucker. Die," the man screamed.

"Holy shit," Albert exclaimed and reached down into his pants pocket. No gun.

Albert stood up and turned his shoulder to the onrushing man who was brandishing the tree limb above his head like a marauding Viking wielding a broad ax. In an instant the man was upon him. Albert braced for the impact, but instead the deranged man ran right past.

"Black bastard. Die! Die!" the man screamed at the squirrel which was several dozen feet from the sanctuary of the chestnut tree. Before it could reach safety the man landed a glancing blow which knocked the animal head over heels in the grass. With a surprisingly fast hand the vagrant then grabbed the squirrel by the tail and slammed it against the tree trunk, once, twice.

"Fucking Mother of God," Albert gasped nervously as the man picked up the limp bleeding body and walked back to the bench.

"Ha, ha, ha," the man laughed as he walked past Albert holding up the dead squirrel like a trophy.

"What the fuck is he going to do with that?" wondered Albert who then decided it might be a good idea to leave the park. He passed homeless shelters, missions, and aid agencies lined up along the streets like pastries on display atop a baker's shelf.

"This must be the principal industry in town, the cash crop," he said staring up at the "Good Shepherd Home". And just who the hell works in these places? Good Samaritan Christian assholes trying to save the world one toothless lost soul at a time? Do-gooders and bleeding hearts? Of course, most of them are the very same jerk-off losers who just yesterday were out on the streets themselves.

"Oh yes, I was a burnt out, crack smoking, butt fucking, homeless moron myself so, you know, it's like awesome how I can relate to these troubled unfortunates. And with the help of tens of thousands of misspent taxpayers dollars I like crawled out of these same streets into a rigged for losers educational program where I earned my diploma in "Dog Fucking" and "Asshole Rehabilitation" before finally landing a useless government job in the "Industry of Perpetual Homelessness." Awesome!"

"Awesome indeed!" Albert continued while checking out a bearded man walking down the street wearing a woman's platform shoes and sporting a ratty fox fur stole around his neck.

"Never mind the temperature, asshole, just as long as you look good," Albert mumbled. "Now what employer no matter how fucking desperate on his worst day would hire any one of these dysfunctional morons to even dig a hole. They couldn't pick up dog shit with a snow shovel. The whole thing is a scam and a planned perpetuation of poverty. No one wants to end this charity breadline because what will happen to all these employees and their useless educations not to mention the staff and executives at the top hauling in hundreds of thousands a year? These people have succeeded where scientists throughout the ages have failed. They've created the perpetual motion machine."

Albert was filled with indignation, but he was also despondent and over whelmed by the enormity of the task before him. His little dream of cleaning up the city was now confronted with grim reality. He was facing an army of sewer rats with only a flat popsicle stick in his hands to beat them off.

At a nearby coffee shop Albert stopped to give himself a boost of energy and combat the feeling of depression that was fast overtaking him. He walked up to the counter when his turn came. A clerk with blue tear drops tattooed on his face and wearing a hair net over a completely bald head looked at Albert and gave him a quick reverse kind of nod. Albert glanced overhead, then behind him. What, he wondered as the man repeated the gesture several more times? Finally the clerk spoke up.

"What do you want, arse-pick? I ain't got all day."

Albert got his order, stumbled outside and down the street gulping his coffee. "Fuck, I don't have nearly enough bullets," he lamented before stopping and leaning up against a building. He slowly slid down the wall balancing his coffee cup in one hand.

A man and woman almost normal looking were passing him when the woman stopped, opened her purse and stepped back to Albert. Looking down on him with an expression of sadness, pity, and a hint of repulsion, she dropped two quarters into his yet half full cup.

"Poor thing,' she said to her companion as she rejoined him. "He looks so damned miserable."

chapter 7

"AND JUST HOW are we supposed to catch this guy?" asked Detective Gignac. "We don't have any leads. We're in the dark. We know the type of gun he uses, and the victims he selects, but that's it. The guy could be anybody and could pop up anywhere. The city is chock-full of potential targets. We got homeless people up the ass."

"No video tape either. Too out of the way for our crime cameras, and there are no businesses nearby so we don't have any private security tapes," added Sergeant Wright.

"Mostly we'd be looking at dark, night time images anyway. Useless. The other issue is that these homeless losers, ah, people, don't own cell phones, eh. Can't call out for help. When he gets them alone, that's it. They're goners. Any trace on the bullet fragments?"

"They're all from the same gun, a .22, but that's it. If we find the gun on him, we got the guy. That's our only hope right now, but we're a long way from that."

"What do you think about the guy's location, his residence, I mean, in relation to the murders?"

"Well," said Detective Hudson, a third lead member of the Toronto Homicide Squad, "the murders are clustered around the West End. We got the one at the Spadina overpass near Lakeshore, and then the two at the Lighting Standards Building on Strachan and the one right across the tracks from that at Garrison Common. That seems to indicate some familiarity with the area at the very least."

"Yeah, and he must have been on foot. Went over the bridge at Strachan and down into the park. But where did he go from there?"

"I've check the streetcar surveillance cameras on the Union and Bathurst cars which turn around at the CNE grounds. I got everything from 6:00 PM to 10:30 PM. It's all pretty crowded for the probable time of death around 9:00 PM. I don't see how we can weed anybody out of all that."

"Please don't use that term." said Sergeant Wright.

"What?"

"Weed." Let's keep "weeds" in the non disclosure category. It could come in handy at some future date. The first murder, our Stinky Eddie, didn't include any weeds. Must have been something he decided to do later. Trying to make a statement. Getting bolder and more confident. How about forensics, fingerprints?"

"The crime lab guys thought they might actually be able to pull some prints off them weeds. Some had a flat surface, but he mashed them all up and destroyed any fingerprints when he forced them down their throats."

"And what about the new condos along Fleet and Fort York and over at City Place? They must have security cameras there too."

"They do, but that's a hell of a lot of viewing and where or when do we begin?"

"Motive?"

"He hates the homeless. That narrows it down to any one of about one million people."

"Yeah, you can add me to the list. I'd kick all them bastards out of the city if I had my way," said Detective Hudson. "Then we wouldn't have this problem and could eliminate another thousand nuisance calls, misdemeanors and felonies per month to boot."

"Just keep that kind of talk to yourself," cautioned Sergeant Wright. "If the press or public get a hold of anything like that they'll cook our goose for us and eat it too. How about any connection amongst the victims? Did they know each other?"

"They all bumped into one another now and again at the shelters and soup kitchens. Just the usual on and off stuff, but no indication that they had anything else in common, no known enemies as such. The two grub balls at the Standards Building were sleeping together of late. The Commons guy we know little about and Stinky there, he was a recluse, hated by just about everyone including his fellow homeless bums. Really, we've got fuck all. The murderer himself is a ghost. We need something to break."

"Something other than our balls. What do we have from the recent step up in patrols? Anything strange come up? Any suspicious?"

"Nothing."

"We're stuck till he strikes again and hopefully fucks up this time or somebody sees him," added Sergeant Wright rather resignedly. "I wonder why he hasn't targeted parts of Yonge Street or all of Parkdale, not to mention Jarvis and Finch. Pretty high density homeless there."

"He's a coward. Doesn't want to run into any gang activity or somebody who can fight back. Are we still concentrating our patrols on the West End, Central West, 56 Division?"

"Pretty much. We only got so many cops. Beyond our own Homicide Squad they ain't giving us much manpower. We're stuck in a bad spot here. If he backs off because of the heat, we may never catch him. If he kills again and gets away, we're going to have a public relations nightmare on our hands."

"Hell, this is a big city. Somebody's got to know this guy," concluded Detective Gignac.

***

At home Sergeant Wright's daughter, Meaghan, was still a problem which his wife let him know about whenever she felt he could handle the extra burden.

"I just don't like the company she's keeping lately. If her grades slip, that's it. She's going to be grounded for the whole summer. Matter of fact, summer school might be an option if for no other reason than to keep her out of trouble."

"You think you can handle this on your own?" replied Sergeant Wright. "I know you're working part time to help out here, but I have to worry about the worst mass murderer in Toronto history right now and it's actually taking up a lot of my time. Also the Captain and Chief of Police are pissing on my head every minute of the day. The whole city is up in arms. And please let's not read the paper for a while. I can't take what the *Star* and that bleeding heart halfwit, Mary Monticello, are writing. Her last article was enough to make me barf."

"You know half that stuff is written just to sell papers. They sensationalize everything now days especially in a big city like Toronto. You never really know what the truth is."

"As if the police aren't the only ones to ignore drug addicts, hookers, and homeless losers," continued the Sergeant. "For Christ's sake, everyone ignores them, passes them on the streets each day and looks the other way. If the cops seriously investigated each battery, assault, rape and death involving these down and out losers, the tax payers would be bitching to the skies that the police budget was out of control. 'Don't you cops have anything better to do?' How often have I heard that refrain? The only time the shit hits the fan is when the homicides pile up, take on a volume that is impossible to ignore. Then the police and other public officials who generally didn't give a rat's ass in the first place put on their caring robes and rant about justice denied and then quickly search the ranks for a scapegoat."

And along those lines Sergeant Wright knew that heads would roll at Toronto Police Headquarters and his was poised to be the first to go down the alley.

"Still, it is a horrible thing what's happening to these homeless people," added Sharon. "You know, there was this guy, I'm pretty sure he was homeless, used to stand on the Southeast corner of Nathan Phillips Square. Everybody called him "the Rat Man" because he had these mice or rats draped around his shoulders and arms. They were actually kind of cute, not like you'd expect, all creepy, and big toothed like, like…"

"Like rats."

"Yeah," Sharon smiled. "Like rats."

"Most guys use puppies. They work a lot better," added Sergeant Wright, Don to his wife and friends.

"But you know, I haven't seen the man lately. There's been a guitar player there instead. I hope nothing's happened to the old guy. He wasn't really bothering anybody. I always gave him a dollar when I passed by."

"So far, I haven't heard anything about a homeless man with rats having been targeted. Then again, who knows? Let me just add that if he lived in Parkdale and wound up dead well then I'm going to be dead myself. Monticello's on a tear right now. She'll go berserk if one of her dear Parkdale neighbors gets bumped off."

"Speaking of the neighbors, ours next door, the Crawfords, said that Meaghan left the house two nights ago when we were at the theater and came home just before us at ten thirty."

"What are they snooping around for?" interjected Don. "They got nothing better to do that stare out their windows watching our children."

"Don, I asked them to keep an eye out for us. Please, they're trying to help. And when you get the chance have another chat with Meaghan if you don't mind. I'm sorry. It's just that she seems to respond better to you."

The phrase, "when you get the chance" didn't sit well with Sergeant Wright though Sharon was obviously oblivious to its significance. "Maybe if you stopped shouting at her for a minute," he replied.

"Not this again. Look, I'm going to my sister's for bridge. Josh is sleeping over at Jason Stockwell's and Meaghan's still grounded remember. And no cell phone. It's in my night stand."

"Gottcha."

"And remember. With all your faults I love you still. Bye."

Discordant rap music with questionable lyrics, at least they seemed questionable from the little Don Wright could understand, poured down from Meaghan's room. If he wasn't so tired and afraid of a confrontation when he was in a bad mood, Don would have gone upstairs. He let the matter drift and headed for the kitchen to grab a beer. Then the doorbell rang.

Don gazed at a slovenly garbed young man dressed entirely in black with a tattoo of a serpent or lizard, maybe a dragon thought Don, encircling the lad's neck. He had what appeared to be a wine cork wedged in one of his ear lobes. The other held a short bolt held in place by two nuts. The boy's left hand had a firm grip on his crotch.

"Genital problems?" asked the Detective before inquiring what the young fellow could possibly want at the Wright residence.

"Just holding up my pants," replied the boy.

"Ever hear of a belt?"

"It's not cool to wear a belt, Sirrr," emphasized the boy. "And is Meaghan home, Pleassse?"

"Meaghan's in her room, but she's grounded. It seems she's been hanging around with the wrong crowd of late."

"Anybody I might know?" asked the lad with a smirk on his face.

"Got a mirror?" answered the Sergeant as he stepped back and shut the door.

"You can't keep her locked up forever," came the voice from the other side.

Don went to the fridge and grabbed a bottle of beer, Steam Whistle. He preferred the local micro breweries. Right now anything wet and cold with alcohol in it would serve the purpose. Anyway, he had to be careful since he could be called out at any moment. Couldn't drive or show up at a crime scene over the limit on the blood/alcohol count. One beer was all he usually allowed himself.

***

At the *Toronto Star*, Mary Monticello followed up on her initial article with an editorial.

"Friends,

Over the years it have been my privilege to know, live among, and write about my Parkdale neighbors. I like them. I hope they like me. Sure, there are times when we are dysfunctional, overburdened, unreasonable and even angry with each other. But through all our difficulties and disagreements we have always been willing and able to compromise. We find common ground. We work together to solve our problems. We strive, sometimes we succeed, often we fail, but never, never, do we turn on one another.

Now there is a killer amongst us. He lives here in Toronto, probably close to Parkdale. Make no mistake, however. He is not one of us. He is not our neighbor. He is not a citizen of this city. He is a heartless, cold blooded killer who has no home, no place to call his own. He is an exile, an outcast. He is ironically the most homeless of all people.

56

My fellow Parkdale friends and Torontonians, let us work together to weed out this monstrous interloper from our midst. Let us keep our guard up, keep an eye out for our friends, and our homeless neighbors. Let's turn his killer's hate against him. Don't let hatred and prejudice triumph. Show this killer just what kind of caring, loving, helpful people we are in Parkdale, in Toronto, in Ontario, and in all of Canada.

Thank you,

Mary Monticello, On Guard for You

P.S. Watch for my future articles dealing with the bedbug menace in Toronto. Exclusive in the *Star*."

chapter 8

ALBERT HAD TO shake off the Allan Gardens experience. This was no time to despair. The ball was rolling and gaining momentum. To stop now would undo everything. "You know what? Sorry, but Toronto does not belong to these insane assholes," Albert stated. "They're not going to take over the city, occupy the streets and abuse respectable citizens. Not on my watch. No, it's time to sweep these lepers out of their open air lairs. Force them at best to stay holed up in basements and airless lofts, hidden from view like the lunatic children of the past. Keep Benjy in the closet."

At night fall Albert grabbed his gun, fastened it to the holster on his inner leg, put the bullet clip in his pocket and stepped outside. "Time to Die."

He rode the streetcar to Queen and Yonge, got off and turned south. He was short of his target area, but he preferred to be guided by fate and chance. When opportunity presented itself, he'd strike. He avoided any well lit corners, businesses, and homeless shelters where security or surveillance cameras might lurk. As a result his path wandered aimlessly up and down various side streets and alleys.

"From corner to corner, I'm looking for you," Albert sang softly as he tried hard to keep track of where he was, but found it increasingly difficult. He'd have to be careful not to get turned around and lost in the unfamiliar territory. Oh well, he could always ask a cop for directions.

Albert resolved to strike hard and fast. No sense knocking off just one loser. He'd hit as many as he could because he'd only have one chance here. After that it would be far too dangerous to return. He wound up turning east on King Street to St. James Cathedral, a beautifully grand and historic building.

"Too bad it's dedicated to religion," moaned Albert as he moved past to the adjoining flower garden which was dark, tree lined and secluded. Albert stopped and in anticipation of some good gardening pulled several dandelions out of the soft earth on the edge of a plot of pansies and petunias. He also slowly pushed the bullet clip into the gun. He knew the local transients would be bedding down for the night while any respectable citizens had already abandoned the area because of its well known dangers. As he made his way down the dim pathways Albert could see one person sleeping on a park bench ahead of him. The homeless man had stuffed his bags under the bench and then cleverly woven his skinny frame through the metal barrier that ran down the middle of the structure which was designed to specifically to thwart the very idea of comfortable slumber. Albert slowed his approach timing it to coincide with the rumbling by of the King Streetcar only several yards away. He then walked up to his target and deposited a point blank shot into the man's head. The figure on the bench lurched forward from the chest up, but was immobilized by his contorted position on the bench. Albert shot him again in the chest and this time stuffed the bitter weed down the man's throat.

"Here, you bastard, have a good taste," and Albert pushed the thick fabric of the sleeping bag down on the vagrant's face while the man chocked on the weed, then twitched in his death throes before finally laying still. Not much satisfaction, but it was one fewer loser.

Close to the street on the nearby sidewalk, obscured by the foliage of several trees and shrubs, a group of people who just disembarked on the corner were strolling past and slowing their pace to admire the flowers still somewhat visible in the lamp lights that ringed the Garden pathways. Albert moved on unseen. He cut through the Garden and the Cathedral grounds and returned to Church Street. "The moving hand has writ, and having writ, moves on." A short ways up he came upon St. Michael's Cathedral.

"Dueling Dungeons of God," he hissed, "St. Mike's and St. James. Each religion trying to outdo, out build the other with only a couple of blocks between them. Oh well, they do call Toronto the city of churches, What a waste of good stone though if you ask me."

He remembered St. Michael's Cathedral in particular from the last Christmas mass he attended there with his wife. The final, fleeting concession. "Boy was she upset when I quit altogether. That stupid, pathetic look she gave me when she had to head out to church on her own. She realized that was it, the beginning of our end. And that ridiculous hat she wore, pathetic, and sad somehow, tilted to one side a little like a kid would wear. Yes, God wouldn't let a woman into his house without a hat on. Men, of course, had to remove theirs. God is a peculiar individual."

"They lock the place at night so as to keep the vermin out," said Albert gazing at St. Mike's. "How charitable. I'll have to file a complaint with the good Father FitzPatrick. This will not look good on our Holy Father's resume. After all, what would Jesus say?"

On to Gerard St. and Allan Gardens, Albert made his way, eyes wide, looking for another target. No one was aroused by the first killing. He still had free reign. Only the occasional couple and scattered groups of people crossed his path. No one took heed of his presence.

"Thank God for cell phones, and iPhones and iPods," he said. "These morons can barely watch where they're going let alone notice whose beside them."

Within the interior of the park he spotted a group of men assembled around a gazebo near the entrance to the old domed conservatory.

"The point being," said Albert, "is you can't have a garden with all these weeds around. They choke out the beauty. They've got to go. It's as elementary as that and it isn't even personal. Just a law of nature."

There appeared to be four or five men, hard to determine the exact number from where Albert stood. "Fuck, it would be great to gun down the whole bunch of assholes at once," he muttered. "But if they didn't all fall neatly in order, that would be a serious problem. What to do? What to do?"

Albert sat on a park bench drumming his foot repeatedly against the ground and contemplating his next move. He was surprisingly calm despite the rapid beating of his heart. No sirens pierced the night. No cop cars sped by. He was still undetected thus far.

Overhead a nighthawk called and swooped, catching insects high above the glow of the park lights. "Preet. Preet. Preet." Albert watched it as it soared, silhouetted against the lighter city sky. "Bird alone, with no mate. Turning cartwheels. Tempting fate. Tell me what's your story. I've got more in common with that bird than with any human here on earth."

Just then three of the men in the group split off leaving one behind.

"Don't bother going up there, pal," said one of the men as they passed Albert who had hoped to remain a bit more unnoticed. "That cheap bastard won't share fuck all with you. But if you got something, look out, it's pass the bottle all around. Selfish cock suck."

Another of the triumvirate turned and shouted back: "Hey Joey, fuck you. Fuck you forever. See if I'll ever be your friend again."

"Thanks," said Albert as the men left the area. He then slowly swung around the pathway and approached the lone remaining vagrant who was now standing up and looking in his direction.

"Hey, what the fuck do you want?" the man asked as Albert walked steadfastly up to him. "I told them others I ain't sharin the bottle no more. Fuckin gulping cock suckers. If they took a sip, Hey, that would be different, but, no, no, they gotta gulp it down like it's water. Well, it ain't water and I ain't sharin with them or with you either so go to hell. How does that sound?"

"Sounds good. How about you lead the way?" replied Albert and he leveled his pistol and fired round after round into the man. "One scotch, one bourbon, one beer." Albert added a final bullet into the convulsing body. But when he stepped back to admire his handiwork and at the same time avoid the blood that was pooling around his feet, he heard loud voices behind him. He turned and saw several men huddled together on the sidewalk and pointing in his direction. The three men who left moments before had returned with two compatriots.

"What's that fucker doing up there with Joey? That mother fucker! Joey's down! He got shot. That was the noise. That fucker shot him."

"It's him," one of the other men shouted in turn. "It's that fucking killer. He's here."

"Not on our turf, you mother fucker. Get him. Get him. Spread out. He can't shoot us all."

Goddamn, Albert staggered back as though hit by a ricochet from one of his own bullets. No time for weeds now. He turned on his heels and ran like a cheap tie-dyed shirt into the night and through the thick darkness of the overhanging tree limbs. His speed and unbalanced momentum gave him the appearance of a sky diver whose parachute hadn't opened. With his arms flaying wildly he had trouble holding on to his revolver. Behind him three of the men pursued.

"Fucking good buddies now. What happened?" Albert spat. He must have crossed a street because he noticed a sudden flood of light. A strolling couple a block away pointed in his direction and stepped into the race. A bloodcurdling cry of "Murder! Stop the murderer," shot up from the angry assemblage. Holy fuck, what had he unleashed? Albert was blind with fear and clutched his gun tightly trying to squeeze some security out of its heavy grip. He couldn't possibly stop and aim without being overrun. Through the darkened sidewalks Albert fled as individuals jumped from dark porches and alleys. Soon crowds merged in hot pursuit. He didn't dare look back, but he could tell from the volume of the ever approaching shouts and curses that his prognosis was not good.

"Son of a bitch, where do they get the energy?" Albert shouted. He dashed along a narrow laneway. It was impossible to tell where the hell he was as he involuntarily stumbled from one side of the alley to the other bouncing off doors like a pinball. He could hear the actual voices of the crowd behind him. They seemed to be everywhere.

"Hey, hey mister. Over here. Here, at the gate. Hurry," a voice cried hoarsely.

"What?" Albert looked around, his head like a Linda Blair double in "The Exorcist".

"They got you trapped. Quick." And a metal gate swung open. Albert slipped through it.

"Don't worry. I'm on your side. I was watching the park. I heard the shots and seen the chase. I know who you are. Come with me. It'll get you through my yard and into the next street. Go into the parking lot there, but stay on the north side. There's a camera at the south entrance near the pay booth. After that you can make your way to Yonge Street and blend in with the crowd."

"Don't look at me," Albert cautioned the man or boy from the sound of his voice.

"I won't, but that don't matter anyway 'cause I wouldn't never say nothing to the cops.

Just tell me," the voice continued as they got to the front of the dark house. "What's it like, eh? I mean they're around here all the time. They piss and shit in our yard and steal our stuff. What's it like to kill one of those fuckers?"

"Well, to tell you the honest truth," said Albert now catching his breath for the first time and tucking away his gun down his pant leg. "It's great. It's the top. It's the fucking Mona Lisa, the Tower of Pisa of all crime."

"Ha, I knew it. OK, go for it, man. Straight ahead."

And Albert was suddenly alone in the street. He followed the boy's directions and soon found himself walking Yonge Street as sirens wailed in the distance surprisingly far from his present location.

"Now what?" someone said while strolling beside Albert.

"Who knows? In this neighborhood it could be anything," he replied before crossing the street and melting into the night time crowd.

chapter 9

DETECTIVE SERGEANT WRIGHT had a blazing headache as he and Detective Gignac traced the flight path of the killer through Allan Gardens, across a street, and finally into the alley where the pursuing men had lost track of him. On the ground below a metal gate they spied a clump of fading greenery. Detective Gignac bent down.

"Weeds," he said to Sergeant Wright. "They're weeds just like the one on the body on the park bench at St. James."

"He obviously stopped here or ducked into this yard," said Sergeant Wright. "Let's go in and knock on the door. Maybe they saw something, anything. I'm desperate."

"Jesus, all this action, killings, chases, and we got fuck all again. Just a bunch of casings which, of course, are all a match with an unknown .22 caliber gun," added Gignac. "Even though we have three or four descriptions now, I'll be damned if any two of them are alike."

"Eye witnesses, they're worse than unreliable. Add the fact that most of them were drunk, stoned and /or stupid and we got worse than fuck all. The press is going to eat us up and spit us out over this. I talked to the Chief this morning. Know what he said to me? 'The homeless are dropping like clay pigeons all over the city. Why don't you and your detectives just walk the streets and listen for the gun shots?'"

"Well, officers," began the mid-aged woman who answered the door to Detective Gignac's knock, "my husband and I were gone to the Sony Centre last night. The Gypsy Kings were in town you know. Great concert. Our son was home alone. Ronnie. Ronnie come down here, please."

"Hey, I was playing my X Box. I didn't hear or see nothin. And you know what, even if I did I wouldn't say a word to you cops because that guy was doing us all a favor. Them bums out there are nothing but trouble. We're always picking up condoms in our back yard and needles and cigarette butts. Just last week we had a couple of queers sucking guys off in the alley next to our garage."

"Ronnie, please, but, you know, officers, my husband found one of them, them men sleeping in the back seat of our car. He drove all the way to work before he noticed the guy. That was when the man messed his pants. It was disgusting. We had to take the car to a professional cleaner."

"Yeah, and you can still smell the shit. And you know what? My mother and father called you cops here more than a dozen times in the past and you know what you did?"

Detective Gignac looked plaintively at the Sergeant, then shook his head.

"Nothing. You did nothing. Said it was all pointless. The neighborhood is just like that and there's nothing nobody can do about it. The only option we have is to move away. Yeah, that was a real big help."

"I'm sorry officers, but my son does have a point. When the children were younger, we used to take them to the Gardens to play, but we had to stop that. The stuff they'd see and the type of people. My God it was terrible. And the dogs! The most vicious dogs."

"And you know I used to help out at the soup kitchen on Sherbourne twice a week, but the people there got so ignorant I couldn't take it. 'What, we had chili last week. The soup isn't hot enough. I'm getting tired of this "stuff". But they didn't say stuff, eh. I tried to explain that we made meals that would stretch so we could feed as many people as possible, but it didn't do no good. And then they stole everything they could: rolls, butter, sugar. You name it. And that's not to mention the harassment. You let it go because of the circumstances, eh, but if that behavior and language happened in an office or business somebody would get fired on the spot. So, I'm sorry officers. We can't help you. We really can't."

"Yeah, that's right and if my father were here now you'd get a earful too except he wouldn't be so polite."

"Well, you know I can sympathize with both of you, but taking the law into your own hands is not the answer," said Sergeant Wright. "We've got two dead men back there; men who were apparently just minding their own business and were murdered nonetheless. We can't have vigilante justice running wild in the city."

"Why not?" added Ronnie. "Somebody should do something."

"Then where does it stop?" added Detective Gignac. "First the homeless, then those on welfare, living in subsidized apartments, the mentally ill, the cripples, the unemployed?"

"All sounds good to me," quipped Ronnie. "But I gotta go. I'm studying ahead of time for school this Fall so I can move out of this shithole neighborhood and get a real life. My parents ain't that lucky 'cause they'll never sell this place, not in a hundred years."

The mother smiled wanly and shrugged her shoulders while slowly closing the door.

"We need citizens to cooperate with the police," Sergeant Wright shouted as the detectives were shut out of the yard. "It's the right thing to do."

"Well, that was productive," said Detective Gignac when they returned to the alley. "I wouldn't be surprised if that little bastard knew something."

"Not much we can do. He's a minor. His parents will shield him. There's nothing worse than knowledge of the law especially in the hands of citizens and criminals. We'll come back though. Maybe they'll have a change of heart."

Because of on going manpower requirements for several other noteworthy unsolved cases, in addition to the recent serial killings, Sergeant Wright's "All In" investigative approach had been modified by Toronto's Chief of Police. The Wellington Street murders which occurred in an affluent area of the city and involved the random murder of three well respected young men in the community still required attention.

Members of the families as well as prominent politicians and clergymen pressured the police daily for action. "We are not talking about a bunch of street bums here. These are important people. I want their murders given top priority," warned Ted De Rosary, the influential city councilor for that district and front runner for the mayor's seat in the next election. "And don't think for a minute you can use these West End homicides as an excuse for procrastination. I for one won't stand for it."

As a result, Sergeant Wright, Detectives Gignac and Hudson now worked with a smaller group of homicide detectives comprised mainly of rookie cops tasked with investigating the homeless murder cases.

Sergeant Wright saw the hand writing on the wall. "It's Donnally, he's throwing me under the bus, cutting my man power, yet expecting a quick arrest. He's got the ear of the Chief. If I don't get this solved and fast, I'll be walking the beat in Scarborough," he confided to his colleague and friend Gignac. "Anyway, right now these two new East End murders are screwing us. It's just what I didn't want to see happen though maybe if the killer was out of his comfort zone, he messed up somehow. What do we have?"

"Well, he's been seen that's for sure, but we don't have much of a description given the quality of our witnesses. Basically we can confidently say he's a white male probably in his forties or fifties. Pretty fit judging from his sprinting out of the park, but I figure with them drunken stumblebums chasing after him even a wooden legged Frankenstein would have escaped. Dressed in dark clothing. Maybe wearing a ball cap. Average to above average in height. Right handed."

"The drunks who left the park, and then came back, they passed this guy on the way out, right? Said something to him?"

"Yeah, yeah, I got that in my notes," said Detective Hudson. "Witness One, Scott Vanderbosch: 'I didn't see his face. It was hid by a ball cap or hoodie. Can't remember. He was kind of tall and he smelled good. He didn't say nothing, just sat there staring up at the sky, eh. I looked too, but didn't see nothing.'"

"Smelled good?" asked Sergeant Wright.

"Yeah, that's what he said. Let me keep going. Witness Number Two: Chuck Lewandowski: 'I couldn't see what he looked like. I was shouting over at Joey 'cause that fucker Joey. I'm sorry now I yelled at him, eh, but he wouldn't pass around his Mogan David. Was keeping it just for himself, but when I got some booze the little fucker right away he's buggin me and callin me a piker if I don't share so that's why I was mad, eh, and left with the others, but now I'm sorry 'cause Joey got shot. Maybe if we all stayed there he would still be alive, you know. That bugs me, eh. Really bugs me.

'Yeah, that guy he was tall, taller than me but hell, I'm only five foot four, eh. My mother when I was a little baby, she was afraid I'd be a fuckin midget and that's why my old man he used to call me Shorty. It stuck so ever since I been called Shorty. You can call me Shorty too. The guy said something to Chuck, but I don't remember what it was.'

"OK," Detective Hudson continued. "There ain't much of use from the next two as I recall. They joined the chase in progress, but were too far away to get a good description. Here, here's the last witness, Witness Number Five, but he was with the original three that were drinking together from the start: 'I remember the guy smelled, eh. He smelled like Aqua Velva. I know because over the years I drank so much of that after shave shit, eh, and Aqua Velva is the best because it's got the highest alcohol content. Packs the most punch and you can't beat the smell on your breath, ha, ha.'"

"Aqua Velva," mused Sergeant Wright. "Is that stuff still around? OK, maybe that's something. How about surveillance?"

"There was a parking lot nearby. He could have passed through, but there's only shadows from the overhead lights. The figures are too far off. The street tapes are packed with images. Hundreds, thousands of people out, and remember we're looking at night time images, very indistinct."

"Patrols pick up anything? We had cop cars speeding everywhere that night."

"No, because we got the first call from St. James regarding a dead body, a shooting victim found on church property at the Garden. The guy was draped across a bench. When we got that second call, some of the patrol cars turned around and took off again, but when they got to the Allan Gardens area they were hopelessly entangled with the witnesses and people chasing the killer. Half the idiots were actually running after each other. One group was beating the hell out of a pedestrian who had nothing to do with the crime. He's in the hospital right now. It was fucking chaos. The bastard's got luck on top of everything else. At the end he could have made his escape on foot, street car, subway, maybe even a cab."

"Check the cabbies working in the area just in case. Maybe they had a fare or saw something suspicious. Mention the smell of that after shave, that Aqua Velva stuff. Sometimes a smell will trigger a memory more than actually seeing something. And another thing. Talking with the Captain and Chief, looks like we might be instituting a curfew, eh. This is an emergency. They're looking midnight to 6 AM. Also any one caught walking around at night after ten o'clock with no valid reason especially in a suspicious area, that person will be stopped, searched and questioned."

"Is that legal?"

"We're going to argue yes, if it comes to that. In extreme circumstances, the overriding concern for public safety takes precedence over personal Charter rights. The same thing was used once or twice before with DNA samples. People in a certain restricted, but suspected group or location, had to submit to testing, like it or not for the same reason we're going to use here."

"Where's this curfew gonna hit, what location, if it does come in? We can't do the whole city."

"They're talking east to west from Church to Roncesvalles/Dundas, and north, south, College to the Queen's Quay, right through the Entertainment District. The Chief and the Mayor are having a meeting with city council and the business community. Should be interesting. For the time being we'll stick with our present patrols, but put more cops on the second shift. I'm pretty sure our boy will lay low for a while. Too hot to handle right now. He knows he almost bought it the other day. What we really need is a break before he gets his second wind."

"Or third," added Gignac.

chapter 10

WHEN ALBERT ENTERED, the City Donut Shop was filled with the din of gossiping customers. Norm was there again, this time with Claudia. Albert wasn't keen on the addition, but he sometimes enjoyed verbally sparing with the woman so he didn't complain. Also assembled around their table were numerous bystanders who were chiming in with their opinions and arguing everything from the most recent murders to capital punishment, socialism and public housing. Albert ordered his usual and sat down at a seat Norm had saved for him. Then a hush fell over the room as the face of Detective Sergeant Wright flashed onto the TV screen.

"Citizens of Toronto, we are confronted today with a dangerous and heartless serial killer, one who has targeted our city's most vulnerable inhabitants, our homeless population. Thus far this murderer has claimed six known victims. Compounding the heinousness of the crime is its cold blooded nature and the random, callous selection of its victims. There is no motive in these killings beyond blind cruelty. As such no one is safe. The next victim could be not only one of the city's unfortunate homeless, but anyone in the wrong place at the wrong time, anyone strolling down the street or sitting on a bench or relaxing on a park lawn.

"Right now the Mayor and city counsel are debating the merits of a West and Central area curfew. We are reluctant at this time to institute one because of the economic harm it would do to our restaurant and lounge businesses which are just now recovering from the recent economic downturn. Further restrictions will undoubtedly prove harmful. We will keep you informed. In the meantime, if you stick to well lighted and heavily trafficked sections of the city, you should be safe. Exercise extreme caution or avoid altogether any dark, isolated area. Travel in groups and take public transportation whenever possible. Otherwise the next victim may be you or someone you love.

"On behalf of the Toronto Police Department I am asking for the help of all citizens. This heartless killer is someone's neighbor, someone's friend, someone's relative and he could be anywhere. From what we know to date he is a white male between the ages of thirty and fifty, medium build and height, right handed. He typically wears dark clothing and a dark baseball cap. He travels on foot. It appears that he focuses his activity in the Central and West End neighborhoods where he might possibly live. Nevertheless, he has killed elsewhere and everyone should be on alert in all areas of the city.

"We have a hotline number flashing across the bottom of this TV screen right now. Please call with any information no matter how insignificant you may think it is. It could be a change in behavior, or attitude, a change in routine. Maybe someone is keeping late hours, appears agitated or suspicious, shies away from former friends. If you know of anyone who keeps a gun, a small .22 caliber gun, give us a call. If someone has had a recent confrontation with a homeless person, or has spoken in an unusually disparaging manner about the poor and homeless, give us a call. In any case, give us a call. We will assess everything and enter any relevant information into our data base. Together with your help I promise we will catch this killer and we will put him away forever. Thank you and stay safe."

"That's bullshit," blurted out Albert as the Sergeant finished. "The guy isn't targeting just anybody. He's specifically after homeless, pain in the ass panhandlers. The cops are just fear mongering, plain and simple. They're spreading panic."

"Hey, you never know. He could make a mistake or branch out," said someone from the crowd.

"He seems to know what he's doing up to this point," added Albert.

"Anyway after this I'm sure you won't see half as many homeless assholes on the streets. I guarantee it," said another customer. "If this guy sticks to his regular targets, he's doing the city a favor."

"Trouble is he ain't getting half enough victims. He should try poisoning the bastards. You know, I figured if someone could plant a bunch of wine bottles around town; filled with some wine but topped off with antifreeze. It's poison, eh. By the time them drunks figured it out, they'd be dead. Or work in a soup kitchen and pour a bottle of arsenic or something into a big vat of chili or soup. Why bother knocking off one bum at a time when you can kill a whole bunch."

"Hey, you guys keep talking like that and someone will report you for fitting the profile."

"Right now that would include just about everyone in here beside the ladies: white, middle aged, medium height and weight, wearing dark clothes. Give me a break. Is that all they got?"

"Oh, they got more, that's for sure. They just don't want to blurt out too much. The cops always keep some shit secret so they can make a match with the killer later. I see that on TV all the time, eh."

"I don't know why I even come in here with you people," said Norm. "Where's the humanity? These people are victims twice over. First of this killer, but also of a cut throat competitive society that sees nothing wrong with kicking them out into the street when their productive working days are over."

"Please, not this socialist crap again," said the store owner.

"Look, people like this are routinely cast aside and forgotten, discarded by the capitalist system. They're a built in army of unemployed."

"Unemployable, you mean."

"No, yeah, but that only comes after they get discouraged, or disabled and then abandon any hope of ever finding a job. Sure sometimes they go to hell with drugs and alcohol, but after years and years of no job prospects what do you expect? I don't care how you look at it, I think every person, if given the option, would rather work than sit around and do nothing. You talk about freedom, but the only freedom that really counts is economic freedom, and no worker has that. They all have to sell their ability to work in order to make a living. If not, they starve."

"I doubt that's true," interjected Albert. "These assholes don't want to work. It's not in their nature. They found the soft way out, they took it, and they want to keep it."

"Maybe we can have a compromise," put in Claudia for the first time. "Help these people out if they are willing to do some retraining or volunteer work to help others."

"Our system is about competition," someone added. "You got to fight, compete with others for good jobs and income, everything. It's like that "Survivor" program. The best ones win. The losers go home. These homeless beggars, they're the losers. Too bad. We don't owe them nothing."

"I've had enough of this," proclaimed Norman rising suddenly out of his chair. "I'm out of here. Are you coming?" he added looking at Claudia. "I know Albert wants to stay and continue with his worker bashing, fascist theories, but I can't take it no more."

"I just want to hear what everyone else has to say. Can't we stay longer?"

"Not me, bye," and Norm walked out of the coffee shop making it a point to give five dollars he couldn't afford to the panhandler at the door.

Claudia just shook her head and looked strangely at Albert, a faint helpless kind of smile on her face.

72

Later that night at Albert's apartment, the phone rang. It was Norm. There was a frantic tone to his voice.

"No, Norm, I don't know where she is," Albert said while straddling Claudia's naked body and watching her frantically shake her head no.

"The last tine I saw her was at the coffee shop this afternoon. We stayed there quite a while, then went our separate ways. In fact, I've got a bit of an upset stomach from all the coffee I drank."

Albert cradled the phone under his chin and abruptly flipped Claudia onto her stomach. He then forced her legs apart with his knees and positioned his cock in the crack of her ass where he rubbed it slowly up and down giving her a preview of his intentions. Then beside her turned face, he repositioned the phone and leaned over to talk into it.

"Well, she did seem upset, but you know Claudia's so used to getting her way with you that she probably didn't appreciate your walking out on her. So now she's gonna punish you by not calling or answering her phone."

Albert stuck his tongue in Claudia's ear and felt her body shudder. He then slowly and deliberately pushed his cock inside her ass. Claudia's eyes bulged as she stared at the telephone a few inches from her lips. Albert spoke again.

"I'm sure she'll call you whenever she gets home. Don't worry. She can't stay quiet for long."

Albert began rocking his cock back and forth inside Claudia's squirming, resisting ass as he worked up another ejaculation.

"Sure, sure Norm. I know you love her and I'm sure she loves you too and wouldn't do anything to hurt you. She'll call and have a perfectly good reason why she didn't contact you earlier. No, I didn't take offense at what you said. That's part of the fun, the interchange of ideas. If we all thought and did the same things, life would be boring. Yes, I'm sure, sure, sure.." he said as he hung up the phone, grabbed Claudia by the back of the neck and finished with her.

"I guess you didn't want to say hello," Albert laughed as tears welled up in Claudia's eyes.

"What am I going to tell Norman?" she asked.

"Whatever you want. It's up to you. I'm sure he'll understand. Tell him you just got horny and decided to fuck his best friend. And you know us guys. We think too much with our cocks to be able to resist. He'll understand."

"It will kill him. You know how depressed he gets, especially of late. I'm worried about him. But he's your friend too. Isn't he?"

"Sure, that's why I think you'd better show up here again and keep me happy. Otherwise I might want to confess to Norm and get this terrible guilt off my chest. Ask his forgiveness. My old Catholic upbringing you know."

Claudia had that helpless, longing look about her that Albert couldn't resist exploiting. It was enjoyable and another exercise of his power and authority even without a gun.

"You bastard. How can you do this? God, how your first wife must have hated you."

"That she did, but she was a wimp like you, and Norman too for that matter. You people have no backbone, no internal fortitude. You can't stand your own company and need other people to give meaning to your pathetic little lives. I'm fine by myself. I don't need or want anybody except for a little entertainment once in a while."

"Thanks for the thought, but that's where Norm and me differ from you. We like to share things, not only love and affection, but interests and experiences too. When I see a good movie or read an interesting book, or walk through a park I want to tell other people about it and get them to have the same fun with it that I did. It makes the whole experience more enjoyable when you have someone to talk to and share it with, not keep it all bottled up inside yourself."

"Have it your way if it makes you feel good. Next time you're here though make sure you wax that pussy of yours. You can make up some excuse to Norm. Say you're trying to get him to pay attention to you. It might even work and he'll take you to bed."

After Claudia left, Albert sat alone and stewed over Sergeant Wright's public message and other media stories. He was especially pissed off at Mary Monticello's articles in the *Toronto Star* which painted a lurid picture of public menace at the hands of the killer.

"Wright's got a job to do, fine, but that bleeding heart bitch, Monticello, I'd gladly shoot her down in the street. However, that would ruin my record and I stand by my record. It's unblemished. Only dead beat deserving asshole losers die and their day has come. The Weed Killer is here, yes, the Weed Killer and he has become death.

"But man alive," Albert interjected with a sigh, "let me admit right now that if that kid had not opened the gate and let me into his yard I would have been dead meat myself. Never escaped. It's hard to shoot your way through a dozen people on a dead run with four bullets left in the clip. Miraculously, when I finally did stumble onto Yonge Street the maddened crowd was too preoccupied with their own little affairs and their electronic devices to notice me panting and pouring sweat like a sumo wrestler at a tango contest and smelling like Sea Biscuit after the Kentucky Derby. I may even have pissed myself a bit."

Albert paced throughout his house as he talked out loud. A Nina Simone record played in the background. He had kept his large collection of vinyl. He liked the slightly indistinct sometimes scratchy sound of the old records. "As long as she keeps it within bounds, she's fine. I can even live with all that black power entitlement bullshit, but spare me the grunting, moaning, and tongue clicking. Jesus that's irritating.

"The other thing is I can't spread myself out all over the goddamn city. When I don't know where the hell I'm going, it's a disaster. I mean, not having a definite target, taking what pops up, that's one thing, but getting lost is another. I can't carry a fucking GPS around with me. On my own turf, downtown, the West End, I can navigate a whole lot better, and I can achieve definite, measureable results. The difference is already obvious. Most of the smog sucking vagrants are gone. The only exceptions are those cocky assholes who bed down right in the open, on some sidewalk, or in front of a busy building like that jerk at our City Donut. He's laying out there right in the middle of the sidewalk, happy as a seagull in a garbage dump and blocking the way for hundreds, thousands of people every day who are rushing to work in order to put food on their tables. Lazy, freeloading bastard, he does it on purpose because he feels he's safe there, invulnerable. Well, guess again asshole. I'll put a spell on you yet because I am the keeper of the flame."

chapter 11

MARY MONTICELLO ATTENDED the Parkdale community meeting chaired by Sergeant Wright. Also seated at the front podium were Mayor Milne along with Rosemary Marchand and Olive Chambers, the MP and MPP for the Parkdale ridings. The assembly was a follow up to Sergeant Wright's prior public announcement. Today the officials were outlining the measures the city would implement in order to offer immediate shelter to the homeless. Mayor Milne gave the first address.

"My fellow citizens, let me start by giving my condolences to the families of the victims of this cold blooded murderer and assure them and you that the city is doing everything possible to apprehend this killer. To help those targeted by this mad man we are opening extra emergency shelters around Toronto to augment the number of beds provided by the usual shelters and hostels. The names of churches and community centers that are open to assist the homeless are listed on the hand out sheet presently being distributed in the hall. More will be placed on the tables at the back and others posted around the city and shown on local TV. We urge all needy people to avail themselves of these shelters. Stay off the streets. Until we apprehend this killer you are in danger. Everyone is in danger."

Mary Monticello next stood up and took the public microphone.

"My fellow Parkdale residents and fellow citizens from across the city. Some of you know me as a reporter, a social aide, and a Meals-on-Wheels volunteer. I'd also like to think of myself as your neighbor and friend. Today I'm sure we all appreciate what the Mayor and city council are doing to assist the homeless in these dire circumstances, but there are also things we can do on our own. Remember, we are a community. We live by the code of cooperation, mutual respect and assistance. Not only should we keep an eye out for our neighbors and especially for the poor unfortunates who live on our streets as I have urged in the past, but we should go a step further.

Let's invite these homeless people into our own homes. The danger is great so should be our response. Let's take them in for a week or two, a month if need be. Let's save them and ourselves from this killer.

"My husband Bob and I would like to start the ball rolling right now by extending a hand to any homeless person in need of a place to stay. See me at the end of the night. I won't let you down and I encourage others to do the same. Yes, you too Mr. Mayor, Counselor Marchand and MP Chambers. Let's all chip in and do the human thing, the Toronto thing, the Parkdale thing."

Shouts of: "That a way Mary. Tell it like it is. We hear you Mary, That's our Mary," rang out from the crowd followed by prolonged applause. Mary was about to sit down, but hesitated then raised her hand and spoke a few final words.

"I just want to add, not as a deterrent, but a word of wise precaution. People, while we're being good neighbors, let's beware of another serious problem here. That problem is bedbugs. Take care to clean up your visitors and their clothing before you give them access to your homes. We don't want to spread this terrible plague any further. It will only add to our discomfort and thwart our humanitarian aims. Thank you once again."

Another lady assumed the microphone.

"Hello, my name is Janet Lockhart and I'm a member of an organization called the Ten- in-Two Committee," she began. "Our Committee initially embarked on an ambitious plan to cut poverty in this city and province by a full ten per cent in two years, hence the name Ten-in-Two. Unfortunately, recent government cut backs blamed on the current recession have forced us to scuttled most of our plans. However, this series of killings has now dramatically underscored the serious problem of homelessness which our committee had made one of its top priorities. Yes, new shelters and soup kitchens need to be established in the face of this crisis, but we also require long term solutions that go well beyond these temporary measures. We need massive investment in affordable housing and a major overhaul in our welfare system, not to mention a comprehensive examination of wealth distribution in this country. But I don't want to get too far ahead of myself. I just want to ask the government representatives here, as well as any concerned citizens, to revitalize the Committee and join with us to work on specific long term solutions to homelessness, hunger, and poverty. I will be here after the meeting to discuss this further. Thank you. I won't take up any more time."

Another person assumed the microphone.

"Hello, my name is Norm, Norm Aspen. I live right now over in Leslieville. You know we've heard about different solutions to this problem of homelessness from taking in boarders to improving public housing. These are good things, but I think we have to examine the entire socio-economic context we all live under in order to understand what we're really up against. Ours is a business oriented society, eh. I would use the word capitalist, but then everyone would start tuning out or heading for the exits. But that's what it is, capitalism and the main thrust of capitalism is making a profit. We're not going to get more low cost housing, not because we don't need it 'cause everyone knows we do need it, eh, but we won't get it because it's not profitable enough. The builders want profits not affordable housing. They'd rather build condos and townhouses and bungalows. That's where the big profits are. These homeless people are just victims of a profit motivated system and ..."

Norm's microphone suddenly went dead. He tapped it a few times with his finger, inquisitively. Then an onstage voice sounded. It was one of the moderators.

"Look, everyone, please. This is essentially a police matter. Let's not expand it beyond that and use a tragic set of circumstances as a cause célèbre for personal or ideological agendas. We do not want some senseless killer out there dictating or even influencing this government or any government's social policy. That would lead to chaos."

"Yeah, why don't you just adopt a homeless person like Mary said," volunteered an audience member addressing Norm who sat down sheepishly. "That would be more of a help than just complaining or talking about some pie in the sky socialist dream."

"This killer can't get away forever. What if we go ahead and build a bunch of houses and apartments and shelters and things and then the police get this guy? Then what?"

"We can still use the housing," put in the Ten-in-Two Committee speaker. "There's a long term need."

"There's a need to get this killer. Let's work on that and leave the rest to our elected politicians."

When the meeting was formally over, the majority of the crowd milled about munching on doughnuts and gulping coffee, the largess provided by the politicians who joined their constituents in discussing the issues of temporary shelters and police protection. No one took up the Ten-in-Two offer or engaged Norm in conversation. Even Albert, who had accompanied his friend said nothing until they were well down Queen Street.

"Well, that was the usual useless bitch session," said Albert. "Sounded like a scat session with your darling Ella Fitzgerald: sweet and melodic, but with no meaning whatsoever. I'm surprised they didn't appoint a commission to study the killings with a white paper report due back in two years."

"Yeah, and you noticed that anyone who offered a suggestion that even hinted at examining the real socio-economic problem, namely capitalism, like that Ten-in-Two woman, was totally ignored. 'Thanks. Next.' Sons of bitches. Just solve the immediate problem, get the killer, and everything else can wait for another day. Affordable housing, welfare, EI, poverty, oh those require long term solutions. We can't tackle them now."

"I got the distinct impression that the cops and our city fathers don't have a clue about this Weed Killer," continued Albert. "Totally incompetent especially this Sergeant Wright, the head of the case though I do feel sorry for the guy. I can imagine he's being dumped on pretty good by his superiors, not to mention the public too."

"Sergeant Wright, Sergeant Wrong. It's no one person's fault. The problem is systemic. That's why I get such a laugh out of the opposition parties in Parliament banging their desks and demanding the resignation of some government minister over a supposed scandal. 'He's got to go. He should resign. The government should remove him immediately.' Really, you've got to be kidding. Replace one asshole with another all working from the same score sheet. What fucking difference does it make? By the way what was that term they used in reference to the killer, "Weed Whacker" or something? When did they start calling him that?"

"What I'd truly like to know," said Albert changing the subject, "is how the cops really feel about these killings. How much sleep they're losing over the demise of such upstanding citizens as Stinky Eddie and a couple of winos sleeping behind a warehouse?"

"Very little I can assure you. Those people have no value to the cops. The police priority is property protection and since the rich have most of the property they get the bulk of the cops' attention. The rest is lip service. I don't know why I torture myself coming out to these ridiculous meetings."

"The donuts were nice and fresh," added Albert with a smile. "Did you try any?"

"No, if I had I'd be throwing up right now. My stomach's in a knot. Were you talking to that Monticello woman afterwards?"

"No, she's an idiot. I wouldn't waste my breath on her. Anyway she's too busy saving the world to bother talking to me. Why?"

"I thought I saw you leaning over her."

"Just reaching for a donut. Her fat ass was in the way."

"Actually, she's got a good shape."

"Hey, keep that up and I'm going to tell Claudia."

"Oh yeah, Claudia. You know I'm worried. She doesn't seem that interested in me anymore. I can tell and I don't want to lose her. I can't lose her. She's the only woman I've been with since my wife left. That breakup almost killed me coming out of the blue like it did. And the kids, they stopped writing back to me long ago. My ex, she poisoned them against me. Made up a bunch of shit. What could I do? I had no money to fight her in court so I gave up."

"You're just imagining it with Claudia. Of course, you could be a little more upbeat, eh. You're so down in the dumps all the time. You're no fun to be with. You're always criticizing things, the capitalist system, and knocking yourself too. Women don't like that. They like a man who is positive, knows what he wants, takes charge of things. Then if he selects them, goes out with them, they feel special. If he doesn't like himself and his life, then they figure by association they're not worth much either."

"How can you not be depressed living in a fucked up world like this? I'm not down or pessimistic. I'm realistic."

"Well, try a twist on the idea of a "willing suspension of disbelief" and call it a "willing suspension of belief". Forget capitalism and its evils for a while."

"I remember reading long ago a biography of the Boston Strangler. Remember him?"

"Yeah, I do. Albert Di Salvo. Killed a bunch of women. Pretended he was some kind of handyman to get into their apartments, then raped and strangled them."

"Well in the book this psychiatrist was interviewed, eh, talking about a patient of his that came in for a therapy session. The guy, this patient, says to the doctor: 'Hey Doc, the world is all fucked up. Nobody cares about anyone else no more. People ignore you in the streets. They cheat and lie, make up stories about you just to make themselves look good and you look bad. There's no trust or honesty anymore.' And the Doc says to the interviewer: 'The real tragedy is that I have to treat this patient as though he's sick, mentally unhinged, when in reality he's absolutely right. It is the world that's all fucked up.'"

"Being right is not the only thing and sometimes it's not the best thing," Albert replied. "Let's stop in the Rex and catch a set. I'll buy you a beer. What do you say?"

***

Immediately after the Parkdale public meeting many people stopped by to pat Mary Monticello on the back and congratulate her on her noble stand.

"Great idea Mary. If I had some extra room in my house, I'd join you and Bob."

"That story you did on Stinky Eddie, terrific. I felt so sorry for the guy."

Mary and Janet Lockhart of the Ten-in-Two Committee bumped into each other on the way out. Actually the volunteer planned the encounter.

"Mary, do you think you could run some stories, one or two, regarding our common cause here? You know, push for concerted, anti-poverty action including long term, affordable housing. I'm really afraid that we'll get so bogged down with anecdotes and individual cases, as horrific as they are, that we will miss an opportunity to broaden our scope. Right now we can't see the poverty forest for the homeless trees."

"Sorry, but I focus on the trees, not the forest," replied Mary. "Individual stories are more interesting. That's what my readers want. The minute you start exploring and explaining economics and broad social issues you lose readers' interest. They tune out."

"Couldn't we at least point them in the right direction?"

"Well, I for one don't presume to know what that right direction is. I'm a practical person and more worried about the immediate problem of getting this killer off the streets and helping my neighbors and friends stay alive in the meantime. Right now you'll have to excuse me. I've got some good-byes to say and later this afternoon I have a tutoring session at Moss Park. Nice talking to you."

Mary watched the woman leave. Then she herself sat back down at the coffee table, chatting and basking in the glow of her reputation and the accolades that her recent stand had won for her. Just then a gentleman stopped by and patted her on the shoulder while bending over to whisper in her ear.

"Nice job, Mary. Very admirable of you to volunteer like that. You've made a great contribution to not only the city, but Parkdale in particular. One day I hope they will appropriately reward you for the great job you're doing."

Two days later Mary Monticello received a letter at her *Star* news desk. There was no return address and it was marked "Personal to Mary". Although Mary didn't know it at the time, of course, the letter was from Albert Champion and it read:

"Dear Bothered and Bewildered Block Head,

Too bad you didn't have time to speak to me the other day at the meeting of the Parkdale Deadwood Society. My God, I haven't seen such a collection of shit assed, spittle chinned, slope headed Neanderthals since I last saw the movie, "Fire." But at least those primitives could manage to fend for themselves which is more than I can say for your homeless charity cases.

"Let me just assure you and any of your employed or retired neighbors that you are NOT my intended targets. Despite the bullshit announcements from our city fathers and Detective Wright I have no intension of ever aiming a gun at any upstanding member of this city. They can go about their business and pleasure with no fear whatsoever. For them things are the way they used to be. Only deadbeat laggards, and homeless assholes taking up space in our beautiful Toronto will die. I am dedicated to eradicating them, the city's human weeds. Night and day I will be the one to pull them out by the root until Toronto is green with civic pride and gainful husbandry. You can call me the Weed Killer and I'm coming to a garden near you.

"I want you to print this letter in the *Toronto Star*. If not, I will gladly forward my future letters to your publishing rivals. I'm sure they will be glad to get them.

Signed, The Weed Killer"

Albert had been careful to use common typing paper that he had bought at Wal-Mart and paid for with cash. The printer he used was also an inexpensive, common brand. Of course, he wore latex gloves when handling any paper; the stamp was self adhesive, and he used a sponge to moisten the envelope also purchased at Wal-Mart though at a different store.

Oh my God, thought Mary when she read the letter which shook in her hand like a wounded bird. And the bastard was at the meeting. Jesus, I can't remember now. There were so many people. But what to do? What to do? A scoop like this. Call the police?

Maybe not so fast. This guy, this cold blooded killer, obviously reached out to me. I doubt he'd talk to anyone else. Probably not. That's surely the sense from this "Personal to Mary" stuff. Yes, I think it's clear I'm the one he wants to confide in. He trusts me.

Mary photocopied the letter and then headed excitedly to her editor's office. The *Star* printed the letter and that same day called the police.

"I don't know about the wisdom in publishing this letter, certainly not without showing it to us first," declared Sergeant Wright. "It gives this lunatic a public platform to spew out his hatred. Furthermore, it frees the average citizen from fear and guilt. If they believe they are not the intended targets of this killer, people might withhold information and refuse to cooperate. Not that it's given us much help up to now, but we want people on our side and on the lookout. We'll have to take this for evidence, you know."

"Certainly and I'm sorry," replied Karen French, the paper's editor in chief, "but it was too big a story to hold back and we think the public has a right to know what's going on. Often in the past, I don't have to tell you this, Detective Wright, but the police have not exactly been forthcoming with information. Need I remind you of the balcony rapist or even the Bernardo case, not to mention the Wellington Street murders. If the victims and the public had known a little more about the criminal activity around them, they could have protected themselves a lot better. I might add I saw the same procedure unfolding with this case.

"Then, of course, later in your investigations, long after much of the damage has been done, you suddenly turn to us and ask for help like you're doing now. 'Please, we need public input and cooperation to solve this terrible crime.' Be that as it may and without further rehashing the past let me assure you that we here at the *Toronto Star* fully intend to cooperate with the police and will keep you informed of any further communication the minute we receive it. Can we agree to work together on this?"

"I trust you've been careful not to handle the letter? Destroy any DNA evidence?" inquired Sergeant Wright.

"Except for when I first opened it and didn't know what it was,' said Mary. "I never thought the killer would write. After that all of us wore latex gloves and treated it like poison which it is in a way."

"We'll have forensics check for prints, DNA, whatever," said Sergeant Wright. "Find out where it was mailed from and when. Also Ms Monticello, do you remember this man approaching you at the meeting? Can you give us a description, anything that might help us out?"

"Believe me when I say I've been wracking my brain trying to remember. There were so many people. I have a habit of talking non-stop, which, I'm sure you've noticed. I'm rather good at it unfortunately. It might have been at the coffee table after the presentation or even outside the building, but it was like leaving church. Everyone was stopping and chatting and offering opinions and judgments. It's all a blur. I just recall a collage of faces, smells, and sounds. Very confusing."

"Smells?"

"You know perfumes, colognes, the coffee, donuts. Everything was mixed together."

"Did we have any surveillance on the scene?" asked Sergeant Wright to his colleague, Detective Gignac.

"No, not specifically, but the press cameras were rolling most of the time. We can check the stations for footage. Something might come up."

"All right, we'll leave it at that, I guess, and get back to you if we find something. And needless to say if he contacts you again call us immediately and don't open any envelopes."

"Before you go, Sergeant," added Karen French. "You don't think Mary is in any danger here, do you? I mean, our cooperating, that's not going to put her in this killer's cross hairs, is it?"

"No, I won't let that happen. We value your cooperation and will go out of our way to protect you. Remember too, by the killer's own written testament, he is not targeting law abiding citizens and he's starting a dialogue with the press through Ms. Monticello so I think you're safe there. Only the homeless are on his radar. They are the ones in danger."

A week later an e-mail arrived on Mary's computer.

"Dear Mary,

Tell Detective Wright he ought to cover the waterfront more often, maybe even the old, abandoned building on Harbor Street behind the Air Canada Centre. I just found some good compost there for the city's garden.

P.S. Thanks for publishing the letter.

Yours truly,

The Weed Killer"

chapter 12

ALBERT HAD WALKED by the old office building one morning in the bright sunshine. It was boarded up and abandoned. The sidewalk outside was damp from a night time shower when Albert noticed a sleeping bag and some wet clothes draped over the spikes of the building's front gate. That led him inside via an unlocked back door.

"Must be the loading bays or stock rooms. Feels like church in here," he sighed to himself, "complete with angelic shafts of light and the distant echo of voices in solemn prayer, but somehow I don't think they're praying, not to any God I know anyway."

"This mother fucker will feed us for days," one man laughed as he and a companion singed the pinfeathers off a dead, crudely plucked Canada goose. "Dumb bastard just stood there, eh. Boink! Good-bye goose. Talk about stupid or what?"

"Ah yes, Strange Fruit, the smell of burning flesh," interrupted Albert. "Don't you insensitive clods know that geese mate for life? Matter of fact, her mate sent me out to look for her. He won't be happy when I tell him what you did."

"What? Who?" the men squinted towards Albert who momentarily stayed within the shadows. When he emerged he was slamming the clip into his gun.

"Fuck man, it's him, the fucking killer. You said we be safe in here," the one man turned to his companion.

"Yeah, what the fuck is up? We ain't outside on the streets. You can't get us in here. It ain't right."

"Right's got nothing to do with it, as my friend Clint would say," laughed Albert. "Let's call it fate instead. You just happened to be here when I was walking by. If I had gone a different route, or if you had been in another building, or if you hadn't put your wet clothes outside in plain view, I never would have ventured in here. Fate."

"Why can't you and your faith just keep going? Forget about us?"

"Faith is another question, but letting the two of you off the hook would undercut the intriguing randomness of our meeting. It's like a starving lion coming upon a crippled gazelle. It's beautiful really and a shame you can't appreciate it."

"We don't know what yer talking about. You don't make no sense."

"Whether or not you two morons understand me is irrelevant."

"What the fuck he talking about? It ain't fair that we goin to be killed for something that don't make no sense."

"The idea that it makes no sense is precisely the sense it makes."

Albert fired two shots into the chest of the man closest to him. He wasn't the greatest shot so at a distance he just aimed at the body proper. The second man turned to run and Albert fired a third time. He missed, but the fleeing man fell anyways and proceeded to frantically crawl away screaming for help. Albert ran up to him and kicked him in the stomach more in an effort to shut him up than to hurt him.

"Jesus, you're black,' Albert called out in surprise. "With all the dirt and filth on your face I couldn't tell. Wow, my first black victim, my first "nigra". You know I always had a laugh thinking about those Southerners and their die hard reluctance to give up on their prejudices, eh. When "nigger" finally became socially unacceptable and was replaced at the time by "negro" those Southerners couldn't stand the change. It just galled them to no end so what did they do? They invented the word "nigra". Son of a bitch. You just have to wonder sometimes. Don't you think?"

"Hey man, let me go. I ain't done nothin, and you, you can show you ain't prejudice too, you know. Give a nigger a chance here. Come on, man. Please."

"Jesus, you just don't get it. If I let you go, it will prove I am prejudiced, giving you your freedom just because of your color. What about the poor slob back there?"

"Fuck him, man. You already shot his ass. He dead."

"But the point here is that both of you are worthless scum. Black, white, brown, or red it doesn't matter. It's not a racial thing. I have a friend. He would understand perfectly well. It's a class thing. You see, you got everything in common with this dead loser and others like him way more than you do with say somebody like Lincoln Alexander, or Oscar Peterson even though they're black like you and your now beginning to decompose buddy over there is white.

"It's the same conclusion that Malcolm X came to about Muslims. When he went to Mecca he saw Muslims of all colors and nationalities. He realized that the whole thing wasn't really a color issue like he figured at first. There was something more to it than that, something deeper. Unfortunately, he died, was assassinated, before could find the answer."

"I don't know no Oscar, or Peter and I never heard of no Talcolm X."

"Malcolm X. Jesus. Had you stayed in school, made something of yourself, maybe you'd be familiar with characters from your own black history, and, of course, you wouldn't be crawling around on the floor here either. But that just proves my point. How about W.E.B. Dubois, or Paul Robeson, Barrack Obama?"

"Yeah, I heard a him, the last one. He down in the States there somewhere."

Albert shook his head in dismay. "I can't say I feel the slightest bit sorry for you. You're just wasting space here on the planet."

"No, no, no," the man pleaded.

Albert fired off three shots, pausing between each one, watching their effect on the prostrate man as he cursed, squirmed, and flailed away with helpless hands.

"Your heavy breathing is pumping way too much carbon dioxide into the atmosphere. You're adding to your already overdone carbon footprint."

A final shot rang out. Albert removed a couple of weeds he had pulled from the building's front lawn and stuffed them inside the gaping mouths of his two latest victims.

"Ugh, complete with bulging eyes and twisted mouth. Anyway, they're both ready for Mr. Wright to gather up. And phew, that sure ain't the smell of magnolias. The boys made a mess in here. No respect for the environment."

On his way home he stopped at the Sanderson Branch of the Toronto Library and typed a message to Mary Monticello at the *Star* using a library card he had lifted from a young boy's packsack several weeks ago. Back at home he burnt the card in his basement.

***

Detectives Gignac and Wright walked across the debris littered ground floor of the old office building. Water dripped into dark pools from some source on the floors above.

"Looks like they were living here for a while. Clothes piled in a couple of shopping carts, dented canned goods, plastic plates and utensils on the shelves, a cut down barrel there for cooking with a chicken wire grille on top."

"What's this?"

"A bird, long neck, probably a goose. They were preparing dinner maybe when he interrupted them. Saw the sleeping bags draped outside. Dead give away, but that worries me."

"Because it means he's on the hunt during the day time now? I thought of that too and us with stepped up night time patrols. He's got us playing the run while he drops back to pass. He's either smart as hell or lucky as a seven."

"That pile of toilet paper over in the corner must be their latrine. Stinks in here. Fucking mess."

"I know they're homeless and all," said Detective Gignac. "But does that mean they have to be complete filthy pigs? All these places, they're shit holes. You go down to Parkdale, and Jarvis, Sherbourne. There's crap and litter everywhere. Can't you be poor and clean and tidy at the same time?"

"I don't know. If you didn't have a job, a family, your own home or apartment, I guess it wouldn't make much difference. Why bother?"

"For your own self respect."

"Without any of those things I mentioned that would be pretty hard too. Well, we're still following behind this guy and picking up the pieces, but the puzzle ain't getting any clearer. That letter of his to the *Star* hasn't helped. It killed the curfew idea though. Once the downtown businessmen read that they lobbied the government hard and fast and convinced them to bury any thought of curfews. What's the sense of a curfew if no one is in danger, no one but those who shouldn't be out on the streets in the first place. Plan B anyone? Hopefully the forensic people will come up with something. Nothing on the TV cameras from the public announcement meeting over in Parkdale, where Monticello, unknowingly met with our Weed Killer?"

"Na da. His letters and e-mails will trip him up though. They always do. His ego will get the best of him."

"Except for that Zodiac Killer down in California. He wrote letters and left clues and the police never did find him. He's still the fuck out there somewhere."

"Maybe he moved here."

"The Zodiac was more into torture. Our guy is like a robot, a heartless Nazi. It's all efficiency with him. He doesn't have any feelings, not even cruelty. He just kills and leaves."

"What about the weeds?"

"Just a signature thing I think. He's marking his territory, his kill, like a dog pissing on a tree."

"Sooner or later, he'll make a mistake. That's why it's important he keeps writing. If he shuts up now and goes underground we may never nab him."

"You know aside from the weed bullshit, if he had done all of these homicides gradually, I mean over time, years, a murder here and a murder there, fuck, we would probably never have known. All these homeless losers, they would have been lost in the shuffle of time and other priorities."

"So why the fuck did he all of a sudden go berserk like this?"

"Fed up. Just fed up like in that old movie where some guy hangs out a window and shouts: 'I'm mad as hell and ain't gonna take it no more.' I think it's like that. I feel the same sometimes myself when all this shit comes down and you can't do a goddamn thing about it. You feel helpless. Look at all the criminals we've put away here in Toronto over the years as an example, the past twenty years say. How many you figure? Thousands, tens of thousands? Has it really changed anything? Has crime dropped? Have we eliminated the gangs, or the drugs, the murderers, prostitution, not to mention the thievery, burglary and fraud?"

"I guess the stats have gone down a bit recently."

"Hey, you know what I mean. It's a never ending cycle. Nothing gets better. There's not even some goal or program that you can feel comfortable reaching for, eh. Everything is just day to day slogging. It's the same thing for your average man in the street, over and over the same bullshit with no real improvement in your life. So you get discouraged and pissed off and then you bump into some fucking jerk who spits on you when you don't hand over your hard earned money, and you snap. I can get it. I can."

"You sorry now you took the Sergeant's job?" asked Detective Gignac. "I mean with all the aggravation dealing with the public, not to mention having to eat shit from the Captain and Chief and the likes of Mary Monticello and Karen French too?"

"It only hurts when I think about it. I had my doubts right from the start to tell you the truth, but I promised Sharon I'd stick it out till I was eligible for early retirement. House will be paid for by then, kids on their own, hopefully, and we'll have enough in the bank to live comfortably."

"By that time the Canadian economy will be in such bad shape your son and daughter will be living in your basement along with their own wives, husbands and kids," laughed Detective Gignac.

"Jesus, don't even kid about that shit," smiled the Sergeant in return. "You know I had a friend up in Sudbury. He was a biology teacher, high school. We were talking about kids leaving home, eh, for good, to start a life of their own. You know when to figure it was the right time and all. He liked to use the example of the mother bear. Biology teacher, like I said. So the mother bear, she instinctively knows when the time is right for the permanent break-up. One day she barks out one of her warning calls and the grown cubs she still has with her scamper up the nearest tree for safety just like she taught them when they were little and still learning the ropes of survival. But this time things are different and the cubs don't hear her all clear call. The mother is silent and when the cubs finally come down on their own, the mother bear ain't nowhere around . She's gone, gone forever. My buddy said that was a lesson from nature we humans could learn from.

Comes a time for the off spring, the kids to leave home. We should embrace the moment, not fight it. It's natural."

"Try telling that to your wife when the time comes."

"Yeah, anyway, lucky thing me and Sharon got our government pension money safely invested. And I did get an offer for the Chief of Police job in Peterborough. Could transfer my pension too. Been thinking about it especially in light of all this bullshit we're going through now. Maybe when it's over. I've got to talk to Sharon. She's pretty keen on Toronto and the new house we've got. Kids have their school and friends too."

"Me, I'm through with the stock market. This overtime is helping though. I got to say that. Maybe it's a good thing we don't catch this guy right away. What's a few more dead homeless assholes anyway?"

"If it weren't for my blood pressure, you'd get my vote on that," Sergeant Wright sighed.

chapter 13

MARY MONTICELLO WAS happy with the release of the Weed Killer's letter in the *Star* especially under her new by-line; "The Weed Killer Talks to Mary". This augmented her status in the paper to new heights. Perhaps a raise would be in the offing, and even a Star Award for reporting and a shot at the coveted Signet Prize honoring the country's most outstanding news journalist. More importantly, she cherished the added prestige bestowed upon her by the people of Toronto, and Parkdale in particular.

"Hey there's Mary, Mary Monticello. The Weed Killer would only talk to her, eh."

"She helped bring down the Weed Killer."

"Good old Mary, she's one of a kind."

"Our hero, Mary. She has done more for this city than anyone I can think of. She should run for Mayor, the Hazel McCallion of Toronto."

"Hell, she'd be perfect for the job. Perfect."

But Mary didn't care for public office. She was a community person and believed in the community spirit, community values, and the grass roots movement. She didn't trust politics at a higher plain. From what she saw that level of government was too far removed from its constituents and too mired in bureaucracy to be effective. Mary's goal was to point out the problems and pitfalls of bureaucrats and government policies as they affected ordinary people. By doing so she intended to shame the offenders into doing the right thing.

One of Mary's favorite targets was the TCHC, the Toronto Community Housing Corporation. It especially galled her that over the years the government body had totally ignored her complaints and vitriolic columns especially her most recent rant about the bedbug infestation overwhelming the city.

"They don't care that their housing is nothing more than a breeding ground for vermin. The only things comfortable in those crap holes are mice, rats, cockroaches and bed bugs."

The release of the Weed Killer letter created a media sensation such as had never been seen in Toronto before. The *Star* ran an extra twenty thousand copies of the "Weed Killer" issue and those were snapped up in an hour. The paper printed editorials and letters to the editor as they flooded onto Mary's desk. The fortunes of the paper, which had waned in the current electronic media age, had been saved. Mary even began a second column featuring interviews with homeless people recently rescued from the streets and housed safely within the newly expanded, if still temporary, city shelters.

Letters to Editor, the *Toronto Star*: "It is chilling to read those brief words of a cold blooded killer. And the thought that this individual actually lives in our wonderful city fills me with horror and shame. This kind of thing happens in the US not in Canada."

"The *Star* shouldn't publish such trash. Giving this man a forum to spout his obviously insane views is beyond distasteful, it's criminal. Nothing can justify such action. Before we know it other insane killers will act out their fantasies knowing there is a willing media there to promulgate their sick views. Terrible."

"As far as I'm concerned, I have no concerns. The killer expressly stated and his actions have proved, that he does not want to kill innocent, law abiding citizens. I am not going to change my ways or habits and stay at home and hide. I will continue to hit the clubs with my friends and have a good time. Let the police handle the Weed Killer. That's their job."

"I don't pretend to know exactly what is going on with this Weed Killer, but I do know that the downtown streets of Toronto have never been more pleasurable to walk down."

"If the government at all levels had done their job and rid the city of the dirty beggars that lined our streets, we wouldn't have the situation like we do right now. This is terrible, murder is terrible, but the city officials share the blame and responsibility."

"Maybe now the Premier and the Mayor will get off their rears and help the homeless get off the streets and into decent housing. Then the problem will go away. Deprive a fire of its fuel and it will die."

"The homeless are people who have fallen on terrible times. We ignored them until they were shot dead on our streets. Now everyone is concerned. Shame on us that it took such a terrible thing to wake us up."

chapter 14

BACK AT HOME Don Wright found no respite from his cares and woes.

"You know, Don, that daughter of yours," began his wife, "she always pulls this pouty, bitchy stuff when you're not around. I come home from work and I'm tired too, but I still have to get supper on the table, clean the house, get her and Joshua settled down, get the homework going. Her constant resistance is hard to put up with, but I don't think giving up and letting her have her way is the answer either. Frankly, she's got me worn out."

"I know, I know, but I'm sitting on the edge right now. Donnally and this Killer, you've got no idea of the pressure. It's like there's a bomb in the squad room with a timer, but no one knows when it's set to go off. All you can hear is the ticking. Tick, tick, tick. I can even hear it in my sleep, not that I can get any sleep in the first place."

Don sat on the couch with his head in his hands looking like an ancient defeated warrior.

"I can't figure out for the life of me why we can't get a lead on this guy," he moaned, speaking to no one in particular. "He's obviously new at the game, an amateur. He should have fucked up long ago. Actually that's probably the problem. He's so new at the game that he's not following any of the rules. He doesn't even know them."

"Don't worry. People are concerned," replied Sharon. "They will notice him somewhere along the line and turn him in. It's terrible what he's doing, just terrible. The public won't stand for it."

"I'm not so sure about that. He's like a goddamn Robin Hood in a perverse sort of way. He's knocking off a bunch of losers that a lot of people hate and would secretly like to get rid of themselves. They just don't have the guts to do it. People respect him for that. I've heard it myself a thousand times. 'The Killer is doing what you cops won't do, get rid of a constant nuisance.' I should never have taken the Sergeant's job. Stupid suggestions about approaches and manpower,

"All in". Why didn't I just shut my mouth. I would have avoided all this bullshit. And I realize a lot of the burden falls on you with the housework and the kids. You know, maybe we should have stayed in Sudbury or we should consider moving to some small town where they don't have all these angry people and problems. Peterborough is a nice place. You wouldn't have to work and I could help out around the house a lot more."

"Please, Don, please. You wanted a nicer place for the kids to grow up in too and be closer to work. Not that it matters 'cause you're working every hour of the day and night and never home anyway. Besides, we've worked all our lives. We deserve a good house, an expensive one. I don't see why we can't have nice things. Gees, I'm going to cry because nothing panned out the way we planned. And now Meaghan, I don't know what I'm going to do with her. I've lost my influence and for some reason she hates me."

"She doesn't hate you. God, you're her mother. But I'll have a talk with her. This bullshit has got to stop. I can't be coming home to this every night either especially with all that crap at work. That fucking killer. He's killing me too."

"Please, the swearing, Don."

The family gathered for supper at six o'clock, one of the few times in recent months that they dined together.

"So, Dad, are you going to catch this guy?" asked Josh. "They call him the Weed Killer, eh, 'cause he says those people he kills are just a bunch of weeds. Everybody's talking about him in school."

"That's disrespectful to refer to people like that, unfortunate people who don't have a home. That's why you and your sister are lucky. You've got a place to stay, be safe, a place with family to love and take care of you," Sharon was quick to put in.

"Some love," muttered Meaghan. "Can't do a thing. I'm not even grounded anymore and I still can't go anywhere."

"There's a killer on the loose," said Don staring at his daughter. "He's leaving bodies all over the city. Pardon us for being concerned about your safety."

"He ain't shooting no kids," replied Meaghan.

"Yeah," put in Joshua. "He just kills the homeless bums that live in the street. Nobody else don't have to worry."

"God, don't they teach grammar in the schools anymore," said Sharon. "And your lack of sympathy for these people. It's terrible!."

"There's clubs set up in different schools and a bunch of web sites about him," continued Joshua.

"What do you mean clubs?" asked Sharon.

"Fan clubs," replied Meaghan. "They got membership cards with a skull and crossbones on them and they hold meetings on the computer and they even go to some of the places where those bums were killed."

"Go to the murder scenes?"

"Yeah, Johnny Cool who used to be in my class before he was expelled, he even collected some of that crime scene tape the cops left. He's got it in his bedroom, a souvenir."

"How do you know what he's got in his bedroom?" inquired Don quickly.

"He told us about it, Dad. Don't get all nervous and suspicious right away. Anyway, Johnny's real good on the computer and he wants to make a computer game out of it. You go around killing the bums and you get points."

"Oh my God," sighed Sharon.

"And that's not all," continued Meaghan warming to the topic and enjoying her parents' discomfort. "Some of the boys are going out and marking the spots where the bums hide out. They paint the letters BSH on a wall, or door, or something nearby so everybody knows a homeless loser's hiding there."

"What does BSH stand for?" asked Sharon with a frightened look on her face, terrified that her own daughter would have knowledge of such things.

"Bum Sleeps Here," answered Meaghan with a smile.

"That's enough. Jesus, what are those friends of yours, sick? Morbid fascination with murder. It just feeds this psycho's ego. Believe me, there's nothing glamorous in what this guy is doing. He's killing innocent people. People who haven't harmed anyone and just want to be left alone. And this Johnny Cool kid, what's he look like anyway? Do I know him?"

"No, he wouldn't be caught dead around no cops. S'got long hair, wears leather a lot, black leather, and high boots. It's the Gothic look, but you wouldn't know anything about that."

"Believe me, I've seen it all. Anyway, I don't want you hanging around with this boy. He sounds like an idiot. Now, eat your supper and let's not talk about this anymore."

"I don't like this stuff."

"Sheppard's Pie, you used to love it," added Sharon somewhat crestfallen.

"It's got meat in it."

"So what? What's wrong with meat all of a sudden?" added Don.

"I'm a vegetarian, that's what."

"A vegetarian, you? You're a vegetarian? When did this happen?"

"Just recent. The way they treat animals is cruel. They keep them all penned up and feed em guts and blood and stuff and shoot them full of drugs. Johnny says most animals grown for food are actually addicts from all the drugs they're given."

"Johnny again. I won't bother pointing out the contradictions here in your defensive argument on behave of the animal kingdom," said Don. "And just what vegetables are to your liking anyway? To my recollection you never were a big fan. Do you like spinach?"

"No!"

"Turnips?"

"No, gross."

"Carrots?"

"Nope."

"Corn?"

"Yeah, I like corn."

"Tomatoes?"

"No, too slimy."

"Cabbage?"

"Ugh, smells like farts."

"Potatoes, cucumbers?"

"I don't mind cucumbers. Potatoes are OK with butter and cheese."

"Butter and cheese are animal products. True vegetarians don't eat them."

"Well maybe I'm not a real true vegetarian right now, not just yet."

"Just so we know what to fix for supper. Sounds like corn, cucumbers and potato casserole are on the menu for tomorrow. Should cut down on the grocery bill."

"Hey, I don't have to eat any of that shit, do I?" chimed in Josh.

"Young man, watch your mouth. I don't know what's happening to this family," lamented Sharon. "I hardly recognize the two of you anymore."

***

Sergeant Wright and Detective Gignac drove south down Bathurst St. on their way to a meeting with the Mayor and city council at city hall. Mary Monticello and Karen French, editor of the *Star*, had been invited to sit in as well.

"That fucking Monticello, I think she's enjoying this more than anything,' said Detective Gignac. "The civic warrior. She's so full of herself."

"Holy Fuck," shouted Sergeant Wright. "Stop the car. Stop the God damn car."

"What?"

"Back up if you can to the corner of Bridgeview. I thought I saw something."

"That was just an abandoned building. Looks like an old shop or factory. There's a string of warehouses along here. The Tarragon Theatre is just down the street."

"Tell me I'm fucking seeing things. What is that on the side of the building?"

"Graffiti, that's all. Nothing new. A little more artistic than most, but we got bigger problems than this to worry about. You doing OK? How are things at home?"

Sergeant Wright sat there open mouthed pointing to the side of the building.

"Those letters, BSH." he whispered. "Do you see them?"

"Well, yes I do. Plain as day. So what? Hey, you sure you're alright?" continued Detective Gignac. "I know you've been keeping some killer hours. Pardon the pun, but…"

Sergeant Wright was already out of the police car and half way to the building. His partner stumbled after him.

"We're gonna be late for the meeting. You know the Chief. He won't be happy. He wants us up front on the case."

The front door was heavily barred, bolted and locked so the two men with Sergeant Wright in the lead moved around back. A push on a door that appeared boarded up opened easily.

"How the fuck did you know he was in here?" asked Detective Gignac incredulously after they found a man's body lying on the floor with a single bullet hole in the head. "You getting clairvoyant on me. Those letters outside. What's with the letters?"

"BSH. Bum Sleeps Here." It's a tip off.. to the killer. Someone informed him of the homeless guy hiding inside the building."

"What? You're kidding. Who, who would do something like that?"

"Call ahead to City Hall and tell them we can't make the meeting. Tell them we discovered another victim and we'll get back to them with the new information. I'll cordon off this building."

Later on, back at their headquarters Sergeant Wright and his squad gathered around the computer. "Look for Weed Killer, or the letters BSH. Websites, info, locations, anything," the Sergeant said to the technical officer in charge.

"Here we go. Didn't take long. There are several sites relating to the Killer. Here's one. 'Weed Killer Fan Club: Become a Member, Kill a Homeless Person'. Here's another, 'Death to Dandelions'. And another, 'Weed Rangers.'"

"Bastards."

"This is getting fucking sick. What the hell's going on?"

While the officers stared at the computer screen Detective Gignac explained the situation at the Bridgeview building and the meaning of the initials.

"Nothing on those letters? Must be keeping that BSH stuff to themselves right now, word of mouth only, or passed between their Blackberries, whatever the little cock suckers are using."

"Well, if they've got any computer smarts they know we can trace them easily enough if they put that shit on their website or blog. Could find themselves open to some kind of accessory to murder charge, or conspiracy maybe. Serious stuff so they're not incriminating themselves. Some of these sites may very well be over the line already."

"Here's another one, 'Acolytes of the Weed Killer'. Has a password, but we should hack that no problem. OK, 'Dandelion'. Not too original. Bingo? Here's your stuff, 'The Official Bum Sleeps Here Site Map. Rat out the Rats!' They got a fucking map of the city, looks like the West End mainly. The red dots indicate the sites of the homeless hideouts. Looks like half a dozen maybe. There's a video here. Check it out."

The officers watched and pointed as a surprisingly distinct and colorful video emerged.

"Is that a crime scene photo from one of the Weed Killer homicides, a naked body with the eyes gouged out and a bullet hole in the head? What the hell? Where did these pictures come from?"

"They're not from our files. Whoever formulated them dug them up from elsewhere and posted them here. There's more. It's starting, some kind of movie."

"This shit is sick."

"Hey, that's inside the Lighting and Standards Building on Strachan St. I recognize that map on the wall and that old fashioned desk and swivel chair. Fucking somebody must have busted in. Yeah, that's a bunch of them dancing around inside, looks like teenagers and fuck, they're naked except for that yellow crime scene tape. Doesn't cover much. Looks like they got red paint, I guess that's supposed to be blood, on their faces and bodies. Idiots! How'd they get in there?"

The detectives watched the images swirl past the camera obscured a bit by the jerky movements of bodies and the poor lighting in the room. Suddenly Sergeant Wright's head snapped back as though hit by a two by four. He stared as a youthful female face paused ever so briefly in front of the camera. Then the face and body disappeared into a large group of naked images circling the perimeter of the room like savages around a bonfire. In the background the same figure turned as the camera purposely but only momentarily zoomed in on her buttock revealing a distinctive butterfly tattoo. The insect had a human skull for a face with red eyes dripping blood.

"Nice ass on that one anyway," declared Detective Hudson.

Sergeant Wright scowled. "Shut that thing off. I get the point. Now alert all precinct cops to this BSH stuff. Have them check those places out immediately and get any poor homeless bastards out of those areas before we have a homicidal epidemic on our hands. I just hope this doesn't get out of hand. My God."

"You thinking copy cats? You think it might escalate into that?"

"We'll be lucky if it hasn't already. Take the bums to any nearby shelter or church that's on our list. Explain the situation, but get these people housed immediately. Then trace that website and see who's behind it. Right now I'm tired, half dead. I'm going home before I collapse like a house of cards."

"What about that meeting with the Mayor and council? They postponed it for only a few hours when we didn't show."

"Tell them what happened. Ask if they want a meeting or the news of a half dozen more homicides on the front pages of the *Star*."

Sergeant Wright swung the front door of his house open and marched heavily into the kitchen. Sharon and Josh were at the table eating supper.

"Where's Meaghan?" he asked sternly.

"She's up in her room. Doesn't like pork chops. You know, the vegetarian thing."

"Come with me," Don said and walked resolutely through the living room and up the stairs to the second level.

"What is it? What's the matter?"

"That goddamn daughter of yours."

"Can I come too," pleaded Josh who followed behind not waiting for an invitation.

"You stay downstairs," Don grimly warned. "And I'm not going to tell you a second time. Got it?"

Josh backed off immediately. "Yeah, I never get to see anything around here."

"Don, Donny what's going on?"

Detective Wright swung the door of his daughter's bedroom open as the girl stood in bewilderment at the foot of her bed.

"What the hell," she shouted. "Don't you people believe in knocking. Christ, I got no privacy here at all."

"And you're about to get a lot less. Turn around and drop your pants. Sharon get in here. Now, drop em."

"Are you crazy?" began Meaghan until she looked directly into her father's eyes and her toned changed. "Hey, Dad, come on. I ain't doin that. I ain't stripping. Isn't that against the law. You're a cop. You shouldn't be doing this."

"I'm your father, and you'll drop those pants or I swear I'll tear them off your ass right here and now."

"Donny, what in the world? Have you lost your mind?" stammered Sharon.

"I want to see that tattoo."

Meaghan quickly sat down on the bed holding the foot rail tightly in her hands. Don stepped up, grabbed her wrists, applied enough pressure for the girl to let go, and then flipped her over on her stomach.

"Sharon, get over here. Get over here and pull down her pants. Just enough for me to see that tattoo. That's all. If not I swear.."

Meaghan screamed. Sharon in a tremble stepped forward. She spoke nervously, her voice cracking, yet with enough force and authority to cause her husband to hesitate.

"Now clam down. Don't do this or we will all regret it. Just tell me what you want, what you're after. For God's sake, calm down. You got us terrified here."

"OK, OK, I'll step outside the room. You, you look at that tattoo and then describe it to me, in detail. I'll be outside. In detail! I want to know exactly what it looks like. You got that?"

"Yes, yes, now leave. Meaghan, Honey, please let me see that tattoo and we can get this over with. I don't know what has gotten into your father, but I'm scared so please."

When Sharon confronted Don in the hallway they could both hear Meaghan crying and screaming in the bedroom.

"Jesus Christ, what in the world came over you?' asked Sharon. "She's heartbroken and scared to death and so frankly am I."

"What did it look like? Tell me. I've got to know. She showed it to you didn't she? You just didn't take her word for it. If you did then..."

"No, no, I saw it. Of course, she showed it to me. I mean the alternative... Jesus! It's a butterfly. That's all. Pretty I guess."

"Oh, Jesus, what color?"

"It's a lot of colors; blue and red, some yellow, pink. The wings, you know."

"And the face itself, anything strange about it? What did it look like?"

"Strange? You mean the face of the butterfly?"

"No, the ears of the elephant on her other ass cheek. Yes, of course, the butterfly. Jesus Christ!"

"Don, I've never seen you like this. You got to get off this Weed Killer case. It's going to kill the whole family. But no, there was nothing unusual about the butterfly's face, just eyes and antennae like a regular goddamn bug."

Don leaned heavily against the hallway wall and held his face in his hands.

"Thank the Lord. I mean I'm sorry, I'm sorry, but I had to know. If that was her, laughing and dancing, naked like that with those fiendish friends of hers, those savages, I don't know what I'd do. What would I do? I have to apologize now. Let me get past you."

"No Jesus, no. Not now. Give it some time. We all need a little time. You can tell her later. Let her calm down."

"I'm not calming down. Not ever," came Meaghan's voice from the bedroom. "And he, he's not my father no more. I hate him. He's a cop too. Yeah, right. He's supposed to protect people. Well, who's going to protect us from him? I never want to see him again as long as I live. And when he's old and all alone he can die in some stinky old nursing home by himself because, because nobody can even stand the sight of him."

At the bottom of the stairs Josh was waiting.

"Hey, is Meaghan grounded again? She in trouble? What's going on?"

Don sat in the kitchen warming an untouched bottle of beer in his hands. Sharon sat opposite, teary eyed and red faced. She had just heard the whole story of the crime scene video at the Lighting and Standards Building from her husband.

"My Lord, Don, what's happened to us? We were such a loving family at one time. And you and Meaghan, you two were inseparable. God, she clung to you like that baby blanket of hers. Remember that, her Biddy? She wouldn't let go of that for love nor money. She was the same with you too. I could hardly pry her out of your arms. At bed time you'd have to read her a half dozen stories before she'd fall asleep. Jesus, I hope we can get over this. That goddamn Weed Killer is killing more than the homeless."

"I know. I'm sorry. I just snapped. This damn case, that idiot kid at the door, and then the video. It all got to me. And she grew up so fast. Where did the time go? She's not my little girl no more. I've lost her and I didn't have time to tell her all the things she needs to know, to protect herself, to grow up strong and confident and safe. Jesus, what a mess."

"Hey, what about me?" came a voice from the corner of the room. "You ain't told me none of that stuff either. I don't want to wind up like Meaghan."

"You," Don smiled at his wife and, without turning around to his son, said. "You, you were such a pain in the back side as a baby, we tried to put you up for adoption, but nobody wanted you."

"Don!" Sharon called out.

"I know. Come here, you. I'm just teasing. You know that. Don't you?"

Josh, sideling up to the table, looked purposely hang doggish.

"Everything's about Meaghan. You guys never worry about me."

"That's not true, son," Don continued. "I worry about you, and Mom, and Meaghan. And I promise you this, that I will never let any harm come to you or any other member of this family, not ever and under no circumstances. I'll be here to protect you because nothing, no job, no house, no Weed Killer is more important than my family. I love you guys. I know I don't say it often enough, but I do."

"You never say it, and another thing" added Josh. "I was just thinking that maybe I could get a new bike this summer. Mine is four years old already, and it can't be made bigger no more 'cause we tried, eh, with the handlebars and seat. It looks like a baby bike. All my friends laugh at it."

"Well, that's out of the question," replied Don. "We don't love you that much. No, just kidding, just kidding. Let me get this case over with first, and then sure enough we can go shopping for a new bike. How's that? Fair enough?"

"Gees, I don't know. How long will that be?"

chapter 15

MARY MONTICELLO HAD always been a helper, a "Catcher in the Rye". She felt her hands on work with Parkdale's poor through her Meals-on-Wheels and other volunteer activities was a good complement to her advocacy on their behalf in her newspaper columns. Every action she took, every person she helped, gave testimony to her belief that individual effort was the key to saving society. "If more people volunteered and got involved we could solve this poverty problem overnight. Apathy and self interest are our biggest foes."

David Chamberlain was first on Mary's meal delivery list today. She had expanded her run to fifteen when the gasoline prices and the general cost of living moved dramatically upward and many volunteers, seniors themselves, cut back on their commitments.

David answered the door with his customary dress pants and sport coat on. The coat was clean, but out dated with padded shoulders, wide lapels and four buttons down the center. His faded blue dress shirt had a ridiculously large collar that appeared to be choking the poor old guy. The thin grey hair on his balding head was combed straight back.

"Come on in. I was expecting you. Right on time, as usual. You know when I was in the advertizing business and had my own office and staff, I was very particular about punctuality. Yes, indeed, I could always tell if a worker was committed, dedicated to his job, by the mere fact of his ability to be on time."

"Well, Mr. Chamberlain, you know I've got a lot of clients. Lots of stops to make so I try to keep to a schedule," replied Mary preparing her getaway in advance. She noted long ago on her first visit that Mr. Chamberlain's kitchen table and chairs were made of chrome with plastic covered cushion seats. Perfect she commented to herself. No bedbugs hiding in there, not that she often availed herself of a rest at a client's table.

"I made some tea," David Chamberlain explained crestfallen by the refusal he saw coming. "Twinings, a good breakfast tea. My father, he had a cup of Twinings every morning of his life and he lived to be ninety-three, you know. He's got ten years on me now."

"Well, you don't look your age at all," said Mary as she deposited the foil wrapped lunch on the table along with some snack items and staples for later.

"What we got today?"

"Meatloaf with mashed potatoes and peas, and applesauce if I remember correctly."

"You know, they make a good meatloaf. I got to hand it to them. Not as good as my wife's. I know I'm prejudiced, but she made the very best meatloaf ever. Had a hard boiled egg right in the middle of it too. Nice slice of meatloaf with that beautiful egg in the center. Was almost too picture perfect to eat. Funny how you remember the little things, eh. And I used to tease her all the time. 'How did you manage to get that egg in there?' I'd say. 'How'd you manage that?' Yes, yes indeed, how did she manage? Now you sure you don't want that tea? I got a whole pot made right here. Can't drink it all myself, you know. Be a shame to let it go to waste."

"Oh, you can always heat it up later, can't you?" Mary quipped.

"Sure, sure I can. You know it's just an excuse. Get's pretty lonely at my age. All my friends, relatives are gone. Died off one by one. I used to read the obituary page, but it got too depressing. Now there's no sense because I don't recognize the names."

Mary moved toward the door.

"I think I'm going to change my name," Don put a half smile on his face. "I'm too close to the start of the alphabet. Zamberlain, that's what I'm aiming for. If I'm last on your list then you won't have to run off so fast."

"It's not done alphabetically Mr. Chamberlain. We plot a route out that's time efficient and has easy access. Sorry." She closed the door behind her.

"Well," said Don Chamberlain as he set a cup up opposite himself at the table and prepared to pour from a fancy china pot. "Tell me Miss Monticello, or Mary if you insist. Do you like your tea weak, or should I let it steep for a while longer?"

Mary Monticello's last meal stop of the day was at Mrs. Begley's apartment. The stench of excrement and urine was noticeable the minute Mary entered the third floor hallway and got worse to almost unbearable as she approached the door of the apartment. She knocked loudly and shouted.

"Mrs. Begley, Mrs. Begley, it's Meals-on-Wheels. Open the door please."

An old lady in a faded green cocktail dress opened the door. Her grey blond hair was disheveled, greasy, and matted with filth. The dress she had on was shiny with wear and bore smears of unknown but scary looking substances over the front and back. The odor in the room physically knocked Mary backwards into the hall.

"Gimme that, and get the hell out of here," the old woman cackled like a crone in an ancient fairytale. She held out a hand lined with dirt and grime. Her long fingernails were so impacted with filth not even a germ could survive under them.

Mary stood stiff at the doorway. There was no chance of entering let alone staying inside the apartment. Mary's flesh crawled with the mere thought of all the bedbugs and other vermin infesting the place. It was plain to see that the old lady's legs and arms were pockmarked with bites and scabs.

"Mrs. Begley, please, let me get you some help. We can take you to a nice home; clean, and safe with people there to help look after you. Please, you can't live like this. Let me help you. I can help you."

"How does, Go to hell sound," the woman replied. "Don't you think I know what you're after? You want me out of here so you can steal all my things, all the stuff I've saved over the years. Then you'll give my home and my things away to someone else. I'll have to live in a little room with no windows and have to share it with people I hate."

"No, no, you'll make friends there. There's people like you. You can share things, do things."

"I don't want to be with people like me. I don't even want to be with me most of the time. No, you want me out of the way because I'm a nuisance for you. But I know the law. You can't get rid of me, and you won't. No, now get the hell out of here before I throw something at you like, like this here bird cage. Found it out on the street the other day. Imagine somebody throwing this out. Why, it's almost brand new. But no, never mind, I need it myself. I'm thinking of getting a bird, a little canary, or a budgie bird maybe. Nice to have a little company around that don't just bitch and complain about you all the time. Yes, I need this cage. I need all my stuff. Can't spare nothing to even throw at you."

Mrs. Begley's apartment appeared to be only about three feet deep from the doorway where Mary Monticello was standing. The rest of the place was a heap of stacked furniture, housewares, clothing, dishes, bric-a-brac and formless, useless odds and ends that defied any meaningful description. A narrow pathway across a soiled threadbare rug snaked through the debris before turning off to the left and disappearing.

The apartment had been cleaned out by the Ministry of Health once before a few years prior because of sanitary and fire hazards. It was slated for a return makeover. Mary was just waiting for the paperwork to clear and the inspectors to show up. Both appeared to be taking an eternity. In the hallway Mary was confronted by Mrs. Begley's neighbors.

"Don't tell us again you can't do nothing," one of them shouted. "This is ridiculous. We can't live here with her. She's destroying the entire building and none of you government assholes will do anything about it. We're dying here."

"I don't work for the government," explained Mary. "But I am trying to do something. It's just that she won't cooperate and that makes it difficult, almost impossible."

"I wish that old bitch would walk out somewhere and run into that killer, the Weed Killer. She's a fucking weed for sure, a stinking weed."

"Yeah, that would be great. I'd pay him for the favor."

"You wouldn't be alone. I bet everyone in this building would be happy as hell if she got bumped off. In fact, I know it. We should take up a collection. Have enough money inside one day, bet you."

Mary walked outside into the fresh air and took a deep breath. Yes, there were plenty of flaws in the system. You can't force anyone out of their home, but if public housing and nursing homes could be better funded and well staffed the immense stigma that surrounded them would disappear. Look at the Lora Chapman Home in Rosedale: private suites, a beautiful dining room, social activities, bussed shopping trips and entertainment excursions, overnight visits with family members and friends. Hell, people want to live there. Problem is, it's a private home and costs an arm and a leg. We need something like that which is affordable, attractive, and free of stigma for the general public to access. We need politicians with the will to get these things done. We need a TCHC that is true to its mandate. Why is it so hard, Mary lamented?

***

"I'll tell you why it's so hard," explained Norm back in the middle of the coffee shop debates at the City Donut Shop on King Street. "It's hard because you morons actually think the government is answerable to you, the voters, the citizens. You think those jerks you elect to Parliament have your interests at heart. Your stupidity is mind boggling. The government, all governments, are answerable to the people who hold economic power in the country. You know, the industrialists, the bankers, builders, the retailers. They call the shots. Look at the environment. Ask anyone and they all will tell you they want clean air, clean water, clean uncontaminated food, clean everything. You name it. But why don't we have all those things if everybody wants them? Because the businesses don't want them, that's why. It costs them money, lost profits. If the government represented the people, then we would have all those clean environmental things, but we don't so do the math."

"I can't believe the government is that callous," said Claudia. "They're people too. It can't all be one big conspiracy."

"Yeah, after all we elect these people, eh. If they don't do a job, we kick them out," added another customer.

"Kick them out and then who do you get in their place? Even if the politicians cared, it's not that they can do anything meaningful," added Norm. "The capitalists hold all the cards. If the politicians don't play the game, the businesses will pack up and leave, set up someplace else. They're doing that even now and you can thank your politicians and their free trade policies for all that too."

"We need politicians with political will. That's what's lacking, the will to change things," volunteered Claudia.

"Capitalism is a railroad," chimed in Norm right away. "You can vary the locomotive's speed, even make it go backwards or forwards, but you can't get it off its economic tracks. It stays on the prescribed route no matter what the engineer or crew do. You just keep an eye on Obama over there in the States. 'Change you can believe in.' Yeah, just watch and see how little he actually manages to get done. When he's finished you won't be able to tell the difference between him and a Republican."

"Maybe people don't want things changed all that much. Maybe we like things the way they are and just want them to operate better. Maybe only a few things need fixing like better housing, or more control over the banks, and more anti-pollution laws too."

"You see," continued Norm clutching his head in his hands. "That's another diversion. All of these problems are treated separately, divided up, so public concerns are not focused on the underlying problem. You got groups that want to clean up the environment. Unions that want to protect jobs and wages. Citizen groups who want to control immigration, up the minimum wage. Groups demanding more public housing especially now with this killer on the loose. One time I counted something like fifteen separate organizations just in the anti-poverty fight alone. In reality they're all fighting different effects of capitalism. It's capitalism stupid! But the government doesn't want you to make the link. No, they rather have you divided and fighting amongst yourselves for hand-outs and charity. It's the old divide and conquer tactic and it still works because you cretins can't ever learn anything from history. Anyway, I've talked enough. I'm about to give up on the whole lot of you. You deserve what you get."

"Come on Norm. You don't mean that," said Claudia.

"I don't know what I mean anymore, but no one gives a damn. You watch. Once this killer is caught the whole question of homelessness, affordable housing, poverty, all that will fade from the public eye and we'll be back where we started, apathetic and alone."

"People care, Norm. I think it's just that they don't know what to do."

"Yeah, a lot of regular folks, the government too, they help other people with charity work and volunteering."

"Sure I take my hat off to those people who do charity work even though I think they're essentially wasting their time. That piecemeal approach don't work. You've got to attack the root of the problem."

"Well, the Weed Killer roots out the problem in his own way," added Albert.

"That's no solution. Even all this killing won't accomplish anything. It won't get the homeless off the streets. At best they will just lay low until he's caught and then resurface when the coast is clear. It's like trying to eradicate cockroaches by stepping on them one by one though I don't mean to insult the homeless like that. I ain't that far from homelessness myself so I got all the sympathy in the world, believe me."

"The killer doesn't have to completely eradicate the homeless," Albert said thoughtfully. "Maybe he started out kind of wild and scattered in his approach, then realized his own limitations. Now if I'm reading him right, he seems to just want to control the problem, restrict it. Drive those dirty losers out of certain parts of the city. Concentrate them in isolated areas where they can exist amidst their own filth and squalor and leave decent people in decent parts of Toronto to live their lives in peace."

"Jesus, Al, you sure you ain't been having coffee with this Weed Killer behind our backs?" commented Norm. "You seem to know a lot about how he thinks."

"Yeah, well I agree about that keeping them all together in one place," commented another customer. "It's like them Jewish ghettos they used to have. You wanted to know where the Jews were? They were in the ghetto. Simple."

"Don't think that ain't happening now," added Norm. "We already got pockets in the city that have a big concentration of homeless people, people in public housing, rooming houses. Places like Parkdale, Mimico, Jarvis and Finch, Gerrard and Sherbourne, the North End. And do you think the police give those areas a lot of attention? Like they give a good goddamn what happens there. As long as them losers fight it out amongst themselves, shoot, rape, rob each other, but keep it in their neighborhood, the cops don't care. Leave them alone to kill themselves off."

"That's good, great as far as I'm concerned," said Albert.

"I'm out of here. Bye," replied Norm.

Claudia gave a quick, expectant look at Albert who immediately glanced away. She got up and followed Norm out of the coffee shop.

***

Mary Monticello discussed the subject with her husband, Bob. They had a small basement apartment which they used to rent before their daughter moved back home after university and occupied the place for one summer. She moved away two years ago and the apartment had been vacant ever since mainly because Mary was paranoid about some-one bringing bedbugs into her house. Now Mary relented for a higher cause. She saw it as her civic duty and the fact that it pained her to do so also indicated to her that it was indeed the proper thing to do.

"It ain't worth much, if you don't suffer for it at least a little, and it's just for a couple of months, mind you," she told her husband. "Until this killer is caught, and that's only a matter of time. He's already shooting his mouth off to us and the police. They'll get him. In the meantime, we're helping out, doing our civic duty. Of course, I want to make sure this homeless person, whoever it may be, does not bring problems in with him or her. Fair is fair because if I see just one of those little creepy crawly blood sucking vermin it's back out on the street for Mr. or Mrs. Homeless."

"I don't know. I was enjoying being just the two of us and getting back to some of our old habits," said Bob with a wink. "We're getting old. Don't know how much longer this will last."

"We haven't hit fifty yet, and remember I'm much younger than you. You're actually pushing the fifty mark while I'm only in my early forties."

"I'm forty-six. You're one year younger than me."

"I was rounding off."

Bob laughed because they had run that routine past each other many times before. "You are beautiful though. I'll admit that in a heart-beat."

"Bob, dear, flattery will get you everywhere, but not now. I've got a meeting with my editor and the police and I'd like to get your agree-ment on this tenant idea."

"As long as we can get some guarantees up front so we don't get stuck with some deadbeat," answered Bob. "If there's any trouble, these losers can be hard to get rid of. Remember my chum, Joe McAdam that I was telling you about? He had a couple living in one of his apartments. This was a few years ago. They looked like good people when he first met them, but then right after the first month they stopped paying the rent. Joe was gonna evict them, eh. No, not so fast the cops told him. It's win-ter. You can't kick people out in the middle of winter, out in the cold. And, if they hand you any money, any portion of the rent at all, you got to let them stay, give them a chance to catch up. After that you must post a notice of eviction around town and in the paper and give them two months warning. Joe, he finally got so pissed off, he let himself into the apartment one day when they were both away and had their stuff thrown out on the street and changed the locks on the doors."

"Gees, Bob, that sounds pretty drastic. The poor people."

"Poor people! They sued Joe. He had to pay damages and let them back into the apartment. Plus he had to come up with their lawyer's fees and his own to boot. He finally give them two thousand dollars to leave. They took it. So with us, Mary, any tenant stays three months max, and there's no use of the yard or driveway. No company especially overnight. I don't want the apartment filled with a pack of losers. The place is furnished pretty well so we don't have to worry about no ratty stuff coming in and we'll insist that all their clothes get washed, sent to a cleaners beforehand. I'll gladly pay."

"OK, I agree. Now, look, I know a few people who are out on their own, living on and off the streets right now. They're good people just had some bad breaks like this guy, Eldridge Johns. He lost his job at a printing shop two years ago, no pension, ran out of EI. I've talked to him at Jason's Coffee Shop on Queen St. Was going to do an article on him. He's a nice man, friendly, not hostile."

"Eldridge? I don't like the sound of that. I'm not prejudiced, mind you, but I'm not out looking for trouble either," stated Bob. "I'm sorry and no single mothers. If you want to make a statement, help the community, that's fine, but let's leave it at that. We've got neighbors to consider too. Don't forget about them."

"Don't worry. Eldridge is white and he has no family, not as far as I know. It shouldn't be long anyways like I said and if the Mayor keeps to his promise and creates more shelters out there then we will be off the hook. We're not taking people in if shelter beds are going empty."

chapter 16

ALBERT HAD MADE it a habit of searching the newspapers, both the *Toronto Star* and the *Globe and Mail*, the TV, and the internet for any information relating to the Weed Killer.

He relished the details, admiring in retrospect his prowess and daring. It also kept him up to date as to what was happening in the community with public reaction, and about police activities and evidence gathered. He knew, for instance, that the police were still purposely withholding information. The weeds in the mouths of his victims were never reported. The homeless young man he gunned down in High Park was not mentioned, nor was the boy who rescued him at Allan Gardens. Moreover, he never saw any reference to the scrawled graffiti letters, BSH, which had accidentally led him to his latest victim and had the potential to target many more.

He was returning from the Tarragon Theatre on Bridgeview Street that night after seeing a performance of "My Name is Rachael Corrie" when he noticed the BSH letters on the side of an abandoned warehouse near the corner of Bathurst. Albert hadn't seen them on the internet as yet and at the time figured they were just some gang insignia or the initials of a graffiti artist until he took a closer look and saw written in very small letters within the capitalized initials the words: "Bum Sleeps Here". The building itself looked interesting from a Weed Killer point of view so he ventured around the back to check it out. That's when he discovered the worthless homeless bastard sleeping inside. Albert came back later that very night equipped for eradication and confronted the man.

"I don't believe it. You were a teacher? How the hell did you wind up like this?"

"What's it to you? You're here too ain't you so I wouldn't be casting no stones. And if you want to rob me let me save you the trouble. I ain't got nothing. And if you're looking for a place to stay get over to the other side of the building. This is my spot. Got it decorated just the way I like. Beat it! I don't want you attracting a bunch of attention.

"Was some young punks fucking around here the other day. They smashed my bottle of wine and stomped on my food rations. Little fuckers. But, hey, no sense losing our cool here, being enemies and everything, eh?" The man paused in his diatribe after assessing Albert's appearance, then continued. "So you got anything to drink on you? I could use a sip. Or how about a smoke? You got any cigarettes?"

"No, I stopped drinking after I got throat cancer. Never smoked. Probably would be dead by now if I did."

"Oh, good, for you," the man replied with no small hint of sarcasm in his voice. "I don't imagine I'll live long enough to worry about any of that shit."

"You're right there, but how come you're not working? I'm curious. Booze got you?"

"Booze got to me afterwards. I was a music teacher until the school I was at dropped the subject. Too expensive for the taxpayers and not part of the core curriculum. Afterwards they had me rotating between a bunch of schools until they figured I wasn't worth it no more. Art, music, even Phys Ed. were all cut. I had only worked two years, no permanent contract, no seniority, so they kicked me out."

"Tough luck, but why didn't you go into something else? Teach in college. Tutor. Get a band going even? You can hear music all around Toronto. It's everywhere."

"Nobody was hiring, you dummy. I tried working the bars. You know what a musician gets for a night's work? They pass a fucking tip bucket. I played at Grossman's a few times. Split two hundred bucks five ways. That went real far towards paying my rent."

"Well, you didn't try hard enough obviously."

"What do you mean by "obviously"? I fucking tried."

"Up north, I heard they're dying for teachers."

"You heard, yeah, you heard. Well, I fucking went up there. You name it: Chapleau, Marathon, Wawa, that fucking goose town, even Manitouwage. All their recently hired teachers are gone. Only the old timers are hanging on. They're closing schools. They're closing hospitals. They're closing whole fucking towns. Give me a break, you fucking know it all. For a while I had some EI money coming in and a couple of buddies whose places I could crash at, but when that ran out, well things got tough; and voila!" The man spread his arms out widely. "My new home. Used to live under the bridge outside but with that fucking Weed Killer on the loose I moved indoors to play it safe, eh. Luxury, wouldn't you say?"

"The trouble is, with people like you around, society will never dig itself out of debt. We'll be supporting you for the rest of your life now. You're a parasite. You need a host, society, the taxpayer, to live off. You have no independent existence."

"What the hell," the man said as he took a step backward. "What are you doing here anyways? What kind of job do you have, you're so critical about me? You don't even look all that hard done by."

"I'm a gardener," Albert said smilingly as he pulled the revolver and ammunition clip from his pants and pushed them together with that reassuring click he so loved to hear.

"Hey, hey, hold it right there. This is bullshit. I fucking tried to get a job. I tried."

"You didn't try hard enough. Otherwise you wouldn't be here. How about retraining? Ever hear of retraining?"

"There ain't enough jobs, I'm telling you. How can you squeeze ten thousand laid off teachers into five hundred jobs? They don't fit. It's got nothing to do with trying. While I was up north I even took the mining course, the Core Program, in Sudbury. Nickel prices were real high and INCO and Falconbridge were hiring. Took two years to finish the course. By that time the nickel market dropped out of sight, the companies got bought out by some foreign firms and then the big strike started. Now nobody's working. If I had a job up there you'd be here preparing to kill some other poor laid off bastard. What's the difference?"

"The difference is that the song is you," and Albert raised his gun.

"It ain't fair. I'm only thirty years old."

"Look at it this way. From a societal point of view the average life span for a male in Canada I believe is something like 72 years. That means for another 42 years the taxpayers would have to support your sorry ass. Think of all the money we just saved them."

"OK, go ahead. Pull the trigger, Mr. Big shot. You like that pun? Feel free to use it. You aren't fooling nobody but yourself. This is about you and your stupid justification for murder. Trying to hide your own sickness by pretending you're some social crusader. You're just a pathetic psycho killer. Fuck you."

Albert shot the man square between the eyes. Then he just stood there for several minutes looking down at the body.

"Jesus, what a waste. Why did you give up on life like that? You can't give up. That's the point. Giving up is for the loser class and that my friend is what you are, were, a loser. Sorry, but you fall squarely into that category. Excuses, you lived with excuses."

Albert then pulled a freshly uprooted plantain out of his pocket and crammed it into the man's mouth. He gathered up the shell casing and left the building. Outside it was dark.

"And there's no moon at all," Albert sang as he walked two blocks before grabbing a streetcar.

I wonder what Norm would say if he ever found out, Albert pondered? Damn, he'd be disappointed, crushed more like it, but he fucking well knows where I stand on the issue. He'd just never figure I could take the next step. He probably never thought Claudia would either. Poor Norm. Poor impotent Norm. Well, sorry, but I wasn't about to sit around like a fool while some hot assed woman who needs banging was left unsatisfied or stand by while these homeless bastards ruined the city. Better to rage, rage against the dying of the light. And if I don't make it in the end, better a dead lion than a live dog.

In his travels by automobile, streetcar, and even on foot Albert spotted other BSH sites around the West End, one or two relatively close to home. Nevertheless, he gave up on them immediately after the Bridgeview murder. Too risky. Obviously other people were in on the meaning of the letters judging from the map he saw on an internet website and the simple fact that somebody was spray painting them on the buildings. If word spread there would be far too much interest and activity around the designated buildings. Police surveillance was sure to follow and the chance of getting caught would be ridiculously high.

"When things get predictable, that's when trouble starts," he admonished himself. "Never knowingly fall into a pattern. The inadvertent mistakes are bad enough."

Albert would have loved to move his activities into Parkdale. It was close by and home to that do-gooder amongst do-gooders, Mary Monticello. Teaching that sanctimonious bitch a lesson would be well worth it. Still, he hesitated. Like the Sherbourne and Allan Gardens area, Parkdale was crawling with people, a predominant portion of them being of the loser variety, but there was indeed safety in numbers. With the alert to his presence on, and Mary in particular warning Parkdale residents to be vigilant, any homicidal attempts there might well backfire and Albert wasn't in the mood for any more marathon runs.

"No. I think I've got a different lesson for our little crusader, a much better idea."

***

Ronnie Bartholomew and his friends gathered in his parents' garage. All were armed with baseball bats, hockey or lacrosse sticks. "Shit that any kid could be carrying around and not attract no attention," said Ronnie. They were dressed in black pants and tee shirts with hoodies covering their faces.

"We'll leave in three groups so we don't attract attention, eh. Meet together at the north end of the park by different routes. When we're all in line, Round-Ups on the left, Orkins in the centre, and the Raiders on the right, I'll give the signal with my club in the air.

"When I drop it down and yell, "Weed Killers, now, bring Hell!" we'll swoop right through the park from one end to the other and club anybody who's sleeping there for the night. It's late enough so nobody but a bunch of losers will be out. Remember, like the Weed Killer himself, we attack only the homeless. If you're not sure, take a pass. When you strike don't fuck around too long in any one spot. Hit fast and hard. You don't have to kill anybody. Break a arm or leg and keep going. We got to move fast. That's the key.

"By the time anyone sounds the alarm we'll be long gone, eh. At the south end we separate into individuals and head right home. We can get on line afterwards and go over the entire attack. Remember the site password is "Blood on the Weeds". Don't share nothing with nobody outside our group. This is our secret club. We're doing this just like the Killer in order to help the city and take back our neighborhood. It's our duty. Onward, Brotherhood of Weed Killers."

chapter 17

SERGEANT WRIGHT CALLED home and told his wife he'd be late again. It had been virtually every night now for seven weeks and there was little chance things would get better soon.

The police just couldn't get anything on the Weed Killer no matter how many times he struck and the Mayor, as well as the Chief of Police and Sergeant Wright's Captain, were on Don's back relentlessly.

"I just can't believe that in all this city population you don't have one somebody who can identify this asshole. He's out in the open for Christ's sake, not hidden away in some torturer's dungeon or house of horrors. This is happening on the streets of Toronto. It's inconceivable that you don't have anything on this guy. He should have been in the lock up long ago," raged Captain Donnally.

The Chief nodded in disgust and added: "Things deteriorate any further, you can be sure that someone will take the rap for this screw up and it sure as hell won't be the Mayor, Captain Donnally or me. I don't know why I listened to you in the first place about your "All In" approach. We're paying for it now. That and your own failure to spot this thing when it first surfaced."

Sergeant Wright was too busy with the case at hand to worry about "taking the rap" as he huddled with his fellow homicide detectives later that day. "Fuck, I'll just quit. I got enough years," he said to Detective Gignac. "They can shove this job and all its pressure up their collective asses. I'll grab something in a little sleepy town over in Southeastern Ontario and finish my career giving out parking tickets and investigating noise complaints. But, you know, I got a bad feeling about this BSH shit that's cropping up. This is going to be a nightmare. Not that we aren't already living through one right now."

"Yeah, I got the same ache in my gut," added Detective Gignac. "People, the public, ain't responding the way they're supposed to, the way we figured they would. That Ronnie kid over at Allan Gardens. I'm sure he saw something, maybe even the killer. He's protecting the guy."

"If nothing breaks we're going to have to look him up again, but can you blame him? Look at that fucking neighborhood. Would you want to live there?"

"When I was a beat cop, I didn't want to even walk there," Detective Gignac laughed. "Fuck, it was rough. Not like the gang turf, but just constant irritation and frustration. There was no let up. And what are you going to do? Lock up half the neighborhood?"

The homicide detectives gathered around their central work station. "OK, let's go over those BSH locations? How many did we uncover altogether, where were they and what did we find?"

"There were five spots with the initials BSH that were confirmed by our patrols. We got the Bridgeview warehouse, a cardboard and plywood shack in Trinity-Bellwoods Park, inside a boarded up bike shop on Queen near Strachan where that theft ring operated, the old Loblaws warehouse on Lakeshore West and just north of that a construction shed at Spadina and Front inside the Concorde City Place Project."

"That's where we found the latest body," added Detective Hudson.

"Another one?" asked Sergeant Wright. "Are you talking about the Brideview homicide? We already counted that one."

"No, this was different, a male victim around fifty years old, bludgeoned to death. He was sleeping in a little used tool and supply shed. Had a bike with him that was found at the foot of Fort York Blvd., the new extension where it dead ends at Bathurst. I doubt it was our man responsible. No weed was found on the body and, of course, no small caliber bullet wound, no gun involved. We convinced the media that it was an unrelated death. They're cooperating in order to prevent a spread of copy cat violence."

"Son of a bitch."

"Copy cats killing the homeless. They're feeding off the Weed Killer. This is exactly what I didn't want to see happen. Now we're in a jack pot. If someone picks up a .22 and joins in the hunt we're really in trouble. Did we manage to move the other BSH people? Are they safe now?"

"All but one. Your chum Mary Monticello got housing for the rest in Parkdale. Scared shitless most of them. I guess they somehow figured they were safe inside, inside any thing. There's a fucking guy living in one of those oversized garbage bins. Says it's a house so the killer won't harm him. We couldn't convince the dumb bastard otherwise. Had to bring him in for petty theft, but he'll be out again in a day. What can we do?"

"I got an idea. Maybe we can use the BSH stuff before we have to go public with it and the horse leaves the barn. For now we got our asses covered by pulling the homeless off the sites. So let's roust out the one remaining vagrant, and take his place. Set up a sting operation. Make it real attractive and accessible to the Killer. And with Mr. Weed Man actually inside a building, he will have no where to run. If he's got that gun on him, it's over. We got his sorry ass. Now, don't let on to anybody, especially the press and more specifically Monticello, about this new BSH information. We want our guy to think this is his private short cut to new victims," said Sergeant Wright.

"Yeah, because the streets are drying up. Most of the homeless bums have been housed, at least temporarily, or they're bunching up for protection, or better yet, skipping town altogether. If he wants to go on killing, this is his best shot as long as he thinks we're in the dark about the initials."

"Hell, he's got to know this BSH shit has limited duration. Pretty soon someone will hack into those Weed Killer sites and expose the information or the people responsible will start talking, bragging about writing those initials. Our killer will feel the scrutiny and then back off. Hopefully that hasn't already happened. He followed the lead once at Bridgeview. Maybe he'll bite again."

"You know I read somewhere that three is some kind of natural number," Detective Hudson said. "People usually try things three times before they give up on them. It's like an instinct."

"Like three strikes?" Detective Gignac smiled. "You a Blue Jays fan?"

"That's not an instinct, but maybe that's part of it. Anyway, I think we can bank on three. He's gonna try it again for sure."

"If he does, then we got him. He won't get to three strikes."

"He better not or we'll be shoveling shit out of the mounted patrol stables at the CNE grounds."

Detectives Wright and Gignac arrived at the old Loblaws warehouse on Lakeshore Boulevard, the spot of the designated sting operation, and waited for the current tenant to arrive.

"His shopping cart is missing, but his bedroll and other shit are still around. Fucking place is massive. Hopefully he's the only one hiding in here."

"Our luck the dumb bastard will be shot on his way back while we stand around waiting for him with our thumbs up our asses," joked Detective Gignac.

"Please, a more positive outlook would be much appreciated."

The detectives heard the rolling clank of the shopping cart with a malfunctioning wheel or two as it struggled up the sidewalk and then into the warehouse driveway. Soon a rawboned, tall man in filthy clothes walked into the large open space. The sun was setting, but the room was still bright enough for him to see the two men immediately in front of him.

"Don't panic," said Sergeant Wright. "We're police officers. You're not under arrest. We're here to help you. The man they call the Weed Killer is in this area so we are going to escort you out, to safety. You can take some personal items, but most of this stuff has to stay behind. We'll keep it locked up for you. Don't worry."

"You ain't locking me up. Stay away. Don't come any closer. Fuck you."

"Hey, buddy, take it easy. We're not taking you to jail. We're here to help you. Don't get all excited. Calm down."

"Calm down. Yeah, I heard that one before. When that bitch of mine called you guys in, calm down, you said. You never wanted to hear my side of the story, just hers. Fuck you. I spent three years in Kingston for that rap and it wasn't my fault. She was fucking around on me. Yeah, that's right, fucking around. I found out. I tried to teach her right from wrong, beat it into her. Tough love, eh. I mean she was my wife and she was fucking around. I had a right."

"Well, the law doesn't exactly work that way, you know, but, Hey, let's not rehash the past right now. Let's concentrate on getting you out of here."

"What do you mean let's not rehash it right now? You bastards never want to hear the guy's side of things. No, it's the fucking woman who gets all the rights. The husband, he just gets the shaft."

"Look, get your stuff or we're taking you in as you are. We don't have time for legal discussions. There's a killer on the loose out there. Let's go."

"Yeah sure, very understanding of you. Sure, sure, I'll get my stuff. One minute."

The man walked hurriedly over to a corner of the room where clothes and garbage were piled high. He rooted around for a moment while the two police men bit their tongues and rolled their eyes in frustration.

"Our luck we gotta get an asshole," commented Detective Gignac. "We should just leave him here. Best thing could happen, he meets up with the Killer."

When the policemen looked back at the homeless man, he was standing in front of them with a sawed off shotgun in his hands. It was leveled directly at Sergeant Wright.

"I don't need your help. I got my own, right here. Now fuck off and leave me alone."

"Son of a bitch, did you have to do that?" moaned Sergeant Wright.

"Now what?" asked Detective Gignac to his superior.

"Move away from me. Make some space between us and draw your gun."

"Put that shotgun down," commanded Sergeant Wright never taking his eyes off the armed vagrant.

"Oh no. Oh no, you don't. Then you cops got all the control. You bastards beat the shit out of me last time. Said I resisted arrest. What was I supposed to do? You were yanking on my arm, twisting it. Hurting me. "

"Look, I'm ordering you to put that gun down. No one is going to hurt you."

"Orders. That's all it is with you cops, orders. You never listen. Well, I ain't going back to jail. Do you hear me? Now you get out and that's a order."

Detective Gignac unsnapped his holster and pulled out his revolver. At almost the same time the man pulled the trigger on the shotgun. Everyone heard an audible click before two resounding blasts lit up the room and knocked the man backward into the pile of refuse.

"Holy mother of fucking God," shouted Sergeant Wright.

"I had to shoot him" said Gignac trembling noticeably. "The dumb bastard would have killed us both. Goddamn it and we were trying to help the worthless prick."

Sergeant Wright examined a shotgun lying next to the victim.

"It's rusty as hell and the shells are damp, soggy almost, too wet to fire. Probably been laying around here for who knows how long. Call it in. Jesus, wait till the press gets a hold of this one."

"Well, it could have been a lot worse. Gunned down by a homeless asshole in a dark, abandoned warehouse. How's that for an obituary? May we rest in peace. By the way, does this count for us or is it one more for the Weed Killer?"

"You're one sick puppy. You know that don't you, Gignac."

***

At the news conference the next day it didn't take long for the daggers, hatchets, and long knives to come out. Sergeant Wright spent the afternoon session dodging the media assault as best he could. He also did it alone since none of Toronto's other ranking police officers made a public appearance that day.

"I have to say," began Mary Monticello, "that I'm very disappointed in the way the Toronto police department has handled this Weed Killer crime spree to date, and now this horrible, horrible tragedy. As you know the Killer has decide to confide in me and correspond exclusively through the *Toronto Star* newspaper where I work. My editor and I ..."

"Is there a question in there somewhere Mary?" asked Sergeant Wright.

"Well sure, OK, with all this information out there and even some communication with the Weed Killer, seems to me that he's leaving himself wide open to capture. I mean walking around the city with a gun and shooting people all over the place. How do you explain your lack of success in apprehending this madman? Have there been any calls from your superiors, Chief Samuals, Mayor Milne, for you to tender your resignation? To be honest, you're not doing a very good job. The number of murders is climbing and yesterday you added to the total yourself."

"No they haven't asked me to turn in my badge. Not at this time anyway, but thanks for asking."

Other reporters entered the fray, firing questions up in no particular order.

"We understand that there were tip offs to the Killer planted around various sites in the city. The initials BSH were used. What do those initials mean?"

"The initials stand for the phrase, "Bum Sleeps Here". As the city's homeless sought refuge from the Weed Killer, some of them took the unfortunate option of moving into abandoned warehouses, factories and stores rather than to approved government shelters.

"Some cruel jokesters then took it upon themselves to identify those hiding spots either for their own criminal follow-up, or to discourage the use of the buildings in that way, or more sinisterly to indicate to the Weed Killer where he could find victims. To date we have not identified any of these sick vandals. It is certainly reprehensible what they did, but frankly I don't know if, other than a misdemeanor vandalism, they are guilty of any crime. In the end, we decided to use one of those sites for an ambush to finally apprehend the Weed Killer. Unfortunately, it did not turn out that way."

"Yes, unfortunately you wound up killing a poor homeless man," added Mary Monticello? "I mean by your own admission he seemed mentally unbalanced. Did you have to shoot him?"

"He had a sawed off shot gun pointed directly at me," Sergeant Wright explained patiently, "and he pulled the trigger. A mentally disabled person is perfectly capable of killing someone. Detective Gignac feared for my life and his own. Indeed, if the shot gun had not misfired I'd probably be dead right now so I want to publically thank Detective Gignac for his prompt and life-saving reaction. Well within keeping I might add of proscribed police protocol. Anyway the SIU will thoroughly investigate the incident and we will answer to their ruling when the time comes."

"What is it about this case that has prevented you so far from nailing down more specific information about the identification of the Killer? He seems to have the entire Toronto police force tied up in knots unable to do anything," ask Bob Coleman from the *Sun*.

"Perpetrators of random acts of violence are the most difficult to track down. There is no direct relationship amongst the victims and the killer and therefore no logical suspect. It's not like a domestic dispute, for example, where we would immediately focus on a spouse, a lover, or a relative. This is what makes these cases so difficult. Plus you have the changing time frame. One minute all the homicides occur at night in out of doors, isolated locations, then they take place during the day and indoors. We have no videos of the crimes taking place. The paper and envelopes in the mailings to the *Star* are all generic and mass produced and contain no DNA evidence, nor was any viable forensic evidence found at the murder scenes. The few eyewitnesses have provided nothing but contradictory evidence. Also several copy cat killers have joined the ranks further complicating matters and on top of it all we are terribly under staffed given the sheer volume of crimes under investigation. I might add that some recent editorials by the *Star* criticizing me and my department have not helped the situation which leads me to perhaps the most frustrating factor of all which is that we are not getting a lot of cooperation from the public. In cases like these the police very often rely upon the eyes and ears of the public to discover what we can't, to unearth clues, and vet suspects and report suspicious goings on. That's not happening in this case. The public has been virtually silent, not because they are afraid as is often the case when gangs are involved for instance. No, here it is plain and simple apathy. People simply don't care because they think they are safe; the killer is not targeting them. It's only the homeless who are being killed and they're a pain in the ass anyway. A lot of people actually view this as a win- win situation as sick as that sounds."

Back at the Homicide Squad's headquarters after the conference Captain Donnally took exception to some of Sergeant Wright's remarks especially those referring to "under staffing".

"Clever Wright, but as of now you can stop the bitching and passing the buck because the department is adding another six detectives to the task force. The Chief is cutting back on the Wellington case which was going nowhere. Our little secret though because the families are still raising hell over our lack of an arrest and the Chief doesn't want the negative publicity. Thanks in large part to your own incompetence the Weed Killer case has grown into our number one priority. Nevertheless, you're still in charge mainly because you're the high profile guy, a familiar face to the public. The Chief is sticking with you even though I recommended that the SIU investigation into your recent shooting incident with Detective Gignac was a good excuse to suspend you from the case. Let's hope we all don't regret it. Anyway, the Chief wants to see a united front out there like we are all on the same page and that includes the public and the press."

"We're not getting any cooperation whatsoever like I mentioned in the press conference and I doubt if we will. The public is not interested in helping us. As far as the news media is concerned, they're using this for their own ends, to sell copy and advertising. They never had such a story before and probably don't want it to end. Monticello is out crusading for more homeless shelters, and extra funding for Parkdale. Any excuse to blow her own trumpet. Actually I think she cares more about bedbugs than she does about nailing this killer."

"Well, we need to show a more positive attitude, like we're making some progress here. We can't have the public losing faith in their police force. That's not acceptable. And the Chief and I will do anything possible to prevent that from happening even if it requires sacrificing an individual here or there along the way if you know what I mean."

"Yeah, I think I get your drift. If I wake up with a weed under my pillow, I'll know for sure. Thanks for the support."

"Nothing personal, Don. I just don't think you're the man for the job. I never felt you deserved that promotion. I've watched you around the office. When me and the other guys stayed late, worked through our weekends, had extra meetings, you went home."

"I got a family."

"We all have families, Sergeant, but we also have a mission in life, an important mission, one that requires sacrifices, sacrifices that you are unwilling to make. You see Sergeant, for you this is a job. For the rest of us it is a commitment, a career. We live for this. You live with it. And if we lose anyone over this fiasco, I'm here to make sure that person is you."

"Right, thanks for the warning and for not making it personal."

***

For his part the Weed Killer responded to the press conference with another letter to the *Star*. He purposely omitted any direct reference to Mary Monticello this time around.

"I want to acknowledge Sergeant Wright and his partner for their weed eradication assistance over at the old Loblaws warehouse. I guess that weed was not for me sorry to say, but I'm not jealous over their involvement. Oh no, I welcome it and all other help in the monumental task confronting not only me, but all of us in the city. So citizens of Toronto by all means come along, come along and lend your hand.

Grab a gun, a club, a rock, and some friends and go out and pick some weeds. Together we can purge our urban garden of the noxious blight that is strangling it. Gardeners of Toronto unite. You have nothing to lose but your weeds."

Yours truly,

The Weed Killer

"P.S. Sergeant Wright. You're so lucky to be having me around to provide such a great service to the City of Toronto. After a little more time, you won't have any weeds left to worry about and I can slip into retirement and not bother you again. The fact that I will still be out there "hiding in the weeds so to speak" will keep the blighted vagrants from returning. I'm on your side. Let's stop battling each other. And thanks again for the help."

chapter 18

MARY WAS HAVING coffee at Jason's Coffee Shop on Queen West with Kristen Summers Clark Johnson of the St. Christopher House, John Beadle of the Affordable Housing Coalition, and the *Star's* editor in chief, Karen French.

"I'm glad you didn't suggest Starbucks," said Mary. "Starbucks is out of the question. The bastards started the invasion of Parkdale with their yuppie store and nose bleed coffee. Now we've got the Bohemian Lofts and Embassy Lofts being erected. Over on King they're planning the Bridgeview Condos. Not to mention that the Gladstone and Drake are already up and running.

"You know I did a series of articles about the last residents of the old Gladstone Hotel. Oh yeah, this was long after the building had been condemned and closed down. There was a whole community of people living in the derelict hotel. They liked it. They looked out for each other. There was no electricity or water, but they pail flushed and chipped in to buy an old generator. They set it up in an unused room with a vent pipe out the window and it ran lights for an entire floor. Just lights. Each person paid what they could afford based on their street earnings and welfare cheques. It was all well organized and cooperative. Then the city decided a private developer was better suited to run the place. Drove all the squatters out except for Old Sally McDermitt. She was the last one standing. Wouldn't leave till she finally took ill and they carted her off to the hospital where she died in less than a week. And you know the best thing about the old place. No bedbugs. That's right, not a one. Imagine that."

"Actually it's a beautifully restored treasure now," chimed in Kristen Summers Clark Johnson looking around rather skeptically at the odd duck characters that surrounded her in the coffee shop. "Quite an attractive edifice."

"And it has helped to revitalize the area, brought jobs too," added Karen French.

"Well, sure, it's a building now, a commercial enterprise, but before that it was a community, a community of independent, free souls who didn't ask for anything or took anything from the government, any government. There was something lost when those people were evicted, something precious. A real human spirit was crushed. It was a shame. To this day I regret the decision to sell that old place. Something more socially useful could have been done with it. Next they will be buying up the apartment buildings and driving every low income person out of the area. Parkdale will lose its unique character. We'll be just like downtown Toronto, a cold, soulless maze of glass and steel where no one knows their neighbor or even cares to know them. As long as I'm around I'm telling you right now I will fight that every step of the way."

"Calm down Mary," chided Karen French cheerfully. "We know about your dedication to your neighborhood and we think that's great. All of us want the same thing. That's why we're here. You've met Kristen and John before, certainly during the jam sessions on poverty we've held at the *Star*. They've been influential in shaping and moving forward the socially progressive policies at the paper. I am personally beholden to both of them for their fine work.

"Now the three of us were discussing ways in which to reinvigorate our anti-poverty campaign and the push for more affordable housing here in Toronto. We've also been in touch with some die hard members of the disbanded Ten-in-Two Committee, like our friend Janet Lockhart, who are still interested in moving forward with our agenda. This Weed Killer mess may provide us with an opening. I think that in the press, the media as a whole, we've been too strongly focused on the criminal aspect of the Weed Killer and his victims. We have erred on the side of sensationalism. Because of that we've overlooked the more pervasive issues of poverty and homelessness which gave rise to this present set of tragic circumstances. You know, as a newspaper which has a long and proud history of defending social justice and fighting poverty, I believe the *Star* should lead the way in redirecting our focus. We've got some making up to do."

"I prefer to examine specific victims and their lives," said Mary. "That brings in the human element, something my readers can identify with personally. I thought that story I did on the death of Jennifer Belcourt was especially poignant. It got a lot of reader reaction."

"Yes, yes, there's no denying that, but I think we have to move beyond that. Our focus has been too narrow."

"We've been battling the poverty issue for years with nothing but set backs to show for it," added Kristen. "The recent government cuts in spending have ruined most of our projects going forward. That's what drove the Ten-in-Two Committee right out of existence and they were a refreshing new ally in our cause. It was a shame."

"I personally think that Committee was too sweeping in their approach," interjected Mary. "They were too focused on the macro rather than the micro. You can't tackle these poverty and wealth redistribution issues in big mouthfuls. You need to take small bites in order to aid in the digestion of the whole. That's what I've always written about and believed in. When a kid studies hard and rises above his background, goes on to graduate from high school and then college and gets that first good job, you can see that progression. It's tangible and rewarding. That's real progress, social progress."

"One day, hopefully soon, this Weed Killer thug will be gone, but the problems of homelessness and poverty that created his victims in the first place will remain and grow a whole new crop of sufferers," said Kristen Summers Clark Johnson. "We have to see that that doesn't happen. We have to seize the moment."

"Problem is that a lot of Torontonians don't give a damn about poverty and homelessness. You can see that in the Editorial section of the *Star*, the Letters to the Editor," stepped in John Beadle.

"Actually I was shocked. The writers seemed to sympathize with the Killer. Certainly they were less than sympathetic to the victims. I think this stems directly from the isolation of the homeless and poor from the general middle class and the more affluent citizens of the city. Except in situations of confrontation, when a homeless person blocks their path asking for money, or runs in front of their car squeegee in hand, or insults them because of a lack of generosity, these groups at different ends of the socio-economic scale rarely interact."

"That's why it's important we push not only for our standard demands for improved benefits and better housing for the poor, but also the idea of integration, social integration, within the housing module," added Kristen Summers Clark Johnson. "We need to have communities, neighborhoods that are cohesive and welcoming and at the same time made up of diverse cultural and economic classes. Look at Parkdale, Mary's beloved home. In large part it has escaped the recent killings. Why? Because the people there are on the look out for one another. They care about their neighbors. This is what we want to emphasize. You in particular, Mary, must appreciate this since you have been instrumental in fostering that goal."

"I've been trying, but it's an uphill fight."

"Yes, we agree. That's why we want to partner with you and the paper to pressure the government into attacking the homeless problem more directly through the use of affordable, integrated housing," continued Kristen Summers Clark Johnson. "We want areas like Parkdale to be maintained as a viable mix with people from all walks of life, not just the poor, or just the rich, but everyone living together in harmony and understanding. Housing is the lynchpin of the anti-poverty battle."

"For too long McGuiness and his municipal counterparts on the Toronto counsel have given the builders in this city carte blanche to build whatever they want, wherever they want without any regard to social consequences. If we are not careful, we are going to wind up with a series of poverty ridden ghettoes on our hands."

"That would be devastating," added John Beadle, "not only in and of itself, but because it would hide the poverty problem from the view of the general public. People wouldn't know or care about what was going on outside their own immediate neighborhoods."

"In this way I believe we can use the Weed Killer," added Karen French. "He has spotlighted the problem of homelessness like nothing else. We just have to expand the light beam beyond the murders themselves to illuminate the way to a permanent solution to the housing problem."

"Yeah, they're treating this Weed Killer situation as if it's solely a law and order issue. We have to show that it's much more than that."

"OK, so here is what we can do to get started on the right track," suggested Kristen Summers Clark Johnson.

"Each of our organizations and affiliated charities will contact a media outlet. We have Karen here and the *Star* already on our side. That's good. And we will state in no uncertain terms that all levels of government are ignoring the wider issues of housing and poverty and thereby contributing directly to these Weed Killer homicides. Let's be forceful."

"I can get pictures from the crime scenes," said Karen French. "We can play up the human angle which is Mary's forte. Headlines like, "People Perish while Politicians Ponder." Or how about, "Death Before Taxes." "Homes or Homicides." "Billions for Business, but only Pennies for Poverty."

"Spoken like a true newspaper editor,"

"Make sure to provide the office and personal phone numbers of all relevant politicians and urge everyone to call and then call yourselves and get your family members to do the same. We have lots of members and sympathizers. Urge them all to write, e-mail and phone."

"And Mary, like I said, we can use your portraits of victims and other anecdotes to provide some personal, human touches, but try to link their dire circumstances more directly to the housing problem."

"How about a public rally, a rally by, of, and for the homeless?"

"But wait a minute. What if the police catch this guy? What happens then?" questioned Mary suddenly. "The government could just drop the ball. Crisis over. Life back to normal."

"Well, that's why we have to link this present danger to the failings of the whole housing situation," reiterated Karen. "We have to move fast and get an ironclad commitment from the government, one they can't back out of no matter what happens with the Weed Killer or the economy for that matter. That has to be our approach and in the meantime this guy, I hate to say it, will hopefully stay on the loose, but maybe just not kill anyone else."

Within a week, the Premier of Ontario, himself under pressure from the Weed Killer murders, met with Karen French and Kristen Summers Clark Johnson in his office. Karen brought Mary Monticello along with her as another advocate for the poor and someone intimately involved in the case of the Weed Killer.

"Now ladies, I must say I was disappointed to see that you have decided to stop working with my office on the anti-poverty issue and instead jumped over our head to the media.

"Of course, your being a newspaper person I can appreciate the logic of the move, but we in government do feel blindsided especially since we were sympathetic to your cause in the first place. You know we've done more to fight poverty than any other government before us. Sure, we had to backtrack on some promises, but times are difficult. The economy is in a state of disrepair. My goodness, it nearly collapsed just a short while ago. Let me remind you, also, that despite these trying times we have continued to press for reform on the housing front. You can't really fault us on that issue."

"Reforms such as?" replied Karen French.

"Well, we've mandated a new comprehensive study on the overall problem and we are moving forward with private partners on some initial funding for a pilot project within the new Lakeshore Development Plan. We already have one developer who said he might be willing to set aside possibly as much as ten per cent of his lower end cost facilities for income based housing."

"The homeless don't have an income," added Mary.

"Ladies this is a start and we're optimistic other builders will get on board. When the time comes, we will commit real budget money for builder incentives and for renovating our present stock of rental housing."

"You gave two Canadian auto companies 18 billion dollars three days after the US government pledged many more billions to bail out those same companies in the States," said Kristen Summers Clark Johnson.

"Yes, but…"

"And you gave 14 million to a film production company and leased them space rent free for three years on their promise to start business in Toronto."

"These are all.."

"You gave a German firm a forgivable government loan for their investment in solar energy panels here in the province, and then amended the rules to allow purchase of that company's foreign made panels by Canadians for their home energy grants," added Karen French.

"Miss French, the economy was falling apart, the jobs of thousands of Canadians, Ontarians, Torontonians were, are at stake. These are working families, not people already out of the system. They have mortgages to pay, education fees, car payments, food to buy and clothing. These are tough times all around."

"Times are toughest for those who have the least. It's about time you acknowledged that fact. We can't have business as usual any more. We have to have a solid government commitment to build low cost, affordable housing right now. And we need you to work directly with our organizations in doing so."

"Ladies, and I'm beginning to use the term loosely, look at it from my perspective. I have to represent all the people of Ontario, that's my mandate. Now you have presented your case, directly, very directly I might add. I know where you're coming from. You're concerned about the poor in this province, the homeless in particular. You want this government to spend millions, tens of millions, maybe even hundreds of millions on the problem, and it is a legitimate issue, a noble goal. I will acknowledge that, but on the other hand I have the industry boys, the builders, coming to me also. They have a different story to tell. 'Give us those same millions and in return we will give you jobs, thousands of good paying, long term, secure jobs. From us, the businesses, you as a government will get corporate tax money and the workers we hire will pay income taxes.

"And this activity will attract even more enterprises to Ontario. Then the government coffers will grow and you can have the money to fund these social programs that the charities and anti-poverty groups are clamoring about. You've got to put the business horse before the welfare cart."

"So, what would you do if you were in my shoes? To me the answer is clear. On your side I have nothing but expenditures and marginal results. With them, the businessmen, I have the same expenses, maybe less, but in return I get a whole lot more, the people of Toronto, of Ontario, get a whole lot more. I hope I've made myself clear."

"In two weeks we are staging a rally here at Queens Park. It will be either to condemn the callous, death dealing inaction on the part of you and your government, or to praise you for your brave, unflinching, unwavering new initiative against poverty, complete with specific funding and identifiable targets and budget allocations for low cost housing," said Karen French.

"Really now, I think you're being unreasonable."

"Yes, you're absolutely right, but that's the only way to get anything done," added Kristen Summers Clark Johnson. "Also please don't miss our special collaboration with CTV next Monday featuring three homeless men from the West End."

"Don't you think you're pushing a little too hard? You can't tug at the public's heart strings forever. Everyone, including the government, has a limit as to what they can reasonably contribute."

"These men, along with many others, are presently sleeping in tents deep in High Park, huddled together for protection and living on discarded food and whatever else they can beg or steal off the streets," replied Karen French. "They're all Afghan war veterans, jobless, penniless and homeless. They've got a few questions for you and the Prime Minister too. Be sure to tune in."

"Well, how did you think it went?" asked Karen French when they emerged outside.

"We hit a nerve that's for sure. I bet he contacts us soon. That veterans' thing got to him. I could see it in his eyes."

"Mary, what did you think?"

"I want to see the specifics. How many homeless into exactly what homes and apartments? Where will they be built? New builds or reconstruction? The TCHC has been useless even harmful for years now. I want to see major reforms there. We've had plenty of promises before and you know what the results have been. I don't trust governments. I trust people."

"Results will come. I'm sure of that and speaking of coming up, what do you have for your Monday article? You said you were bringing an outline with you?"

Mary handed a typed sheet over to her editor who gave it a quick perusal.

"Mary, this, this is about bedbugs?"

"Sure, yeah. Bedbugs are the scourge of the city right now. They're devastating apartments and especially, as you'll notice if you read on, especially low income and TCHC run apartments."

"I'm not exactly following the logic here. I thought you were going to profile that Weed Killer victim over at St. James Garden, the guy who had been evicted from his public housing room because he somehow forgot to pay the rent. Government bureaucracy failed to notify him in time and he got kicked out in the street. Wound up on the park bench where the Weed Killer found him. That would be a great tie in with our new thrust. You know, linking the Weed Killer directly to the housing issue."

"I thought about that, but this bedbug thing has fallen off the radar of late. It's too important to be ignored. If the government is going to provide housing for the poor, well they better get going on the bedbug issue as well, don't you think? We don't want to see people pulled off the streets only to be put into bedbug ridden apartments. If you talk to these homeless people like I do on an almost daily basis, you'll realize that one of the main reasons they avoid public housing in the first place, and prefer to sleep on the streets is…"

"Bedbugs?"

"Right on, bedbugs. It's a big problem."

"Hey girls, what do you say we grab lunch," interjected Karen. "On the *Star*. I could actually use a drink right now."

chapter 19

ALBERT READ THE newspaper with renewed glee and self satisfaction. He couldn't get enough of his letters and the furor they created. He was in charge and everyone waited to see what he would do and say next. It felt good to finally have a purpose in life, a purpose that was worthwhile and garnered attention from others. He was the Weed Killer. "Look on my works, ye mighty, and despair."

***

At Sergeant Wright's house Sharon's bridge club was finishing up their last game, a situation that could easily take another hour or so. In large part Don knew that his wife had invited the group over to help heal the rift between the two of them which still simmered over his treatment of their daughter. It was difficult to maintain hard feelings when there was company around. The situation demanded good manners at least for show and often from that there flowed renewed understanding and a return to affection. The group of woman greeted Don warmly and sympathetically when he returned late from work.

"Hi, Don, you look beat. Case taking its toll I guess. Don't worry. You'll get the bastard."

"It's been horrible, really horrible," said Sharon. "You girls don't know the half of it. There's some supper in the oven, Honey," she continued smiling at her husband.

"Thanks," he smiled back. "I'll get right at it. I'm starving. Been a long day."

"And night," his wife added.

Josh walked into the kitchen and grabbed an ice cream bar from the freezer. "Hey, Dad."

"Hi, son. How's the ball game coming?"

"Good, only struck out twice. Got a walk."

"Great, things are looking up. How's your sister doing?"

"She hates you and wishes you were dead."

"Thanks Josh. I needed that."

"Don't worry Dad. I still think you're OK."

"What more can a father ask for?"

"Give that bike idea of mine any more thought?"

"Yeah, I have. Looking good. I just need a bit more time. Maybe this weekend we can scout around. For now you can check some bikes out with your friends and narrow down the choices."

"You mean it? Great."

"Sure, let's keep a limit on it of about fifty dollars though. How's that?"

Josh spun around in his tracks like a figure skater in a short rink.

"Just kidding, kidding," added Don quickly. He couldn't afford any more misunderstandings even of the humorous variety.

As Don put his dishes into the dish washer, he could hear the women gathering their belongings. The card playing was over and the ladies were heading home. Good-byes were exchanged and the door opened and closed several times, then Sharon came into the kitchen. The couple once again exchanged wan smiles.

"I'm sorry," he said. "I know I haven't been much of a husband or father lately. This case, and the job are killing me and if I wind up losing my family over this, I, I…"

"It's OK. Don't fret and don't talk crazy. We've been through a lot and we'll get through this, Meaghan too. Time will heal this, but you know I wanted to tell you something, something I discovered while talking with the girls tonight. Of course, we were discussing the killer, the Weed Killer. It's on everyone's mind so it's impossible to avoid, even though, you know, I tried to change the subject a thousand times if not more."

"You don't have to explain," replied Don. "I understand."

"Well, Susan had some clippings from the newspaper about the Weed Killer, his letters to the *Star*. I know I said I wouldn't follow any of the case and I don't want to get you upset, but…"

Sharon could see her husband's eyes kind of roll back in his head and his expression change slightly.

"I'm sorry, but I think this might be important."

"No, no, it's OK. I shouldn't shut you out. It's not right. Go ahead. I'm listening. What is it?"

"I noticed something while reading the Weed Killer's letters in the *Star* and that e-mail they posted. Susan passed them around as we were talking. You know, some of the women are volunteers for charity. They knew, or heard about the individual victims from the streets and soup kitchens where they work. Anyway, I don't know if it has any significance, but I just couldn't let it go without saying something. Maybe it's just to make me feel I'm contributing, helping you out in some small way. I'm not sure."

"That's certainly a worthy thought, Honey, so what is it you've noticed?"

"You know that I like jazz, jazz music, eh? Something you're not crazy about, but I know you indulge me and I appreciate that, those concerts and the clubs. I've seen the pained look on your face. Myself, I've been like that since I was a kid. I just loved jazz music. I don't know why, but I just took to it. When other kids my age were listening to Elvis and Buddy Holly I was into Miles Davis and Lester Young. And, you know, I know so many songs. Jesus, I can sing along with anything they play in the clubs or on the radio."

"Right, been there with you and I've teased you myself often enough."

"OK, so what I'm getting at is that I noticed in those letters in the *Star* a lot of lyrics to songs, jazz tunes. When the Weed Killer writes, he uses words from jazz classics. I mean he doesn't come right out and underline them or anything. They're just kind of interspersed in his sentences as though he uses them unconsciously like they're part of his everyday speech."

"Really," Don seemed suddenly more interested. "You're sure about this? It couldn't be coincidence?"

"I don't think so. Here, I kept Susan's copies of the letters and I underlined the phrases and words. Take a look. See here from that first letter he wrote, the salutation, 'Dear Bothered and Bewildered.' That's from a popular jazz classic called, "Bewitched, Bothered and Bewildered", and then 'Things are indeed the way they used to be.' That's a variation taken from a popular jazz song, an instrumental called, "Things Ain't the Way They Used to Be." I don't remember who wrote it, but I've heard it a hundred times. And 'Chances are,' and 'Night and day I am the one.' That's Cole Porter's "Night and Day."

"Hmm, Day and Night, that's a common expression. Everybody says that."

"Everybody says Day and Night, not Night and Day. That's from the song." Sharon began to sing: "Night and Day, you are the one. Only you beneath the moon and under the sun. Whether near to me or far…"

Don smiled broadly. "OK, I get it. Don't give up your day job."

"There's more too. From his second letter where he tells you to 'cover the waterfront for another body.' Billie Holiday made that song a classic, "I Cover the Waterfront." And then the last letter, 'Come on along, come on along.' That obviously refers to the old chestnut,

"Alexander's Ragtime Band". And then there's the phrases, 'You're so lucky to be having me around' and 'I'm not jealous' and 'I guess that weed was not for me.' Those are lyrics from the songs, "Time After Time," "But Not for Me," and "I Get Jealous." This guy's a jazz fan. I'm sure of it."

"Sharon, let me ask you this. If someone was interested in listening to good jazz, where exactly, say on the West End or the downtown, would they go?"

"The absolutely best club with the best and the most jazz in Toronto is the Rex Hotel. It's just west of University on Queen Street. You've been there once or twice with me though you probably don't remember. It's quite popular and has a regular and loyal following."

"Is that right? And let me just say I'm sorry for the miserable mood I've been in lately. I'm telling you once this case is over, I'm seriously thinking of resigning if it's alright with you, of course. I'll retire and write a book or I can take that job in Peterborough. You like Peterborough don't you? You said you did at one time."

"Sure, I'm with you. No matter what, I'm with you. I always have been and always will be. Hey, I'll be your secretary, sit on your lap and take dictation."

"Wow, I'm looking forward to that," Don looked straight at his wife. "Have I told you lately that I love you?"

"I know you do and, by the way, that's from a jazz song too."

chapter 20

FATHER FITZPATRICK OF St. Michael's Cathedral in conjunction with Bishop Gomlak of St. James held a special commemorative mass for the two men killed in the St. James and Allan Gardens neighborhoods, both murdered on the same tragic night. The church was full and the service broadcast throughout the city on local TV. The Premier and the Mayor and the Chief of Police were present along with scores of other Toronto dignitaries many of whom spoke at the service.

Albert watched from home. He had read too often and seen on the various television crime shows the practice of the authorities of video taping such gatherings in an attempt to spot the criminal who despite his best judgment could not help but view the proceedings in person. He would not fall into that trap being mindful of the chance he took back in June when he attended the Parkdale meeting with Norman.

What Albert found especially irritating was listening to Father FitzPatrick and that phony, pause for effect, delivery the good Father adopted when lecturing his flock. The priest's superciliousness was as evident as the miter perched on his head.

"Who can take a moron who wears a hat like that seriously," Albert sputtered out loud.

"Medieval malarkey. God, what crap. A modern, scientific society ruled by the beliefs and mores of a two thousand year old sheep herding culture. The whole world back then was proscribed by a tiny sliver of land that made up about one fifth of what is now our Middle East. You've got to be kidding. And there was my stupid wife waltzing through it all with ashes on her forehead and "the flesh and blood" of Jesus in her mouth and not a doubt in her mind. No wonder they call it a flock. Vive Christopher Hitchens! God is not great, the understatement of the century.

"Maybe, it's time to pay the good Father FitzPatrick a visit," Albert mused. "No sense throwing another letter in the mail. That sanctimonious asshole isn't worth the postage."

"Bless me Father for I have sinned." Albert could see the silhouette of the priest sitting opposite him separated by that dark screen. He remembered the routine well enough from his youth. Lord, how that crap sticks with you. Give me a boy and I'll give you the man.

Yes, those fucking Jesuits knew what they were talking about. The emotions flooded back: the fear, the shame, the anxiety. I was actually making sins up, little venial ones, to pad out my list of transgressions, give it some substance and perhaps distract the priest from the more serious flaws like, like what? Eating meat on a Friday? That was always a favorite of mine. My Protestants buddies were chowing down on hamburgers while I had to swallow dry, tasteless fish sticks. That fucking Captain High Liner, I wanted to shove that pipe of his right up his fat ass.

Albert hesitated now. Maybe he shouldn't have bothered with his little visit. What was to be gained except for some proud revenge? A knocking on the panel startled him out of his reverie.

"Go ahead, my son. I'm waiting."

My son. Father. Holy Ghost. One big happy family. God is three. God is also one. Try that out in math class and see how far you get, Albert thought before speaking. "I heard your sermon on the TV the other day, Father," Albert dragged out the last word. "Very moving, your concern for the homeless, even to someone like me."

"Like you?"

"Yes, I'm the Weed Killer in the flesh so to speak. I shot that man in St. James' Garden and the other one too that same night up at Allan Gardens. I shot all of them."

Albert saw the shadow of the priest leap up amid a loud thumping and bumping sound as the clergyman struggled for balance.

"Don't panic," Albert reassured him. "I'm not here to harm you. But if you leave or try to get a look at me I will gun down those people still waiting their turn in the pews outside. You can have their deaths on your conscience. Now settle down. I want to unburden myself."

Albert heard the puffing breath of the priest as the man sat back down. He was portly, Father FitzPatrick, a regular Friar Tuck.

"Yes, yes, my son," began the priest trying to control himself and collect his thoughts. "It was a horrible thing you did, but our Lord is a forgiving Lord. Above all else he loves his children, all of them. But you know, you must renounce your sins. Wash the devil from your life and ask God for forgiveness. In line with that you must also turn yourself in, of course, and face the consequences of your actions. Only then will you be truly forgiven."

"I didn't know I had to turn myself in to the police to get forgiveness. Isn't that what confession and penance are all about? Aren't I supposed to pray to God, say so many Our Fathers and Hail Marys and be forgiven? I don't remember anything specifically about turning oneself in. Where did that come from?"

"In a just society, man's laws on earth mirror God's mandates in Heaven. You must pay homage to both. Thou shalt not kill is a commandment from God and from our own humane laws."

"Strange, but I've heard many sermons from you and other priests over the years. In all that time you never mentioned thou shalt not kill when it came to war or fighting terrorism. All that Jesus, Prince of Peace bullshit! I guess that doesn't apply to soldiers or governments when they're slaughtering heathens in the Middle East, or how about capital punishment down in the States or your own Catholic past when you burned people at the stake with a wink and a nod and the sign of the cross?"

"I don't condone war and the past can not be undone. We often can not control earthly matters. We have to trust in the judgment of our elected leaders, and in the hidden wisdom of the Lord. After all, we do not know what his master plan is."

"How convenient, and I guess God has plans for me. Matter of fact, in a way he's actually responsible for these killings. After all, he could have stopped me whenever he wanted."

"But you are forgetting free will, my son. God gave you the ability to know right from wrong and to act accordingly. That's why you're here, isn't it? Your conscience is bothering you because you know you have sinned, sinned against God and your fellow man, and ultimately against your own Godlike soul."

Wow, thought Albert, once these mumbo jumbo artists get cranking out this religious bullshit, it's a diuretic nonstop. I wonder if he actually believes this crap himself.

"That may be true although let me confess, if you will, that I really have no remorse. I did it my way and I'd kill those losers all over again if I had the chance except I'd stop and relish it a bit more. But I don't have all day here. The point is this. In your neat little world of dishing out responsibility, what right do I, or anyone else, have to impose my free will and its consequences on innocent people? Answer that. Why does God allow me to ruin the lives of others in the exercise of my own free will? Sure, I could face eternal damnation if you like, but what about those I killed and their loved ones? Even if they will get rewarded in heaven what right did I have to destroy their admittedly short, though still precious lives on earth? Flying high in April, shot down in May. Does my exercise of free will supersede their right to life? How does God balance that out?"

"I don't presume to understand all that God does."

"I bet you don't. But here's another thing. You can console yourself with the belief that these poor souls, these toothless, homeless, loveless assholes are now rocking in the bosom of the Lord. I did them a favor. All you Catholic bleeding hearts are so anxious to be with God I don't understand why you fight so hard against death and dying. Why not just accept it and be happy? I remember the good Father Browning, Monsignor Browning, your predecessor here at St. Michael's. He was a patient at Princess Margaret Hospital and one of the first bone marrow recipients in Canada. His parishioners and other Catholics throughout the city all got themselves tested as possible donors just to save his sorry ass. When one finally matched up, the operation was done amid a big publicity hoopla. That actually bought the good father a couple of years of life during which time, I might add, he pissed up who knows how much more government health care money trying to avoid a direct meeting with the Lord. Why not forgo the treatment, pray instead, and take the consequences? St. Jude Hospital, Mt. Sinai, St. Joseph's, they're all contradictory to your faith, hypocritical I might add. If you believe in the healing power of God why bother with earthly intermediaries like doctors and hospitals? Go to the source and take your chances with the one in ultimate control. You priests are the real hypocrites and yet you're going to condemn me.

"Now let me tell you I know what it's like to be in a bad spot, in a hospital dying. I've heard all the supplications, the entreaties. 'Oh Lord, if I beat this cancer I will praise your word and help others to see the true path of salvation.' And, 'I just want to see my kids grow up, my poor kids. What will they do without me? If I could only see them in high school, graduate from college, and, you know, eh, get married and have children of their own. I want to be a grandmother. It's not fair, Lord. Why me? Why me? What did I ever do to deserve this?'

"Well, let me tell you, my pledge was different, very different. 'If I beat this cancer, I promise I will embark on a holy mission, a jihad, to rid the City of Toronto of its homeless hordes, those ragged, toothless, filthy individuals who have milked the system, plagued the law abiding citizenry, befouled the streets and bankrupted the city. I will gun down as many as I can, until I run out of bullets, or they run out of town.' So there you have it. Who am I to argue with the Lord? He kept me alive to do what I pledged, what I have to do. Now, I've enjoyed these few stolen moments with you, but remember I've given this confession in confidence so I don't expect you to go blabbing it out to the cops.

"Don't talk about me when I'm gone. I might even come back and give you a second chance to work out my redemption. If I find out you squealed, however, I'll take it out on more of God's little homeless dar-

lings and I won't shy away from telling the newspapers that I was motivated by you. Remember, with all my faults you have to love me still. Also,
if I see that confessional door open so much as a crack when I leave, I
will empty my gun into your parishioners."

Albert was glad Father FitzPatrick did not call his bluff at that
moment because Albert didn't have his gun with him. Nevertheless, the
first thing the good Father did was in fact call the police. Albert was at
the coffee shop across the street having a sandwich when he saw the
cruiser drive up.

"OK, Father, if that's the way you want it. The next one's on you."

chapter 21

NORM AND ALBERT sat at the back of the Rex having a leisurely drink and a bite to eat.

"Food's good here, not to mention the quality and variety of the music," commented Albert. "If this place ever goes the way of the Montreal Bistro, it would be a tragedy. And we lost the Top of the Senator too. It's getting bleak around town, harder and harder to find good jazz venues."

"Not everybody could afford the prices at the Bistro although I'll grant you the music was great. I saved up all year just to go there once. It was a special treat," said Norm.

The two men only peripherally listened to the band, Bohemian Swing. Norm, of course, was primarily a blues man and Albert preferred the Be Bob jazz style of the '40s which was far removed from the present gypsy jazz playing in the background.

"It must be a current craze or something," said Albert. "All these Django Reinhardt clones. There's Club Django, Abbie's Meltdown, Bohemian Swing. Once in a while, fine, but Jesus take it easy, eh. The jazz violin is another resurrected sensation. Everyone wants to be Stephan Grappelli all over again. You know he and Reinhardt were contemporaries and did some gigs and recordings together, but Grappelli couldn't stand Reinhardt. Hated him."

"Why's that? I'd figure their love of music would bring them closer together."

"I don't know, but Django was something of a fop, eh. Always well dressed and he had that David Niven kind of moustache, not to mention the fact that he was a big hit with the Nazis even though he himself was a gypsy."

"Didn't they gas all the gypsies back then?"

"Exactly, so you got to wonder and maybe Grappelli did too."

"It's the same thing happens to restaurants. It's all a big follow the leader fad," added Norm. "Right now it's Thai food. Years ago you never even heard of the stuff. Now every second restaurant serves Thai food."

"Too hot for me after my radiation treatments."

"Oh, I like the stuff, and at least it's cheap. Some of the places in the city, I honestly don't know who can afford to eat in them. You know, when I used to get the *Star* every day and they had those Carrey Lintz food columns evaluating the different restaurants, most of the time I didn't even understand what in the hell that son of a bitch was talking about. The goddamn terms he used to describe the food: arugula, terrine, caramelized this and that. I can't pronounce or remember most of them now. And the prices! Dinner for two with tip and a glass of wine, $230. Are you kidding me? He rolls them prices off his tongue like they were sweet cherries. Who can afford that kind of food?

"When I was first dating my wife, I took her to a fancy Italian restaurant, Perrone's or something like that. I wanted to impress her, eh. Was over on Queen West. The entire fucking menu was written in Italian. I was staring at it and wondering, what in the hell is all this stuff? I had no idea. The waiter had to interpret the whole menu for us. 'What's this? And this? What was that again?' I felt like an idiot. At least here they have not only good music, but good, simple food too at a reasonable price."

"It's the same with wines," added Albert. "I can't drink them now, but even back then I could never appreciate what I was drinking. I couldn't discern the underpinnings of oak and tannin with a hint of black cherry and apricot, a light nose of lavender, a slight aftertaste of bitter walnut."

"Most of those assholes just drink wine because they think it makes them look sophisticated. And the mark up will kill you. At least Claudia isn't snooty. She likes beer."

"And how is Claudia doing of late? I haven't seen her with you for a while, here or at City Donut's."

"I don't know. I think she's fooling around on me. She's acting different. Talks different as if she's my mother or older sister not the way it used to be when we first met, eh. I can't quite put my finger on it. She even smells different somehow. New perfume maybe. It's hard to explain. Of course, it's not that we're going steady like a couple of high school kids or anything like that. I couldn't blame her if she was seeing somebody else. The trouble is I'm so fucking paranoid especially if I'm off my meds that I start imagining things. She was pretty hot stuff when we first met, eh. Like I told you she was real energetic and even liked the rough, kinky stuff. Yeah, that threw me for a loop."

"I remember you saying she wanted to do it in front of mirrors and liked to be tied up and get her ass spanked. I thought, right on! My man Norm is scoring big time. I was proud of you."

"When she figured out that I couldn't really keep up with her, not to embarrass me I think, she cooled it, and after that we'd just sleep together, not doing nothing, eh. It was nice though to lay their hugging and talking till we fell asleep. Last little while she hasn't been into that either. Says she's got stuff to do at home and can't spend the night."

"She does still work you know. Maybe she's got responsibilities and is tired after a hard day on the job. What does she do again?"

"She's like a loan officer at a bank downtown, Royal Bank. Just got full time work a while ago. Trouble is I ain't got a lot of money of my own to take her nowheres. She says it doesn't bother her, but I'm sure a woman, every woman wants to be wined and dined once in a while. A chance to get all dressed up, eh. Someone like you could afford that, but not me. I've taken her to the Spit once and to the CHIN Picnic, Harbourfront for the different festivals. They're free, eh. If you live in the city and you don't have a lot of money, you find out and enjoy what's free and make do with that."

Both men made it a habit to sit at the back of the large, long Rex bar room whenever they planned on any sustained conversation.

"One thing I can't stand is someone talking loud through an entire performance," said Norm. "It's an insult to the band and the rest of the audience."

"That's what I loved the most about the old Montreal Bistro," added Albert. "their silent policy. Absolutely no talking during the band's performance. It should be like that everywhere. Now today, Norm old buddy, to prevent us from getting into an argument let's agree to keep economics and politics out of our conversation. No more capitalist bashing."

"Agreed. I'm getting sick of it myself. Trouble is you can't have any kind of a real dialogue anymore. Nobody listens to the other guy's point of view. I've watched discussions on TV and at public meetings not to mention my own conversations. On certain points you could tell people were not that far apart in their views. It wouldn't have taken much to reach an agreement, but, Ha, fat chance of that happening. At the last minute they'd suddenly become stubborn and simply say, 'This is what I believe. I don't care what evidence you've got.'"

"Sure, people spend more time trying to find holes in the other guy's argument than they do in actually listening and discovering points of agreement."

"It's all about winning the argument. Finding out the truth has got nothing to do with it anymore. That's what I love about science, and the scientific method. When a scientist puts forward an idea, a theory, he challenges other scientists to find fault with it. He even reexamines it over and over again himself looking for flaws. And then, and this is the important thing, when a problem is discovered the guy doesn't go all ballistic and start denying the other scientist's evidence. No, he checks it out and if the other guy is right, then he accepts that and changes or even discards his own theory. It's a community effort of scientists who all play by the same rules. You don't see that anywhere else and it should be the standard, not the exception."

"It's mainly the religious idiots who block that kind of logical reasoning. Some of those Born Again Christians still believe that the Earth is 5,000 years old and that cave men hunted dinosaurs. And that's not the worst part. Oh no, the worst part is that they want that religious shit pushed on other people as the truth and even taught in the schools."

"Capitalism is the same. People believe that this is the best of all possible systems, economically and socially. They don't think beyond that to what else might be possible. It's the same narrow point of view like you said with them religious fanatics."

"I think we're drifting off into politics, economics again," Albert smiled.

The waitress stopped by and asked if the men wanted another drink. Albert nodded.

"To change the topic then, another thing I noticed," Norm put in. "When I'm alone in here, the service is only so-so. It's not that the waitresses ignore me or anything like that, but they sure don't hustle and I know why. It's because I don't tip that much, eh. Ten per cent, that's all I can afford. I told one of them that last year. 'Sorry, when you're on a limited budget you can't afford too much of a tip.' She smiled, kind of a, 'Sure thing, you cheap asshole' smile. But when you're here, Oh boy, big change because they know you're a big tipper. What do you leave, fifteen per cent?"

"Twenty."

"Holy fuck, there you go again. That's another reason it's hard to talk to people, even guys like you about capitalism, and poverty, and homelessness. You don't care. You don't care because you got it pretty good especially when you look around and see other people like me; no permanent job, no house, or car, no prospects. We're divided like the black slaves of the Old South. You're one of the house slaves and figure you got it good and look down on me and the field slaves as inferior. You got a stake in the system and buy into its inequalities. You probably take credit for your superior position and figure everyone else is undeserving. Even though you're a victim too you don't know it and actually serve as a prop to the status quo. I hate to say it, but you're a lot like that fucking Weed Killer to tell you the truth. You both got the same attitude."

"Man, Norm, calm down. You're flying off on a tangent again. Let's listen to the music. Here come our drinks."

"That's another thing," said Norm nodding at the approaching waitress. "What these people need is a union. All these bar and restaurant workers, those in retail, the clothing stores and banks, they all need a union. One of the large Ontario unions, national unions ought to come in here and organize these people, help them out. Cancel that. Fucking unions today are useless, self absorbed and protectionist. They have no social vision beyond their own membership. Hell, even in a specific industry there's no union cohesiveness, no solidarity. Take the railroads. You'd think there would be one union representing all the railroad workers. No, there's about ten even within the same railroad not to mention the whole industry. You got a union for electricians, a separate one for construction workers, running trades, repair and maintenance men, inside office workers, conductors, engineers. And you'd think that if one was on strike, the others would automatically go out too? No way. They got separate contracts that expire at different times and with different conditions. Can you imagine anything so fucking stupid? This is unionism today. Sell out unionism I call it. In the old days of the IWW this kind of crap would never be tolerated. An attack on one was an attack on all. If you tried to cross a picket line back then you took your life in your hands. Every union member knew whose side he or she was on and they stuck together like brothers and sisters. Nowadays you're afraid to mention you're even in a union and you make apologies if you're identified as a member. Bull shit!"

Albert rocked back in his chair and pressed his hand to his head. "Norm, old chum, you've got to give up on this bitterness. It's eating you up."

"You sound like Claudia now," Norm went on. "But you see how everything is set up to screw the workers. We got a minimum wage here in Ontario. A lot of people fought hard and long to get that established and increased over the years. But guess what? It doesn't apply to part time workers like those in the hospitality industry like our waitresses here. They're on a different scale. They can be paid virtually any pathetic wage. That's why the tips are so important because these workers can't live on their wages alone. And that's why you get better service than a guy like me. I don't blame them."

Albert smiled at the young waitress as she set the drinks on the table. "You'll have to forgive my friend here. He's pretty hot under the collar. He needs something cool."

Just then Albert noticed a man awkwardly making his way through the large crowd. The person moved uneasily, hesitantly. He looked familiar somehow, but Albert certainly had not seen the man here at the Rex before.

"Excuse me. Pardon me. Sorry."

Albert nudged Norm. "Hey, that guy there at the post near the bar, who is he? Looks familiar."

"I know him too," said Norm. "Give me a minute, ah, ah. Jesus, you know. It's that cop, the lead detective on the Weed Killer case. Yes, Wright, Detective Sergeant Wright."

"Sure enough. He looks different in regular clothes, civilian clothes. What in the hell is he doing here I wonder?" replied Albert. "Doesn't seem all that interested in the music, not listening or even glancing at the band. Now he's talking to one of the owners behind the cash. I'll be right back. Got to use the washroom."

With Albert's luck while he stood there at the urinal, the washroom door opened and none other than Sergeant Wright walked down the steps. In the mirror the two men looked straight at each other. Albert smiled and nodded, then quickly zipped up and turned to leave.

"Good band today?" Sergeant Wright asked.

"If you enjoy that style. They play every Saturday afternoon, this month anyway, but the place has good music seven days a week. Of course, you can hit something you don't like every now and then. Just avoid the night time weekend venues if you're not sure. There's a cover charge."

"You seem to know a lot about the place. Come here often?"

"Not really, I don't get around much anymore and would hardly consider myself a regular. Anyway, enjoy the show," and Albert left.

A while later Sergeant Wright emerged and strolled around the back area of the bar room. He nodded knowingly to Albert, then stopped at his table and stared at Norm who returned his glance with a friendly, "Hello".

"Do I know you from somewhere?" asked the police officer. "You look vaguely familiar. I'm pretty good with faces. Comes with the job. I'm Sergeant Wright of the Toronto Homicide Squad." He showed the two men his badge.

"Well," said Norm. "I did attend that public meeting over in Parkdale when you were there talking about the Weed Killer. Mary Monticello was in attendance too amongst others. I got up and spoke a few words about the real cause of our homeless problem."

"And that would be?"

"Capitalism."

"Oh, yeah, of course. I do remember now. You had some problems with your microphone."

"That's right. You got it."

Sergeant Wright smiled sympathetically and then turned to Albert. "How about you? Were you there too?"

"No, I'm not the social activist that Norm is. I keep my nose out of those affairs. The police can handle crime on their own."

"Well, they sure as hell aren't doing a very good job of it, are they?" said Norm rhetorically.

"On that note I think I'll take my leave," said the Sergeant. "You men enjoy the music."

"No manners," commented Norm as the man exited via the side door. "You'd think the asshole would have waited for the set to end. I hate when people do that. It's disrespectful."

"I'm sure he didn't know any better," replied Albert. "He probably never gets out."

"Yeah, what's he doing here anyway? Doesn't he have a dozen or so murder cases to solve?"

"Maybe he's solving one now," answered Albert.

"And, Hey, how come you told him you weren't there at the meeting with me?"

"None of his business. Anyway, I don't want to take the chance of being put on some government subversive list along with you. They might jail the both of us if they think we're trying to overthrow the government."

"Ha, I wouldn't doubt it. But a revolution doesn't have to involve violence. You can vote people out and take control peacefully if you're sufficiently well organized."

***

Albert had studied the homeless "doorman" at the City Donut Shop ever since the vagrant showed up this past winter. "Thank you anyway. Have a nice day." Man, did that irritate the shit out of Albert. A polite bum, how fucking noble! When the man was not standing at the coffee shop with his coffee cup in hand, he was bedded down on the opposite King Street West sidewalk comfortably tucked in his sleeping bag with a pillow, cigarettes, water bottles and fruit juice packs. Occasionally he ate the sandwich, banana or apple provided by the itinerate charity workers after which he invariably tossed the scraps, peels and cores onto the sidewalk.

"You think he'd bother to at least roll over to that little garden area just off the sidewalk for a little more privacy," noted Albert. "But hell no, because then people wouldn't have to trip over him and smell his shitty shorts, the nervy bastard. But maybe the times they are a changing."

152

A new condo was being built across John Street from the City Donut, the Film Festival Towers. High end stuff. The pile driver banged all day long, carpenters nailed up walls and fencing. The noise level was high and large crowds of people crossed to the south side of King to avoid the construction. This packed the sidewalk and forced people to divert around the oft sleeping homeless man like creek water around a partially submerged log.

"A dead head," muttered Albert as he formulated his plan. "Yes, the cops are still mostly focused on their night patrols and their stake outs at derelict buildings and warehouses although I think they gave up on the BSH sites. Thank God I dodged that bullet. The sons of bitches were waiting for me sure enough. Good old Sergeant Wright. He ain't giving up. Anyway, the clued out bastards will never, ever expect something so bold. It should shake them up again for sure, but it's got to be done perfectly. Nothing left to chance."

Albert labored at his kitchen table with his curtains carefully drawn. He didn't keep them that way all the time. Too suspicious he figured. Just be cautious and don't do anything out in the open, like clean and load the gun. Albert cut the bottom off a small plastic Coke bottle, and taped the spout end to the barrel of his pistol. Then he took another larger two liter bottle covered it in a thin smear of butter and wrapped the main body around with several layers of wet papier-mache made with newspaper, the *Toronto Star* naturally. When the papier-mache hardened he pulled the bottle out giving him a hollow tube open at both ends.

Before he left his house, Albert stuck the .22 revolver with the Coke bottle silencer about two thirds inside of the papier mache tube leaving room for his hand to grip the trigger. Keeping the end of his home made silencer clear, he packed solidly around the rest of the barrel with damp City Donut serviettes which he had taken over time from the John Street shop. He remembered the scene from the Godfather when young Corleone shot the Black Hand kingpin in the apartment hallway and the towel he had wrapped around the gun caught fire.

"Nothing like trying to walk down King Street with a flaming newspaper in your hand," he laughed. "Oh, this Officer? It's nothing. I just butted out a cigarette inside the sports section."

Albert draped the open front pages of this week's Now magazine over the entire fabrication. He crimped the pages in front of the firing hole and put a few staples into the overhanging loose pages so the whole thing wouldn't fall apart in the heat of the moment. Finally he threw a light jacket over the bundle and left the house looking like he was carrying a newspaper along with the wind breaker folded over his arm.

On King Street the sidewalks were packed with hurrying pedestrians bent on their lunch time destinations and oblivious to all around them. Most of them were also wired for sound, noted Albert. It all made the crime so much easier. Sleeping Beauty napped until one o'clock so he could maximize the irritation factor by blocking the sidewalk thought Albert. Then the man ran across the street to City Donut when customers coming out of the coffee shop were at their peak. On Wednesdays when the Royal Alexandra and Princess of Wales theatres ran their matinees, the immediate area was even more jammed with both foot and vehicular traffic.

Albert walked through Metro Park slightly before noon and joined the throngs moving west on King Street. The crowd twisted and swayed, slithering like a multi-legged human centipede down the sidewalk. It split around obstacles such as light posts and trees and parking meters like a flow of liquid mercury only to join parts again and form a united stream farther along the route.

A steady pound, pound, pounding resounded from the construction site as the steel foundation plates were hammered into the ground. Albert knew all the city surveillance street cameras were well behind him. He only had to worry about his fellow travelers. As usual they were oblivious to his presence and to almost everything else around them. To them he was just a fellow worker carrying a newspaper to read on his lunch hour. The sublime and very useful indifference of the city, thought Albert. Good. With his hand tucked inside the *Now* magazine and poised on the trigger Albert slowed his pace until the rhythmic banging at the condo site resumed. Boom! Boom! Boom! He then stepped across the slumbering man whose face was hidden by a drawn hoodie and Bang! Bang!

Bang! without missing a beat he fired three shots into the sleeping bag square into the chest area approximating where the man's heart was located. Small puffs of fabric jumped from the sleeping bag like kernels of heated pop corn. A hand protruding from a dirty shirt sleeve silently crushed an empty Starbuck's cup.

These were the only signs of movement from the figure on the ground as Albert and the crowd surged past. Minutes later Albert entered City Donut and gave a nod to the few regulars he knew by sight. Norm wasn't around, but Albert did expect Claudia later. They had arranged to show up at separate times to throw off suspicion if Norm had decided to make an appearance. Also her presence might prove important if events took a bad turn, reasoned Albert. He then ducked into the washroom. Inside the toilet stall Albert pulled the *Now* magazine off his papier-mache newspaper roll and spilled out the three spent shells and put them in his pocket. He had been careful to leave space for their ejection inside his plaster tube. He then banged the structure against the inside of the bowl, waited for the plaster like material to

154

soften in the water and then he shredded the remaining serviettes and flushed it all down the toilet. He did it in two attempts to make sure the drain didn't clog. He stuck his revolver in its usual leg holster and emerged from the washroom with the magazine and jacket in his hand just as he had entered.

"I'll have the usual," Albert said to the clerk/owner and folded the *Now* pages and deposited them into the garbage purposely bypassing the recycling bin just in case. He momentarily held on to the small Coke bottle before letting it also drop into the receptacle so it sat separately from the rest of the debris.

Claudia entered about ten minutes later. At roughly the same time a commotion erupted across the street. "Someone's been shot," a cry went up. "It's that poor homeless guy on King Street. He's bleeding. He's been shot. He's dead. It's the killer. The Weed Killer was here."

"Oh my God," cried Claudia as the coffee house customers rushed to the windows and door to check out the situation. In minutes two police cars and several patrolmen who had been directing traffic around the nearby construction site showed up.

"I'm glad you got here on time," said Albert to Claudia. "A little earlier you might have run right into this mess. Here, have a sip of my coffee. It will settle you down. We better go. This is no place for a woman, too gruesome. But, wow, right here on a busy street in the middle of the day. The killer must have nerves of steel."

"The poor dead man," replied Claudia after she left with Albert amid the turmoil. "He was the guy at the door wasn't he, the man who held it open all the time? My God, to lose his life like this, shot down with all these people around and nobody saw nothing. Nobody did nothing. What's going on in this city? How could it happen?"

Albert glanced back at the City Donut entrance as he and Claudia moved west down King Street. He saw the owner standing there with a wide smile on his face. Far up the street, several blocks away the police were positioned on the corners stopping pedestrians. Just ahead of Albert and Claudia a lone man was held back. "Just a moment, sir. We'd like a word with you if you don't mind."

When the police looked at Albert and Claudia holding hands, they waved them through.

"You can go. We're just questioning a few men here as a matter of precaution. You two needn't worry. Have a nice day."

"You're shaking," said Claudia to Albert. "You see. You're not as hard hearted as you'd like me to think after all. The poor man's death affected you too. You just won't admit it."

Back at his house, after surreptitiously stashing his gun and bullet clip, Albert put Claudia through her routine with extra vigor.

"How can you do this to me?" she kept asking as he manhandled her insultingly. "How can you do this?"

"It's easy. Because I can and because you like it."

When they were done, the two lay side by side but not touching on the bed. Albert noticed that Claudia was sobbing and sniffling and her breathing seemed labored.

"What's the matter? You crying?"

"That's part of it, the part I'm used to, the way you mistreat me. I can't believe I put up with it. Sometimes I just want to scream, stupid me, but I also must be allergic to something, maybe the cologne you're wearing. Every time I get close to you I get the same reaction; runny nose, watery, itchy eyes. My luck to have both you and your after shave slowly killing me at the same time. What is it you're wearing anyway?"

"Aqua Velva, I got it from my ex long ago. It was a regular Christmas present. I still have a couple of bottles. She said it always reminded her of me. I imagine that's not a positive thing anymore for her. I don't mind the smell myself, but, what the hell, if it bothers you I'll stop using it. That's the kind of guy I am."

"Yes, you're all heart, no doubt about it. That picture on the living room table is that her, your ex-wife?"

"Yeah."

"I guess you must still have some feelings for her since you got her picture sitting there out in the open?"

"You might say that, but you'd be wrong. Did you notice that ledger book opened in front of it?"

"Doing some accounting work?"

"No, I keep the two of them out like that so every time I pass them by I can thank my lucky stars that they are both out of my life for good, the wife and the job. These foolish things, eh. It makes my day."

"I should have known better than to think some affection might creep into that stone heart of yours. You do have a cute little house though for a bachelor, nice and clean. You got someone who comes in once in a while to tidy it up?"

"No, I'm perfectly capable of looking after the place myself. Anyway, I don't like other people snooping around my stuff."

"You're too paranoid, secretive really. What are you afraid of? You know, when I stop to think about it, I don't know all that much about you except the little bit of beans you've spilled and what Norm has told me. For all I know you could be a rapist or serial killer."

"The rapist part I could go for. Matter of fact, I've got a little game I think you'll like. Put my bath rope on and come here in the kitchen. I want you to pretend you're doing the dishes, then…"

"Oh no, come on Albert. Please. Can't we just lay here and talk for a while longer? I'm still a little sore."

chapter 22

"CURLEY IS GONE," by Mary Monticello, *Toronto Star* columnist

"Our beloved Curly is gone, killed, murdered, taken away from us in broad daylight on one of the busiest streets in Toronto. No longer will his smiling, albeit tooth compromised, face light up our days, nor his cheerful, 'Have a nice day,' send us off to work or play with a happy heart. Curley is gone, murdered as hundreds walked by oblivious to his grim fate. I, for one, however, will mourn Curley. I will put on my widow's weeds and cry for Curley. And in this deep grief, I won't be alone. Make no mistake because there are others out there just like me. Others too with a warm heart and open mind, others who could see beyond the man's dirty hands and face, the rotten teeth and soiled clothes, and the occasional, when provoked, belligerent behavior. Others who saw a beautiful inner soul beneath the rough exterior, a soul now gone.

"Yes, Charlie, the butcher at Kensington Market where Curley occasionally found himself, is one of those others. 'I'd always get a big smile and a friendly slap on the back from Curley when I'd hand him some of my meats when I cleaned out the shelves at the end of the month. Talk about happy. And that stuff was still good, mind you. It can go beyond the expiry date, no problem. It's just these goddamn ministry health rules, so stupid, fussy, eh. Except for chicken. I'll admit that. Chicken can be a problem. I always told Curley and the others, if it smells a little bad cook it right away and cook the shit out of it. That way maybe it will taste a bit "off" but it won't make you sick, eh.'

"Yes, Greg and David over at the Brewer's Retail on Queen St. they were part of the others too, always happy to help Curley with adding up his deposit return. 'Yeah, old Curley,' said David, 'he'd more often than not get his total screwed up, eh. Thought he deserved more than was really coming to him. He could get pretty nasty about it sometimes, but that was old Curley. Me and the other guys, we just laughed it off and sometimes threw in a buck or two from our own pockets just to keep him happy.

Won't be the same without Curley out front no more. That's for sure.'

"And yes, Father FitzPatrick was another who didn't mind handing Curley a few dollars for an hour's worth of work cutting grass or weeding the garden at St. Michael's Cathedral. And there was Saftir too at City Donut across the street from the site of Curley's premature demise. Saftir always let Curley use the washroom there and tossed him a few stale donuts in exchange for Curley's polite door work. 'He was cheerful guy when he wasn't just total drunk, you know. He'd wash in the bathroom. That's OK because it's hard to kick someone out, eh. Looks bad. Lots of customer, they know Curley and now they ask, 'Where's that Curley?' Yeah, Curley, I knowed him good.'

"So dear readers in a way Curley is still with us, in our hearts and our minds. May it always be that way so this cruel and heartless killer can not totally destroy all that makes Toronto great. We miss you Curley, but we won't forget you. And finally let's hope that the Toronto police will redouble their efforts to get this killer off our streets. We owe it not only to ourselves, but to all the Curlys out there.

P.S. Whoever the poor unfortunate was that picked up some of Curly's personal possessions there on King Street, Beware the Bedbugs."

***

"Sergeant Wright, please have a seat." Despite the polite offering there was no hint of kindness in the voice of the Captain Donnally. Opposite Don's immediate superior sat Police Chief Samuals, Mayor Milne, several city councilors, two of them from the downtown and West End areas of the city. Also in attendance were OPP Captain Newman, and two men Sergeant Wright had never seen before. They were dressed like civilians although they sat with the two senior police officers.

Detective Gignac, who normally would have been on suspension during the SIU investigation into the Loblaws shooting, accompanied Detective Wright and sat beside him at the lone front table. Gignac, like his Sergeant, was still on active duty because of his importance to the Weed Killer case.

"Needless to say, Detective Wright," Captain Donnally began, "Police Chief Samuals and I, not to mention the mayor and the city council, some of whom are present here today, aren't too pleased with your progress on the Weed Killer homicides. No, let me change that, we're not too pleased with your complete and total lack of progress on the Weed Killer case. We haven't had any breaking news from your office, any reports of progress, for weeks now. All we seem to get are informationless updates and pleas to the public for assistance while the body count builds. For Christ's sake, man, the public is looking to us for answers and assistance not the other way around. If you were doing your job, you wouldn't need the goddamn public."

"Thank you Captain," said Chief Samuals. "Now, I'm not going to say much here this afternoon. I think Captain Donnally has summed up my feelings pretty well. Let me just reiterate that we need some progress here. The pressure is building to put the RCMP in charge, take matters out of the Toronto Police Force's hands. I don't have to tell you what a black eye to our organization such a move would mean. It would be devastating. But let's allow Sergeant Wright to take a minute and tell us just where the case stands to date. Right now I believe we've had ten murders or is it eleven? I've lost count. Am I right?"

"Yes, sir. ten that we know of."

"Please, Sergeant. Don't get me more upset than I already am. Can we realistically settle on ten?"

"OK."

"So, for these ten murders, which I might add is a record for a single killer here in Toronto, or anywhere else on the east coast of the country for that matter, what suspects are you looking at, Sergeant?"

"None. We have had several men confess to being the Weed Killer, but they were all lying. Why people do that I'll never know, but it was an easy thing to check because of some pertinent evidence that we have withheld from the public. None of these men could identify that evidence. Therefore, I'm sorry to say, we have no suspects."

"I don't necessarily mean definitive, there but for a bit of forensics comes a conviction, suspects. Just persons of interest if you like."

"We don't really have any of those either."

"Goddamn, man, what do we have?" shouted Mayor Milne. "We're getting crucified in the media over this fiasco."

"Not much, Sir. First of all for motive, the killer hates the homeless. That's hardly a uniquely identifiable characteristic. In a city of this size there have to be thousands, tens of thousands with the same attitude. Then, of course, the homicides are totally random. We've got no pool of relatives, enemies or friends to sort through as possible suspects. And to our knowledge there has never been a survivor who can give us any detailed information about the killer. Also you heard my news conference the other day. We don't have any tangible evidence either, no forensics, DNA, only a few drunken eyewitnesses who have given totally conflicting statements. The only common elements were that the killer was Caucasian and wore dark clothing and used the same .22 caliber gun in all the killings.

"Father FitzPatrick at St. Michael's was one individual who actually spoke to the Weed Killer in person, but only in the darkness of a

Catholic confessional and frankly he was far too nervous to make any
meaningful observations about the Killer's mannerisms, or the way he
spoke, nothing. The poor cleric almost had a heart attack from the
ordeal. The police who arrived at the church after his emergency call
had to summons an ambulance for the priest. Then there was another
possible eyewitness, the young Bartholomew boy in the Allan Gardens
neighborhood, but he has refused to speak to the police. His parents
have him lawyered up."

"Jesus, that's ridiculous."

"Ridiculous yes, but not illegal. And that's another problem we're
having. A lot of the public actually sympathizes with the Killer. They're
rooting for him and like what he's doing. As a result we are not getting
a lot of cooperation."

"Yes," interrupted Councilor Marchand. "And a recent *Star* poll
showed that 65 per cent of the public believes the Weed Killer has done
more to clean up downtown Toronto in the last four months than the
police have done over the past ten years."

"I can't comment on that aspect of the case," continued Sergeant
Wright. "That is not my responsibility, nor my call."

"Thanks for that, Councilor," replied Chief Samuals. "I read the
poll myself, but appreciate the reminder nonetheless. However, back to
the cases at hand. Sergeant Wright, this last killing right on King St. in
broad daylight, come on, you have to have something on that?"

"We drew a blank again. No witnesses. Evidently there was a hell of
a crowd moving through the area, fast, oblivious. They were accustomed
to seeing the homeless victim sleeping there on the sidewalk for months
before the killing. They evidently regarded him as part of the scenery. The
hot dog vendor on the corner saw no one suspicious. It was lunch time.
The City Donut across the street was packed. People coming and going
like crazy. There was a noisy, busy construction site on the corner that
added to the commotion and confusion. No doubt the killer was counting
on that to mask the sound of any gunshots. We have no police security
cameras in that area except for the cameras at the two theatres across the
street which were focused on the lobbies. They didn't give us anything."

"Jesus, I've heard enough, more than enough," said Police Chief
Samuals. "We won't bother grilling you on the shooting death of another
homeless man this time by you and your partner here. The Special Investigations Unit is looking into that. But really Detective, you've gotten us
into a fine mess. You've been on the force for how long now?"

"Five years here in Toronto. Seems like five hundred at the
moment."

"Well, despite your past contributions to the Toronto Police
Department, we have given serious consideration to relieving you of

duty or at least transferring you to some other case. Unfortunately, the little that is known about the Weed Killer file seems to be in your hands and you're the public face of the case. Other than that, and certainly on my own personal recommendation, you would have been out of here yesterday. But don't get too confident. It could still happen especially with the press starting to turn against us and you in particular. It was a mistake to let the *Star* in on a lot of our information. As of today I am appointing Captain Donnally as your active overseer in the Weed Killer case. He will report directly to me."

There were a few nods of agreement and a general murmur throughout the room.

"Another thing, Sergeant, I'd like to introduce you to a couple of men who have been sitting in with us this afternoon. This is Sergeant Romano from the OPP and Detective Sadjak from the Toronto Bureau of the RCMP. They are criminal profilers and I will turn the meeting over to them. The rest of us will adjourn for a separate session. I hope your meeting will be productive. These men have my full confidence and I expect you will take their findings to heart. After they are finished, I understand that Father FitzPatrick from St. Michael's Cathedral would like a word with you."

Sergeant Wright nodded affirmatively.

"He's waiting outside the room. When you are done with the police profilers, you can invite him in. That's all. Good luck, you obviously need it."

Detective Gignac gave Sergeant Wright an understanding, sympathetic glance, one that also conveyed the unmistakable idea that he was very glad indeed that it was his superior not him on the hot seat.

The Toronto detectives then settled down with the two profilers who had been given the Weed Killer's file to date as well as all the letters and e-mails he had written. They also had interviewed Father FitzPatrick and had a make shift transcript of the priest's talk with the Killer. They had the forensic and investigative clues at their disposal including for the first time the information regarding the weeds stuffed in the mouths of the victims and the Aqua Velva after shave mentioned in the Allan Gardens report. The Toronto police were desperate and couldn't take the chance that withholding any information would come back to bite them in the ass. Although the profilers had some interpretations in dispute, the men did agreed upon an overall picture of the Killer.

"He's middle aged, probably no older than fifty, given his physical endurance at the Allan Gardens killings and his subsequent flight through the streets. He's well educated, good vocabulary and with a somewhat stilted way of expressing himself, and probably well groomed, i.e. the Aqua Velva though "under dressed" when he makes his "rounds" in order to blend in with crowds. Has familiarity with Toronto streets especially in the city's West End. Probably lives in the neighborhood or has lived there in the recent past.

"He resents authority so he is probably a younger sibling, maybe the youngest in a large family. He might have had an abusive father, or maybe a grandfather whom he resented. That's why he targets mainly older white men. Also, perhaps there was a history of alcoholism and/ or abuse in his family to which he is rebelling. He is a self made man most likely from humble if not poor background to which he has much resentment. Hence his attack on the homeless who he sees as the end game for his own feared destiny or the reality of his parents' lives. The weeds indicate an overt hatred for his victims and a need to humiliate and degrade them. He also wants to display their worthlessness for the world to see as well as to showcase his own power. He most likely holds or held a position of authority in his chosen field.

"Those BSH sites were a distraction. He took momentarily advantage, but the idea was not his. He abandoned it quickly, but his caution is noteworthy. Since his letters have been published in the papers and readers encouraged to compare them to the writings and speech of people they know and no one has come forward, he is probably a loner with few friends. His family lives elsewhere and/or has not had contact with him for quite a while. Probably never married or now divorced. Well off. Catholic from what Father FitzPatrick has said, but non practicing because he's scornful of church authority. May be a former altar boy. Also from the priest's testimony, the Killer is a former cancer patient with a serious life threatening diagnosis going back perhaps ten years. Good chance he was hospitalized in the GTA. The possibility exists that the story is fabricated.

"He appears to be a crack shot, maybe ex-military. Could frequent gun ranges, perhaps a member of a gun club, but probably resigned due to his killing spree. The gun is fairly common, compact and low volume. Enjoys killing and sees it as a mission of high merit. Will continue to kill until he's apprehended. His eventual capture is probably a foregone conclusion. The real question is, how many others will he kill before he is stopped because he won't stop. He enjoys it too much."

"Frankly I'm not sure about this shit," said Detective Gignac to Sergeant Wright when the two police profilers left the room. "Most of that stuff seems self evident or impossible to verify. What do we need them for?"

"They help make us look like we don't know what the hell we're doing. Anyway, to keep the Captain and Chief happy, not to mention the media, bundle this shit up best you can into a report and issue it to the press. It will show our cooperation. Leave out the weed stuffing

info and the after shave. We'll hang on to that. I don't want him changing any of his habits and we will need that information later to separate
the wheat from the chaff and finally nail this guy. The lab also said they
lifted a print, a very partial print, off one of the shiny leaves of a weed in
the Harbor Street murders, just like at the Lighting Standards Building.
If the leaf was a bit broader, they think they might have had something
really useful. Anyway, they are trying to combine the two to get one useful print that can stand up as evidence. I got another lead I'm exploring
kind of on my own. Not sure about it yet, but I'll let you know if it mate-
rializes into solid evidence."

Just then there was a knock on the door and Father FitzPatrick
stuck his head inside the room. "I have someone waiting outside that I'd
like you to meet as Police Chief Samuals mentioned," said the priest as
he then stepped into the room. "Now please give her a chance. I think
she can be of assistance. I met this fine lady at St. Michael's many years
ago when she was on a pilgrimage through various holy sites in North
America and I've grown to admire her. She knows the Lord and commu-
nicates with his angels. I know you police don't necessarily believe in this
stuff, and I don't pretend to understand how she does it, but Madame
Sigourney can see things that others miss. I'm positive she can be of
assistance in this matter."

"What? Who do you mean?"

"Please, not some psycho soothsayer or clairvoyant."

"Your chief said it was alright. Please, just hear her out. What harm
can it do? You've got the profilers' statement which she hasn't heard.
Let's see how they match up."

"Or don't match up."

"Certainly," said the priest who then opened the door and escorted
a portly, blond, older woman into the room. She wore a full length red
dress and a red scarf with matching red shoes. She genuflected to the
clergyman upon entering.

"Fucking, little red riding hood," muttered Detective Gignac to his
superior.

"Detectives, this is Madame Sigourney and she'd like to share some
things with you," said Father FitzPatrick.

Madame Sigourney took a seat proffered to her by Sergeant Wright
and proceeded to hold her face in her hands before speaking in an odd,
high pitched, faraway sounding voice as though she was a child speaking
into a soda straw.

"While I moved along the buildings and the park where the people
were killed, I sensed the presence of a man, a man of pure evil, a man at
war with God. The man moved as if in a dream descending from a height
and then walking deliberately down an alley. I realized that he had been

previously seated up high on a bicycle where he kept his weapon and other instruments of crime in a sack behind the seat. I saw the setting sun at his back as it cast a long black shadow down the lane where he traveled splashing through blood. A cold wind was blowing and his jacket, more like a cape, was open, but he felt no discomfort.

"He lives alone, but with many others around him. He has a garden and tends to it meticulously. I see flowers and plants surrounding him. He's obsessed with weeds and eradicates them mercilessly.

"I saw him in a church laughing while the holy statues shed tears of blood," Madame Sigourney continued her body shivering and her hands shaking. "He was a religious man, but has turned his back on God. He has killed before for many years and in many different places. Some of his victims have never been found. He is on a mission to make God sad by killing God's most vulnerable children and he makes no apologies for what he's done. He feels no remorse."

"Do you know what he looks like?" Detective Gignac interrupted.

Madame Sigourney glanced up with a look of patient irritation like a parent listening to the repetitive inane questions of a small child. She then closed her eyes and continued.

"He is a white man with no family. He is of East European decent. As a young adult he changed his name because he was embarrassed by its foreign sound. Tall, slim build with a full head of hair, but he wears a baseball cap or something with a marking on the front. I saw the letter "A". And there's a tattoo or a birthmark on his body which he tries to keep hidden. It's the mark of the devil."

At this Madame Sigourney fell silent. Detective Gignac and Sergeant Wright looked at each other and around the room, then hunched their shoulders simultaneously.

"Well, that's all very interesting Miss Sigourney. Anything else you think we should know?" said Sergeant Wright.

"Yes, the killer is strongly attracted to men."

"What do you mean? That he's a homosexual?"

"Yes, but he doesn't know it himself. That is why he is so angry; why he kills so many men."

When she was finished, Madame Sigourney got up and left with a bow once again to the good Father. Outside the police station a cab waited for her.

"Well, what did you make of that? She had him figured out pretty good don't you think?" said the priest. "You know I didn't want to say anything before hand but Madame Sigourney helped the Niagara police with the Bernardo case. Oh yes, she was the first to suggest that there were two perpetrators involved in the kidnappings and murders and that there were previous victims."

"Wow, that is something," said Detective Gignac with a wry smile on his face. "In this case I'm not sure what she has to offer. Nothing she said has any verifiable validity."

"Really, you think not? What about him being surrounded by people? I'm sure she's referring to a high rise or a development somewhere on the West End, that sun setting thing. And having killed before with some victims as yet unknown, what do you make of that?"

"The chances are he has killed others that we don't know about."

"And the religious stuff. From what I heard in the confessional I figured he was a Catholic for sure. She couldn't have known that."

"With all due respect, she does know you, Father" added Detective Gignac. "You could easily have said something to her by accident or by implication and our killer did murder a man right in St. James Gardens, a logical link to religion and he did seek you out in the confessional at St. Michael's, a Catholic church, your church."

"Gentlemen, forgive me but as officers of the law," continued Father Fitzpatrick, "you are used to dealing in concrete facts, tangible things, elements of the real world. What we have here in Madame Sigourney is a spiritualist, a medium. She is a person who bridges two worlds, one which you know intimately, but the other you admittedly know nothing about. And I think you would have to admit that there is something out there beyond the concrete world of man. After all what is God about if not spirituality? Madame Sigourney appears to be able to tap into that other world. What harm can there be in using the information she uniquely possesses? You ought to check out that bicycle thing and the A on the ball cap, not to mention the tattoos."

Sergeant Wright mollified his clerical companion with the promise to have his detectives look into Madame Sigourney's visions and combine that with the information provided by the government profilers.

"Given all that I'm sure we can come up with some great new leads," he reassured Father FitzPatrick on his way out.

"I'm in plenty of trouble as it is and now I've got to deal with this thunder struck clergyman and his red robed tea leaf reader. Didn't I see a movie about that somewhere, some midget fortune teller," said Sergeant Wright to his partner after the priest had left the room.

"I think that was "The Poltergeist" one of those horror movies."

"This is enough of a horror movie in its own right. I wish I could write myself out of the script."

"Well, you might get your wish. The Chief almost granted it to you this afternoon."

"I'm ready. I'm burnt out. I think the thing that really bugs me is the fact that none of these assholes really gives a shit about the homeless killings, not deep down. The Chief, Donnally, the mayor, even

McGuiness, they've ignored the homeless for years, never had a program to deal with them one way or another. They should have either helped them or kicked them the hell out of the city when they had the chance."

"I prefer the latter approach myself. Mollycoddling these losers is more than I can take," said Detective Gignac. "Only problem with you resigning is that I'm the one they're gonna stick with the case. I'll be the new you. Donnally is too smart to take control because with control comes responsibility and he sure doesn't want that."

"OK then, so let's follow up on this psychic stuff. I want you to put out an all points bulletin looking for a tattooed closet queer Catholic Caucasian wearing a baseball cap with an A on it and riding a bicycle to a nearby community garden with a packsack full of dandelions and a .22 caliber handgun," said Sergeant Wright. "Jesus, at times I feel like just going home and swallowing my gun."

Detective Gignac laughed out loud, "Don't say that, that suicidal stuff. Reminds me of my father. He got himself all depressed one night, after a bit of boozing I might add, and blurted out to his doctor the next day that he was feeling so low he was thinking of just ending it all. So guess what?"

"What?" replied Don Wright with an exaggerated lifting of his eye brows.

"The old man winds up in a mental ward, an involuntary admission. He was so pissed off and humiliated he started ranting and raving proclaiming his innocence and sanity and demanding to be released. Of course, the more he bitched and moaned, the more they figured he really was crazy so they wouldn't let the poor bugger out. Matter of fact, they almost did drive him off the deep end before I finally showed up and arranged for his release. He died six months later."

"Jesus, OK, I'll keep that in mind."

"But what about that gardening stuff she talked about?" added Detective Gignac.

"The guy calls himself the Weed Killer for Christ's sake. It's not a magical leap to figure in gardens and flowers, but that's got nothing to do specifically with weeds in the mouths of victims. If she came up with that, believe me, I'd be listening. Same thing with that cologne he wears. I do think the profilers are right about the BSH sites though. He bit once only, then let it go. Too bad we didn't realize that earlier. Sure would have saved us a lot of grief not to mention an internal police investigation."

"You can thank Three Strike Hudson" for that one,' said Detective Gignac.

"I am convinced of a few other facts. First of all, the guy must live in the West End or the downtown. There's just too much activity centered in those areas. He's familiar with the territory. Also he probably figured, and rightly so, that if he can't clean up the entire City of Toronto he can at least scare the homeless away from his own turf. And he obviously got turned around and disoriented on the East Side because he wasn't sure where the hell he was going. If it hadn't been for that goddamn Bartholomew kid, the mob might have had him.

"Next, the guy must read the *Toronto Star*. With his letters appearing in there and all the stories about him and the editorials I'm sure he can't resist. He's too conceited and wouldn't want to miss even a single issue. So check up on every *Star* subscription that exits in those two areas. Get me a list and another one containing every and all male cancer patients aged forty to sixty who underwent cancer surgery in any Toronto hospital during the past twenty years. Then check out all the Catholic divorces that took place within the same time frame. Again restrict it to the West End and downtown parishes for now. Finally check the gun registry for .22 caliber handgun and track any ammunition purchases over the last year."

"Seems like a hell of a lot of work. What's it gonna tell us when it's all said and done?"

"You know Steve, this is unfortunately what police work is all about; checking mundane details and sometimes going with hunches. In New York City you know how they finally caught the notorious Son of Sam Killer?

Detective Gignac shook his head.

"They matched a parking ticket to the time and place of one of the homicides. Bang. Sam Berkowitz. Who would have figured? So let's get going with all this stuff, even if we've been over the territory before and see where it takes us. I want the names of anyone who appears on those lists. Get Hudson and the guys on it right away."

"There's one other thing about this guy," added Detective Gignac as he turned to leave the room.

"What's that?" asked Sergeant Wright.

"He's lucky, goddamn plain lucky, but one day his luck will run out and everything will fall into place and we'll get him."

For now Sergeant Wright kept the idea of the jazz lyrics in the Weed Killer's correspondence to himself. He figured it would be best if there was some information, some insight, that he alone possessed and which he could pull out later if the going got any rougher with his superiors.

"Any rougher road than this and it'll bounce me right through the roof and out of a job."

chapter 23

ALBERT RE-READ HIS latest missive to the *Toronto Star* before mailing it out.

"I must say that I get jealous when I look at Mary Monticello and her Parkdale neighbors and all the love and concern they show for one another. Congratulations! And because of my admiration I am declaring Parkdale a neutral ground. From now on no homeless person will be harassed in Parkdale. It is off my target list. Everyone there is safe and you can all thank Mary Monticello for this turn of events. Mary did it. Hurray for Mary."

Signed,

The Weed Killer"

"There sweet Mary, I've put a spell on you, but you don't know it yet. This should feed your ego long enough to distract you. Good luck and good morning heartache," Albert chuckled as he sat in his kitchen drinking a cup of coffee and reading the paper, the *Star* of course.

"I should change the wallpaper in here. Maureen picked this out. I never noticed how ugly it was until now. I deserve something new and better in keeping with my new elevated station in life. Perhaps I should renovate the entire house, new paint jobs in the rooms, new furniture, how about a mirror on the ceiling in the bedroom? Yes, Claudia would go for that, I think, although she has been acting a bit moody of late. Must be that time of month. Women!"

***

If his value at work had deteriorated to junk status, at least Sergeant Wright went home feeling better about his welcome within the family. Although he was still in deep shit with his daughter who point blank refused to even be in the same room with him, his wife had certainly come around and forgiven him.

"And mother and daughter have found each other again," Don sighed, "That's something in itself. At least I can take credit for that."

Don was unexpectedly greeted at the front door by Sharon, a welcome surprise, but there was clearly something wrong. His wife was hysterical. Tears ran down her face when she tried to speak.

"She, she's not here, Meaghan. I think she's run away. I've called all, all her friends. She wasn't at Amber's last night. Never showed up. Never intended to I guess from what Amber said."

"Just don't tell me she's with that loser, Johnny Cool. That son of a bitch I should have shot him in our doorway when I had the chance."

"She's been skipping school too. Probably meeting up with him and since he doesn't go to school God knows where they're hanging out or what they're doing."

"He don't live at home no more either," Josh put in half sobbing. "I wasn't supposed to say nothing. He and some friends live under the Bathurst Bridge. They got like a fort there."

"My God, is Meaghan with them?"

"I don't know, but she was planning to run away with Johnny. He's the only one who understands her and loves her too, she said, but I didn't want to hear all that mushy stuff so I didn't listen no more."

"Son of a bitch," Sergeant Wright turned on his heels and headed back out the door.

"I'm going with you," shouted his wife.

"No way. I've got the police car."

"She won't come to you, so you may as well forget about going alone."

"Can I come?" asked Josh.

The looks from both parents at the same time gave Josh his answer without a word being spoken.

"Jesus Christ, I don't get to do nothing around here."

"Watch your language," warned Sharon as she closed the door behind her. "Stay home and lock the doors."

chapter 24

ELDRIDGE JOHNS MOVED into the Monticellos' basement apartment. The man had no possessions other than a large packsack filled with clothes, a few snacks and a bottle of Tabasco sauce.

"Kills the flavor of stuff that's maybe gone a little bad and ain't too good tasting, eh. And I want to thank the two of yous for being so good to me," said Eldridge to his hosts. "I heard about good people like yous, but I never met any till now. Thanks."

"We're glad to help our neighbors, and here in Parkdale everyone is a neighbor," said Mary. "But remember, you have a shower and I laid out some of our older towels that you can use. They're still plenty fluffy and they've all been cleaned."

"I never was one for washing up," admitted Eldridge. "Not much water available on the streets and when it's winter out, well you know. Plus I don't got a lot of extra clothes."

"There's plenty of hot water here so you just help yourself," said Mary with a sick smile on her face.

"And I've got some clothes that I think will fit you too," added Bob. "Those you got on I think it would be best if you just threw them out."

"But I'm pretty fond of these duds. They're good; tough fabric, you know. I feel comfortable in them. I don't really want to get rid of all my stuff."

"Well, if you'll just throw them out in the hall there," suggested Mary. "I'll wash them up for you and give them right back. In the meantime, you can wear Bob's old stuff. You wouldn't want to dirty up all the nice clean sheets and furniture we've got down here for you, would you now?"

Eldridge gave them a look that indicated he didn't much care about the quality or state of the furniture. Not that he was malicious. It just didn't mean anything to him.

172

"And there's a few groceries in the cupboards and in the refrigerator to get you started," said Bob.

"I don't know too much about buying or cooking no food either. I usually don't eat no breakfast and go to the free lunches over at the Salvation Army or St. Christopher's and once in a while there at Osgood Hall too. After that, at night, I just eat whatever I can get my hands on."

"I can take you shopping until you get the hang of things on your own. There's a No Frills Store on Dundas," said Bob. "That's probably your best bet. Sometimes we've got more than we need upstairs and Mary's used to feeding three. Once in a while we can have you .. ."

Mary shot Bob with a look that could wilt fresh cabbage.

"What Bob means is that once in a while we can send something down for you. Then you can eat it at your leisure, whenever you want."

"That would be real nice 'cause like I said I ain't so good at cooking stuff." It was evident that Eldridge had not made the best of first impressions. Still Mary was not discouraged. She was focused on a new column idea based on the best seller "Evenings with Morley". Yes, she thought, could be a weekend feature in the Saturday or Sunday edition. "Evenings with Eldridge". Good ring to that. Might also work itself up into a book deal. Yes, that was certainly a possibility.

"It's a fine thing you're doing," said a neighbor during that first week as Mary left the house for work at the *Star* office. "I don't think I could do it myself, mind you. Me and Diane we value our privacy too much. But good luck to you and Bob and if you need anything let us know."

"Anybody else on the block take in a homeless person?" asked Mary.

"Not that I know of, No. Over on Trenton Terrace I heard there's one family took in a homeless lady. There's some talk that the city is supposed to remodel the old Britain Building and turn it into low cost apartments. There's going to be a meeting about that and other ideas at the end of the month. Government is stepping up to the plate with some long term plans to get new housing started. Guess your pressure is adding up to some real changes."

"Just doing what I can," replied Mary with a self satisfied smile.

Mary and Bob had to purchase an addition garbage can to accommodate their new tenant.

Bob wasn't particularly pleased with the run around he got from the city. "Do they really care about someone having too many garbage cans? By the time I get this resolved Eldridge will be long gone, or he better be."

When Mary read the Weed Killer's letter, the one declaring Parkdale a no kill zone and praising its residents in general and Mary in particular for their sense of civic responsibility, she was delighted and perversely proud. She did not fully comprehend its repercussions. Then the homeless started showing up, lots of homeless.

"What's going on?" Mary asked Eldridge one day as they stood outside of Jason's Coffee Shop on Queen Street and noticed a large crowd milling around on both sides of the street.

"Holy shit," said Eldridge suddenly. "There's Marty and Booger Tommy over at the Queen Street Coffee Shop. Hey. Marty, you old cock sucker! I used to hang around with them after I lost my apartment. Hey! They had a real neat little lean-to set up over behind the Arts Building on Queen. Real cozy inside, made out of fiberglass panels, eh. When the sun would shine, it would just glow all green and yellow, cheerful as hell and warm too. Had one a them old time kerosene stoves in there for the winter. Got it from some railroad guys, eh, and let me tell you, when they say kerosene, they mean kerosene.

"Booger Tommy one day he got a hold of some white gas, naphtha gas, that they use in them Coleman lanterns, eh. He was a little hammered up and didn't read the label or probably wouldn't a known the difference anyway. Fuck, blew the door and top right off that stove and sent them flying threw those fiberglass panels like they was tissue paper. Yeah, them two were great guys. Took me in no questions asked, eh. I'm going over to say hello."

"I won't bother to ask you how he got his name," Mary stammered after Eldridge crossed the street. As she stood there bewildered someone else called out to Mary.

"It's the Weed Killer."

"What? They got him?" asked Mary, disoriented at first.

"No, fuck no. He's responsible for this. Said Parkdale was goal. He won't touch no homeless persons here, eh. Everybody's safe so everybody's moving to Parkdale. It's the promised land."

"Yeah, Mary, ain't you Mary Monticello? I seen your picture in the papers. We can thank you for this," added a ragged passerby. "We're free. Free at last. Thank God Almighty, we're free at last."

The next week showed the full extent of that freedom as almost every vacant lot in Parkdale, every inch of alley space, every parking and vacant lot was filled with the homeless. Tent cities sprang up everywhere. Lean-tos and cardboard structures appeared behind businesses and warehouses. Any vacant structure became an instant apartment building.

The city and charitable groups set up soup kitchens in former construction offices and bus shelters. Food trucks were virtually bumper to bumper along the streets both day and night giving out sandwiches, fresh fruit, and juice boxes and water bottles. Litter was knee deep and dogs barked throughout the night. Police officers were pulled from other parts of the city to maintain law and order and direct traffic which often came to a complete stand still with scooters, shopping carts, wagons and myriad make shift vehicles pulled by the combined homeless of Toronto flooding the streets.

"My God, what in the hell has happened to our beloved Parkdale? It looks like a war zone," said Bob as he accompanied Mary to an emergency meeting at the Parkdale Mission on Queen Street West. The public assembly had originally been designated as an information session to discuss the Ontario government's new strategy to combat homelessness in the city. Now it refocused on the emergency situation in Parkdale.

"My God," gasped Mary. "Where on the Lord's green earth did all these dogs come from? Bob I'm afraid. They look vicious as hell and half of them aren't on leashes."

"The homeless," replied Bob. "A lot of them have dogs for protection, and when the Weed Killer came around, well, that many more people got them. They're here now thanks in large part to you."

"Please," replied Mary. "That's not my fault."

"Some people will say it is. You know, Mary, sometimes it's not a bad idea to adopt a low profile. You don't have to be out there front and center all the time."

Just then a large pit bull ran past the couple and attacked a miniature poodle being walked by Mrs. Ferguson, their neighbor from the corner. The poor woman shrieked and tried to pull her pet free, but the weight of the two tangled dogs stiffened the leather leash into solid resistance. When it was finally free, there was only a disembodied dog's head attached to it. Mrs. Ferguson leaned against a nearby street light in a faint.

"Fluffy," she whimpered. "Fluffy."

"Goddamn it, Balls," shouted a bedraggled man running up and kicking at the pit bull.

"What the fuck is wrong with you? Heel. I told you to heel, you cock sucker."

The man turned to Mary and her husband. Mrs. Ferguson had already wilted to the ground.

"Don't worry. Don't worry," the man said to them. "He's real good with people, eh. He just hates other animals. Bad dog, Balls. Bad, mother fucker."

"Where am I?" asked Mary. "What planet is this?"

Mary helped Mrs. Ferguson to her feet while Bob discreetly kicked Fluffy's bloodied head out into the street, hiding it behind the curb to spare the poor woman another look at her mangled pet.

"I'll take Mrs. Ferguson home," said Bob. "You go to the meeting yourself." It was a good idea that Bob did not attend because the bitterness against his wife was on open display and his protective instincts may have gotten him into unwanted trouble with his neighbors.

"There's that bitch now, Mrs. Good Samaritan. Happy with the way things turned out?"

"Yeah, Parkdale's a shining example of all that's good in Toronto. We can't even walk down the streets anymore. Where the hell are we supposed to put all these people?"

The police and government representatives at the meeting were overwhelmed. It was impossible to establish any order. Sergeant Wright was the first to try.

"Please, ladies and gentlemen, let's get organized here. Let's work together. We have a common problem that needs solution."

"You got a problem and a big one," someone in the crowd shouted back. "And if you can't figure out what to do, we will."

People who fought for and at least momentarily grabbed the microphones set up on each side of the room shouted different points of view.

"We've got to help these people. We've got them all together. Let's do something."

"We got them all together, yeah, but they're all together in Parkdale. Other people live here too, eh, tax payers, law abiding citizens."

"We love Parkdale," shouted a homeless man. "If the government would just give us a helping hand, eh, I'm sure we wouldn't mind living here permanent."

"A permanent army of the homeless! Just what we need."

"There are plenty of empty buildings here that could easily be fixed up to house these poor people and it would create jobs in Parkdale. We could use jobs here and even put some of these poor people to work. It would be a win win."

"Hey, wait a minute now. I didn't come here for no work. Forget that shit."

"We already got the nut house on Queen Street. Parkdale will be turned into a wasteland of poverty and lunacy. No self respecting citizen will want to live here. We'll never be able to sell our homes. They'll be worthless."

"If you cops had done your job and caught the Weed Killer, none of this would have happened."

The catcalls that had greeted Mary upon entering discouraged her from taking a seat. Instead she elected to position herself at the back of the room near an exit. She also spotted her editor, Karen French, standing there. Karen motioned her over and together they withdrew to the adjacent hallway out of the view of the assembly.

"Jesus, I actually feel sorry for poor Sergeant Wright up there," said Karen. "He looks beaten. My last editorial hit him pretty hard before we switched our focus to the overall housing issue. Now that doesn't look good either. The government is taking back its latest commitments to us because of this new crisis in Parkdale. Said they're putting all their attention and resources here. We're finished before we even got started. I can't believe it. It's happening again. And you, Jesus, you must be going crazy living here. It's a madhouse."

"I'm shaking. I don't recognize the place anymore. These aren't Parkdale people. They're, they're animals. They have no respect for others. None. Sunday I was at Jameson and King Street. The usual Parkdale people were out holding their little garage sales, you know, all kinds of stuff set up on the ground and on tables. They sold lemonade and other drinks too. A little street party. Have it every weekend, sometimes more often. I was looking through some stuff, just being friendly 'cause it's a chance to chat and learn what's going on in the neighborhood, eh. I don't think a lot of people actually buy stuff. Then suddenly a crowd of, of idiots comes swushing through like a tsunami just grabbing stuff, knocking tables over, and stealing everything. There were so many of them we couldn't stop them. When they were gone, there was nothing left. It was like locusts had descended on a cornfield. We all stood there with our mouths open. It was terrible, terrible!"

"I'll walk you home after the meeting. Some of these people, I swear, they must have just been let out of the Addiction Center on a day pass. They're completely unreasonable and hostile."

"So, all your, our plans?"

"Gone."

"The homeless march that Kristen and Don were organizing? Wasn't it this past weekend? I couldn't attend. I apologize, but Bob and I were having an argument with our new tenant. He had invited a couple of his homeless chums to move into our apartment and stay with him. They were a miserable lot I must say. Filthy and I'm sure they were just crawling with bedbugs. I had to call 911."

"Wasn't he the homeless guy you were going to profile in a new column? We talked about it, I remember."

"Yeah, but you can forget that now. The man is impossible to reason with and he can't remember anything. What he can recall is useless trivia. It's amazing. You know I was hoping to gather some insights with this guy, sort of lessons of life that we could share with my readers. Warm human stories that would move others to sympathy and then action. God, was I ever naïve. He's still living at our place, but we did manage to get the others tossed out before they could get comfortable. Poor Bob. I talked him into the whole thing. Now it's turned into a disaster."

"The march turned into a disaster as well," said Karen French. "We should have cancelled it. The Weed Killer had just made his announcement which, of course, we promptly printed in the *Star*. As a result every goddamn homeless person within the GTA was here in Parkdale and not at Queen's Park for our rally. Talk about irony. That letter sabotaged not only the march, but our entire agenda. The homeless were safe so they didn't care anymore. A lot of organizations backed out too: the Coalition Against Homelessness, Citizens Fighting Poverty, the Committee Against Unfair Housing Practices, Citizens Against Poverty, Co-op Housing Tenants for Fairness in Housing, and the Anti-Poverty League, amongst a half dozen other groups. So we had only a few activists left. John and Kristen were there and Janet Lockhart from the old Ten-in-Two Committee. The government had a fence set up around Queen's Park so all we did was march within the perimeter and chant a few slogans. It was embarrassingly pathetic really. I'm beginning to wonder about the efficacy of these marches anyway. I mean, what do they accomplish? They're so ineffective, so innocuous that even the government doesn't really worry about them. They give us a permit, set up a speaker's corner and even designate a safe little marching route, and off we go. Little wind up robots. Have a good time. It's ridiculous, just a way to let off some steam."

"And what happened to the interview with the Afghan war vets over at High Park? I didn't see a thing on TV. Did I miss that too?"

"No, McGuiness sent his Minister of Culture and Community Affairs, Bitterman, personally out to High Park with a camera crew and offered the poor down and out bastards temporary jobs with Toronto Parks. Said that the minute he was made aware of the situation he rushed right over to help "our valued veterans". Made a big deal out of it."

"Thank God I missed that one. I would have thrown up," replied Mary.

"Yeah, the Parkdale sanctuary that the Weed Killer declared has ruined everything. Funny, but I never saw it coming. Tuesday we got a notice from the Premier's office telling us that all our latest requests were unattainable in light of this emergency in Parkdale. Beyond that there's no money, nada, they said so don't even bother asking for any. Now there's talk of bringing in the army to restore order."

"Great, military brutally coming up. The homeless are going to get it one way or another. Anyway, you know I wasn't crazy about the approach you and the others were taking," Mary continued. "I like my way better. It's not dependent on collective action so it's more likely to succeed."

"Maybe you're right, but it's a better bet we're all doomed. The other day I was looking through the *Star's* archives," replied Karen. "Over the years, and I'm going back decades now, the paper has run article after article after series of articles defining and attacking the poverty problem. There's a long list of writers and editors who fought the good fight in the past. How noble I thought at the time, but you know what? I'm not so sure now. The same issues keep coming up again and again throughout all those years. I could have taken any one of those articles, updated the wording, stripped out the colloquialisms, and republished the article today and it would be just as relevant because bloody well nothing substantial has changed. We haven't learned a thing. We are wasting our time with these stupid, useless reforms and petitions to the government. They're all meaningless."

Mary and Karen stuck their heads back in the meeting room as order was finally restored. Mayor Milne had the floor. The crowd quieted.

"Ladies and Gentlemen, this sudden and overwhelming influx of migrant homeless people into Parkdale has created an emergency situation unparalleled in our city's history and certainly one which none of us could have foreseen. Immediately prior to this crisis and spurred on by the tragic killings our city had witnessed I along with Premier McGuiness and representatives of the federal government had been tirelessly working together and with numerous volunteer groups on programs and plans for the relief of our current housing problem and for concrete steps to help alleviate poverty in this city and province. These were well thought out, long term, incremental steps aimed at measurable poverty reduction. Unfortunately, those ambitious plans must be put on hold in order for us to tackle this new emergency. I ask for those of you who have worked hard and were optimistic for new government action on the poverty issue to step back and give us time to handle this new problem. After that I can assure all of you that we as your government will refocus and dedicate our time and energies, and yes, money to tackle the poverty and housing problems head on and end them once and for all. Thank you.

"Now Minister Bitterman will outline the measures just put in place to combat this dangerous over crowding situation here in Parkdale. Please pay attention and don't be alarmed. Most of these measures will be temporary in nature."

"I give up," Karen French said. "It's useless. I feel like going out on the streets away from Parkdale somewhere, dressing in rags, and lying down in a sleeping bag and having the Weed Killer shoot me. The hell with it all."

On her way out of the building, a black woman caught Mary's eye. She looked familiar in appearance to the mother of one of her former student charges, a young boy named Anquin Jeffreys. Of course, after a while those women all looked the same, Mary mused, not in a stereotyped manner because of their color or race, no nothing as superficial as that. They all looked the same because they all came from that same crowded cesspool of poverty which gave them a trademarked appearance of hang dog despair and vacant eyed hopelessness.

She remembered those past evenings with Anquin's mother lingering nearby during the study sessions. The woman, captivated by curiosity, but held back by shame and pride was herself illiterate and beyond schooling. Burdened with the simple task of survival she could do nothing to help her son and precious little to aid herself. Anquin had great difficulty with his studies. He struggled mightily despite Mary's almost desperate efforts to help and encourage him.

"Yes, Anquin, at least you've begun to write in simple, straight forward sentences, and your spelling has gotten better, a lot better."

Anquin was in Grade 10, but reading at the equivalent level of a Fifth Grader. His comprehension was virtually non-existent and his math skills worse. To even call them skills was comparable to calling finger painting, fine art. But that did little to deter Mary.

"If you can reach even one child," Mary said, "that is an accomplishment to be proud of. You can build on that. One student at a time, one small step at a time. It may not look like you've moved forward a whole lot until you look back to where you came from. Then you realize, yes, this is progress. We're making real progress."

That progress came to a halt when Anquin was shot dead during some misunderstanding over a pair of sneakers. Mary remembered walking through the Lost Park Projects after leaving Anquin's mother's apartment that fateful day. She looked around at the youth who threw worn basketballs at netless hoops on the broken courtyards, the boys who dealt drugs, teased the girls in their youth then raped them later in life, stole money and clothes, intimidated, lied, and survived. Above all they survived. It was a tough life.

Mary saw a world of Anquins around her that day of sadness and for a brief moment even she despaired as she did once again this day observing the woman leaving the Parkdale Mission.

chapter 25

RONNIE BARTHOLOMEW WHITTLED down his active Weed Killer posse to three members, a more manageable number. "We can't take the chance of any snitches popping up in our gang, squealing. With too many guys involved it's hard to keep control."

"Nobody's gonna snitch. It's against the club code, and they know the consequences," said Ronnie's second in command, a boy named Darren.

"I'm with Darren. We ain't got no tattle tales in our gang," said Cory, the last of the triumvirate.

"That's good and you guys have to remember," said Ronnie, "we're Canadians. We got rights. You don't have to talk to no cops about nothing even if they arrest you, especially if they arrest you. My dad told me all about it. Trouble is people don't know their rights and start spilling the beans. The criminals, they been through all that before, and got friends that know all the legal shit too, so they get off. It's us poor, average, law abiding citizens that get the shaft.

"So, the fewer the better now that we're gonna ratchet up the action. I don't know about you, but I'm tired of just whacking these guys and scaring them off only for them to come back later on. We got to send a real message, some serious shit's got to go down otherwise we ain't nothing but a bunch of loud mouths, beating up on a few drunks and homeless losers."

"What you talking about?"

Darren nudged Cory with his elbow. "He's talking about finishing off one of these assholes, not just roughing them up. And I'm with you, Ronnie boy."

"Hey, let's not get too carried away, eh. We beat the shit out of a couple of them bastards. One guy was even in the hospital for three days. That's a good enough lesson if you ask me."

"Wow, golly, in the hospital, ain't that something," replied Ronnie. "How about we aim a little higher next time, like the morgue. I know the Weed Killer. He's a man of action, not talk. He was right here in this yard telling me how it's done, the thrill of the kill, and all kinds of shit like that, eh. He was talking to me, up close and personal and all the time them bastards were out hunting him and we stood here talking for probably twenty minutes. He was cool, relaxed, never worried. It was like we was chatting about the Leafs or a Blue Jays' game."

"Man, that's awesome."

"That was when he gunned down that pack of bastards at Allan Gardens, eh? I heard they all jumped him, but he fucking fought them off, then shot everyone of the cock suckers. The police said he shot one, but I heard they covered up the fact that there were really six killed. He's a crack shot, eh. One homeless loser for each bullet he had. I asked him what it was like, to kill somebody, eh," continued Ronnie.

"Fuck man, I wish I had been there at the time. What he say? What he say?"

"He said it was a thrill of a lifetime. Ain't nothing like it in the world. So that's what I want now, man. I want that thrill, eh."

"Yeah, dude, me too. I'm with you. Awesome shit."

"That's what turned me on to the Club idea. The guy's a fucking hero; fighting for the little guys like you and me and our parents who got to put up with all these losers shitting up our neighborhoods. If the cops can't or won't do nothing, then the little man has to take things into his own hands."

"Hey, you guys, I don't want to kill nobody. Go that far."

"Well then, Cory, when we get to the Gardens you can stand guard at the north end and keep a look out for us, or you can sneak off into a dark corner somewhere and jerk off. Then you won't know nothing about nothing happening."

"Just stay alert," added Darren reassuringly. "You'll be alright. Just text us if the cops or somebody's coming our way. Me and Ronnie will go through the park and check things out."

Ronnie and Darren walked through Allen Gardens. The park was quiet.

"Everybody's fucking over at Parkdale" said Darren. "That's where we should go. The losers are piled up there like cigarette butts in front of the Crazy House.

"No way, man. That's off limits. You read that letter. The Weed Killer declared Parkdale a no kill zone so we got to respect his wishes. You got to go by the rules, otherwise it's just anarchy. That's what the Killer told me himself."

"OK, man, I'm with you. And, hey, what we gonna do if we find somebody here, a fucking loser to knock off? We ain't got nothing to kill him with."

"We didn't bring nothing on purpose, remember? Carrying weapons around is dangerous. It's visible, dude. It's clues and tells the cops we got a premeditated motive. We just use something laying around. That way if we get caught we can say that the guy jumped us, eh, that we had to fight for our lives. It was fucking him or us. We had no choice. Now keep an eye out. Like that over there. That tree's got some dead limbs and these benches they often got a loose seat board or a railing. We can pry those free and use them like clubs."

"Awesome, man."

***

Albert had been aware of the homeless activity under the Bathurst Bridge for a long time and he seethed with indignation over it. "The sons of bitches, right under my nose, right in the middle of my no fly zone and that despite my fucking generosity in declaring Parkdale a free base for the homeless. That isn't enough? I haven't done enough to be reasonable? Do stars fall on Alabama? It's an insult. Do you know who I am? Do you know who you're dealing with?"

One dark night Albert settled down next to the ember glow of a dying fire under that very Bathurst Street Bridge. He stoked the fire to life with wood from broken palettes and scrap lumber piled nearby and obviously scavenged from the adjacent construction site at Concorde City Place. He deposited his .22 revolver, loaded and wrapped in a plastic bag, under a rock at his side. If the cops came, he'd pretend to be homeless himself. He left all his ID at home. Then they'd just hustle him off, warning him for his own safety. The cops, such stupidity. They were no match for him. It wasn't long before a group of youths arrived from along the well worn pathway. They gave Albert a quick look over before figuring an old man like that had to be homeless himself and harmless. He didn't fit the Killer's profile recently posted around town and flashed across every bar and restaurant screen in the area. Albert himself took the precaution of stealthily grabbing his gun back from its hiding place and putting it under his shirt as he sat on the edge of darkness watching the youngsters settle a bit uneasily around the fire.

"When I was a kid," he told them in an effort to ease their suspicions. "Me and my friends, we built forts out in the fields. Lots of open fields and vacant lots back then, eh. And we'd make fires and roast potatoes. Yeah, let the fire die down and flip the potatoes into the coals and bury them. Then we chatted and joked around and told ghost stories. If we forgot about the potatoes, they'd burn down to a little cinder with a nugget of nice white hot potato flesh in the middle. If we watched what we were doing, we'd be rewarded with a virtual meal. Yes, summer time and the livin was easy. Ha, I remember Mike Stakowski, he'd bring salt and butter out with him. Me, I kind of thought that spoiled it a bit. Too sophisticated. By the way, what are you kids doing out here alone? Don't you know there's a killer on the loose in the city?"

There were four of them, youngsters, but weeds nonetheless figured Albert as he eyed the group up across the light of the fire. Seedlings that would grow into noxious adult plants if given the chance. He had seen too many of them throughout the summer season and he knew he'd have no qualms about killing them. After all, a weed was a weed.

"Speak for yourself, old man. Why should we worry?" said one boy who seemed to be the ringleader of the group. "There's four of us, and we got knifes and clubs. You're the one who should worry."

There was a slight tone of menace in the youth's voice which Albert was quick to note. Two girls were paired with the boys. One couple looked familiar, but in the darkness it was hard to tell exactly where he had seen them before. The girl was twinkling with body rings, studs and earrings. She had numerous tattoos on her amply exposed flesh.

"What me worry?" said Albert with a grin. "I don't think anyone is going to bother me although I've had my share of hard luck and sorrow. For a while everything bad seemed to happen to me, but I got my life straightened around. It's got a purpose now. I feel better."

"Yeah, it looks like you're straightened around sure enough," laughed one of the boys who opened four beers from a six pack and passed them around, not offering any to Albert. They talked amongst themselves.

"That's OK," Albert said in jest. "I don't drink."

"We've got almost enough money to travel west right now," said the dark garbed leader. "Don't want to drag our asses here in Toronto because of Meaghan's old man, eh, Mr. Detective. Hey old man," the boy turned towards Albert. "Did you know that you're in the company of a important person, almost a celebrity? Yeah, this here is Meaghan Wright, baby daughter of the one and only Sergeant Wright, the Weed Killer hunter except he don't hunt too good. He'll be out looking for her so tomorrow morning it's hasta la vista, baby."

He returned his attention to his friends.

"When this old codger leaves, and I sure hope he leaves soon, we can take our spots high up on the side of the bridge. That way we can watch if anyone comes around. Put out the fire too. Meaghan and me will sleep together. Hope we don't keep you up."

Albert noted that Meaghan looked rather meek and afraid.

"Yeah, but after that we switch off," said the other boy. "Remember, share and share alike."

"Oh, I like that," said the tattooed girl. "Johnny Cool for me."

"Hey," said Meaghan pleadingly to the leader. "I don't want nobody but you Johnny. I thought you loved me. I don't want to be with him. I want you, only you. I love you."

"Hey, Randy's my number one. We're all in this together. Don't worry. You'll get used to it."

"And more too," said the other girl. "We don't get enough money begging then you and me got to do what it takes."

"What it takes?"

The other three laughed before Johnny Cool spoke up.

"Don't rush her guys. She's cool. She'll do what she's told," and he gave the girl Meaghan a playful but strong slap on the face. The girl started to sob. When her companions turned their attention to the old man, she quickly reached her hand into her purse, then pulled it out again.

"That's really no way to treat a lady," said Albert. "You kids going out west to work? Out in the oil fields maybe? I might be heading there myself. Lots of jobs."

"We ain't kids and we ain't going no where to work, Grandpa. Working is for losers. We're going to form a band. Get some money and buy a couple of guitars and a drum kit. I'm good with computers so we can cut our own CDs."

"Yeah, I don't need much to keep me going. I got my bitch to do the dirty work," added the other boy.

"Rebels, eh," said Albert. "I remember those days, days of rebellion, the anti-war movement, protest songs, fight the system, Uncle Charley. I got a buddy who's still in the trenches even after all these years."

"You are crazy, old man. That's a stupid waste of time. If it don't help you personally, don't do it. What's the point? You only live once."

"Hey mister," said the tattooed girl to Albert. "Tell us one of them ghost stories you said you used to tell around the camp fire when you were a kid. You remember any of them? I like ghost stories."

"That's for babies. Make believe stuff," said the boy, Randy.

"Still, it would be fun. It's dark. Kind of spooky, eh?"

"Well, OK then," replied Albert recognizing the couple now as the squeegee kids he had met on his way to the Spit earlier in the summer. The girl had jumped in his car beside him. "Once upon a time..."

"I love stories that begin like that, once upon a time," said the girl. "They don't tell stories like that no more."

"Good thing too," said Johnny Cool. "Old fashioned bullshit."

"Anyway, once upon a time," continued Albert. "A group of homeless young friends was sitting around a campfire just like this one. It was in a deserted place along a dark railroad track kind of like the setting here. In the distance the outline of buildings could be seen with their dark, silent windows staring out like lifeless, hollow eyes. Cats yowled in the blackness and in the distance dogs were barking and a far off train whistled mournfully in the night, the Night Train. The Night Train comes again."

The youngsters instinctively turned their heads in the direction of a lonely whistle that sounded almost in sync with the man's story. Johnny got up and threw some wood on the fire making it flare up momentarily in a shower of sparks one of which landed on his bare arm.

"Ouch," he winced brushing it off quickly.

"Play with fire till your fingers burn, but when you've got no where else to turn, don't go to strangers. Come to me."

The youngsters all looked back at Albert who was now smiling at them.

"Ask not for whom the bell tolls," Albert added then continued with his story. "Even though summer was still upon them it somehow felt cold so the friends huddled together and moved closer to the fire trying to keep warm sort of like you're doing now. Then a silence fell over the group like a funeral shroud dropping over a pale corpse, and the flames of the fire drooped as though doused with a cold mist. The moaning of the wind picked up and a feeling of foreboding came over the group.

"They looked at each other as if for the first time and each wondered to himself just what they were doing there in that desolate place with no prospects for the future, no hopes, and no dreams. And then they noticed for the first time a man standing in the shadows just beyond the light of the fire. He was very tall and old and quiet like a statue draped in worn clothing. A stranger in the night. His hands were hidden behind his back."

"Like you?" laughed Randy nervously.

"Yes," said Albert standing up. "Exactly like me."

"Where you from anyway?' asked Johnny Cool. "You from Toronto?"

"That's the same question one of the boys asked in the story," continued Albert mixing the present situation with the past time of the tale.

"'No,' the man replied. 'I came in with the wind.'"

"'And it's a goddamn cold wind too,' said one of the lads.'"

"'The wayward wind,' the man said. 'They say that the devil rides on the wayward wind.'"

"Ha, yeah, that's a good one," the tattooed girl said nervously. "But Jesus, I'm freezing. It don't seem like it should be so cold, but I'm freezing here."

"It's always cold when you die," Albert replied.

"Don't talk stupid, old man," Randy interjected. "You're scaring the girls with your bull shit talk."

"Too late for that," replied Albert. "It tolls for thee."

"You're crazy, you old bastard."

"Is, is this part of the story?" asked Meaghan standing up and looking around. "What? I mean who's telling this?"

"The friends tried to get up, but somehow they couldn't move," Albert continued in the confused time frame of his story. "The girls began to cry because deep inside they knew what the old man was going to do. They had suspected it the minute he showed up. They felt it in their hearts and souls. Their bones ached with the emptiness and cold of their coming deaths."

"I felt the same way when I saw you here," shouted the tattooed girl pointing at Albert. "I swear I did. The cold because you're him ain't you. You're him! The Weed Killer!"

Albert pulled the gun out from under his shirt. He shot Johnny Cool and the other boy first, twice each, then the tattooed girl who sat with her mouth wide open and her hands hiding her eyes sobbing uncontrollably. Meaghan stood up disoriented and terrified.

"What, what's happening? Why? Who? Mister, no, no. Don't. Hey, Johnny, Johnny was right. My daddy is a policeman. If you hurt me, he'll get you. He will. You better not hurt me. I want my mommy, my daddy. Please."

"Shut up," and Albert threw her on the ground next to the three others. "Keep your face down in the dirt and don't look up at me or make a sound."

Albert then walked across the bodies of Johnny Cool and Randy and the tattooed girl and put an extra bullet in their heads. He holstered his gun and turned away for a few minutes. When he returned, he kicked Meaghan onto her backside and threw three uprooted weeds at her feet.

"Get up and stuff them into the mouths of your friends."

Meaghan broke down crying, trembling and shaking her head.

"No, no! My God, you killed them. They never did nothing to you and you just killed them. My daddy…"

"I don't give a flying fuck about your old man except he's got my sympathy for having a moron like you for a daughter. Now do as I say or I'll dig up a fourth weed for your benefit. Hurry up."

Meaghan was crying and vomiting as she groped with her eyes closed for the twisted mouths of her dead companions. With each insertion of a weed she squealed in revulsion and helpless despair. Then a phone rang, the distant sound coming from the ground, the girl's purse.

Meaghan turned and frantically lunged for the handbag. Albert beat her to it and, pulling his hand inside his sleeve, lifted out the cell phone.

"Meaghan? Well, no, I'm sorry but Meaghan's busy right now. Oh, correction, I see she's done. Just stuffed that last weed in her boyfriend's bloody mouth. You may talk to her now. Here, here she is."

"Daddy, daddy, help me. He, he, killed everybody; Johnny and the, the others. They're all dead. He shot them. Just shot them. Help me. Daddy help. I'm sorry. I'm so sorry."

Albert took the phone out of the girl's hand and gave her a slap.

"Just a little discipline," he said to Sergeant Wright on the cell phone. "Something you should have done long ago. Now don't get all excited. I've got a little proposition for you. It will probably help both of us because I'm sure by now you're just as fed up dealing with me as I am with you. So I figure we can have a little pact, just the two of us. Ain't nobody's business if we do, eh. I understand that you're a man of your word. I've heard you say that on more than one occasion so the deal goes like this.

"Right now your idiot daughter is staring at the barrel of my gun. All I have to do is pull the trigger, jam a weed in her bloody mouth and make this trio here laying at my feet a quartet. No problem. But, and this is a big but, so think it over, but I'll forego the pleasure in exchange for your pledge to quit this case, resign from the Toronto police force and in your retirement offer no assistance of any kind to your former police officer friends. I know you cops have kept some evidence to yourselves like the weed situation and that body I dumped in the lake at the Red Path Sugar refinery. I haven't seen anything in the media about either of those. You're obviously up to something significant so it can only help my cause if you, as the head honcho, step out of the picture.

"I know you don't have any choice at this moment. Nevertheless, I'm doing you a favor out of good faith and my own free will. Later the burden will fall on you to keep your part of the bargain. So when you have your daughter back in your arms, remember this moment and how helpless you were and how I saved you and your family. That will be the true test of your promise because a bargain with the Devil is still a bargain. Alright then, and good-bye Sergeant, I hope we don't meet again."

"Now be still," he cautioned Meaghan as he tossed the phone into the fire. "Your father, along with every cop in the city, is out looking for you. They'll be here shortly."

Albert hesitated a moment and looked down at the girl whose face was wet with tears and softly illuminated by the adjacent fire. She was quite beautiful with a turned up nose and bright blue eyes. "Say hello to him for me and remind him he owes me one for sparing his little pug nose dream and while you're at it you can thank your pretty polka dots and moonbeams that you still have a home to go to."

chapter 26

SERGEANT WRIGHT RAN down the ramp toward the western entrance of old Fort York. At the bottom just before it turned from a sidewalk to a well worn dirt path he saw an unearthed weed, dirt still clinging to its roots, sitting in the pool of light from an overhead street lamp. His heart pounded and he lost his breath. He kicked the weed aside, drew his gun and continued down the dark line that marked the pathway through the high weeds below the Bathurst Bridge and onward through a torn gap in the security fencing. He had told his wife to stay in the car, but he could hear her footfalls and heavy breathing behind him. As he espied the fire in the near distance, he called out his daughter's name.

"Meaghan! Meaghan! Are you there? Answer me, please."

He heard her scream and while still running, quicker now, he raised his gun and fired three times into the air.

"I'm here, baby. We're here. We've got the place surrounded. Hang on. We're coming."

Sergeant Wright stopped in the dimly illuminated area surrounding the fire. The flickering flames pulsated like an open heart. He could see the bodies lined up on the ground. The last one was his daughter's leaning on her elbows and screaming uncontrollably. He rushed to her followed immediately by his wife who crouched beside her daughter and ran an immediate inspection across her body examining every detail for some flaw or wound as though the girl was a newborn just delivered in the hospital.

"You're alive,' Sharon cried. "All this blood. My God, I thought, I thought…"

"Daddy, I'm so sorry," Meaghan pleaded. "He killed them. He was here. He just shot them all."

Sergeant Wright called 911 as well as his station. In minutes the ambulance and police cars arrived.

"What's up, Sergeant? Is he around? Where do we start?"

"I, I don't know. He's long gone. Check the area I guess. I've got to go, my daughter needs help."

"But, this is a crime scene and we need to...."

"You need to officer. I told you, I've got to go. You're in charge. Do what you want."

"What the fuck's with him," the officer said as Sergeant Wright took his wife and daughter away. "Hey, we got to interview her. She's a witness."

"I'll do the interviewing on my own. You got a problem with that, officer?"

"No, I'll take it up with Detective Gignac. I see him coming here with some other homicide detectives."

"Good, you do that. Don't ask. They will fill you in," Sergeant Wright said to a bewildered Gignac as the men passed each other on the darkened path. "I've got to go. It's all yours."

"Yeah, sure Sarge, I understand. I got it."

***

Don Wright sat on his living room couch, his daughter's sleeping head in his lap. Across from him his wife had her arms wrapped around her knees and rocked gently in an armchair. She smiled reassuringly at her husband. Josh slept on the floor his eyes wet from crying.

"She'll get over it," Don told his wife. "It will take a long time, but she'll get over it. She's alive. That's the main thing, the only thing. He didn't shoot her. All the others are dead, but he let her go."

"He knew who she was, that you were her father, didn't he? Did that matter? What did he say on the phone? You never told me."

"We struck a bargain. Meaghan for my resignation. Simple."

"What? You agreed?"

"What the fuck was I supposed to say? No dice. Go ahead. Put a bullet in my only daughter's head and ram a stinking weed in her mouth. No, I took the deal. I'd do it again a thousand times over."

"Oh Don, I'm sorry. I don't know why I said that. That's not what I meant, but you were under duress, unbelievable stress. What else could you have said? He, the Killer, he must have known you were in an impossible spot."

"Yes he did, and that was precisely the point. It's not that I'm afraid he'll come after her again, no. I know he won't even though the guy's a ghost. He's gunning people down in broad daylight for Christ's sake and we don't have a single solid clue as to who the fuck he is. You'd think we'd actually run into the guy on sheer percentages, he's out there that often. No, he knew exactly what he was doing. He would have killed her. I don't have any doubt about that, but on the strength of my word, he let her go. I have to respect that now. He knew I would. I had and have no choice.

"And you want to know the truth of it? No one down there on the city force really gives a shit about these homeless assholes and you can include me in that group too. If it wasn't for the bleeding heart press, and the social workers and do-gooders, the Mary Monticellos of the world, as much of this stuff as possible would have been swept under the rug long ago. I can't begin to tell you how many times that's happened in the past. Keep the violent crime confined to the poor, dysfunctional neighborhoods they always told us. Don't let it spread outward. Nobody gives a shit as long as it stays quarantined in the ghetto. The trouble was this whole Weed Killer mess got too big too fast and once the liberal assed press got a hold of it, it was game over.

"Similar thing happened in that Tom Chouder case which we handled last year. I don't know if you remember it. I was bent out of shape over that one too. Nothing like this Weed Killer stuff though, that's for sure, Anyway that case got into the public domain also and ran wild. This Chouder, a homeless bum sleeping out in the rain, got beaten up and killed by three service men, military guys serving our country. Sure it was tragic, but who really suffered? Chouder? He was a walking corpse at the time; sick, sleeping on park benches, eating out of garbage cans, ignoring offers of help. He hardly ever spoke to people even those who knew him. What kind of life was he living? What contribution did he make to society? What was the loss? If he had died of exposure that night, there would have been a brief back page story in the *Star* and then nothing just as it should have been. And the guys who beat him up, killed him? What about them? Three promising careers ruined. Families destroyed. They were drunk and didn't know what they were doing. Why should they suffer for the rest of their lives?

"And the whole thing would have been unsolved too if not for some goody two shoed, gay knob gobbling asshole strolling home in the middle of the night. He had to see the whole thing and rat on the service men. His civic duty. Yeah, right. Does anyone actually think those three poor guys were some kind of chronic offenders, that they would have attacked and killed anyone else in the future? Hardly. They probably would have learned a lesson and turned their lives around and been productive members of society. But not now, no, now they're completely screwed and for what, Tom Chouder and a wandering queer? Ain't that justice. So now the Weed Killer, he can thin out the whole city for all I care. I'm not going to sacrifice my family. We've suffered enough. In the long run you might say he even did me a favour. I'm off the police force."

Don extricated himself from under his daughter's exhausted body and laid her head back down softly on the sofa. Sharon moved over to take her husband's place beside Meaghan. She stroked the girl's hair.

"And another thing," Don went on, unable to stop talking. "I remember a relative of Chouder's come screaming into the station once the story got out. How could we have ignored the poor soul all those years and not been there to help him in his hour of need? After all, he was a human being with feelings, and family, and hopes. Oh yeah, she was going to sue the police force, the city, form a class action suit with the family members of other murder victims.

"Then I asked her just what was her relationship with the deceased. Oh, it was her brother, step brother actually and she was just crushed by his untimely death. Crushed? And when did you see him last? She couldn't remember exactly, one year, maybe two. I thought to myself; you self-righteous asshole, you couldn't be bothered to visit or help the guy, your own brother, when he needed you. You were content to let him rot on the street living on a cardboard mat and eating garbage, and blaming us for his problems. But now that you think there's a possibility of making some money off the poor deadbeat, suddenly you're crying a river of tears. Yeah, real sincere. These are the jackass citizens we are beholden to, we work for. Fuck them. I'm out of it."

"You know, at first I felt so sorry for those other poor kids, those three," said Sharon, "but then I thought, if one of them had survived and our Meaghan was dead, I'd never forgive them, the Killer, myself or you. That would have been the end of this family just like the Mahaffey case. That poor mother. She'll never, ever be the same again. Yes, I'm sorry, but if the others had to die in order for Meaghan to live, too bad. I'll take that deal. I guess I'm with you on that. That bastard Johnny Cool or whatever his ridiculous name was, I'd have taken your gun out and killed him myself for getting her into that madness. The Weed Killer saved me the trouble."

"The move out of the city will do us all good, Meaghan in particular."

"It's fine with Josh too. Frankly, this scared the hell out of him. It really doesn't matter where we live as long as we're together and happy and safe," said Sharon. "I frankly don't care one little bit about no fancy house. What difference does it make anyway what kind of house you have? You do the same things wherever you live. I just want my family safe and together."

"Just out of curiosity," Don put in. "Not that I actually give a damn anymore, but the Weed Killer said something to Meaghan about "pig nose dream" and "polka dots and moonlight." Does any of that ring a bell from your jazz song repertoire?"

Sharon smiled weakly. "Yes, they're lyrics again. It's actually "pug nose dream" from a song called "Polka Dots and Moonbeams," not moonlight. It's a jazz classic. The Weed Killer is a fan no doubt about it."

chapter 27

"I CAN'T BELIEVE just how goddamn easy this all has been," said Albert to himself the day after the Bathurst shooting as he sat in his living room listening to Billie Holiday and the Verve Years, one of his favorite albums.

"I don't really care for the strings," he digressed. "But she loved them so I will indulge her wishes. Basically I like a jazz quartet with a singer. Got to have a singer. Anyway, I walked right down to the bridge, no nerves, steady as can be, shot those worthless young bastards after a little story telling time, and then strolled out again without encountering even a goddamn cricket. All of that and a life saving chat with my long time pal, Sergeant Wright to boot. What are the chances of that happening? If I was a religious man, I'd be lighting candles right now and booking a pilgrimage. That reminds me. I wonder how Father Fitz-Patrick is doing? I should pay him a visit and maybe thin out his homeless flock a bit more just to show him I care. He still owes me one for that Judas Iscariot trick he pulled."

The living room was small and almost devoid of furniture. Albert liked things simple and uncluttered: a short couch, one easy chair, an end table and lamp, plus one bookcase. Albert had given away his extensive library years ago. "Why bother and continue to buy books when the Toronto Public Library has millions of book at any and everyone's beck and call? Doesn't make sense. Impractical. The tax write off didn't hurt either.

Albert also got rid of the myriad knickknacks his wife had deposited on virtually every surface in the house. She left without them and never inquired after them again. China, porcelain figurines, antique glassware and jewelry. One time he had caught one of his high end hooker/escort invitees stuffing a silver salt cellar into her purse. Nice trick. He got to fuck her up the ass for free when he threatened to turn her into her agency. He let her keep the item anyway. "A good will gesture."

Besides, that incident had prompted him to clean out the house.

The experience was liberating. Now he just had the wife's framed picture and some embroidered towels. "More than enough. Except for Claudia, I told everyone she had died, cancer. That elicits a lot more sympathy and the occasional freebee extra."

Reviewing his latest exploit Albert realized that his success in gunning down the Bathurst Bridge crowd was greatly aided by the fact that nearly every cop in Toronto was patrolling Parkdale and trying to keep order there. Talk was now in the air of the army being called out to help implement a government plan to force, or strongly cajole, the homeless out of the city.

"This is all I ever wanted," said Albert. "It perfectly complements my own mission. Look at everything I did. It was all predicated on driving the homeless leeching losers out of Toronto. And, and this is important, and in doing so I refused to waver from my self imposed guidelines. I never shot anyone other than the most obviously deserving losers.

"Too bad if some of them were young like this last bunch. If they fit the criteria, they had to die. I did spare the Wright girl. Yes, I did because there was reasonable doubt that she was really homeless. She had options and a fair chance of changing her ways so I let her go. No hesitation, no questions. I made the exception where it was warranted. Is that fair? Is it? I'll let Sergeant Wright answer that for me. And I also went out of my way to explain what I was doing and reassure the honest and upright citizens of Toronto that they had nothing to fear in me and they could go about their daily lives in complete freedom. What the fuck more could you ask for, eh?"

In response to an avalanche of outrage and disgust from the public as well as the media over his latest murders Albert felt compelled to write another letter to the *Star*. Much to his satisfaction Mary Monticello's tedious columns about saving the homeless and ridding the city of bedbugs had been recently suspended mainly because of the turmoil in Parkdale. Poor Mary was out on a "protracted and long deserved sabbatical from her duties which had driven her to the point of exhaustion" according to the paper itself. So Albert sent off another missive.

"Fellow Torontonians,

Don't trouble yourselves with the recent loss of three worthless garden variety weeds. Yes, they were young, but they were rude, useless, and irredeemable. They were thieves and beggars, dirty and diseased. They lived like the parasites they were preying upon the gainfully employed, generous, honest citizens of Toronto. Don't weep in sympathy for them and don't blame me. I am on your side.

"Finally, my pledge to Mary Monticello remains steadfast. No harm will come to any homeless person living in Parkdale. The blood of any murder victim there is not on my hands. Vale.

The Weed Killer

P.S. Tell Sergeant Wright that when we both retire we should meet up at Allan Gardens and compare notes. You know, just friends then, adversaries no more. I think we may have a lot of good stories to tell each other."

Albert mailed the missive on his way to the Toronto Islands where he checked in at the Island View Bed and Breakfast for a three day stay. If the cops were going to make a move on his "tip" about the sugar refinery on the lake , he'd know about it in the next couple of days. Then he could also determine if his trust in Sergeant Wright was justified.

He brought along a good book to read, "The Painted Bird" by Jerzey Kosinski and his binoculars and bird identification books for some intensive bird-watching, something he hadn't done for a while and missed.

"Any good sightings lately," he inquired of the owner who showed him to his room, a pleasant spot overlooking a flower laden garden and water feature filled with chirping gold finches and chickadees.

"Well, you will be glad to hear that down the end of the street right here we have three pairs of purple martins nesting. We put our martin house up for six straight years and we finally hit pay dirt."

"Wow, that's great. I'll have to tell my pal Norm about this."

"Yes, we've had quite a few visitors coming through because of the martins. We also have two families of swans, mute swans, along the shoreline a bit farther east."

"Good, I'm here for a few days so I should get a taste of things. Any notable shore birds?"

"The usual plovers, and sandpipers. We did have some greater yellow legs in the Spring, but they moved on. There are cardinals at the feeder every morning and house finches, of course, and we did have a towhee earlier as well, but I haven't seen him for a while. If you like to sleep in, I hope they don't wake you up."

"No, they're music to my ears. I'll probably sleep longer, the Lullaby of Bird Land so to speak. Lot's of warblers around too I imagine?" added Albert. "I love the little devils although with all this greenery it will be hard to spot them. I think as I've gotten older I have less patience too, not to mention failing eyesight."

The lady smiled. "My husband tells me I have the same problem."

"Where is your husband anyway? I haven't seen him around."

"He works during the day on the mainland at the Hyatt Hotel, a summer job. Be back some time tonight. The bed and breakfast is closed in the winter. We go to Florida. You know, you ought to try it here during the migrations. A lot of people go to the Spit, but we have a lot of stop overs here as well. If you want I can bring you a little bit of lunch today. You're our only guest."

Every day after breakfast and for the offer of an extra fee Albert enjoyed the "special services" of his island landlady.

"Jesus, do you have to be so rough? Don't leave any marks, please. I don't want my husband to see them."

"That's your problem. Do you want the cash or not?"

The woman nodded while Albert stuffed her panties into her mouth. "Now bend your knees and spread your legs. Wider." In the afternoon Albert sat on the thick shoreline grass with his binoculars and books. He positioned himself directly across the channel from the Red Path Sugar refinery and intermittently scanned the far shore for activity.

"Watching the detective. He's so cute, cute, cute," Albert sang softly to himself.

Three day's worth of observing netted him several dozen bird species, but no police activity across the harbor.

"Looks like he kept his word. Wow, an honest cop. Too bad I forced him off the homicide squad after all, but "that's life" as Old Blue Eyes would say and self preservation comes first."

***

While Albert Champion was culling weeds under the Bathurst Bridge and holidaying on the Islands, the Village of Parkdale led the entire nation in violent crime: assaults, rapes, burglaries, break and enters, and battery. There were even three homicides unrelated to the Weed Killer activity as such. Toronto police on foot, horseback and bicycle and patrol cars augmented by OPP cruisers were everywhere. Citizens armed with bats and hockey sticks marched down the streets trying to keep order and protect their property.

"You people can't sit on our steps. This is private property. We pay taxes here, you know. Please, get off the steps and out of my front yard."

"We're just restin here for a minute. It's hot, we thought we'd relax. We ain't doing no harm. What's wrong with you people? We thought that Parkdale people was real friendly. Hey, by the way, you got anything to drink inside?"

"We'll give you some water. Then will you leave?"

"When I said drink, I didn't mean a drink of water for fuck sake."

Neighbors soon gathered on one side of a house where an argument was taking place and a troop of homeless mustered on the other. A fight broke out. The police were called and responded in a matter of minutes.

"OK, if they won't let us sit on their steps, what about the curb? That's the street, eh. That's public property, ain't it?" proclaimed an unshaven man with no shirt who acted as spoke person for his group.

"Yes, that's true," said a police constable.

"Good, we'll just sit there then. All of us and these cock sucks can't do nothing about it, right?"

"Not as long as you don't break any laws, that's right." The policeman turned to the homeowners and their allies and shrugged his shoulders. "Sorry, but he's right."

"Oh well, aren't you cops just a perfect solution to the problem. Look at this street, this neighborhood. It's a total shit hole since these, these vagrants arrived. What about all this litter and the excrement and piss in the streets? My neighbor here, right here Mrs. Markham, she had lovely flowers blooming on her front lawn. Right there; petunias, impatiens, geraniums. What do you see now? Nothing, nothing but brown leaves and wilted stems. These sons of bitches have been pissing on them steadily for weeks. The flowers are all goddamn dead! I seen him right there, that one, pissing in her yard just fifteen minutes ago."

"It wasn't me."

"Sure as hell was. You see anyone else around here wearing a red plastic fireman's hat? Don't tell me it wasn't you."

"It wasn't. You can't prove it. I, I give my hat to a chum of mine. Lent it to him for a hour."

"Why don't you cops do something?" said the Parkdale neighbor. "Arrest him."

"I'm sorry, but it's just his word against yours right now. You have to catch him in the act, then call us."

"Oh yeah, and I suppose he's gonna just stand there with his dripping dick hanging out of his pants waiting for your arrival. Give me a break."

"Yeah, you know what we need here in Parkdale? We need the Weed Killer. He'd clean this place up in a hurry."

"And you can thank that bitch Mary Monticello for his absence too. We got all these worthless derelict litter-bugging assholes in return. Some tradeoff that turned out to be."

That night a brick was thrown through Mary and Bob Monticello's front window. It had a note wrapped around it.

"Get out of town, homeless loving bitch. Find some bed bug ridden flop house on Finch and Jane where you can be with more of your kind."

Mary was a mess, and rarely left the house. For a while she did all her news articles from home and e-mailed them into the office, then one day she had a heart to heart with Karen French.

"Mary, I think it would be best if you just took an extended leave of absence. It would do you a lot of good. Take the pressure off, don't you think? And frankly we're all suffering here. I'm not one to give in to pressure. You know that, but as of today we have lost over three hundred subscribers in the Parkdale neighborhood and our outdoor news stands have without exception been vandalized or destroyed. A lot of stores are also refusing to handle the paper. Once this all dies down and I'm sure it will eventually, well then you can resume your duties. Go ahead, take the time off. You deserve it."

Mary took her editor up on the offer knowing that although it was couched in terms of recovery and recuperation, it was more of a lay off than a sabbatical leave. She turned her attention to her mentoring program and started tutoring a boy who was a Lost Park neighbor of her former student, Anquin Jefferies. It would also help to focus her attention outside of Parkdale for a while.

The new boy's name was Kiwana Jones and like Anquin he was sixteen years old and also like Anquin he struggled mightily with his studies. Mary helped him with a sort of preliminary high school curriculum which if successfully completed would allow the boy to enter Grade Nine in the coming school year.

This I can do, Mary reassured herself. I don't have to worry about the interference of others and I can chart my own progress with Kiwana and although it's been only two weeks now and four sessions, I can see we are moving ahead. He's actually doing better than Anquin at this stage of the game.

One day Kiwana did not show up for his tutorial at the Lincoln Alexander Community center so Mary phoned his apartment.

"I'm kinda sick, stomach hurts." said Kiwana. "And I don't think I'm doing too good with all this school shit anyways. I can't get the last math stuff. You know when yous got a whole bunch of different numbers all lined up and yous got to figure out what number come next, that shit. What difference do it make? Nobody's got numbers that be all, all fucked up like that. What happened to one, two, three? What was wrong with that shit? I can't do this shit no more."

"Kiwana first of all you shouldn't get yourself excited like this, and of course, swearing is not allowed and doesn't help matters anyway. But maybe I could stop by your apartment and help you out with today's lesson. I mean, I already have the time set aside. I know where you live. Is your mother or step father at home?"

"Yeah, she here cleaning up after supper."

"Good, then we can work at the kitchen table. That would be the best place to study, bright and away from the TV and other distractions."

Mary had been to the apartment once in the past when she stopped by to introduce herself to the family and to get Kiwana orientated to his new program. As a matter of policy doing school work at a student's apartment was allowed only under extraordinary circumstances such as illness or disability. At the same time Mary was there she also carefully eyed the apartment. From her preliminary scouting she concluded that the kitchen was the cleanest part of the house, from a bedbug perspective, of course. The furniture was plastic and chrome, safe.

When Mary showed up, there was no one in the apartment except Kiwana. He seemed nervous, sweating. Jesus, maybe he really was sick thought Mary. She looked around the kitchen. There were dirty dishes and pots and pans covering the table, counter top and spilling out of the sink. There were no books in sight.

"Where's your mom?" Mary asked. "You said she was here."

"She gone out for groceries and stuff. We all out."

Just then the buzzer rang and Kiwana stood up to answer it. "Yeah, OK, sure, I be right down. That be my mom now, she at the back door and need help with her packages. I got to go down. Might as well walk you back out 'cause I ain't gonna have no time to do no studying no more or nothin like that by the time we gets the stuff put away and we has our supper."

Mary winched at the grammar and the boy's rambling sentences. Another look at the table convinced her that staying was a lost cause and Kiwana was right about the time line too. Mary had promised her husband she'd come right home after the lessons. If she was late, Bob would worry and come looking for her especially in light of the recent problems in Parkdale. He didn't like her walking home alone from the streetcar and often met her at the corner. Mary turned around and accompanied Kiwana back out of the apartment.

"OK, Kiwana, but I'm going to leave tonight's lesson here on this chair by the door. Give it a try, please, for me, and we'll pick up again on Monday, OK?'

"Sure, for you I'll do it," said the boy with a smile.

Down in the lobby Kiwana stopped Mary as she was about to leave the building. "Hey, you mind comin down here to the door for a minute and hold it open for me and my mom. She say she got a lot of bags to bring up."

Mary glanced at her watch. "Sure, I can do that. You know you're lucky Kiwana. You have a mother who cares for you, takes care of you. That's more than a lot of children can say."

"I ain't no child," said Kiwana as they reached the bottom of the stairwell. At that point he pushed open a door marked "Recyclables" and grabbing Mary roughly by her arm pulled her in behind him.

"What?" Mary gasped as the door closed and she stood facing another young black boy.

Kiwana immediately pinned her arms behind her.

"Hey, man, you done it, man," said the other boy gleefully, "just like you said. This be my first white bitch too. Fuckin cool, man. You the man, Kiwana."

"Kiwana what are you… What?"

Next thing Mary knew there was a knife pressed against her throat.

"Shut up and get your clothes off, bitch. Smart ass white teacher bitch gonna preach to me about no learning. We gonna learn you some lessons right here and now. Black meat lessons."

"Kiwana, don't. Don't do this. Please. You're gonna be sorry. You're gonna throw away all the good work we've done. You were progressing, making real gains. I can help you. Please! My God!"

"Shut up and get these clothes off. Don't make no noise. I slit yer throat and you bleed to death before nobody can help you." In the meantime the other boy stepped forward and started ripping Mary's blouse off while Kiwana from behind cut her belt and the elastic around her skirt with his knife and pulled the rest of her outer clothing along with her panties down to the floor.

"Ooo, wee, that some good looking white pussy there," said the other boy. "You right man, you can see everything on these white bitches, eh. I'm gonna get me one permanent white pussy for a girlfriend after we take care of the teacher lady here."

"Please Kiwana. Don't. Jesus Christ, this can't be happening. Bob! Bob!"

Kiwana tipped over an old dirty mattress that was leaning against the storage room wall.

He spun the naked Mary around, slapped her hard in the face and pushed her onto the mattress' spotted and stained surface. Mary recoiled in horror. The other boy pulled her arms over her head and knelt on them all the while holding a knife to her throat with one hand and feverishly raking and squeezing her breasts with the other.

"Spread yer legs, bitch. Wider for my man Kiwana, or I cut yer face open like a watermelon."

Kiwana pulled his pants down and jumped on Mary. He pumped feverishly and awkwardly inside of her. He was rough and unpracticed. Mary sobbed and pleaded. When the boy was done, he switched places with his friend.

"I be ready for seconds the minute you done," he added. "This teacher bitch got me goin."

When the two were done, they forced Mary over on her stomach and sodomized her. Despite her face being half buried in the urine soaked, dirt encrusted fabric she could plainly discern spots of dried blood and squashed insect bodies pock-marking the filthy mattress. She gasped in horror and vomited. When one of the boys grabbed her hair and lifted her head off the mattress to cut her throat, the last thing she saw was the word "Bedbogs" scribbled in big black letters on the mattress underneath her face.

Mary's body was discovered that evening by the building's superintendent. Within hours Kiwana and his friend were arrested for her murder. They were apprehended outside of Melvin the Jewelry Buyer's where they had just sold Mary's rings, necklace and bracelet.

"It was all her fault, man. She called me and Kiwana dumb nigger boys. We don't put up with that shit. We be men. White bitch comin in our building like that, she askin for trouble. And we be juvees too. You can't lock us up. No way, man."

chapter 28

"WELL, YOU CAN tell he's well educated. That's for sure," began Detective Gignac. "Look at the vocabulary and that Latin word, "Vale". Means good-bye. I looked it up and remember that confrontation with Father FitzPatrick? What was that all about except he's angry about religion. I tell you he's got a strong religious, Roman Catholic, background."

"So what exactly does that give us?" asked Detective Hudson. "I don't see that doin much good."

"That near death experience the Killer told the priest about. Before he quit, Don figured that the hospital records would yield something. I was just about to parcel out some of that stuff, but then the Captain called me in about Don and my replacing him and I lost track. And don't forget I've had to attend those internal sessions too about our shooting at the Loblaws warehouse. So now, Hudson, you check the hospital records for someone, a guy, who beat cancer maybe five, ten years back. Make that twenty and see if you can match it up with a residence on the West End and any *Toronto Star* subscription holders in the same area. You can use the notes in my desk there to get started.

"Also Don's daughter, Meaghan, mentioned the Weed Killer telling the group some kind of story before he killed them. Maybe there's an educational link and the reference to the Devil riding on the wind, that's religion again. Maybe he's a former teacher and, or a Catholic school student. Maybe an altar boy who was abused by a priest. We should check that too."

"Was Don's daughter able to give us anything else? She's the only survivor, ever," said Detective Hudson who was now second in command under the newly appointed Sergeant Gignac.

"Only the usual stuff that we got already. He was white, older. No accent of any kind. Tall, dressed in black, old clothes. Talked about old times, camping and the antiwar movement. He was planning to go out west, but that could have been some kind of distraction. That's the trouble, we don't know if he's planting false leads or slipping up on stuff. He referred to some childhood friend of his, but the girl couldn't remember the name except that it was Polish sounding or Ukrainian. And he was calm throughout everything. Never tipped his hand even though a couple of the kids were worried about him right from the start. Unfortunately, they waited too long and by then it was too late to run or confront him with their extra numbers. He just shot them calm as could be. Meaghan had no idea what was going down until he started shooting."

"Why did he spare her?"

"He knew she was Don's daughter, eh. One of the boys blurted it out. Could be he was saving her for something special to send a message to Don and us, but when her cell phone started ringing, he got spooked off. He realized we could track those things and figured we were on the way, getting near."

"Did you tell her to keep the weed information to herself right now."

"Don't worry, Don's taking care of it even though he's out of the force. She ain't talking to anybody that's for sure. Rough shape right now."

"Poor Don. Still, I don't think he should have resigned like that. Should have stuck it out. Any chance he's coming back? Maybe after a little lay off or some soul searching?"

"I doubt it and I don't blame him. All the bullshit that's fallen on his head. He took most of it on himself, kept us out of it saying he was principally to blame since he headed the task force. Who needs the grief? Plus his family was all screwed up, eh. They couldn't take it no more. And I don't know for sure, but something happened there at the Bathurst Bridge with the Weed Killer. Don don't say much about it, but there's something between the two of them, him and the Killer."

"I hear he's moving out of the city completely."

"Yeah, I heard that too. Going to Peterborough. Good luck to him and his family."

"And one other thing. Don's daughter said the Killer smelled sweet when he was bending over her and talking, was like flowers in a funeral parlor. Of course, given what had just happened, you know, the connection with death and funerals was logical, eh."

"Yeah, that or he was wearing some cheap after shave. I remember something said about that over at the Allan Gardens murder scene, one of the witnesses. I forget the name of it now. I'll check the notes from that night and find out. I'd like to go out and buy a bottle if it's still around. See what that shit smells like. You and the men get on the rest of the evidence."

***

"Norm, I wish you weren't so depressed all the time," pleaded Claudia. "You've got to shake out of it. You've been in bed for three days in a row. Your employers are leaving messages that if you don't show up soon, they'll have to get someone else for the house and office cleanings. I filled in once already, but I can't do no more. And the ice cream stand said one more day and that's it. This is their busy season. They've got to make their money now."

"Oh yes, make money. Isn't that what it's all about, making money?" mumbled Norm from virtually under his covers. "Heaven forbid if you aren't making money. I mean what else in life is there besides making money? You know if we had a sane society, people would express themselves in other ways. Write poetry, pen a novel, write a song, join a band, volunteer at a nursing home or hospital, travel, go bird-watching for fuck sake. But no, no. You've got to make money, money, money, money. You're not a success unless you make lots and lots of money. Isn't that the first thing people ask when you meet. What do you do, or roughly translated, how much money do you earn so I know if it's worth my while to make your acquaintance."

"That makes the world go around, I guess," said Claudia.

"Not my world, thank you. And you don't have to pretend you're part of that world anymore either. I know you're seeing someone else. I can tell. It's not that difficult."

"Honestly Norm, you're so paranoid it's pathetic."

"Thanks for the diagnosis. I appreciate it."

"If you'd just stop obsessing about everything and go out and live life, you'd get so much more out of it. I mean you've got good ideas, interests, but instead of following them, you just lay in bed and brood. If you don't care about the money, there are other things you can do like you just said. Look at Albert, he's never bored or brooding. You should take a cue from him, maybe. He's your friend."

"Maybe, maybe I don't want to be like him, Mr. Assertive, Mr. Opinionated. He's so self confident he gets on my nerves. By the way, I was wondering about something. You know the name, Weed Killer? Who came up with that name and when was it first used? I don't remember it early on when the killings first started."

"Gees, I don't know. I think it was when that letter appeared in the *Star.* That's what he called himself, the Weed Killer. Albert would probably know. Ask Albert."

"Yes Albert again. And when it comes to brooding, let me just say that it suits me. How can you do otherwise? The country, the world is going to hell. Capitalism is ruining everything and nobody cares, nobody even knows what's going on and that includes your know it all chum, Albert. You're all so focused on your own little space, your own little lives, that you can't see, let alone understand, what's happening around you."

"People are struggling to make a living. You can't blame them. Other than that they want to enjoy themselves. There has to be more to life than just working. You said so yourself."

"But there isn't anything more to life than working under this system. You have to work, there's no choice. That's the problem. Without work you're nothing."

"If you're so concerned, why don't you fight for your beliefs? Join a political party, the NDP, or help out with some community group that shares your ideas."

"I tried that, the Socialist Labor Party. They had great ideas. Put the workers in control of everything: production, distribution, political organization, the whole shooting match. Workers do all the meaningful work in society anyway so why shouldn't they also call the shots and get the benefits? Without workers nothing would, would work.

"But I'll tell you what happened with that. I still remember like it was yesterday. The Party, its Toronto Branch, had rented the Lithuanian Hall over on Bloor and Parkside Street to hold a bunch of lectures. The lectures were sort of like question and answer sessions about socialism and some of Marx's ideas on the capitalist economy, eh."

"Well, that certainly sounds like a start."

"Yeah, a start and finish. I had prepared a whole bunch of notes 'cause I was part of the panel that was supposed to handle the questions and answers."

"How did it go?"

"Not so good. The hall held about a hundred and fifty people, but there were only ten in attendance and all of them were either Socialist Labor Party members or sympathizers. Pathetic. I mean there are only about two, three dozen card carrying members throughout all of Canada anyway and we couldn't attract not even one new comer. Jesus, out of plain old curiosity alone you'd think we'd pull in at least one person. Fuck me."

"Well, you've got to start somewhere. Little steps, eh. Every journey starts with a single step."

"Please. Anyway a few days later I was passing that same Lithuanian Hall and there was a huge crowd outside, hundreds of people pushing and shouting, trying to get into the building. I asked what was going on, what was creating the big fuss? Turned out it was a lecture and a slide show about UFOs and so called documented evidence of alien visitors to Earth. All of those fucking morons were lining up to hear about space ships visiting Earth with little green men running around and conducting experiments on people and transporting them back and forth across the universe. I couldn't believe it.

"Yeah, just days before there I was trying like hell to get people, one person even, to come in and at least listen to the possibility that the capitalist system was corrupt and needed meaningful reform. But, no, no way, that proposition was ridiculous. What was I, some kind of idiot, some nut case? People didn't have time for stupidity like that. They were busy finding out about those UFOs that crash landed in Roswell, New Mexico where the U.S. government had alien bodies hidden away in a secret lab and stored pieces of the actual space ship. That was it. I quit!

"So yes, I've given up. Thank you very much, but at least I have the satisfaction of knowing that I understand the truth. It's sad but humorous to watch the rest of you wallow around in ignorance trying to make sense of it all. Right now I'm with the Emperor Claudius. Give me the poisonous mushroom. Let the Neros of the world take over."

"Really Norm, you're impossible when you get in one of these moods. I can't nurse you along any more. When you snap out of it, give me a call. I'll be waiting."

"Sure, go ahead. Get out. Go over to your lover and get yourself fucked. That's what you want isn't it, to get fucked and spanked. Albert was right. You like the rough stuff and I can't give it to you so you're leaving. Well, leave. See if I care. I hope he beats the shit out of you whoever he is."

Norm snuck out of his bed as Claudia descended the stairs. He peeked from behind his curtain, watching her walk down the street. When she turned to look back, he hid against the wall only to follow her once again when she resumed her journey.

"She walking out of my life and I'm just standing here like an idiot. My God, how pathetic, how fucking pathetic."

chapter 29

ALBERT'S DOORBELL RANG. "Hi, me again," said Claudia. "I'm worried about Norm. I saw him today and he's in one of his moods again. It's getting serious. Maybe you can talk some sense into him."

"Yeah, sure enough. I'll mark it down as the fiftieth thing to do on my list of this year's chores."

"You're such a bastard. I don't know why I come here. All I get is abuse."

"Maybe that's all you deserve. Step inside, get your clothes off. Let me get my belt. I want to redden your ass good before I put you through your routine."

Claudia's face and backside were soon the color of ripe beef steak tomatoes as Albert spanked her hard taking his time between blows to rub the leather belt across the rising welts on her ass.

"Has Norm seen you lately? Did he like your little shaved pussy? What did you tell him?" Albert asked as he slid a chair next to the woman.

"I didn't say anything," Claudia replied taking a deep breath. "He hasn't touched me in a month. He doesn't know for sure that I'm seeing someone, but he's got his suspicions. He's not stupid, but you're the last man he'd ever suspect. Believe me."

"Too bad. It might perk the old bastard up. Now put your leg on the chair and spread your pussy, wide till it hurts. More. Use both hands," and he whacked her hard with the belt again.

"How, how can you do this to me? Why?" she whined.

Albert administered another slap without answering. Then he grabbed Claudia by the forearm and escorted her into the bedroom and pushed her to her knees in front of the full length mirror there.

"Down." he said. "That's it. Look up at me and start sucking. Ah, yes. Now reach back and spread your ass cheeks and turn a bit so I can see you in the mirror."

When he was coming in her mouth, Albert plunged his cock farther down Claudia's throat as her head bucked and saliva poured from the corners of her mouth. Albert didn't withdraw until he was totally finished. Then he made her lick up the few drops of semen that had spilled onto the floor.

"That's it. Good girl," he said as he patted her head. "Now get in bed with your head on the pillow and your ass in the air. I'll finish you up after I get myself a drink of water. My throat's dry."

Later in the night Claudia quietly slipped out of bed and started to dress in the darkness.

"Where you going?" asked Albert sleepily shaking himself awake. "What's the rush? You don't have to leave till morning. Get back in here. I'm not done with you yet."

"Well, I'm done and I'm leaving. I can't stand it no more," replied Claudia. "I haven't slept all night waiting for you to stop snoring and maybe roll over and show me a little affection, a hug or even a pat on the bum after you got your anger and frustration out of the way. I thought the other night that you were beginning to mellow a bit when we fell asleep holding each other. Must have been an oversight on your part because there's obviously no tenderness in your heart. You're too self absorbed to share any affection. You don't care about anyone, not me, not Norm.

"I told you often enough that Norm needs someone to talk to, someone other than me. He respects you despite your warped opinions. The least you could do is go over there and talk to him once in a while. What have you been doing that's so important you ignore probably the only friend you've got? Certainly, you're one of the few friends he's got. He needs you. You could show him some consideration. He won't listen to me. I'm worried. I'm afraid he's going to do something crazy."

"Jesus, settle down. I like the guy even though his liberal, bleeding heart philosophy is hard to take."

"At least he believes in something. That's more than I can say for you, or myself for that matter. That's probably why I torture myself with you. Punishment I guess."

"Don't overdo the self pity, but getting back to Norm. You know he's like some fanatical hockey fan cheering for his favorite, but losing home team. He's tried and tried for years to convince people he's right about capitalism and to show them the true path of socialism. He's cheered, cajoled, and pleaded, reasoned, and even scolded, but no one listened. Instead of rallying around his inspirational messages the people ignored him. In other words the team kept losing so he stopped trying and like a lot of fans who feel betrayed, he turned on his own team, his friends. He started booing them and ridiculing them, hating them because they had let him down, because they hadn't fulfilled his expectations. They didn't win the Stanley Cup so now they're a bunch of worthless losers who deserve the defeat they brought on themselves. It's another way of passing the buck. It's the same thing you're doing with me now. You want me to try to help Norm because you failed and gave up. Nevertheless, to keep you happy I'll stop by tomorrow or the next day and see how he's doing. Maybe get him out bird-watching at the Spit."

"Oh, he'd like that. He often talks about the times the two of you had up there. I never would have thought a bunch of birds could bring such pleasure to someone. God knows I tried without much luck. I could never see anything through them binoculars. The birds, they kept moving around."

"Well, birds don't bother you, or intrude on your life. They just make it more enjoyable. Summer's fading fast now. Before you know it, it'll be autumn and the warblers will have changed their plumage and the migrations begun. Then we'll have to wait a whole damn year to see the little darlings again. I should get one last look at them myself, a final good-bye. Yeah, Norm too. He'd like that. So then why don't you stay? You can leave in the morning."

"No, maybe another time. I can't get Norm out of my mind. I feel like I've deserted him just for the perverse thrill of being with you. For a moment I was going to say that I was as bad as you, but that's not true. I'm not putting that on myself. No one can top you in the stone hearted department."

"Ha, a heart like a rock cast in the sea, that's good. But, you know what, it's always us bad guys people remember, eh, the bad guys. When I was a kid, I had one uncle who was a real pain in the ass for the family. He was drunk all the time, lying to everyone. He borrowed money from my father and other relatives and never repaid it. Got into arguments and fights. He was even in jail once. Oh yeah, a real prick. But you know what? Whenever the family got together, who was always the topic of conversation?

"Why, Uncle John, of course. Even to this day I have only vague recollections of my other uncles and aunts, but Uncle John, his image is as clear as a bell. You see, no one remembers, or cares about all the good people in the world. It's the bad ones who get the attention. Think of Germany. How many chancellors of Germany can you list, how many leaders? Not many I'd bet, but I'm sure you and everyone else knows one guy really well, Adolph Hitler. How about leaders of Iraq? Iran? Anyone know an Italian leader other than Mussolini? Ever hear of Jack the Ripper, Count Dracula, Willie Picton, Charles Manson? I rest my case. If you feel that way about me at least I'm in noteworthy company."

"I feel sorry for you," Claudia continued shaking her head. "You're not half the man Norman is because being a man means not only taking but giving too and I'm afraid you don't how to give. Norm cares for people and wants to help. He's just been so beaten down and frustrated that he can't handle life anymore. That's where you can come in and finally do some good, but I'll believe that when I see it. Right now, sweet dreams. I know the way out."

Albert watched Claudia walk through his yard to the street beyond. The wind billowed her skirt and threw her hair back. He thought of the day his wife, Maureen, left him. The same scene, the same sad wind blowing. Neither woman really wanted to leave and Albert knew it. His wife had loved him, loved him way beyond his deserving and deep somewhere in his heart he knew that he loved her too, and maybe it was the same with Claudia, but he couldn't force himself to show the affection both of them longed for and needed. For some perverse reason he preferred to let them slip away. Maybe he was punishing himself too.

***

Albert called Norm a number of times during the next few days. "Jesus, when I want the son of a bitch he's a Kirkland Warbler. Every other time he's a Starling at my feeder. I thought he was in bed brooding. Still, I better stop by. Make an effort or Claudia will have a shit fit."

There was no answer at Norm's front door. "Probably hiding under the sheets. Well, it is early. I'll drive down to the Spit on my own and then head back here later. Take him out for lunch. He probably could use a good meal."

Albert pulled into his usual spot. The community gardens across the road were burgeoning with vegetables, not like the sterile stalks he had seen early in Spring. Lettuce, cabbage, beets, carrots, beans, both yellow and green, sprouted everywhere from the fertile composted earth. Peas swayed in profusion from awkward homemade poles and cucumbers and squash trailed across the ground. Albert rolled up his windows, locked the doors and instinctively popped open the glove box.

"Son of a bitch. What the fuck? Am I getting senile?" he said as he stared at the .22 sitting in plain sight. Then he remembered that he always stored it there, along with his stock of ammunition, whenever Claudia came to visit. Locked in the glove box, locked in the car, locked behind his driveway gate. He didn't want her discovering it in the house.

Albert looked around. In the bright morning sunlight several gardeners were already tending to their plots. The hot dog man was setting up and a couple of bike riders and skate boarders zipped by beating the afternoon heat with a brisk morning trip down the Spit. Albert owned a large 9 X set of Bushnell binoculars with a zoom lens. He didn't trust leaving the gun in the untended car, too many people around this time and he had grown far too paranoid over the summer, so he stuffed the loaded revolver into the oversized case, slung the case over his head and shoulder and carried the glasses in his hand. He put the extra bullets in his pocket.

"No sense taking a chance at this stage in the game. Last time I left the gun here inside the car I worried all day until I got back."

Albert briefly walked the beachfront looking for the usual shore birds before making his way inland toward the lighthouse. "At least those assholes with the blue tarp are gone. Authorities must have driven them out. You can't just set up a shit hole of a campsite right on the water like that. Ruins the view for everybody, not to mention polluting the lake."

Albert preferred taking the more deserted side roads en route. They were quieter and offered better bird-watching. As he wandered along, he thought of the good times he had had at the Spit over the years. Yes, he had neglected his bird-watching this summer and hardly did any reading either. That's why he so enjoyed his little hiatus at the Island Bed and Breakfast. He should do a lot more of that kind of thing. Trouble was his mission had gotten in the way. All his energy and all his thoughts and plans had been consumed by his driving ambition to rid Toronto of the homeless scourge. The mission wound up taking over his life.

"Maybe it's time I gave it up?" he said. "I've done about all I can do. A lot of the homeless are gone. Those who are left are packed into Parkdale like cat bird chicks in a warbler's nest. I heard even they are waiting to be shipped out. The city and province are providing bus tickets along with a stipend of a hundred dollars on the written promise that the losers not return. I guess I certainly made an impression. They'll never forget me. Never. I'll go down in the annals of Toronto history. The Weed Killer, who was that man? Where did he come from and where did he go? Down Route 66. Lost and a mystery forever. That's the way it should be. That's the way it will be."

Albert turned down a dirt pathway that led to Norm's favorite haunt, that little dead end turn around facing a quiet bay which was connected to the main lake by a narrow and shallow reed choked shoal. The two of them had originally spotted a few cranes feeding there years ago, sandhill cranes, a big discovery and one that made both their live lists. From that day forth it had been Norm's favorite spot. Albert admired it also.

"Jesus Christ," said Albert breaking his reverie and stopping dead in his tracks. In front of him, barely hidden behind a screen of shrubs and willows just off the dead end gravel path, was that same old blue tarp make shift tent that had been formerly sitting on the beach. "Those fucking bastards, the rotten pricks, they moved over here. I don't believe it. Of all the goddamn places to pick!"

Albert pulled out his gun compelled by immediate anger and an instinctive reaction to kill. He couldn't help himself. It was by now an ingrained, compulsive response detached from thought. He looked around, then walked cautiously up to the tattered tent. It was indeed the same raggedly assed set up he had seen along the beach earlier in the summer, but here in this spot it took on a particularly sacrilegious appearance. A hibachi and bag of charcoal sat near the entrance. A cooler and Rubber Made container along with a case of water bottles stood in the shade of the trees.

"Won't be long before the place is littered with shit and garbage. Norm's place, damn it. Is nothing sacred?"

Through the semi open flap in the front and with the bright morning sun shining through the back of the tent, Albert could see someone stirring inside, sitting up beside an elevated bedroll or sleeping bag. Albert checked around again. There was no one in sight and given the secluded nature of the location no one could possibly see him. Everything was quiet except for a distant but still noticeable raucous din from the cormorant colony a ways up the main road. Deep, washed out ruts precluded any bicyclist from travelling down the gravel pathway and Albert had not seen anyone walking on the main road above the turn around.

He stepped forward until he could see the distinct silhouette of the man standing, awkwardly hunched over in the low ceiling of the tent. For some reason he thought of Norm. What would his friend think of Albert murdering someone right here on the Spit, at Norm's sanctuary no less? Undoubtedly the mortal sin of murder would outweigh the venial transgression of trespassing especially in Norm's socialist oriented mind. Still, rules were rules and this was a clear violation of the Weed Killer's bible.

"This sure isn't Parkdale for God's sake" hissed Albert. "Haven't I given enough? You can't be satisfied with Parkdale? That's the problem with you people. You get a little and then you want more and more, and then some. Never satisfied."

When the figure stretched in the translucent light of the tent, Albert fired three times. Without a sound, the man's body fell to the floor like a dead tree toppling in the forest. At the same time two mallards and a blue winged teal flushed from the bay grasses and sailed off with whistling wings.

Albert was tempted to step in and finish the man off if he was still alive. The symbolic coup de grace of the weed placement was also needed and various species grew in profusion all around him, but instead Albert hesitated. Something stopped him. On the pole at the entrance to the tent a pair of binoculars was slung and a worn Peterson book lay on the threshold. Albert got a strange feeling of foreboding. He hadn't wanted this kill anyway, but he was provoked and was given no choice. Now he just wanted to get away like a frightened sparrow who saw the shadow of a kestrel pass over his open perch.

"Come fly with me. Come fly. Let's fly away." Albert fled propelled by an unseen force, an unexplained panic. His heart pounded. Out on the open road above the tent site, with no one around, Albert stopped and took a few deep breaths.

"Jesus, what the hell is wrong with me? Calm down old boy. Calm down. This isn't Allan Gardens. No one is after you. Relax."

He purposely slowed his pace and soon began to feel better, calmer, relieved, a feeling that increased geometrically with each step he took away from the murder scene. Before he had gone even halfway to the lighthouse Albert's anxiety had ebbed and he resolved once again and this time for good that he was done with killing.

"Yes, I think my body and my nerves are telling me something here such as, the party's over. It's time to pack up and go. Let's face it. It's been a miracle that I got away with so much for so long. I don't know if it was my own skill or lack thereof on the part of the police, or just plain luck that led me to so many victims and then allowed me to turn around and get clean away?"

Albert remembered a post World War II interview with one of Hitler's army generals. The officer was asked why he, the troops, and indeed the entire country had blindly followed Der Furher's disastrous course and never once questioned its wisdom. The man replied; "Because he was right all the time until, of course, he was wrong and then it was too late."

Well, he, Albert Champion, wasn't going to fall into that trap taking that one step too far. There were hints already that the tide was turning against him. Sergeant Wright wasn't walking through the Rex in order to enjoy the music and bask in the ambiance of a bar room. No, something was up for sure. That was why he had to get Wright off the case.

"So now, aside from one or two more redundant killings, what could possibly be left for the mighty Weed Killer? Getting caught, that's what."

Furthermore, the Spit was actually the perfect place to get rid of a murder weapon. Fate or call it good luck again. All around him was uninhabited wet land, field and water. Nobody would ever find a gun in this environment. It would be hidden forever just like his own murderous identity. Albert confidently made his way to the cormorant colony.

It was alive with activity as the adult birds and their summer offspring darkened the blue sky in long sorties back and forth into the lake for food.

"It's easy to understand the evolution from dinosaurs," said Albert. "The ugly sons of bitches look so reptilian, so snakelike there's no mistaking the connection."

Below the cormorants, the blackened rookery swayed fragilely and skeletally, its trees dead and dying from the foul excretions of thousands of birds. The noise was both frightening and exhilarating. Albert moved past the warning signs to the shore of the lake and into the fringe of the noisy colony. Gulls by the thousands flew around him. Had it been weeks earlier they probably would have killed him in their attempts to protect their young. But the grey, mottled adolescents were now fending mainly for themselves though some late bloomers still harassed a weary parent for food.

Albert hesitated with the gun in his hand. It was like saying good-bye to a cherished lover, a dear friend, one who never asked but always gave when called upon. Vale, old chum, he said and tossed the revolver as far out as he could manage. Surprisingly, it flew through the air like a vertical boomerang climbing in a high arc and then descending with a bigger than expected splash. It hit virtually on the shore of a small grassy island which was sitting adjacent to the largest congregation of the nesting cormorants.

"Jesus," Albert looked hurriedly around him wondering if his action had attracted any attention. No one was around. "Thank God," he muttered, then chuckled. "Could have landed in deeper water, but what the hell. Nothing out here but a bunch of birds and they won't talk." He then grabbed a couple of handfuls of bullets and threw them after the gun. They pebbled the surface of the water like so many heavy raindrops. The cartridge box he buried in the ground. It would deteriorate quickly and with it his criminal persona.

The Weed Killer? Who's the Weed Killer? The image and the man could drift into legend and Albert could start his life anew. Get back with Claudia. Sure, sure, he could treat her a lot better, and he would. Yes, he would and lay off the rough stuff too. She wasn't a bad woman, kind, a little simple minded maybe, naïve would be a better word. She could provide for some great sex and decent companionship. He could live with that. And Norm, he could be a good friend to Norm too. What the hell, their conversations were interesting, and they did enjoy music and bird-watching. So an enjoyable life was in the offing, a return to positive values now that his mission was officially over.

Albert walked mechanically down the road lost in thoughts of the future and listening to the bird calls and songs around him. "The young ones learning to sing," he mused. It was a beautiful day, the dawning of a new era for him. There were very few people in the immediate area: the bird-watchers, bikers, and hikers having been absorbed by the vastness and diversity of the Spit. Then suddenly, out of the corner of his eye, Albert perceived something lurching toward him. He flinched and turned his shoulder just in time to avoid a blind side collision.

"What the hell?" he shouted as his long absent friend, Norm, jumped forward and threw his arms around Albert in a strong, grasping, almost stifling bear hug. "Whoa, I'm glad to see you too, pal," joked Albert, mistaking his buddy's action for affection until the body squeeze Norm had applied suddenly lost its power and Norm slumped slowly to the ground. It was then that Albert noticed the blood.

"Norm, Norman?" Albert looked beyond his friend's body at an intermittent but obvious trail of blood that led downward along a winding rutted trail to the shore of a quiet, half hidden bay. The scene was familiar. Then he knew.

"Oh my God. Help! Help!" he shouted. "Someone call 911. Help." Inside a few minutes Albert was surrounded by people who materialized out of nowhere. Some mind clouded indefinite time later police and paramedics arrived and Norm's lifeless body was placed on a stretcher and taken away while Albert stood transfixed in a sightless daze.

"Sorry," said Detective Gignac. "Sorry, but I've got to ask you some more questions, important questions. Please pay attention. Now I understand from what you've said already that you and the deceased.... the victim here, knew each other. You were friends."

Albert nodded.

"Can you tell me what happened? Were you with the .... your friend when the shooting occurred? What did you see? What did the killer look like?"

"I, I wasn't here at the time of the shooting. I was coming back from the lighthouse. Norm wasn't home. I figured he was just out somewhere, walking maybe. He was troubled of late, about Claudia, and you know, capitalism, the whole rotten system. And now this. How did this happen? Why didn't I see him?"

"He was living down there in a tent," Detective Gignac pointed toward the rutted road and the far off water. "You would never have known it was there if you hadn't seen it before. Hidden. The killer must have watched him for a while, a couple of days maybe, stalked him, then today, he finished him off. It's probably a good thing you didn't show up an hour or so earlier. You might have been killed too. We have detectives checking the area and there's a roadblock at the entrance in case the killer is still around."

218

"No, no, he, the killer, the Weed Killer, he only kills the homeless, eh. You know losers, social leeches. Not Norm, not me."

"I don't know about you, but your friend here was homeless. Been living on the Spit for several days. A lot of people have seen him coming and going, carrying groceries. The guy at the hot dog stand knows him by sight. So did you see anyone suspicious walking around, perhaps lingering in this particular area, or leaving here in a hurry?"

"Jesus, I don't know. I was concentrating on the birds. Sure there were people around, eh, biking, skating, just walking. I never figured on anything like this happening. I didn't know Norm was here. I can't understand it. He's got an apartment in Leslieville. He's not homeless."

"I'm only telling you what I heard, that he's been living here for a while. Can you give me your address and phone number? I'm sure we'd like to talk to you further once you've recovered from the shock or maybe you can stop by the station. Whichever you want. It's up to you?"

"Sure, sure, no problem. He was my friend, eh. Anything I can do to help."

"One more thing," said Detective Gignac rather pointedly. "I'm afraid I'll have to pat you down. You understand with the Weed Killer on the loose the police have been granted a certain latitude by the courts. This applies even to mandatory DNA sampling, but we don't need that now so if you don't mind this will only take a second."

Before Albert could respond, the police officer knelt down and starting with Albert's ankle, gave him a quick squeeze along his legs, groin, waist, back, and ending at his armpits.

"There, over and done with, you're clean," smiled Detective Gignac. "I hope I didn't insult you with that, but, you know, duty calls."

"No, no problem," Albert replied only just beginning to realize he had escaped almost certain detection by the skin of his teeth. Jesus, what if he hadn't just thrown away his .22 at the cormorant colony? Maybe he was blessed after all. Fate was certainly on his side, but Norm, Norm. He stared around, his mind and eyes drawing a blank.

"You OK?" asked Detective Gignac.

"Yeah, I guess. I'm just sort of stunned by all that's happened."

Albert threw his blood stained shirt into a garbage bin which stood next to his parking spot at the entrance to the Spit. He couldn't stand the sticky stiff texture that touched his skin and he wrinkled his nose and breathed shallowly as the sweet metallic smell of blood, Norm's blood, flooded his nostrils. He felt as though the dark red, almost black liquid had penetrated the fabric and burned into his very flesh. He retched repeatedly.

"I feel like a fucking vampire splashed with holy water. Jesus." Albert got into his car wearing only his underwear. His pants were in the trunk. He didn't want blood on the car seat and he had no coverings or blankets to put down. If he got stopped by the cops, he would have one hell of an excuse.

At home he spent an hour in the shower until the water cooled and drove him out. His hands were shaking as he sat at his kitchen table holding a cup of tea. He rarely drank coffee at home saving it for a treat when he was at City Donut. Albert put on a Billie Holiday record, but quickly replaced it with "The Best of Sarah Vaughan" which he didn't like all that much. He knew that whatever he chose to play would forever be tainted with what had happened on the Spit this day so he didn't want to ruin one of his standards.

"Her fucking vocal acrobatics with all that high pitched screeching and low bellowing is perfect for the mood I'm in. If I never listen to this again, I won't bemoan the loss. The bitch is one small step above that scatting idiot, Ella Fitzgerald. I wonder if I should I call Claudia? What will I say? What can I say? Jesus, that fucking Norm has got me in a fine mess, just when I was about to begin my life anew."

The next day Albert readied himself for that trip to Sergeant Gignac's office. He sure as hell didn't want the detective sitting down in his living room, looking around and asking questions. No sir, not here. After a shot of straight vodka which seared his throat Albert took another prolonged shower, his third in two days. While dressing in fresh clothes, he resurrected his old cologne. "I don't have to worry about Claudia and her allergies now. She's the least of my problems," he muttered and splashed extra on his face along with a goodly smear of antiperspirant deodorant under his armpits to mask any nervousness he might evince at the police station.

Throughout his preparations to leave that afternoon two images haunted Albert's mind; one was that of a man standing awkwardly in the bright sunlight of a tattered tent. That silhouette, did it look familiar somehow, should it have, and the Peterson book and the binoculars? Then the second shape, grotesque, slumped and dying in his arms with a strange, bewildered expression on its face. Did Norm know? Did he somehow figure it out? That look, what was it? Jesus!

"If you stare at them, the eyes will open." Albert remembered the picture of St. Veronica's veil and those words below it as the image hung on his mother's bedroom wall. "And of all the fucking stupid moves, why did you have to come up with that one, camping out on the Spit?" he went off again raising his voice to no one. "The fucking Weed Killer was still on the loose. He hadn't gone anywhere. Why didn't you put up that stupid fucking tent in Parkdale. Parkdale was a free zone. It was written right in the newspaper. Hey asshole, don't you read the fucking paper?"

Albert poured himself another vodka and left his house. The guy's no genius, he mused about Detective Gignac. I'm sure they have no suspicions about me, but still anything can happen. I've got to be alert and act normal and hopefully Wright was a man of his word and kept his mouth shut. From what I saw, or rather didn't see, at the sugar refinery I think he passed the test. Vale, Sergeant Wright.

chapter 30

Detective Gignac greeted Albert warmly.

"First of all let me again express my sympathy to you about your friend. We're in the process of contacting his family. Sorry to put you through this misery, but it's best to get things straight and written down while events are still fresh in your mind. So you're a West-ender, eh? Niagara Street you said. You like that part of town?"

"It's busy with lots of restaurants and shops. People everywhere. I like that although I'm more of an observer than a participant. Lots of different characters walking around the area, but I enjoy the lake and the festivals at Harbourfront too. Always something happening, something to see and do."

"Your wife? She go out with you a lot? You married? I guess I should ask that first. I didn't see a ring, but that's not always an indication."

"Used to be. I prefer to be single. More freedom."

"Divorced?"

"Legally separated. My wife is a dyed in the wool Catholic. They don't believe in divorce. For me, no harm done, separated or divorced as long as I'm free of her."

"Yeah, I know what you mean. I'm on my second right now. You're close to Parkdale too, eh. What do you think about what happened there, that safe zone the Weed Killer set up?"

"His decision, I guess. There are enough loser types, weirdoes there. I imagine he could have gone crazy in Parkdale if he wanted to take advantage of the situation. Happy hunting grounds for a killer like that. You know I myself thought for a moment that maybe the killer was actually fooling everyone, that once he got all them homeless losers in one place he'd mastermind some huge attack."

"Wow, that would have been something. Thank God you're not the Weed Killer. Actually, I've got a theory myself about Parkdale. You want to hear it?"

"Sure, I guess."

"I think that Mary Monticello's living there had a lot to do with it. The Killer didn't have much respect for Mary, eh. No, there was a certain tone of irritation in some of his letters to the *Star*. Even I could pick it out. When I thought about it more, I came to realize it was kind of a cruel joke. The overcrowding that occurred, the fights and crimes, the tons of litter and hundreds of complaints and those curfews. It was Mary's fall from grace. The Weed Killer did that on purpose."

"Who does have respect for that woman anyway?" added Albert. "She's a grandstander, champion of the poor and oppressed."

"You don't seem to have too high an opinion of Mary Monticello either."

"I just read her columns in the paper. That's all."

"When is she in there anyway?" asked Detective Gignac. "She a regular columnist? I hate to admit it, but I'm not a reader of the local papers. They're tough to take sometimes. You know with the police criticism and all."

"Yes, I can certainly understand that," continued Albert. "Actually Mary's column appears every Monday, Wednesday, and Friday. She had some extra stuff there for a while in the Saturday edition, a new series about a homeless guy she and her husband took in. It was cancelled recently. I think Mary was having some personal problems."

Detective Gignac leaned over close to Albert so much so that Albert instinctively moved away.

"Something wrong?"

"No, just wondering what kind of after shave you have on."

"I don't know the name. Got a couple of bottles in the medicine cabinet. The wife used to give them to me as presents. You know Christmas, birthdays. She liked the smell, eh. I got enough left over to last a lifetime probably. Why?"

"Oh nothing. I thought it smelled good. Was thinking of buying some myself. I couldn't help but notice your neck there too, eh. Looks kind of raw and raspy on that one side. Have some kind of an operation?"

"No, that's, ah, shingles. Subsiding now, but it can be bad enough at times I'll tell you. Hurts like hell. I'm on painkillers. Anyway, you wanted to talk to me about Norm out there on the Spit. Terrible. I still can't get over it."

"Yes, yes, of course. I guess I got a bit sidetracked. Police habit. OK, so when you were bird-watching out there on your way to the lighthouse, did you pass that washed out path that led down to your friend's camp site?"

chapter 31

"WHAT EXACTLY DOES that jerk-off think he's doing," said one of the research assistants to the other? "Can't he read? He's way the fuck past the warning signs."

"I don't know. He's either a Blue Jays pitcher practicing his windup or he's about to toss something in the water. He's pretty near aiming right at us."

"Maybe he's a disgruntled sports fisherman and wants us to recommend a culling of the rookery. You know some of those guys are real assholes, fucking eco- terrorists. You sure he ain't holding a bomb."

"No, he doesn't even know we're here. Our viewport is facing away from him. He can't see shit."

Just then a splash erupted on the water near the edge of the camouflaged blind.

"Good arm. I'll give him that. Almost reached us. What was it?"

"Don't know, but it's right off the shore here. Can't be six inches of water. I'm gonna take a look. The minute he leaves I'm stepping out."

"Fuck no, we ain't spooking the birds no more than we have to. Look at them all in the air now because of that dummy. Let's do our job first. We can check that out when we leave in the evening if it ain't too dark. Make a mental note. And what the fuck is he doing now? He's got the young ones flapping like puddle ducks in a pond. In another minute the gulls will kill him."

"Is that some kind of feed he's sprinkling on the water? He's not poisoning them, eh? Hey, asshole, they eat fish. I swear I'm fucking happy to be working with birds. At least they operate on predictable instinct. With people you never know what in the hell they're going to do. Remind me when we leave to check that shit out. I don't want any harm to come to these babies. By the way, what you doing after the grant runs out? Got any prospects?"

"No, I'm hoping they extend this research for another eight weeks or I'm going to be mighty short of cash come the winter."

chapter 32

CLAUDIA NEVER RETURNED any of Albert's phone calls, but a letter from her arrived a few days after Norm's death.

"You killed Norman. I know you did. More so than the Weed Killer, it was you with your heartless negligence. Norm was suffering. He needed you, his friend, but you couldn't be bothered. You stole me away and used me to amuse yourself. Never gave any thought to me or Norm's feelings. Hopefully, he never knew what you, or we, were up too. I can't forgive myself and I'll never forgive you. Poor Norm dying like that. I read the whole account in the paper and it's all over the news. Shot down like a dog. Too bad the last thing he saw in life was you. He would have been better off staring at the killer. At least he'd know him for what he was, not a cheating, heartless liar who masqueraded as his friend.

P.S. His funeral was yesterday. Too bad you couldn't make it."

"Well, fuck you too," said Albert. "Give me a hooker any day, no commitments, no promises to keep. Loveless love, you can't beat it. I should never have gotten involved in the first place. I knew I was taking a chance. As if I need her, that lame brained loser. But shit, I should have gone to the funeral. Looks bad, me being Norm's best friend and all. I'll just say it was too much for me. I couldn't bear the heartache and I'm still suffering from post traumatic shock. Yeah, that's good, post traumatic shock. That should work."

For the next several nights Albert walked the streets without real purpose, wondering, remembering, and sometimes regretting. The sidewalks, parks, and lanes held lots of people going about their business and pleasure, people with homes and purpose in life, people free from worry because they were exempt from the Weed Killer's wrath. For their part the homeless had abandoned the downtown neighborhoods and much of the rest of the city. Toronto's temporarily expanded social housing network, primed for this crisis, had absorbed a fair number of the remaining homeless while a remnant remained in Parkdale tormenting the residents and exasperating governmental efforts to corral and deport them. Strict new city bylaws which prevented loitering in any Toronto park or public place effectively stopped the homeless blight from regaining lost ground.

Within this context it was Albert who felt lost, but he was also afraid, worried for the first time about his own freedom. That new Sergeant, Gignac, he knew something. Albert could sense it from the interviews. Perhaps in another letter to the *Star* Albert should publically admit that the Weed Killer was done, retired along with his nemesis Sergeant Wright. Maybe it would take the pressure off.

"Of course, I can't do that because, despite the new laws, the vagrant sons of bitches would only creep back again like maggots onto a squirrel carcass. One minute nothing, then total infestation. No wonder at one time people believed in spontaneous generation. No, they have got to believe I'm still around and ready for action. Keeps em guessing and keeps them the hell off Toronto streets."

Albert got drawn by a sense of nostalgia to revisit his old killing fields and soon spent his afternoons and evenings walking through the scenes of his crimes and pausing to relive the action and emotional excitement that occurred there.

"Stinky Eddie. What a fucking loser," mused Albert out loud. "That picture of him in the paper really got to me, pissed me off. Him standing there with that stunned fucking look on his face, the disheveled hair and those wild eyes. 'What, who me?' I could shoot that fucker all over again just thinking about him. Regrets, 'No, je ne regret pas' with apologies to Edith Piaf."

Albert found the old office building on Harbor Street near the Air Canada Center where he had shot the goose cookers. Some faded and torn police tape blowing across a parking lot was all that was left of the crime. A sign proclaimed the coming of a new condo complex.

"These foolish things remind me of you. And Norm? Well, he was an idiot with all his pouting and cry baby moaning. Capitalism this and capitalism that. Jesus, grow up and take some responsibility. Life is tough, so what. Overcome it. Be a man."

Albert walked cautiously down the lane behind the Lighting Standards Building, even more deserted now than back in the early summer when he gunned down the duel losers.

"You say either, and I say eye-ther. You say neither and I say neye-ther. Either, eye-ther, neither, neye-ther, but I didn't call the whole thing off. Did I?"

"You said you'd kill only one of us. Oh, sorry. I lied. Ha, two idiots. I mean they've got to be kidding. Who in the world would ever miss these useless losers? I'm sure even their relatives, those few that would even admit some sort of kinship, were happy they were dead."

In the throes of his enjoyable reverie Albert became aware of someone approaching, a group of people actually, talking loudly. Albert squeezed behind the utility garage which backed up against the railroad tracks below. Beyond that was Garrison Common where he had shot that homeless, self appointed keeper of the greens, Common Johnny.

"Yeah, well yer trespassing. This is my park. I own it by squatter's right of self possession. I was here first. You can go over to the other side of the wall, dead man's wall, but not here. Fuck off or I'll summon the legions of Hell to drive you out. Oh yeah, look out mother fucker, they will come at my command. You'll be sorry. I've done it before. Behold. Behold."

Before Johnny could get to his third "Behold" out, Albert shot him twice. "Behold this, asshole!"

Common Johnny died thrashing around on the ground and spitting blood and calling upon the angels of darkness to destroy his enemies before Albert choked the final breath out of him with a stuffed weed. Now Albert leaned against the garage wall listening to the conversation of the assembling crowd at the Lighting Standards Building.

"Gather around. Gather around. Over here, there's room here, but don't stand there. That's where the victims were killed. Their bodies were sprawled against that wall. If you look closely you can still see the blood stains."

Shuffling sounds and gasps rose from the apparent crowd of people. What the hell, Albert wondered as he craned his head to listen.

"Yes, ladies and gentlemen, the police presume this was actually the Weed Killer's third assault and his first multiple murder. This is where Jennifer Belcourt and John Potts, aka Lefty, were savagely shot. The forensic report and police investigation showed that Lefty tried to position his body in front of that of his girlfriend, Jenny. He was shot first and in a gallant dying gesture he leaned over to shield his lover from the bullets that were to come.

"Police hypothesize that the Weed Killer then tormented the woman, perhaps exposed and fondled her in an attempt at humiliating her. Her clothing showed signs of undress. The buttons on her blouse were undone and her pants unzipped. The weeds in her mouth showed signs of tearing and chewing indicating that she was still alive when they were forcefully inserted. Further proof of the Killer's inhumanity."

Albert heard groans and gasps issue from the crowd.

"Police reports paint a picture of the Weed Killer as being simply efficient and dispassionate and showing no signs of engaging or torturing his victims. I beg to differ. I've studied the Weed Killer and his homicides in great detail and I can assure you he was anything but matter of fact and efficient. He was cruel. I would go so far as to say he sexually tortured his female victims. Yes, I believe the police are hiding signs or evidence of fellatio. The weeds were a cover up to hide this fact. You won't want to miss the details of the Bathurst Bridge killings which involved two young, beautiful girls one of whom survived the ordeal, but to this day is so traumatized by what happened to her and her friends that she has become totally mute, unable to communicate in any way but through sign language. Through our contacts with sources within the Toronto Police Department, however, we have secret information which we will share with you. That, and more, later in our tour."

Jesus, what the fuck is this idiot talking about? Who is he? Some sort of tour guide thought Albert as he tentatively stepped from his hiding spot as the gathering of people moved away? The distant voice of the guide continued faintly.

"This tour, unlike some others you may find around the city, this tour covers the more insidiously cruel, often sexual, and I might add, untold details of the Weed Killer's modus operandi. That is why there is a slightly higher fee for our excursion. We give you a lot more detail. Now stay together. We are going to walk over the bridge into Garrison Common, the scene of the Killer's next murder, planned and carried out in tandem with this double homicide."

Albert caught a glimpse of the crowd, about a dozen people, walking noisily over the Strachan Bridge as he rounded the deserted buildings and moved out onto the street.

"Son of a bitch, these assholes are making money off my handiwork. I put my life on the line, got rid of the city's parasites, and everyone else benefits while I live in fear of getting caught and spending the rest of my life in jail. Oh yeah, that's a great deal."

Just when he banged his fist upon the street railing, a car pulled up. A brief siren sounded and a blue light flashed. Before he knew it, a police officer jumped out of the car and accosted him.

"What the fuck?"

"Please sir, just put your hands up and don't move. Don't move."

"Officers, what's the matter? I was just looking around. This is where it happened, right? One of the murders, by that that killer, the Weed Killer. I was wondering. And by the way, a whole group of people doing exactly the same thing left here a minute ago. Matter of fact, you can spot them now going down into Garrison Common. Over there."

"Yeah, we saw them," replied the cop as his partner emerged from the car and ran his hands down Albert's body obviously checking him for weapons. Thank goodness, Albert thought.

"If you don't mind coming with us, we have a few questions for you."

Down at the station Albert met Detective Gignac again. "He's OK, Officer," Detective Gignac said while closing his desk drawer and offering Albert a seat directly opposite him. "He was with his friend over at the Spit during the last killing. He's a victim himself in a way. Meant no harm at the murder scene, I'm sure."

When the officer left, Detective Gignac turned to Albert. "They were acting on orders, eh. Looking for anyone suspicious hanging around the murder scenes. You know the old expression about the criminal always returning to the scene of the crime. Actually it's true in more than half the cases. Believe it or not.

"Anyway," proceeded Detective Gignac, "I'm glad you're here. We've received a lot of new critical evidence lately. For the very first time on this case I think I can actually say that I'm optimistic so I wanted to talk to you a bit further about the events at the Spit the other day. Now do you recall anything peculiar about that day, any suspicious characters hanging around?"

"It's the Spit, eh," replied Albert. "There are always strange characters hanging around."

"Sure enough and while you're here," continued Detective Gignac, handing Albert several large black and white photographs, "I wonder if you'd mind looking at these pictures."

Albert hesitated a moment.

"Something wrong?" asked Detective Gignac.

"Are these suspects? I didn't think there were any actual pictures of the Weed Killer because, you know, he always avoided surveillance cameras and all that."

"They're just what we call, persons of interest."

"Not suspects?"

"Persons of interest. If you wouldn't mind," the detective nodded at the photos.

"These look like mug shots. You sure you haven't arrested anybody? I mean I'd do anything to get that bastard put away for what he did to my friend and all."

"No arrests yet, but I think we're getting close, and, of course, everything has to be done properly. We don't want this guy getting off on any sort of legal technicality, so anybody look familiar? Take your time. Don't be afraid. They won't bite you."

Albert smiled back and thumbed through the eight or so photos in front of him handling them rather gingerly, then he shook his head, No.

"OK then, I'll take those back. Maybe they'll be of some use later on. By the way, out there on the Spit, did you notice any homeless people around," said Detective Gignac changing the subject and trying to alleviate some of Albert's apparent anxiety.

"No. I don't think it's too fertile a ground for begging and stuff. Pretty remote."

"Used to be a couple that lived on the beach, near the entrance when you first walk into the Spit. Ever see them?"

"Can't say I have," Albert lied. "I usually don't go near the water itself. I'm not that good at shore birds, eh. Hadn't been to the Spit for a while either. I mean before that day."

"Busy?"

"Yes."

"I thought you were retired, but it don't matter. Oh yeah, bird-watching. I forgot. Was your friend a bird-watcher too?"

"Oh yeah, and he was good. Knew his stuff. He could identify a lot more species just by their songs than I can. I'm more visual, though I do know some songs and calls too."

"Ever do any bird-watching at High Park, Albert? Is that a good area to spot birds? Better than the Leslie Street Spit?"

"Ah, I haven't been there recently. Years ago I went a few times and yes, it's a pretty good spot, but I prefer the Spit."

"By the way, just out of curiosity, what do you think of that big cormorant colony at the end of the Spit? I couldn't believe it when I was there, the noise alone, eh. Had to see them for myself. Was talking to a couple of people. I guess them birds, the cormorants, they come back every year to the same spot to nest. Some people don't care for them too much either? I guess they can eat a lot of fish. I don't know too much about them myself."

"Really detective, you should take more of an interest in things around you, even birds. It adds depth and meaning to your life. Cormorants, yes, I guess they take their share of fish, but they eat small species not game fish. I never minded them. Neither did Norm. Yeah, bird-watching will never be the same without him. Poor Norm. I wish I could have done more to save him."

"Do you know a woman named Claudia? She was a close friend of Norman's. Said she knew you too."

"Yes, I've met her a few times, over at City Donut's and Norm's place."

"She described your relationship in far more, shall I say, intimate terms."

"Well, I didn't want to have to say that, not that way. A lady's reputation and all."

"Not good to lie to the police, Albert," laughed Detective Gignac good naturedly. "But, hey don't beat yourself up about Norman. There was nothing you could have done. Once the Weed Killer targeted a victim, it was all over. Only one person ever survived to tell about it. That was our own Sergeant Wright's daughter. Her three friends were killed, but she was spared. Shortly afterwards the Sergeant quit the force. Otherwise it would have been him not me here interviewing you."

"Yes," Albert replied. "I heard that. Why did he quit anyways?"

"I don't think that information was actually made public," Detective Gignac replied. "But, if you ask me, he was just burned out, took a lot of abuse both inside and outside the department and that incident with his daughter that was the last straw I guess."

"Yes, I'm sure that must have got him thinking," added Albert. "I wouldn't put up with it either, not for a bunch of homeless people who.." Albert trailed off before continuing. "I imagine he's still working with you guys here in some capacity. Probably sort of a consultant, eh?"

"I'm not at liberty to discuss that Albert," replied Detective Gignac. "Let's just say Sergeant Wright is happy to be uninvolved with the Weed Killer case. Anyway, more bout you. I'm curious. When you traveled to the Spit for all that bird-watching, how did you get there? What route did you take?"

Albert explained his usual drive down Lakeshore Boulevard and his parking spot at the entrance to the Spit. However, the questions, as well as Detective Gignac's attitude, aroused Albert's suspicions once again and he immediately became evasive and nervous.

"I can tell you're still upset by all this," said Detective Gignac. "I think we can call it a day. After one more meeting we should conclude our business."

"One more? Don't you have everything you need already? What more information can I possibly give you?"

Detective Gignac smiled. "I'll be the judge of that, Albert, and by the way, be careful snooping around those old murder scenes and places off the beaten path. We've had a lot of copy cat activity around the city including a couple of actual murders. A lot of people fantasize about being the Weed Killer."

"Yes, but there is only one real Weed Killer. I don't imagine you guys have ever seen the likes of him."

"True enough, and remember, he's still on the loose, eh, but hopefully not for long."

When Albert left, Detective Gignac reached into the open drawer of his desk and took out a tape recorder and switched it off. He then carefully slipped the line up photos into a large envelope and called one of the police clerks.

"Here, take these over to the lab and have them checked for fingerprints. They'll find mine, but I want the others from our recent guest here lifted and compared to any and all partials that were gathered from the crime scenes. Then one other thing. Give Father FitzPatrick over at St. Michael's a call. Ask him if he's got some time today. Won't take long."

Detective Gignac then picked up the phone and quickly called a number.

"Hey, Don, It's Steve. Yeah, how you doin? The family? Meaghan coming around OK? That's good. Now listen. I think we got some good leads on our man. OK, my man. Yeah, lots of crazy shit, but looks like luck is finally on our side. I know you're out of the loop and don't want to get dragged back in and I respect that. However, you know if this goes to court you're going to have to testify and Meaghan too. If we can make this case air tight, well, we might be able to spare both of you the trouble, and anyway our boy won't get out of prison ever and you and your family won't have to worry. So with that in mind I'd like to ask you one quick favor. No, right now over the phone. I want you to listen to something and tell me what you think. When you're done I'm going to run it past Father FitzPatick too. Listen up."

As Detective Gignac played his interrogation tape to his old friend and colleague over the phone, another detective motioned for his attention. Detective Gignac leaned away from his desk.

"What? I'm very busy right now. Can't it wait for one goddamn minute?"

"I don't know, but this guy's been here before. He wants to talk directly to Sergeant Wright. I explained to the dumb fuck that Wright is not available. You know I didn't want to get into a lengthy explanation with him. It's none of this moron's business. Now he's back and says it's important and he wants Wright and only Wright. He's got something to show him, says it's very important, but won't tell me what it is. Thinks it might be worth some kind of reward. What do you want me to do with him?"

"Give me a minute here. Jesus. OK, Don, does that voice sound familiar? You think we can use this? I mean, it's only part of the evidence, but if we put everything together and get a warrant I'm optimistic. It's still basically circumstantial, but it's building up to a pretty solid case. No, I won't make a move until it's a lock. Promise."

Detective Gignac put the phone down and turned to his fellow officer. "This guy you've got, where's he from? What's he do?"

"He's a college kid working on some sort of stupid bird study. I don't know."

"Bird study? What kind of bird?"

"Hey, what do I know about birds? They got feathers and fly. What else is there? He told me the name, but I can't remember, Commanders, or Commodores, something like that I think."

"Cormorants?"

"Yeah, that could be it. Yeah."

"Cormorants, like those nesting at the Leslie Street Spit where the latest murder just took place?"

"Hey, I don't know nothing about no birds at the Spit. What's that got to do with the Weed Killer?"

"Detective, if you took more of any interest in things around you, birds included, you would not only add a little more depth and interest to your life, but you'd make a better police officer as well. Now let's have a talk with this man of yours."

chapter 33

ALBERT RESUMED HIS habit of taking long night time walks and surreptitiously visiting his old killing grounds. He seemed unable to focus on anything. The music didn't interest him. He hadn't been to the Rex in ages. Bird-watching was out, that was for sure. Maybe a trip is what he needed, yes, a trip, a holiday. Get away from it all.

"I don't think I have to worry a lot about the Weed Killer," he smiled, "even though he is still on the loose. Oh, golly gee, the Weed Killer. Thanks Sergeant, for the warning."

Funny, when Sergeant Wright left the police force, Albert had felt that the greatest threat to his freedom had been removed. Yes, the meeting at the Rex was a watershed and showed that Wright was making up ground towards him. However, that little murder spree under the Bathurst Bridge had worked perfectly in Albert's favor when Meaghan Wright fell into his hands. He never figured on Gignac though, the underling, but the guy was obviously on to something. Albert didn't like the questions he asked and the subtle hints he dropped about the case being closed soon, and their meetings being very helpful to that end.

"Persons of interest, what was that all about? There are no goddamn persons of interest. I'm the only person of interest because I'm the only killer. Finger prints?" Albert wondered aloud. "Is that what those photos were about? But what could he possibly compare them to? I never left any prints. I'm sure of that. Maybe on the gun, but that's gone, rusting away in the middle of Lake Ontario. You know maybe I should have kept it after all. Not for more murders even though a few more wouldn't have hurt, but for the final showdown. Every story that has a conflict has a climax and what better way to go out than in a blaze of glory with guns firing away like Butch Cassidy and the Sundance Kid or Bonnie and Clyde? Something with drama in it. Maybe I could hold up in the house with Claudia as hostage. That way I could have the pleasure of torturing her first.

238

No need to worry about being caught then. Wouldn't it be great to see her pleading for her life with my .22 shoved up her ass. That bitch. The nerve of her lecturing me."

But now without his weapon he was facing the possibility of a very ignominious end, carted away in cuffs, hangdog, and beaten down, to spend the rest of his retirement years rotting in prison where no birds sang. Fuck, what a fate! It was late at night and Albert cut the corner of his street on his way home by walking through a small parkette. Toronto had a lot of parks and parkettes, another thing about the city that Albert loved. "Round midnight. Old Dobbin heading back to the barn while the young colts and fillies are just getting their prancing legs limbered up for a night on the town. Ah youth, too bad it's wasted on the young."

Near the sidewalk he noticed two young boys hiding behind a tree. They were whispering and pointing down the street actually in the direction of Albert's house though the building was not visible from their vantage point.

"Hey!" Albert startled the lads who jumped a foot in the air. "What are you two doing here? Hiding and then trying to scare people? You could give someone a heart attack, especially an old guy like me. Shouldn't you two be at home, in bed even? A little late to be out prowling around a dark park. Don't you two know that there's a killer on the loose?"

"Jesus Christ, mister, you scared the shit out of us," one boy said, a bit young Albert thought to be using such language. "Yeah, well the Weed Killer, he lives right on our street, down at Number 36," the boy continued. "That's why we're here, watching. The cops they're gonna bust him tonight."

"What? How do you two little pip-squeaks know that?"

"For your information Mr. Smarty Pants, the cops surrounded the guy's house. They're hiding in the yard and them unmarked cop cars on the street. They came to our apartment and all the others around to tell us to stay inside. It could get dangerous. Yeah, our parents think we're upstairs in our bedrooms right now, but we want to see the action."

"I seen the guy, the Weed Killer, lots of times," said the other boy. "He's a vampire, eh. Only comes out at night. He wears a mask and a black cape and sucks the blood out of his victims. The cops don't say nothing about that though 'cause they don't want to get the people all scared and start a big panic."

"Yeah, I bet they don't even get him, that he escapes or else takes a bunch of them cops with him. He's the Weed Killer, you know. He leads a charming life. That's what my father said. Should be lots of gun fire. You better get behind a tree yourself Mister."

Albert stuck his head out and glanced down the street. It looked unusually quiet and dark.

"They said to keep our house lights off."

Albert stood there dumbfounded. It can't be, he reasoned. Wright wasn't even on the case anymore. You mean to say that idiot Gignac figured this all out in a week. That is impossible unless that bastard Wright lied to me and stayed active or is helping them out behind the scenes. But no, he wasn't at the police station. Never showed up on the Spit and there was no activity on the false lead I planted about the body off the Sugar Mill. What in the hell is going on?

Albert backed off behind the boys. He felt suddenly alone and vulnerable, naked. "I'm leaving. It's too dangerous here."

"Scaredy-cat," one of the boys whispered.

"Hey, that cap of yours, can I have, buy that off you? Here's twenty bucks."

"Sure thing. It's old and the Argos suck anyways."

Albert pulled the brim of the cap down low over his eyes and walked slowly out the back end of the parkette. He was physically weak in the knees from the news he had just heard.

He wandered aimlessly, stumbling in the dark even though no obstacles presented themselves along his path. Where would he go? What could he do to get out of this jam? His car was back at the house. How did this happen?

"Maybe they can arrest me, but can they convict me in a court of law with no real evidence? Where are the witnesses, the forensics, the DNA, the fingerprints? Where's the fucking gun? They don't have anything. You got nothing Gignac, nothing!"

He made his way straight down Queen Street preferring to be in the crowds rather than alone, safety in numbers. He kept walking and walking. What else could he do? He finally passed St. James Church and the Garden late at night, early morning really then he turned mechanically towards St. Michael's Cathedral. There on the corner he noticed a large sign on the lawn. "St. Michael's Outreach Program".

"In response to the current city wide tragedy and taking our cue from the teachings and example of our Lord Jesus Christ, St. Michael's Parish has instituted a comprehensive program to feed, house, and clothe our unfortunate homeless brethren. The supplementary Parish Hall and rectory basement have been converted to men's and women's dormitories. Luncheon meals are served in the main Hall from Noon to 2:00 PM. Clothing drives and distribution are held in conjunction with the Salvation Army Centre at 333 Queen St. East every Saturday AM.

Bingo remains every Thursday at 9:00 PM. Weekly Grand Prize $1000. Proceeds support the Outreach Program and Other Charitable Church Functions.

Signed, Father Andrew FitzPatrick"

"That pious, do-gooding son of a bitch," snorted Albert. "Too bad I don't have my gun. It would be nice to see the expression on his face when he wakes up one morning with a bunch of deadbeats pushing up daisies on his front lawn."

The night turned chilly as the wind shifted out of the north. Albert continued on to Sherbourne Street and the Allan Gardens area.

"What the fuck day is it?" he said out loud. "I don't even know what day it is, and where exactly am I? Not too many people around here."

The Allan Gardens neighborhood was a lot quieter than during his former scouting and hunting sojourns. He could hear the screech of that night hawk which flew unseen over his head. Was it the late hour or the fear of death that kept people off the streets? The few people he did notice were staying close to apartments and rooming houses, standing in driveways or sitting on porch steps and chairs. No one was roaming around. This was certainly not the raucous, partying, disorganized crowd he had first encountered.

"Oh yes, I know this place now. A long walk. It is looking better though," said Albert as he entered the park proper. "I take full credit. I salvaged this place. I saved the city. Maybe instead of trying to lock me up, they ought to congratulate me. Thank you Mr. Weed Killer. Take a bow. Even Parkdale is quiet and the future looks good. Vive Toronto. Vive Toronto libre!"

Albert found a bench and stretched his legs out, put his hands behind his head. He could see the moon swaying in and out of view behind the thickly leaved branches of the park trees.

"Ooo, Ooo, Ooo, what a little moonlight can do. Ooo, Ooo, Ooo, what a little moonlight can do for you," he sang and closed his eyes. "Jesus," he shot back up immediately and looked at his watch. "It's two in the morning. I'm sleeping on a goddamn park bench. For fuck's sake, I'm homeless!"

"Thanks for the information, asshole," Albert heard a voice behind him. He turned around to catch a glimpse of movement before a loud thud and blinding pain struck him over the head. He couldn't speak the impact was so strong, but he did hear another voice, speaking from far away.

"Hit the old fucker again. Quick before he can fight back, before somebody comes."

Then numbness and Albert was laying on the ground staring up at two smiling, youthful faces.

"I, I know you from somewhere," he barely breathed.

"Ha," the boy in question laughed. "Yeah, you're probably one of the assholes who's been shitting in my backyard. You're just another homeless cock sucking loser by your own admission."

"No," Albert moaned. Then he heard more than felt numerous blows pummeling his body and an acrid wetness spilling over him.

"Get him in the face," a disembodied voice called. "Yeah, that's good, cool. Choke on my piss you old fucker. Now, let's finish him off good, real good."

"The devil rides on the wayward wind," said the old man sitting around the fire which despite its bright flames did not seem to shed any heat. Billie Holliday sang in the background, "Life is like a faucet. It turns off and on. And just when you think it's on, baby, it has turned off and go-o-o-onne."

***

No one claimed Albert's body. All efforts to contact his wife, to whom he was still legally married, prove futile. Claudia never answered any of Detective Gignac's phone calls. The body was cremated and the ashes scattered in an unknown site to prevent vandals and groupies from targeting it. Memorials for the victims were erected at the sites of the murders and plaques in their honor were installed in the walls of public housing and service buildings throughout Toronto. In Parkdale on the corner of Queen and Cowan provincial leaders, city officials, the media and the public gathered in a newly restored building for a well publicized event. Premier McGuiness addressed the crowd.

"Mayor Milne, Police Chief Samuals, Captain Gignac, and fellow Ontarians and Torontonians, it is my pleasure today to commemorate the opening of this wonderful new facility here in Parkdale. Named in honor of the late Mary Monticello, it will house twenty formerly homeless individuals and ten single parents and their children. Mary's husband Bob is here with us today. Bob, take a bow please. Thank you and thanks to Mary I'm sure. She was a remarkable individual and a selfless crusader for the rights of Toronto's poor. For that she will always be remembered.

"As you came into this wonderful edifice today, you probably noticed the bricks above the lobby entrance. They are inscribed with the names of all those poor unfortunates who lost their lives in the tragic murder spree that rocked our city last year and whose sacrifice led to the reconstruction of this structure. May it stand forever as a testament to their lives and to the value we as a people put on the lives of every one of our citizens, rich and poor alike. What the late president of the United States, John F. Kennedy, once said about the City of Berlin,

I think can be safely transposed to our present location when I say with deep sincerity, nothing could make a person prouder than to state, I am a Torontonian.

"In closing today let me reaffirm that it was and still is our intent as your government to open many more such facilities. However, as you all know, we are still in the grips of a stubborn economic downturn. Although conditions are slowly improving, we still do not have the where-withal to tackle this problem with the resources it requires and deserves.

Not to mention the fact that our summer long battle with this terrible adversary, this heartless murderer, has dramatically drained the city's coffers. But rest assured, when factors warrant, my government will make poverty reduction and new affordable housing construction our top priorities. In preparation for that I would today like to announce the formation of a new Ontario commission to thoroughly investigate the housing problem in this province and city. It will be our guide into the future.

"Now, ladies and gentlemen let's stop and reflect on the good news before us, this grand new building, and thank you again for your attendance today. Coffee and donuts are being served in the basement hall.

The End

0 1341 1571729 7

CPSIA information can be obtained at www.ICGtesting.com
Printed in the USA
LVOW12s2129270614

392146LV00011B/207/P

9 781484 081181